2

Aug 19/2016

Cameron Munroe

The Genesis

The Genesis

The Beginning

Cameron Munroe

Rev. date: 07/01/2016

To order additional copies of this book, contact:
Xlibris
1-888-795-4274
www.Xlibris.com
Orders@Xlibris.com
736389

CHAPTER ONE

I woke up feeling my heart pounding underneath my ribs. I was soaking in bed, sweat was dripping from all parts of my body. I felt it drip into my eyes and off my chin. I sat up and wiped my forehead with the blanket. It was as if I had just stepped out of a sauna.

Recalling this last dream, it was somehow connected to the previous dreams I had over the last week or two. They were all intense, although none was as intense as this last one.

Remembering the odd feelings and reactions to the dreams, there were visions of a multitude of different aliens. Most were helping us grow and helping us with the struggles the Earth was going through.

There was also a feeling of lightness, almost like floating, experienced after the last dream.

Recalling the dream, it happened during the daytime, just after I had finished lunch and was sitting, relaxing, although, I believed it had only lasted for maybe a minute. The feeling of light-headedness, I felt was as if I could float across the room. The last dream was so intense, I did feel different but quite good, Overall, it was a feeling of wellness, not something bad or harmful.

In this last dream, I was physically floating in what could only be described as a sphere. An unbelievable light was emanating from my very essence. It was tingling throughout my body. Never had I ever experienced anything quite like it. It felt like I was talking, no, not really, maybe communicating, with someone, but to whom? This last dream seemed so real. So real it was as though I was there, but where was there?

Exhaling slowly as I rolled back over, the sweat dried from my body as my muscles relaxed. I looked at the alarm clock—2:38. *It is Saturday morning, and I don't have to work today*, I thought. *Why can't I sleep? This is my time to kick back, relax, and enjoy myself.*

Suddenly, I found myself wide awake, thinking of this most recent dream. Grabbing my pillow, I flipped it over, laying my head on the cool side of it, sinking comfortably back down. I was slowly forgetting my dream as I once again relaxed, ready to slip into a deep slumber.

I was methodically relaxing every muscle, trying to get back to sleep, when this overpowering urge to get fresh air outside came over me, almost to the extent of like a claustrophobic attack, although I had never experienced a claustrophobic attack before. I had a feeling that I had to go outside. *I guess this dream really rattled me*, I thought. I found that my breathing became shallow, very labored, and with such an intensity. Breathing slowly and deeply, I regained my composure, shaking myself as my breathing also returned back to normal. As soon as it came over me, it quickly disappeared.

"Maybe I should hop into the truck and go down to the lake. Yes, yes, that's a good idea." Shaking my head, I muttered, "Go back to sleep, you idiot!" as I laid my head back onto the pillow, closing my eyes.

The strange compulsion came over me again, realizing that I had just given into myself. I found myself sitting on the side of the bed.

"This is strange!" It was as though I was having a premonition or déjà vu. It was almost as if I had done this before, not the getting out of bed, but it was as if something was about to happen. A feeling of anticipation came over me. *Odd*, I thought. *What could I be anticipating?*

Thinking to myself, *Maybe . . . there's a reason for me to go there. Oh well, can't get to sleep anyway.* Giving into my thoughts rather than logic since it was still the middle of the night, I stretched my arms, waking myself up even more.

Leaning forward, I reached over and grabbed my jeans lying on the dresser. Stepping into the legs of the jeans, I stood as I pulled them on. Opening the first drawer, I pulled out a pair of socks. Out of the second drawer, I grabbed a plain white T-shirt.

Walking out to the kitchen, I stopped and grabbed my jacket from the closet.

I had no idea why it was important to go out at this ridiculous time of the morning, yet strangely, I for some reason, knew I had to. Still carrying my shirt and socks, I sat, pulling my socks on, then reaching over, I pulled on my runners, then my T-shirt, and last my jacket. Pulling my keys from my pocket, I opened the front door. Feeling the rush of cool fresh air hitting my warm body, it felt accelerating, waking me up completely.

Heading to my favorite spot to sit and contemplate, I turned into the secluded lake road, following the road to a little knoll overlooking the lake.

The night was remarkably clear, silhouetting the trees and hills of the surrounding landscape with a soft lighted glow from the large full moon. The night stars could be made out, as there was not a cloud in the sky. The light from the moon allowed the smallest details to be visible. It was surprisingly quiet. The wild animals that usually were so abundant in this particular area seemed to be all asleep. Through the half-open window, the loon's lonely eerie call echoed serenely from the lake, indicating that all the animals were not asleep. All across the immediate landscape, it was such a remarkable peaceful moment, a real pleasure to witness such serenity.

Placing the truck into park, I readjusted the seat, leaning it back into a more comfortable observing position. Relaxing, soaking up the scenery, still wondering why it was somehow important to be out here in the middle of the night, knowing something profound was going to happen.

Out of the corner of my eye, I spotted three moving lights, similar to yard lights, spaced evenly apart in perfect formation. They were moving across the landscape from my left side. I quickly adjusted my position, as I looked out the driver's side window. They were coming over the hills, rising and dipping as the lights followed the lay of the land.

Shocked, initially with seeing the lights on such a clear night, I sloughed it off, as the lights where probably helicopters, or maybe planes. The lights though, had my full attention as well it was the only thing moving. I thought it was odd though, that there didn't seem to be any flashing lights.

"Oh . . . there's a red light." I was thinking it but verbalized the words unconsciously just a quick flash of red moved between the left light and the middle light. Since the three lights were getting closer, I realized that the red light had moved behind the second light, then it went behind the third light. The three lights with the red light moving behind the lights traveled past the front window, still with no sound of planes or no visible images of a plane. They kept moving to the west.

No, I thought, *it can't be a plane*. They must be helicopters, as they had just stopped to the right side of the truck. They were still visible in the front window, just about to the frame of the truck window, almost to the point that it would have disappeared had they moved any farther.

They just sat there, not moving. The little red light moved from a position behind the right light to position itself behind the center light as the three lights moved back east, in the direction they had come from. Moving to the left, I watched the lights through the front windshield. The lights stopped again directly in front of me. This time, they moved in a straight line toward the truck to about a hundred feet in front of me.

Checking the radio to see if there was any static on the radio, I noted that it was fine. The strangest sensation came over my body as I suddenly became completely powerless. The most notable sensation was that the hair on the back of my neck started to rise, a sensation that I had never experienced before. My hair was standing up and out, kind of like the hair on the back of a scared dog or a cat, exactly as I felt, scared. A feeling of complete and utter helplessness came over me as everything seemed to go fuzzy.

Comprehending a small portion of what was happening to me, similar to looking through a thick fog, this unbelievable pain was surging through my body, bringing me out of an almost hypnotic-like state, a state that still allowed me to realize that I was hurting. This humanoid-like person was in the middle of sticking a tube into my urinary tract.

It was as if I was in a fog, yet the burning pain was extremely painful, so painful that nothing would stop me from gaining my senses and trying to defend myself.

"What the hell are you doing to me?" I couldn't see very much. Yet someone in front of me placed a hand on my naked shoulder. I could feel several hands on my arms, as they pushed me back against a cold steel bench. Things started to go a little fuzzy again like going to sleep when you are going under anesthesia. "Why are you hurting me?" I asked, slurring my words as I slowly felt the pain subside. It was as though I was again in a deep groggy sleep, too groggy to be fully sure of what was going on.

It felt as if it was a second later, I found myself walking down a hallway. I could make out a figure of a person walking beside me, and as the fuzziness slowly left me, this person slowly came into focus. First thing that flashed through my mind was that it looked as though the person had an odd-shaped helmet on. Although as I looked closer, I realized that it was not a helmet but a very large head from a human perspective and yet not unpleasant in an overall look. This humanoid had very large black eyes that sloped toward small slits, which were openings for a small nose. Below was small delicate thin lips forming a mouth, centered in the middle of a very pointed chin. I realized that this person was only about three to four feet tall and was dressed in a simple dress yet a definite type of uniform over a small childlike slender body.

Subconsciously, I wanted to know why they had hurt me so badly.

Something in my mind softened my angry, hostile thoughts of what I wanted to say. Instead, I found myself politely asking, "Why did you have to hurt me like that? The other times, you never hurt me before."

Wow, why would I say that, how did I know them, or that I had been through this before? I still needed or insisted on an explanation.

Turning its head slightly, recognizing the hostile question, somehow this person was still in control of my emotions as if reading my mind. Showing no fear or emotion of any kind, I noticed that I could easily have hurt this small frail-like person if I decided to.

Calmly, the person explained, "We had to run tests and take some samples that will help us to help you."

I was surprised, as it was a pleasant female's voice, and taking a second look, I could tell there was a definite attraction to me.

Softening my tone of anger again, I politely asked, "What kind of tests?"

She turned to me and was about to start to explain when another person, almost a replica of the lady standing beside me, came down the hall, interrupting our conversation.

"We had to do some tests to make sure that you were the right one," interrupted a man dressed in a male uniform suit, the same colors as this female, coming down the stainless steel-looking hallway. "My name is Jescan, I am here to help you," he said very politely. "You have had a very unique experience, and we are here to help you to realize the importance of this event. I will explain everything in due time," answered the strange little man called Jescan. He directed me down a hallway, leaving the lady who moved in the opposite direction, rounding the corner.

I somehow knew that deep down, she had something to do with the pain that was inflicted on me and would, I felt sure in time tell me why. Strange. It was as though I knew there was something besides the pain that she was hiding.

I could feel the sensations of g-forces on my body, feeling as you would in an elevator on the way up, straight up. Moments after it started, it returned to a normal state once again. "Again, where am I and who are you? What just happened?" I found I was overwhelmed with a multitude of questions needing immediate answers.

"You are now give or take, about a hundred miles above your Earth. You have been selected by a power greater than we are. The task is to now, discover the things that you already possess but are not aware of yet. I will be your mentor . . . but it is more than likely I will learn more from you than you will from me." Anticipating my next question, he added, "What just happened is that the ship has just left the planet surface. We have just left the atmosphere.

The gravity plates restored the normal gravitational pull of the pressure inside the ship, allowing you to feel normal without the weightlessness of space." The man reached down and picked a round baseball-sized object lying as though it had fallen by the rapid ascent and placed it on the wall.

"Come, let me show you our ship. Be careful. You will still find that you feel much lighter than you are used to," he said, motioning to a door that opened from what seemed a solid seamless sheet of metal.

Not feeling threatened in any way by this man excitedly, I thought, *Neat, just like out of the science fiction movies,* as I found that I almost bounced as I took my first step in space.

"We ran all the tests that was required for this unique situation," he said, interrupting his conversation again as he motioned to a window port. "This, of course is the lift where you were brought from the surface. This other room is the control room. You may want to take a look at the planet. It is an interesting-looking planet from this distance."

I looked out into solid blackness. Looming out of the blackness was the very bluish-green planet Earth. The planet was truly blue.

Although it seemed surprisingly small, floating in the vastness of space, it was unbelievably breathtaking. I realized how really small we or Earth was. I could see North America, South America, parts of China and Australia. Although I could as people had said, make out the Great Wall of China as it faintly zigzagged across the continent, making a line from the ocean through the land outlining China, I was surprised at the length of the wall.

Looking at the whole planet, I was surprised to see the number of man-made satellites floating around the planet, as I didn't realize that there were so many.

My concentration returned to the planet itself. I could see the clouds moving into and around a low-pressure storm out in the ocean with the clouds moving into the center of the storm. I was unbelievably moved emotionally and physically. I felt very small, indeed, as we moved what seemed very slowly away from the planet yet speed-wise probably very fast though space.

The moon loomed beside us as we approached close enough to see the large crater-riddled satellite. How desolate and uninviting it looked. The dark side of the moon started to come into view as we traveled farther out into space. I was not sure, as the movement and conversation of people in the control room distracted me, but I could have sworn that for a few moments, the moon passed by surprisingly fast and was now very small. I thought that I could see the shimmering of lights on the backside of the moon. Maybe I was seeing things. I again questioned myself if this could be happening or if this another intense dream. "When am I going to wake up?"

Turning, I noticed the other men, all dressed in the same suits, almost like looking at replicas of the first man calling himself Jescan. "Does everyone look the same?" I asked, looking a bit perplexed. "I mean, that you all look alike."

Taking a closer look, I could see several differences. Realizing how foolish I must have sounded, made me feel even more foolish.

"Yes, we do look alike, but as you have already discovered, we do have differences . . . many sometimes," Jescan answered. "This is our crew. Captain Ryan, First Officer Riley, Medical Officer Evelyn, watching the monitor is Engineer Kyle." Each nodded as their names were introduced.

I nodded politely to each when I suddenly noticed that Jescan never moved his lips. "You . . . you never moved your lips!"

"Yes, you too have been communicating in the same manner even though you didn't consciously realize it," stated Jescan. "You have experienced several things in the past few minutes. Very shortly, I will be showing you things that you only recently thought about, especially in and during your dreams, especially lately."

"How is it done?" I asked, referring to the voiceless speech, totally fascinated yet posing a different surprise question. "What do you know about my dreams?" I was suddenly defensive, as what he had said finely struck me.

"You will find out all the answers of why and how, but first you must have some patience." Pausing momentarily, Jescan turned and looked at me. "Yes, you inadvertently have used it several times. Even as a young person, you had used your ability of nonverbal communication, even though you were not aware that it was you, and sometimes they would answer you. Most humans have the ability, but have not used it." Jescan stood tall, almost stretching, I observed. Maybe because of the statement I said before, about them all looking alike, I got the impression that it was his natural stance, awkward as it looked.

Turning and looking at a bit taller, slimmer person I suddenly realized that it was the female that I had first encountered on my arrival. I commented, "I believe we have met before. I still have several questions that I would like answered," I said, recalling the last statement that I had made to her about not being hurt before. Had I encountered her before?

"Yes, in time she will answer your questions," Jescan said, changing the subject. "This is our destination," he said, pointing to a chart on the monitor. "We are presently here, represented by this flashing light. It will take several of your Earth hours to arrive at Edan, our home planet. You will have these hours to discover all the things that you find fascinating and interesting. It is time, though to start your preparation for your arrival. There will be several things that you will want to know before you arrive."

"I feel like I have been kidnapped. What is so important that you have to take me to your planet, and for what reason?" I asked, suddenly realizing what had just happened in the past few minutes, or could it have been longer, maybe hours? Looking at my watch, it was now 6:10 a.m. A little over three hours had past. Actually, that was a lot of time that I do not remember.

Jescan continued, "You have out of all in the universe, been the first to have made contact with what we call this other plane, or different universe or dimension, because you have been subconsciously communicating with the dimension, mostly in a dream-like state, actually from a young age flashes to start with, then more each time from a thought in the beginning to full sentences.

"This is a very unique dimension we have been able through our technology and with the objects that have connected to or communicated with four other planes or dimensions. Although not completely successful, we have estimated that there have been four distinctly different communication links. In all cases, we could not determine the exact link. In all such cases it was speculated that there could be up to six planes. We named our three-dimensional plane the first plane and so far, four others have intermittently been in contact with us. This link that you have demonstrated is, or we believe to be the final link. You have somehow linked with an entity occupying the same space and time but on a different parallel plane, at least in theory.

Our people received information on you a few years ago, and we have been observing you ever since. This entity though, is trying to break through to your conscious mind, and it has sent anomalies throughout the universe. We know very little about this plane, as you are the very first to have linked up with this particular plane. With the use of some new technology, we have been able to monitor your connections with this plane." Jescan changed his tone and spoke softly and slowly. "We have many unanswered questions surrounding this link, indications that allow us to think that it is safe to communicate with it, but to be on the safe side, we decided to document this new phenomena. This is to verify to the universe that its intentions are good and not harmful as some has speculated.

"You have a right to know that there may be risks involved. This is why we have decided to help this entity to communicate to you under the protection of a regulator to monitor you in this event. We know that it is our place to ensure a safe transformation and offer as much help as we can."

Digesting all that was being said, I stated, "You mean to tell me that my mind has linked with another being from another place, I mean plane, yet occupying the same space and it is trying to communicate with me? How is this possible? It sounds ludicrous." I reached down and pinched myself to see if I was dreaming. "Yes . . . I definitely was not dreaming," I said as I started rubbing the spot I had just pinched. I definitely was awake.

"We occasionally over the years have received distortions in the universe, and we monitor them and try to open communication links with other planes. If there is a pending disaster in one of the planes, then there is eminent disaster in all the other planes. We have detected and linked with four other such planes besides ourselves. Yours will be the link with what we believe to be the sixth plane and should be the final one, at least that is the speculation arrived at by our scientists."

"Who are you, people?" I interjected, realizing that this was so bizarre.

"We go by many names, depending on which part of the universe you are from. Our planet is called Edan. We are the observers, or the protectors of the universe. With this link, you will grow to protect this new dimension as well as our dimension, and you will prevent several problems that occur in all the dimensions. We now know how you came to be and much of your past. Although your life will be forever changed from this day forward, it is supposed to be this way."

Pondering what was just said, the reality seemingly exploded in my head. "It's supposed to be this way, what do you do to protect the universe . . . is this for real?"

"We are striving to make certain that the universe survives the way that it is supposed to and we correct things that are not supposed to be, although in the past we have made many mistakes. In this case, it is helping what is supposed to be . . . and you are a part of that," replied Jescan.

"I will be able to return to Earth, won't I?" I asked as a feeling of detachment overcame my conscious mind.

"You will return . . . except much more knowledgeable and more aware of the things that are not known by anyone else. There will be some adjustments that will happen. We believe that this entity is trying to communicate with you having knowledge that is unique, and if we understand this knowledge correctly, it could well be that it can and will extend our time in the universe indefinitely."

"Interesting. What do you know about this entity?" I interrupted, almost like I knew the answer, as if this was something that I somehow knew almost like the premonitions I had experienced sitting on my bed.

Jescan looked patiently almost hesitating, as if not sure that he should tell me now. "We know that this plane has several unique properties that you will understand and are able to use. Other planes have informed us of some of the abilities of this plane. There is a limited documentation on it when we arrive. The most important information that we have obtained is that you will travel though the matrix of time.

This plane is believed to be the entity that holds the universe together or the key to the universe. The time has arrived for them to reveal themselves to our plane, you in particular. The quadrant that they exist in is where an intelligent species originally started and hundreds of thousands of years later included the same quadrant that Earth is in. You are the individual unequivocally chosen, although nothing ever just happens. Your destiny has been written from the beginning of time. We knew of your importance in the history of man, but we did not know how you became this person.

We are privileged to be part of this joining and are able to piece together other things that we could not understand why they are as they are."

"And I thought I was just a normal guy . . . normal," I said, almost comprehending the ramifications of what he was saying. "This does put some purpose to my life, I guess."

The possibilities rushed through my mind. "Awesome. What do I do?" I asked, excited at the prospect. Parts of the dreams were starting to make sense now. I could feel this other plane so much stronger now.

"That I cannot tell you and no one will be able to, because it changes so often that it is even being written as we speak. We should get ready for our arrival. The council of observers is preparing for your arrival. Let me show you where you can get ready," he answered as he walked toward the seamless door that we had entered from.

"Neat, how is that done? Are all the walls like that? How do you know where the doors are?" I questioned as I wonderingly followed him, noting a red box above the door.

"We use a special metal that is electrically charged by a cue from our movements, which opens and closes the ports. Of course, only where the designated opening is which the red light box above the opening indicate. Each door is set at appropriate locations, and the ship senses the movement within the room. With the different alloys, combined with the ship's sensors that we have developed, the door liquefies and then solidifies as soon as the person has passed though."

Stopping in front of a door, the door melted away. I could see the liquid running along the bottom to a tube and could see it as it was vacuumed up, and the liquid was directed up and around to the top of the door. As we moved through the door into the elevator, the tube released the liquid, and it solidified into a solid, completely seamless wall again.

It felt strange as there was no physical pull, as I could feel us move but with no sensation of movement. The door suddenly opened, exposing a shiny well-lit hallway.

Jescan moved down the hallway and stopped just about halfway down, again the door marked by a light fixture just above the door melted open again. He motioned for me to enter.

Looking in, it was a surprisingly spacious room with a comfortable-looking bed, chair and table and obviously must be a dresser with a mirror above. Hanging on the walls, some geometric-shaped plaques of no particular design with multicolored textures, although simple were pleasant to the eye. A light fixture signifying a door to another room off the main room, was on the far wall.

Jescan moved in front of the door, exposing a compact bathroom. I suddenly realized that I was wearing clothes quite different from what I had been wearing. I had a suit similar to Jescan's, and after the initial surprise I realized that they were very comfortable. So comfortable that it seemed to move as I moved, never creasing or bunching up even at the bend in the elbow, where usually the material of a shirt tends to show creases. It seems as if they stretched or contracted to the shape that I held my arm, as though it was a second skin with no creases as it loosely hugged my body. I suddenly recalled, in the back of my mind, the memory of that fuzzy hypnotic sensation when I woke up with such great pain. I recall that I had no clothes on then. The burning returned as my thoughts returned to the pain that I had endured.

"What happened to my clothes? How did I get these clothes on without my knowledge?" I directed at Jescan.

"This type of clothing reflects the electrical fields generated by the ship. Your other clothing would attract the electricity. If exposed for too long it could possibly combust, causing burns to your body. For your protection, we exchanged your clothes for these ones," explained Jescan. "There is a selection of different styles but still appropriate clothing if you like in the closet," Jescan said as he slid the closet door open by a handle that was indented in the metal. The door blended into the metal as it opened to his touch. "You have a choice of different styles, or you can wear more conventional clothing similar to yours that you came in, from your planet although made of a protective material. If you do not like what you have on which is very acceptable, or these are very acceptable," he said, gesturing with his hand to a limited row of clothes, "this should be adequate."

"I feel almost like a prisoner, yet I'm being treated like a very important guest." Is there something I am missing? I was not getting any bad feeling from these people, yet it somehow sounded too ludicrous. "Some of these clothes are really excellent," I said as I looked at the line of cloths. "Is the dress formal or causal?"

"Please, I assure you that you are not a prisoner. You are probably the most important guest ever to arrive at Edan, and you can dress in whatever you feel most comfortable. We do not have as on Earth, a formal dress code here. All are acceptable for any occasion."

"I have no idea what to expect, who will be there am I meeting important people, or what . . . ?" I asked, looking bewildered.

"I believe this one will do, as it is similar to what you have worn in the past," Jescan said as he took out an off-white T-shirt and a pair of pants, denim in look. Reaching down, he pulled out a pair of runners and reach up top for a pair of socks.

Pausing at the last statement, I pondered what he had just said. "You mean, I have been here before and these," I said, pointing to the clothes that looked similar to my own original clothes, "are what I wear?"

"You have in the past been here on several occasions, but this is the first of many for you, meaning all the other times have been after this initial encounter. I will now, with plenty of time before we arrive let you have a shower and get dressed," he said, turning as he exited the room the door melting behind him as it closed.

"Wild. I'm meeting people for the first time, and they have all met me before . . . Wild," I said as I slipped out of my clothes.

It was a short time after I had showered that standing in the nude, I could feel a tingling sensation as if I were in a dream again. It was similar to holding your hand onto an electrically charged ball to make your hairs frizz out.

Moving toward the bed, I started to get into the clothes that were lying on the bed. "Not too shabby, if I do say myself," I said, looking at myself in the mirror hanging above the dresser.

Looking around, I still felt overwhelmed. *How is this possible?*

CHAPTER TWO

I was sitting comfortably on the bed, contemplating what had happened in the last seven hours, sifting through the entire bizarre and strange things that had just happened to me. I found though that I was calm and relaxed, totally comfortable almost like I was supposed to be exactly where I was. Somehow the dreams that I had, were somehow falling into place as flashes of the events that had happened or about to happen. These flashes though, did not seem to make any sense, as they only lasted maybe a fraction of a second, if that.

I somehow had a feeling that I was exactly where I was supposed to be, as though I knew this was my destiny. Maybe what Jescan had said was going to my head, and I was fantasizing that it might actually be true.

At least it would be neat to be a part of the helix of time. "I could actually see how life started. I could see the beginning of time for that matter, see what is in store in the future," I said, shaking my head as I was trying to make sense of all this. I was amazed at my composed accommodating attitude surprising myself, as I thought that I should have been frantically trying to escape!

I felt strange and looking down, could see a small light emanating from my body. I could feel a slight lightness and found that I could move in a floating motion across the room. This was like a few seconds, maybe less. I really was not sure.

Suddenly, I heard a buzzing sound almost like an old alarm clock that I once had, breaking my concentration.

"What the hell . . . oh . . . the door," I said, cocking my head as I realized that I had no idea how to open the door. "The door . . . How do you open the door?"

I jumped so fast. I inadvertently leaped turning a somersault, literally as I was not used to the buoyancy of space, triggering the sensor. The door opened, and I slowly sailed in the air, half tackling, half crashing into Jescan knocking him over sending him down the hallway, all in what could only be explained as in slow motion. As I rolled off the back wall, I bowled over another person standing by the elevator. Completely taken by surprise the person braced, holding on to me and slowly collapsed underneath my body, absorbing my momentum with me landing directly on top of this person.

The gender of this person was still indistinguishably hard to decide, at least in the initial encounter as we rolled from one side to the other, although there was no doubt in my mind as we finally come to rest in front of the elevator.

"Are you all right?" I questioned, blushing at the intimate position I found myself.

Realizing that although it must have looked hilarious, one of the unique factors of space is that things tend to float, and other than the initial surprise followed by the slow motion like bounce, we landed very gently . . . to my amazement.

Strange exciting feelings came over me, as I could feel the closeness and the scent of her body. It was as though I could sense every chemical that her body released. Looking into her large eyes, I realized that this was the lady that I had first met after my strange abduction. I could sense that she too was concerned for me, as I detected a concerned look, as she was hoping that I was not injured.

"Are you all right?" I asked once again. Sensing that she wanted to tell me something that she was withholding, I passed it off as her infatuation.

"Yes, are you?" she questioned back genuinely concerned.

Jescan, analyzing the situation, was relieved to see no harm had come to anyone and in a diplomatically charming way almost laughingly, tried to make the best of my situation. "I see that getting used to space will take a few more hours, perhaps. We are about to arrive," announced Jescan as he picked himself up, reaching out to help Evelyn and me to our feet.

Totally embarrassed, I too was helping her as we resumed the normal standing position once more, postulating looks back and forth as though we were too embarrassed even to talk, especially with the chemical attraction that had just happened between us.

"Well, I see that you have met Evelyn once again. We did need to use the elevator anyway," Jescan stated slowly as he observed the two of us, surprised at the reactions of both her and me. As he entered the elevator, he turned and waited for us to enter.

Following Evelyn, I cautiously stepped forward into the lift, my eyes still fixed on her eyes. This interest in this alien lady was somewhat different from what I had ever anticipated or could ever have expected. The chemistry exchange of hormones, as well as I had just landed upon her sprawled all over her in a very compromising position.

"Here we go, hey," I said as I moved slowly almost blushing at my feelings for her, as I caught Jescan looking back and forth between us.

Making sure that I didn't go further than I wanted to, I stood toward the back of the elevator. "What is expected of me?" I queried, holding on to the edges of the lift.

"You will be transported to a study area that has been equipped with the necessary equipment that will be required. You will be introduced to your team as soon as we arrive," Jescan said, exiting from the lift and stepping into the transport room.

I followed Jescan, not knowing what to expect but anticipating what was to happen, as it felt like I knew this was supposed to happen.

Standing on one of the oval rings, everything started to go blurry as I could feel myself breaking up, slowly . . . obscurely . . . disappearing.

Suddenly I found myself looking out into a room, that had seven people similar in looks to Jescan. I looked at each one, still amazed at how they all looked alike although the height was slightly different.

I thought about what another race of people would think of us earthlings. Maybe we all looked alike to them.

Jescan looked at me then back at the people. "This is Adam. Adam, I would like to introduce you to your team. This is the leader of the group, Jesse, his assistant Arian, coworkers Moran, Yenta, Allay,

Yuma, and Leone." Each nodded as they were introduced. "I will turn you over to Jesse, as he is the expert in this area. I will be an adviser and consultant, but mostly an observer."

Jesse, stepped forward and held his hand out. "Pleasure meeting you again," he said, stopping as he realized that I had no way of knowing him. Starting again very apologetically, he said, "Although at this point in time, you are not aware of it yet. As Jescan mentioned to you that you are well known by most of our people, it is an honor to be here on this historic day."

"I get the impression that is not all bad then?" I said, contemplating my bewilderment, feeling as though I had amnesia or something.

I noticed that I could feel a mild tingling. Goose bumps started to appear on my arms and body. It strangely seemed to creep all over my body. *There must have been some equipment generating an electric field or something*, I thought. "I have to admit, most of this is a little overwhelming to say the least. I still have some major questions, and I still wonder if I am going to wake up and find that this is all a dream."

Recalling the most recent dream, I suddenly recognized this man . . . What part of my life does he know, or play in it? I couldn't remember. Reaching out my hand, I shook his strong handshake.

Somehow I knew it was an acquaintance, not someone who I knew.

"Let me reassure you that this is not a dream and yes it is not bad, usually quite the opposite, a little unconventional at times as history will reveal but nonetheless, very interesting." Jesse smiled as he motioned to sit on a chair. "This chair will act as a buffer to ease the shock of the initial communication. The first contact will cause shock waves possibly throughout the universe. We are here to balance things and buffer the possible shock to your system.

"According to the little we know, this will affect several aspects of this plane. It has been speculated with the communication from the other planes that it will also affect all the other planes. Jescan informed you, that this is the last plane that we think we will encounter. This is the link that could possibly be the one that allows life to be extended past the inevitable end of the universe, as we know it possibly doubling, maybe even tripling our existence.

This chair, with the information from your tests that were run on you when you first came aboard the ship, is now set to the biological synapses of your brain. This will cause an electrical endocrine link directly to your synapses of your right and left brain simultaneously, which apparently is important to the linking. Which has been indirectly explained to us by your future self and the other planes?

They tell us, has been directly influenced by the initial contact plane or the sixth plane. Which is the one plane that we have not been able to communicate with? Although we know from the communication with the other planes as well as drawing from our history that it is the final plane, the sixth plane.

"When you sit in this chair, there will be an immediate response that will cause radical changes to you. Your time is very close, as you have felt and this will increase your knowledge beyond anything that we in this room could ever only imagine. Are you ready?" explained Jesse.

"No time like the present!" I commented as I approached the chair, anticipating what was to happen. Strangely, it felt very right. It was what I was destined to do. I was not able to shake my last recent dream, as it flashed images so fast I could only sense them, not see them. It was as if I knew what was to happen, my body completely ready.

The chair reminded me of a dentist's chair, except where the light usually was, there was a helmet-shaped object overhead, kind of like a hairdressers helmet.

I felt an electric charge tingling in my temples, throughout my mind, down though my body and clear down to my toes. As I sat on the chair, a burning sensation slowly started to penetrate into every fiber of my body.

The men quickly pulled the helmet over my head as I sat back into the very comfortable seat. Feeling like fireworks were exploding in my mind, every essence of my being felt like it was on fire. *Did I make a mistake in doing this . . . the pain, the unbelievable pain?* I questioned myself momentarily, having second thoughts. *What have I gotten myself into?*

I heard sounds, pure musical notes, starting in the center of my head resonating through every synapse within my skull and along my upper backbone, along my neck to the top of my shoulders.

A clear musical voice imitating perfect English diction emerged, sounding as if it was echoing, similar to the sounds that you would expect to hear in a cave if someone was talking.

We are the future of all the different planes enveloping all of the universes, this joining of us, combines all the existing planes. All our existing planes . . . now have combined. This makes you the key to time and space intertwined together forevermore, enhancing our individual universes forever. Your time of enlightenment has now begun. It will improve all life in all your universes. We are now combining our minds in a continual never-ending circle of information, always connected.

We are now forever connected with the use of all our intellect, experiences, and knowledge sharing the sameness of our individual minds.

We are combined and now make up the matrix of all time and space.

With this link of our minds, is the final link that will justify our very existence.

This is the beginning of our combined energy to deal with the tasks that we will encounter. This is the beginning and will begin the needed healing of the planes, de-cloaking the ignorance that has limited each plane's potential, and of all the life forms within each.

We can now open the communication links with all the planes of space and time. We can now preserve the universe indefinitely. No mortal shall be capable of understanding all that we will be capable of. We now have powers beyond anything conceived by each individual plane.

The powers can and shall only be used for preserving and protecting, for the good of all life forms. This shall be the deciding factor. This is the code that will allow us to live throughout eternity. Any deviation shall change all our destinies. No matter where, we are connected, we shall be there to help, guide and counsel one another. We shall enhance one another's powers.

The buffer chair, the protectors have constructed, has diverted a lot of unavoidable ripples though time, although not enough to stop some seismic rifts, activated by the disturbance in the time matrix. None will cause serious destruction, as you will be able to correct these. You are one now with a link of six, allowing for an infinite number of planes within the individual planes, and with the knowledge and control of time, within your plane as well as the intimate bond that you share with the other five planes. This is the beginning . . . Behold . . . this is the time of enlightenment.

I could feel the burning, in what seemed like every nerve of my body slowly subsiding, as I was able to now relax my muscles that were as tight as could be. It did leave a feeling like my head was exploding with millions of little electrical sparks. Thoughts appeared in my mind, so fast yet vividly remembered. As the thoughts appeared, it was being filed into areas of my mind that felt strangely new. I could feel ripples surging through my body, almost like convulsions. I felt the nerves, just below the epidermis, tingling surprisingly pleasant yet the only comparison could be mild static electric sparks, each one with varying degrees of intensity. Each synapse was expanding as the sparks flew across the minuscule space between the nerve endings, bouncing from one to the other. Over millions of nerve endings were sparking in every nerve of my body, so many nerves that I didn't even realize existed within my body. I could sense the millions of nerves, all seemingly talking to one another. It was amazing how much chemical-induced information could be stored within the spaces of the synapses.

The transformation seemed to be lasting forever, yet through real time was only maybe a few minutes at the most. The random thoughts became conscious concepts that, in turn pulled all the concepts together into a knowing of the answers of the universe, encompassing far beyond the physical confines of the universe. How and why the different planes linked together would now become an important reality.

I now understood why they were so closely interconnected and how life can be affected in one plane and yet in another plane may have a catastrophic effect changing life forever in the other dimension.

I could hear music, and the placement of the notes started to made sense to me, surprised at how it related to the physics of the universe, as all elements resonated a sound that can be interpreted whether they were combined with other atoms making up the different elements.

Travel through time was not anything like I expected, as it was not dealing with time as I had once thought. Time was a concept used to pass from one instance to the next and was all relative to the concept, but it was the chemical evolution of the atoms that stayed constant although altered occasionally with the connection with other atoms, but throughout time, the atom's nucleus stayed constant. It was the simple aging or rejuvenation of the atoms that time travel was based upon. It became so clearly obvious, as if I had known it all my life.

Light started dancing in my head, which converted into music, and each note became an important character. Certain musical notes seemed to pull everything together. I realized that the versions that I was receiving had a subtle difference in each of the other planes, and music or sound waves seemed to be a constant between planes, although they perceived it differently, and within the different confines of the music, it allowed communication to be possible, in a way like talking to someone in a different language but through translation is understood.

The ability to take matter and convert the molecular structure into becoming a totally different molecule, completely different in the chemical properties, seemed so easy. Complex tasks seemed so, . . . so very easy.

My body seemed to be adjusting to the extraordinary changes as the tingling subsided yet, appropriately was still very present.

Jesse pulled the helmet off. "How are you doing? I recommend you sit for a little while." Taking my wrist, he started to take my pulse.

Realizing what he was doing, I immediately slowed my pulse to normal, surprising even me. "I am all right physically, although my body feels like every part is more than alive, which I have no doubt it is," I said laughingly as I slowly sat up. I could feel the energy radiating from my body and became aware that there was a silvery-golden glow surrounding me. I found myself floating. As I rolled my shoulders and stretched my arms and my legs, I inadvertently started to float upward, realizing that I was nearing the ceiling. I with a simple thought, found myself landing up right on the floor. "Awesome . . . Awesome!" I said out loud. Gathering my composure, I looked at the people around me as they watched with complete reverence.

Regaining my composure, the glow slowly subsided. "I was told that I have caused some disturbances throughout the universe. Let's see what has happened?"

Jescan stepped forward. "There seems to be ripples or waves passing through the universe. Our computers are just collecting the information. They are still moving . . . This is remarkable. The ripples seem to be causing time to go backward. Look at our chronometer . . . It's going backward."

Hearing musical notes in the areas just below and behind both my ears, spreading up to the top of my brain, I realized that all five planes were communicating with me. Although all planes were trying to talk at the same time, to isolate and understand each plane was remarkably clear, and I found that I could, in turn, talk to each plane almost simultaneously. *We have inadvertently reversed time, sending all time, including the time in each of the different planes. Listening to the different planes, it was very clear that I was the only one who could reverse the ripples since they had emulated from my joining. For every minute, the ripples increased in velocity, speeding the reverse of time.*

My body started to tingle, as I could feel the energy leaving my body in waves. Although I could not see the ripples, they seemed to come to me very clearly. Quickly scanning the monitors to confirm what my senses were telling me, I could see the ripples coming to a standstill and started moving forward till it reached the point where it should be, confirming that what I could sense was really happening.

The power of the ripples was remarkable. "Wow. It really works," I commented, totally impressed with myself.

Opening my hands, palms up forming a cupped position, a light streamed from me even going through the ceiling of the study area, forming a circle above my head starting to emanate around the rest of my body as the room almost became indistinguishable, as the light was so bright that objects blended together under the intense light.

The people around me could not be seen, as they covered their eyes because of the intensity of the light, dropped to their knees. This being a self-induced energy release, was accelerating as the minutes progressed. An ultimate feeling of power came over me as every nerve in my body was alive, and it felt awesome. The responses came in from the other five planes, informing me that time was starting to reconfigure to the regular universal time. Images of the beginning of time zoomed past the evolution of time, events flashing before my eyes. In the next few moments there was an amazingly bright light, bringing the remarkable inauguration of the now combined six planes. Fragmented bits of light formed together, yet separately each containing visual information from each plane or images of the time as it is supposed to be.

Slowly they started to move together, appearing from all the planes. The light became focused around six large distinct shapes starting to form between my two outstretched palms. There were six individual crystals that started forming, each one representing one of the planes. Slowly, as they floated individually in front of me, the six large pieces started to attract to each of the other five pieces, each a compatible shape to the other five keys of life.

They started to bond together, surprisingly shrinking as they started forming a sixty-six faceted diamond-shaped stone the size of a large walnut or the size of a silver dollar. Finally, the light returned to normal as I cupped the diamond-like crystal in my hands. I was now holding the history, the very beginning, the very existence. It was a culmination of all the six planes, and I was the sole guardian of this precious treasure, holding it gently in the palm of my hand.

Observing the people in the room, they started to regain their composer, both fear and relief showing in their eyes as they were readjusting to the normal light.

"What just happened?" they all asked almost in unison, as their attention was quickly drawn to and focused on the newly formed diamond-shaped stone.

"This should solve the slight glitch in time," I commented as my mind wondered at what was to be done next. With a short period of consideration, I came up with the most important essential, that I would need to carry out the many things that at this moment seemed so pressing. "I would like to if possible, request the use of a ship. Is that possible?

Jescan, I would like to study what has happened with the data that the computer has on the surrounding universe just to make certain that time is back to normal with no residual effects of the ripples."

Smiling, Jescan gave me the data as it arrived. "These seem to be the most affected. They seem to be correcting themselves thanks to you, thinking that we would be doing this again and possibly a few times till the time would slow and go the other way."

"There were five other planes that had a lot to do with the corrections. I was just in the right place at the right time," I said, smiling to myself, thinking that it was a remarkable feeling although it still felt like I was the same person, although I knew I had forever been changed.

My thoughts wondered . . . With all the questions that I had ever wondered about, I now realized that I was capable of discovering them for myself. Even though I could tell how everything was formed, intertwined in the web of live becoming aware of all the intelligent life within the universe, still my first desire is to experience the beginning of life on Earth, then somewhere within the universe, to be able to experience the first new beginnings of life that begin to exist after the big bang—what about before the big bang and what about the beginning of man, as evolution has developed so many specimens, humans being one of the newest species.

What was the first atom that developed into life? What is in the future? What is in store for mankind? Where is the place I should be seeing first? What happened to man to allow the development of the intellects that has allowed man to excel to present day? How far will man excel? Is there a point when man will reach the point of complete knowledge? In a way, I felt the same as before yet knowing all the newfound information, suddenly my life was radically different.

My desire to start on my quest was very pronounced and was forefront in my thoughts, although it would make sense if I could have the time to build a ship that could be my domain. All in all, I knew that it would take longer than I wanted to stay and wait here. The thought occurred to me that it might be possible to use one of the Edan's ships as a temporary means to move around.

The need for transportation was important, as I wanted to get going right now. So I asked, "Is there possibly a ship available, one that I could borrow temporarily?"

It was as though my words fell on deaf ears, although I could sense that they were simply avoiding the answer that I was requesting.

Walking over to the desk I reached for a piece of paper, and I jotted down some items that I thought might be useful. "How soon can you get these things?" I asked, presenting the slip to Jescan.

"I think about fifteen to thirty minutes maybe a little longer, and we have your new ship ready and waiting," he answered smiling almost beaming, as he knew I would be pleased that I was not being ignored.

"You already knew that I needed a ship." Thinking of all the planning and research these people had gone through with a limited communication link with the four other planes, gathering as much information as was possible. "Your people have done remarkably well, and on top of everything else, you say it is a new ship.

"Oh yes . . . You said that I had been here before. Did I initiate the building of the ship?" I said, nodding unconsciously as I realized that this would be the ship that I had been dreaming about, understanding now that it was actually the sixth plane communicating with me in a very musically precise way. "As soon as these materials are ready, can you put them in my ship and call me when they are ready?"

Jesse stepped forward. "I will get this right away. But first you must eat," he said, noticing that trays of food were being brought in and placed on the counters. Taking the list with him, he motioned the group into a huddle.

"Jescan, do you have a status of all the planets before my connection with the other planes?" I asked, grabbing a sandwich.

"Yes, all the information was downloaded into your ship. All the information from our recorded beginning to the present is in your computer. The ship was designed specifically for you indirectly and mostly through the communication of the fifth plane, but initiated by you, keeping in mind that until now your destiny was still being formed," Jescan answered, pondering. "But there is a duty that you must perform before you depart, and after you eat."

Following Jescan I suddenly realized that this is the strange destiny which I had been dreaming about for the past few months, including just before I was picked up. The dream was the initial connection with the sixth plane, the last plane to the matrix. I now have acquired the connections to the other four planes through the joining, which I until today had no connection too even in my dreams. I am now the connecting point of all six planes. The welfare of this plane is now my soul destiny. As I finished my lunch that they had brought for me, I realized I was hungrier than I thought.

Opening a door to a long tunnel, Jescan smiled as he turned, looking into my eyes penetratingly with the large deep black eyes, characteristically distinctive of his race, as it was a normal practice to circumcise their newborn children's eyelids giving them unusually large eyes. Beaming with pride as he was the one to escort me to the new ship, he said, "This is the passage to your ship, and we have arranged a little ceremony and watching the honored privilege of you christening your ship to be recorded for all time."

"Oh . . ." I paused to mull over what Jescan was saying. "Really. I thought the ship would have already been named?"

"We do know of the name that you have chosen, but we cannot tell you the name. That is your decision. I am certain you will make the right choice."

As we walked down the passageway, there was a light that could be seen at the end of the tunnel a brilliant white light, and the forms of people could be seen hustling into position as we approached the entrance of the dock.

Entering the room, a large delegation of people clapping their hands circled the entire room, leaving a path that led to a podium on the far side of the room.

Approaching the podium as I contemplated the name that I would most like, the group stopped clapping, the room became silent. I could sense the friendly warmth of the people as I positioned myself behind the podium. "I am honored that you have made me feel so welcomed, and I have the privilege of christening this ship. I will be going to many places, places that will possibly change the destiny of the universe, and before arriving here at this place called Edan I had a dream that I could not figure out. Since I have arrived here, my dreams has been put into perspective. The universe was simply on a random path with no direction, so to say. This is no longer the case. The universe has finally reached the point of growth that it will perpetuate itself and carry on infinitely into the future. This is the turning point for life as we know it, and it is forever changed.

This ship represents a new beginning, a rebirth of living creatures evolving into a compatible society with a place and a right for every living creature to exist.

My purpose is to preserve what we have, and the good in things shall be the deciding factor." Turning I picked the container filled with a vintage bubbly liquid similar to a champagne on Earth, and a long cord attached to the side of the ship, holding it up behind my head, ready to hurdle it and said, "I christen thee in the name of humanity, *Genesis*," and I released the bottle as it sailed over the edge, down to the ship smashing as it stuck the side.

The people gathered on the platform and began to clap and cheer as the liquid from the bottle flowed down the side of the ship. Jescan, still clapping approached me. "You must now imprint your hand and voice into the computer, as this is the key to enter the *Genesis*."

The raised platform lowered to the side of the ship and came to a stop, gently touching the side of the ship. I placed my hand on the square-shaped plate on the side of the ship. I could sense the scanning of my handprint and the biological makeup of my body being processed. "My name is Adam, and I take command of this ship named *Genesis*."

The door opened, and I had my first view of the inside of the *Genesis*. I looked into a large round room with several doors behind the fairly large circular console in the middle with the boxes of supplies I had requested stacked neatly beside the controls, kind of reminded me of a receptionist's desk in an office tower, except a bit bigger.

I, followed by Jescan entered the ship. It was as though I had always been there and knew every aspect of the ship, its capabilities and its potential. Things were as familiar as entering my home on Earth. A very comfortable feeling came over me.

Sitting at the console, I leaned over to check the contents of the boxes pulling out the contents of some, setting them carefully on the console, set about constructing a stand on a metallic rod extending from the console. Jescan watched intently as I completed the final step.

A globe-shaped ball slid over the rod, then removing the six connected crystals from my pocket, I set the diamond-shaped stone at the crown of the globe. The crystal seemed to melt into the metallic globe, radiating a reddish-blue light as it transformed the globe into a glitter of small multi-colored lights, with static electricity moving across the surface as though it was alive, completely enveloping every part of the ship.

I could hear the other planes explaining that I had to do something first before I proceeded on my personal quest. The coordinates flashed through my mind.

"Let's take it for a spin. Some things need to be corrected still," I said as I repositioned myself on the very comfortable captain's chair in front of the console. "The *Genesis*'s maiden voyage," I commented. The board on the console was very familiar. Every nerve was actively alive in my body, the anticipation was overwhelming.

Jescan watched in wonderment as the door closed automatically,

I opened the viewing screens and looked out at the people on the platform.

Touching the crystal, the buttons on the console started flashing setting the coordinates to Earth, and even though I knew what to expect, suddenly the people disappeared, and the landscape of a barren volcanic molten-shaped land, uninhabited land with only the ocean that undulated up and down below the ledge, although desolate black and reddish hills loomed above the valley that we had landed on, I somehow could feel the presence of life.

The sky was laden with dark-blue to almost black clouds, glowing red at the bottoms of the billowing thunderheads as the light was reflecting through the thick rain-filled clouds. The sun was almost at the horizon still high enough to be hidden by the clouds, and a large rainbow loomed across the far end of the valley. The terrain was stark and naked, void of the dense vegetation I was used to seeing and somehow expecting. It was overwhelming.

The thick rain pelted the barren inhospitable countryside. The oceans and craggy edges teamed with creatures so strange and unique, animals that looked like they were from a different planet and not of our planet Earth, animals that looked so ridiculous although in sync with the barren desolate background of rocks and mountains and windy rainy black terrain, some streaks of reds from the iron and brownish-black dirt.

Overlooking the beach, there was a teaming abundance of life mostly from bacteria forms of life to amoeba forms as well. There was a moss type of algae very thick in the water. As well, there were strange tube like creatures. One of the creatures had a huge head, a long tube like mouth with suction-like cups attached to a ridiculously long stretched neck, that was attached to a small round body with short fin like appendages, and a large single suction cup that was obviously used to attach itself to prey as well as hold it. Well its head arched around able to grab hold of the prey, devouring it after it had grabbed its prey, coiled around its catch, and ingested it whole.

Music started to sound in my head. *Your first initial task begins here. A musical voice suddenly came from within my head. There will be a disturbance in all our planes. It will be affecting your plane in twenty four hours. This is what will happen. The music started to play in my head with a different beat and a visual picture of a collision of a huge rogue comet the size of mars colliding with the planet. "This is an image of what is about to happen to your Earth. You must gather as many species, and shelter as many as possible as complete annihilation is imminent. You will have to move very fast, as the collision is imminent and all our planes are affected, especially the second plane. This is the single most important event that involves all the planes. Loss of life can be prevented. The task is now in your hands.* The voice simply stopped as fast as it had come.

Jescan reached over and put his hand on my shoulder. "Is everything okay? You have been in sort of a trance for the last few minutes."

"Yes . . . yes, everything is all right with me. Nothing like jumping into the frying pan," I commented. "But the planet is not. We must collect as many animals and plants as possible. I will prepare an area,"

I said, realizing the immense size of area that would be required. "The size will be a small planet. The continent will have to have enough water and with less land to contain all forms of life. I will prepare a space.

Please plot a course that will cover the entire planet without any doubling back, but overlapping, on each side. We shall start beaming them aboard as soon as I give you the command."

Moving to the back of the control room, although the ship was familiar to me, I really had not thought of what lay in the remainder of the ship. Opening a door, I entered a hallway with several doors off each side. I think the second door on the left will do, as I really had no idea what was in the room. *Yes*, I thought, *the room is empty. It will be just perfect.* As I raised my hands, energy started to illuminate from the palms and fingertips of my hands, surprising me as the sensation was unexpected.

Slowly, at first a planet started to form, and as it grew the room seemed to also grow, as the space was expanding to meet the size required. This was a surprising experience, as I somehow knew that the area of the room from the outside was not changing, only the inside was expanding. Returning to the control room, I looked over the coordinates Jescan had prepared.

As I sat him down in front of the console pointing to the proper buttons, "this one controls the coverage, and this controls the animals transported to the location here on the Geneses, which will be cataloging and classifying each species recording everything that is transported. As we travel along we will be making the widest sweep possible there can be nothing left on the planet, and if we are lucky this spiral course you have plotted will work. This is an excellent route.

We will start in the north and work our way south. This is remarkable, as there is no ice." As I looked out the viewing window, I somehow thought of the north and south as always being cold. There is snow on the highest peaks of the mountains, but none in the large open plains and valleys. Since there is minable or no land life, we will start with the plants and the animals in this Arctic Ocean. Take as much water as you can. Then we shall include in our sweep the land animals if there are any and plants as we reach the surrounding land. These animals are so different from what I had expected."

Touching several of the controls on the console, I readjusted the transporter range. "The transporter is set so that the animals will be placed at different locations, depending on the needs and according to species and compatibility of living with other species. The transporter computer will catalog, keeping track of them and transporting them back after the danger to the earth has subsided. Let's do it!" I said, smiling as I sat in the chair glancing at my watch showing that four hours had passed. There were twenty hours left to completely cover the planet.

Jescan stared at the coordinates, not really believing what he was looking at, although not questioning what he had been told, as the number of the coordinates was similar to maybe the size of a medium planet, although the coordinates that it was being utilized were all contained in a space of about twelve feet by twelve feet, maybe less. If a comparison could be made, the coordinates were taking from a large planet and placing it in the space, the size of a garden shed. Shaking his head, he proceeded with the transporting of all the life on the planet.

Turning to Jescan, smiling at the perplexed look on his face, I said, "I will be in the back room. The ship will stay on course. If you need me, just holler."

Placing myself on a high point on the miniature planet, all around me creatures that had not been seen in any book or for that matter, rarely in any archeology finds such unique life forms, I noticed that most every animal was an invertebrate, strangely shaped as they arrived, very few animals that had made the transition to land yet although there surprisingly was some actually breathing air and some Occasionally climbing out on the beaches and rocks. The animals were so shocked at the change that they were totally subdued, even the plentiful sea animals were totally subdued, and I observed them and felt very comfortable. I adjusted the light shining around the false planet. The planet filled up the lowlands with water and started to run into the crevices forming freshwater lakes and ponds in the upper land areas and salty seawater in the lower areas. The land started to look very much like what Earth looked like, except the plants and animals were in closer proximity yet there was surprisingly few disturbances as though the animals being disrupted and displaced to this artificial land were enough to settle them down into a submissive, very passive group of animals.

Jescan came over the speaker and reported that all life, including a large portion of the water, some fresh as well as mostly salt water had been completely transported and that there was something that I needed to look at.

Knowing that it was probably the meteorite, I realized that I had not explained the situation to Jescan. "I will be right there," I said, leaving the room with the artificial planet. I re-entered the console room.

"Jescan, what is the status of the meteorite?" I asked as I looked into a very concerned face. "Could I be reading your face properly in that you possibly would like to leave?"

"Yes!" he answered in a very short, excited response.

Looking up to the sky, all I could see was a massive planet-sized object moving straight at us. It was so close that I could see the landscape of the meteorite clearly, showing a crater-filled landscape with valleys and mountains and small as well as huge craters as it had picked up an amazing amount of debris as it had circled the sun, and I could tell it was with no atmosphere.

Touching the controls, we moved out into space exposing the immense meteorite looming ominously. It was so large it blocked out all the sky and because of the gravitational pull, was heading straight for the earth.

Watching the massive planet-sized asteroid starting to enter the Earth's atmosphere, something made me look at the console. "What was the reverse trajectory of this asteroid?" I soon realized that the meteorite had been circling in a close parallel outer orbit for millions of years and because it was so close, the gravitational pull had finally dawn it closer and closer. We were watching the final orbit as individual celestial objects, over the eons the asteroid as well as

Earth had been picking up the floating debris, growing in size with each additional chunk, gaining more gravitational pull with each additional one. The same as the meteorite and Earth had done over millions of years.

In what seemed like slow motion, it crashed into the earth allowing tons of debris shooting out into space. It collided as the mantle cracked on both planets. Both had a liquid molten core as both mantles cracked all over, causing the liquid to flow freely together. The smaller being combined with the larger, sending out a crown-like circle around the collision, shooting debris out of the atmosphere and into space. At this range, it looked like several large pieces moving out from the planet moving out till the gravity of the planet started to have an effect on the debris, which was because of the gravitational pull and rotation of the planet. It quickly formed a big ball of molten lava, surprisingly restricting how far the debris moved out into space as it slowed, as the gravity from the planet kept most of it from leaving the area surrounding the planet.

These chunks of debris immediately formed similar to a crown-like ring, except it was still being added to as the planet became one large molten blob, causing all the water to evaporate, causing the atmosphere to become saturated with huge clouds as it was raining, but was evaporating as soon as it hit the molten planet. The debris outside the atmosphere collided together as some were huge chunks that were still hot. Molten chunks attracted because of the larger pieces having more gravitational influence, which would become several chunks floating around the planet Earth, even now starting to collide together.

We sat watching this unbelievable transformation as this planet we called Earth grew in front of us. The center core was seemingly unaffected, as I could sense it simply increased in size as the friction of the two planet's collided, causing higher temperatures still though allowing the cooler lava to circulate around it. There was one more observation that I noted. There was so much debris in the atmosphere that the sun was sufficiently blocked from the earth, which allowed for a needed cooling period that the planet needed to reach a point whereby it could one day support life once more.

The ocean in the horizon was almost completely evaporated with some pockets being caught inside the lava causing huge releases of gas into the atmosphere, starting large lava flows or volcano flows as some had the volcano sides and look, forming a cone shape.

I was surprised as well. The large asteroid had a large deposit of huge chunks of ice, adding a sizable volume of water to the overall water of the planet. Steam rose from the planet as it blocked out almost all the site of the planet itself, as all water evaporated as soon as it touched the molten lava.

Musical sounds came again, *They suggested that I look at Mars for a temporary storage place for earth's life, and it would help out the third plane that in the future is a factor that allows life to exist on Mars, after the life from Earth is removed, with a small residual that is left behind as well as asteroids and possibly comets will allow for the life on Mars to begin even in this plane, but especially in the third plane.*

"Well, time to check this out," I said as I touched the globe, and the lights started to load in the coordinates. "Welcome to Mars. Let's check outside," I said as I opened the viewing windows as we moved over the land.

Mars was remarkably like Earth in many ways, even large bodies of water flowing over the land, although I could tell there were no life forms in the water or on land. It was completely sterile. Knowing the urgency of plane three, the need was important.

Water was plentiful on Mars. It had an atmosphere, as there were heavy clouds with plenty of rain in them, and with the additional water on the artificial planet, there would be plenty of room for the life forms to survive on Mars till Earth could once again support life.

Thinking to myself, *We should start a gene pool and save two of each of the species and suspend them for study at some future date in time.*

Touching the controls, we started to transport the living life forms to compatible areas on the planet. After the last life form had been transported, we toured the planet.

The oceans seemed to be doing very well and the microorganisms, including the algae were multiplying at an accelerated rate. The new life was in a very comfortable situation, as I knew it would be several hundreds of years before Earth would cool down enough for life to exist, due to the increased temperature leftover from the collision of the asteroid and the debris and water that would not be normal for several hundreds of years. "Let's check out Earth," I said as I touched the globe and the console lit up, it buzzed us that we had arrived in orbit around Earth.

The realization that there was no moon had not even really occurred to me, yet this was the actual formation or the start of the moon. Adding to the cloudy debris still floating around the planet, residue from the beginning of the solar system had formed around the sun, and this debris would eventually be attracted by gravitation adding to the mass of the new satellite till one day it would become the size that we would be so familiar with. I was so amazed and surprised as I watched with total and complete amazement and fascination.

The meteorite actually had struck the side of the planet, and the angle was just right to have knocked off a portion of the bulge on the southern region, which before the collision gave the planet an odd bulging pear-shape look. The earth became a sea of molten lava as it gushed out black lava smoke spewing the black residue as the water cooled the red hot lava. The molten ball of matter projected out in a circular motion still controlled by the gravity of Earth. It was as though the new moon reached a point that the pull of the gravity from

Earth and the weightlessness of space allowed the moon to come to a slow motionless standstill, and although it looked like the new moon had quickly settled into a slow revolution around the earth was starting to gather the cloudy debris as it circled around the earth, that was still very evident around the still very young planet.

The new satellite became stationary in a relatively short time and did not rotate like the earth did. The entire moon still rotated around the planet, but the one side stayed fixed to Earth thus, only one side of the moon could be visible to Earth at any given time. It soon reached a comfortable equilibrium with the Earth's gravity and the new satellite's gravity, which allowed to slow in a comfortable motion, which I could sense was on a route that, over time would move it fractionally still farther away from the planet till it finally would reach it's somewhat stable distance that we know it to be in the future. This would cause major tides on the earth's surface initially which over time, would slow down as the moon moving slightly over time farther from the planet, fixing a geocentric orbit around the earth.

"I think that it is going to be a while before we will be able to reintroduce our passengers back to their home. Let's have the computer log these species and find out when we will be able to send them back to a livable Earth. Let's go two hundred years into the future," I said as I touched the controls, and a buzzer sounded our arrival.

"I recall reading in school that the earliest form of life exchanged genes at an accelerated rate and that mutations of these genes occurred in an orgy of reproduction never rivaled in any other period on Earth.

The species on the planet Mars is the source of the entire DNA or the backbone of all life on Earth, man included." Looking at Jescan I said, "In all the writings, this has never been recorded, not sure it should, but history should know this! Not even your people have ever recorded this event.

Creatures that had been in the room, small though they may be in terms of evolution, most still being microscopic, each of them is presently invertebrates, yet a lot have started what will eventually be rudimentary external skeletons. The majority is animals that would resemble some modern-day animals.

It is surprising the small animals as in comparison to the huge creatures in the future massive creatures, are not yet containing a bone, with only cartilage someday holding massive bodies together.

Unique creatures monster-like in appearance, if a description was possible recalling the pictures of monsters in the books I had read as a child, these remarkable animals that we took out of the oceans now swimming in the oceans on the planet Mars, somewhat comparable to jellyfish or to a modern version of a small slug or possibly like octopus without the stability of cartilage, down to the microscopic plankton even to the smallest virus, may be the link of all life in an infinite timeframe. These creatures are the genesis of all life in this sector, or should I say plane."

Contemplating the words that I had just said knowing the answers, I still questioned myself, not realizing the significance of the words but somehow understanding what I should be doing. All that I had known before my transformation was that the viruses played an important role because they contained only one half of the DNA strand called RNA. To actually see how everything started was what I would like to experience. I knew I would have to consider the possibility, maybe someday soon.

"We should start a gene pool and save two of each of the species and suspend them for study at some future date in time."

Jescan looked at me and with a slight pause, said, "Our people have been collecting specimens since our meeting with you, and our technology within limits has allowed us too. You are right in the statement that this has never been recorded before in any form, as nothing was or is capable of recording these events until now, and the ability has never been available till you came along.

You see there are many important facts or information including situations that you have brought to our people that had never been presented to an educated, literate society before and traveling through time is something that only you now possess, had never been possible until you arrived. The changes that you have started in saving these animals and plants have already been written in the books, and the historical records are in the museums so my people can marvel at the unique creatures. We were aware of them even before you or myself were born.

We just never knew where you came from and I found out that it was me the moment we took off from home base. I really had no idea that this was in store for me. Although my name is very common among my people, my name I thought was after the man who first went with you. Little did I realize that it was me. I should have realized it when we picked you up, I suppose that I had a twinge of wanting to be that person, but it did not occur to me till we took off."

Considering what Jescan had said, I focused my thoughts on the lifeless planet below and said, "It is time to replace the animals and plants although there is new water forming in the overheated humid atmosphere the oceans must be replenished. It would be a major slowdown if the animals and plants had to form all over again. Let's check on the status of the earth."

The planet was in a state that could not sustain life yet, the thick debris of dust and particles had not yet filtered back through the thin atmosphere of Earth, and although Earth was cooling down slightly the violent volcanic action still was restricting the sun's ability to filter through to the surface. I decided that we would travel to the estimated date that life could once again survive, the time was in the thousand sixty-fifth year from the date of the collision. Sitting down to the controls I reset the controls of the *Genesis*, and a little buzzing sound from the computer announced that we had arrived.

Opening the viewing screen, I looked out to a sterile lifeless planet with water and rock and a thick layer of dust over everything.

The sun though was shining and the rain that was constantly cleaning the atmosphere needed the regeneration and recycling of the plants and animals. "Let's start the sensors to cover the oceans first and then the land. First, let's check for life signs as there may or could be new life formed from the chunks of ice from the meteorite," I said, knowing the possibility that new life could be present.

Our task is to retrieve the life on Mars. Setting for a date only a few centuries after we had dropped them off, I touched the globe, and the buzzer sounded that we had arrived in an orbit around Mars.

As we traveled over the landscape of the planet scanning the surface as we covered the amazing red landscape before we recover all the life, I said, "We should land and maybe check it out."

Landing on a bluff overlooking the ocean I double-checked that there was enough oxygen, and no harmful particulates were in the air.

Jescan said, smiling, "I was wondering if you would ever take a break and have time to appreciate what you have done."

I too now realized that we had done a lot and should be appreciated. "Good plan," I said as I opened the door letting in a refreshing gust of fresh air.

Stepping out I could sense the abundance of oxygen in the air and realized that the algae had produced so much oxygen. It was a pleasant feeling as I reveled in the sensation of having a breeze blowing lightly in my face and the purity of the air. It was so relaxing.

"I think we should take a walk," I said as I headed toward the ocean. Noting that I could step almost twice as far as I could on Earth, being that the gravitational pull was less than that of the earth, it was a great feeling as I could jump very high with very little effort, super feeling.

Jescan and I had a view of the edge of the ocean and could see the water was a vivid blue-green color, some more blue as the water was deeper, where the water was shallower was a striking green tone and noticing that the bottom of the sea could be seen from both the shallower area to the deepest almost as though you were looking through a magnifying glass it was so clear.

Jescan moved down closer to the edge of the sea, and pulled out of his jacket some sample beakers taking samples of the water.

It was going to be dusk in a few hours. I suggested, "How about we set up a camp here in this clearing on the beach? What do you think?"

"I would like that. Will be a nice break from being in the Genesis."

Going back we collected what we would like and again went down to the beach, setting up a nice little camp.

Sitting on one of the chairs we brought with my feet raised as well, a gust of wind blew off the sea and felt amazing. This was such a wonderful feeling. I could appreciate the view and could kick back and relax. A very good feeling indeed.

I could see the algae in large patches floating on the top of the sea and noticed that there were several clumps some large and some small, even in the small area that I could see.

Along the edge I could see the water moving as some animals were trying to get something to eat or trying to get away from being eaten. It really was very peaceful with no sounds other than the waves coming into the beach and the breeze blowing across the land. This was the most peaceful a place as you could want.

Jescan was enjoying the break as well and was looking at the sea.

"We should bring some food and have something to eat. It is so nice here," he said.

"Great idea."

"Be right back," stated Jescan as he headed off to get something to eat for us.

Sitting back, I looked up at the sky seeing very light wispy clouds knowing that we would not be rained upon, what a clear view of the blueness of the sky.

Jescan returned with enough sandwiches to feed five people. I smiled, knowing that we had not eaten for quite a while and actually was very hungry seeing the food. Settling down with a sandwich in my hand, I started to eat realizing how hungry I was. Looking over at Jescan, he was devouring his sandwich as well.

We were just finishing the last of the sandwiches as the sun went down. Suddenly, it became cool very fast. As it got darker it got colder.

"Think we should go back and get some sleep where it is warm," I said, as the planet had very large temperature shifts from day to night as we were experiencing firsthand.

Waking up, I heard Jescan rustling in the console room. Getting up,

I entered the console room. "You're up early. Did you have a good sleep?"

"Sure did, and how about you? I was just checking the samples of the water. Everything was as normal as could be. It still amazes me how the microorganisms purify the water so well. What would you like to do first?"

"Well, let's start by plotting a course to cover the entire planet," I stated.

"All ready for you, although double-check them," Jescan quickly answered with a smile on his face.

Reaching for the globe, I said, "Then let's get it done." The console lit up, and watching outside we could see us moving across the landscape of this red planet. "I will be in the other room. Let me know when it is completed," I said, proceeding to the second room down the hallway.

Watching as the life forms arrived, there were many more of them. Some had changed as expected, but they were still mostly microorganisms. Some of the larger ones in a way, looked stranger than the first time they had been teleported, and monsters although small would still fit as a description of them. Turning around I heard the door open noticing Jescan.

"The transfer is complete now, and we left the same amount of water that the planet had, give or take," said Jescan.

"Okay, let's get back to earth," I said, smiling. There is no time like the present. "Earth is waiting."

Taking a check before starting the process, we discovered from the computer results that there even in the harshest of conditions, life had started. All was recorded and samples of the new life were taken as samples of all life to be recorded.

I had noticed that there was one distinct landmass, and the rest was mostly oceans with only a few islands present where there had been or still were volcanic actions happening.

Jescan started the process, and I watched the seas form first landing like little fountains as the water materialized, causing little waves everywhere.

Then the land once again started to fill up with plants and animals still very docile from the unique experience of the changes that they had in their life that was only a matter of a few hours, although they had no idea that they were now approximately a thousand sixty-five years later. They were now free to roam and multiply or perish if that was its destiny, but the reality was that life once again had a chance to continue to evolve changing as the need arose.

The room was empty except for the suspended specimens left on the artificial planet. The earth was once more alive, and even though there were still debris in the atmosphere, the earth was still recovering clumsily yet somehow with the extra moisture from the oceans, allowing the rain clouds to build up faster. The earth taking it in stride was remarkable. How easy the planet was assuming a natural order once again. "Jescan, let's take a walk," I said, setting the landing destination to the highest peak overlooking the ocean, which had the most amount of area visible to the eye.

"I would be honored," he said as he opened the door.

The earth had been reintroduced for three days now and the sky was clear and the day was warm and humid.

There were swamps everywhere and being a rare day with no rain for several hours, it was a perfect day.

The air had a pure clean smell, with the humid air and its distinct smell. With the animals and plants resuming their roles in the sea and the mostly uninhabited land that they had been born to live on, the beauty of the land was spectacular although very barren and desolate.

The continent surprisingly was still mainly one landmass since the spectacular meteorite collision, although the fault lines had developed because of the moon's influence and would eventually over millions of years, form the continent that was more like the earth that I knew radically different from this if a comparison could be made.

There were earthquakes occurring on a regular basis everywhere, the volcanoes were popping up, causing trimmers that could be felt everywhere as the earth was somewhat still adjusting to the change of mass, still trying to equalize itself out. This is time when the fault lines would start their never-ending parting, separating in an endless journey forever striving to renew itself over time, changing forever. The continental drifts would flow for the rest of eternity and with the addition of the new satellite, the pull of the moon started its perpetual movement rhythmic motion of the tender top crust of the earth, forming ebbs and tides of the oceans obviously more severe than I had ever seen from my time as the moon was so much closer.

Jescan stopped on the top of a knoll and without looking at me, questioned, "Will the earth ever get back to the purity of this air and water, and will the land ever again achieve a state of serenity like this?" He recalled the state of the planet from his time.

"This is my first travel in time, and the power that I have acquired is still new to me. The answer to your question is one that I cannot answer yet. I can only speculate like you only hope that man will not destroy everything but for now, I would say that the answer would probably be no, although I hope that I can make a difference." I answered, taking a large deep breath. "It is time to take the *Genesis* and leave now."

"Yes, I know," he said as he turned, considering the last conversation, deep in his own thoughts.

We both walked slowly back to the *Genesis* soaking in the ambiance of the countryside. Even as the earth shook with such a vengeance, we knew what was in store for the planet.

CHAPTER THREE

The *Genesis* was on its way once again, and the buzzing sounded our arrival.

I opened the view screen. The land was somewhat desolate and volcanoes were erupting and the smoke floating in the air, volcano dust lay like snow over everything. Yet this looked totally natural. One would not have guessed that life even existed on this planet.

How are you? said a voice coming from the center lower back of my brain, almost like listening to music in digital surround sound on an IMAX theater or in a concert hall.

This stop is to answer some important questions that you must seem to be able to make the judgments in the future. It will also answer the questions you have been wondering about and as we all have in our own planes. The question you have been asking is how and when life began.

This will be the start. This will be the beginning of your practical side of all the knowledge. Take this time to learn the capabilities of your newly discovered powers. Later, as you become accustomed to your new powers, time will allow you to correct some things that were not supposed to have happened, such as from the initial contact, but you have all the time that you need to solve them after you have witnessed firsthand, your immediate questions. This is your beginning and discover period. You are starting at the beginning of life on your planet. I too will be able to observe through you as well as you will observe through my observations in this plane as well as in all the other planes. Since our joining, we have acquired immense powers that we must each, take this time to learn our newly acquired powers and capabilities.

At this period, it is imperative that you do not leave the ship without using sterile fields around you, including the automatic sterile shell that has been placed around our ships that is a permanent part of the matrix.

This so as not to change or influence life in any way, as this is the way it started and should not be contaminated. This will hold for the next few stops until life is well established. Use the ship as your legs, not as your base to return to. You must not contaminate this sterile environment. The music stoped.

I looked up at Jescan casually sitting, looking straight into my eyes.

"This," I said, understanding his thoughts, "is something that I had asked for. I have always wanted to know the origin of life, and now we are about to find out how life began on Earth. This is the time in history that life is about to begin. This is just before the Achaean period."

"This is so much more than I expected. I can hardly believe that I am with you and will be able to witness such a historical event."

"Let's move the ship around and survey the earth." Sitting down to the controls, we moved slowly up and in a westerly direction. The ground was continually shaking, as volcanoes were spewing moving red molten lava. The air was overwhelmingly humid, according to the monitor's sensors. This was due to the heat of the molten lava hitting and heating water to cause large pools of boiling water, water being the residual from the ice comets, adding large quantities of water to the oceans and ponds and in some of the older areas were the extinct volcanoes survived. There were pools of water, large cooler waters.

I could see the fragments of debris from space entering the atmosphere sounding like a hailstorm of sorts, at points although the atmosphere was thin, it still was enough to cause several particles to burn on entry. It was like floating through a thick fog, yet there was no fog.

It was as if we were in a constant rain, yet there were no raindrops to speak of, only the thick layer of humidity or water hanging in the air. This was the ultimate vertigo or suspended water particles, 100 percent humidity.

Pulling up higher, we could see the light crust dark in the middle and lines of moving red lava exposing the larger planet with a very thin crust covering, thicker where the oceans had formed, thinner where the volcanic areas were. The volcanic dust was moistened as soon as it hit the atmosphere. Although the dust was white and looked like snow, the truth is that it was more like mud than dust. Everything was moist. In some areas, it was almost like soup, thick with dust and water. Off in the distance, the ocean could be seen cooling the land as it crashed against the volcanic walls. The ocean seemed strange. There was no life, no seashells or seaweed, or driftwood. It seemed empty and very desolate.

"What are we looking for?" Jescan asked as we looked out on a totally virgin ocean and a mass of volcanoes that dominated the landscape.

"To be honest, I am not certain. My understanding from my schooling is that life started as one-celled animals and plants, so we will use the ship's computers to analyze the water samples that we will take at random locations. The possibility is that it happens all over the planet, or we could find that it is isolated in one area. We should start taking samples of all the water and samples of the older volcanic ash."

As each sample came in and was analyzed, each one being sterile, we stored them in order and location collected. We carried on around the planet.

Then suddenly one large meteorite hit the isolated large sea, which we were headed for. The meteorite was a huge chunk of ice. We could see the ice hit the sea, and even though there were large particles flying over the land around us, the ice came back to the top of the surface as we came close. The ship automatically took a sample.

As we came into range, the samples showed the magnetic attraction of the molecules that were contained within many of the ice chunks. The ice was so ready to join with other molecules that it formed many links, relying on the ship's sensors as they were microscopic in size, forming long and some wide, as several were connecting randomly some that coiled together. As more molecules bonded with them, the more the strands lengthened.

The strands that had bonded in the water started to vibrate depending on the atoms with the bonded elements, moved as if by contraction because the water was warm enough the molecules could maneuver freely. Although not living as yet, it could mean life had started. "Mmmm . . ., These little magnetically charged strands contained all the essential chemicals of organic life, but could this possibly be one of the starting points of non organic becoming organic living matter?"

In almost all areas, there were violent thunderstorms with lightning striking all around. Would these relentless electrically charged storms have been the start of life with these vibrating bonded chemical actually floating around but not inter-reacting with one another, as it seemed like they actually repelled one another and did not connect with one another, although some still joined as they were not big like some of the others? We found ourselves mesmerized as the storm approached.

The lightning was all around us now, as a major storm mass was descending upon us.

Yes . . . this could be the spot that life might have started, with the bonded molecules floating around, still life was just floating around vibrating. My question is, how did it get to be a reproducing life form?

Life would then begin, as I realized that in the water samples that the computer had collected, they contained small amounts of the little linked atoms. They were microscopic sized polarized gametes, nonliving atoms that had a south and a north polarity. These little gametes, attracted others as we saw with the bonding forming what I would say, could be a colony of, or a string of atoms. I thought as I watched the vibrating atoms.

The electrically charged thunder storm that was moving towards us with the main storm heading in our direction. Closely watching the storm, I could somehow sense all the chemicals reacting to the electrical storm as the gametes were becoming overexcited. "This could be what we are looking for."

"You mean that the life on this planet started with little polarized atoms? Not from a chemical reaction?" came a surprised question from Jescan.

"There is still a chemical reaction needed to start the process, and this could be the storm," I said, contemplating how to proceed.

"Computer. Monitor and analyze the water in general areas of the sea where the bonded particles are floating. Check anything that has a chemical vibration in the water, especially the carbon atoms. Visually display on screen, and magnify."

A fuzzy blur of atoms moving very rapidly in and out of focus completely amazed us as we watched a group of little polarized atoms connecting and disconnecting. The closer the lightning came, so did the static electric field, causing and exciting the carbon atoms present in the bonded molecules, and caused the gametes or polarized atoms to become more excited, moving in and out of the screen. As the lightning struck the water, the little molecules seemed to not really melt together but more like bond together, and as they did so, there was a helical formation within a membrane of polarized molecules, which surrounded a clump of organized strands of single-stranded helix-formed atoms, utilizing several chemicals obtained from within the bonded molecules, RNA had now arrived.

Watching intently, they seemed attracted to other molecules similar to themselves. The thin layer around one another slowed the process, in some they bonded to one another forming a longer strand but in some, the one that broke through the one strand was disassembled and was reassembled in the exact replica of the other RNA strand, then they would separate, leaving two identical RNA's. several bonded in small bunches.

Still watching intently, in a small few the RNA's completely broke apart into the atomic state, due to the static electrically charged atmosphere, then unbelievably inside the shell a single strand formed, known as a telomere, followed rapidly by the rejoining of the atoms as the double helix formed for the first time. The first DNA's had just arrived!

Well, we were watching several formed as they darted back and forth. As more combined we could see the formation of telomeres alongside the DNA strands, which would lock in the sequence of the DNA, causing it to reproduce only in the sequence of the original DNA. As this one-celled microorganism consumed or rather enveloped more, some of the telomeres and DNA strands attached and became longer strands.

This all happened within hours of the initial formation of the RNA's arrival. *Totally amazing*, I thought, *truly amazing*. When life started, it was amazing how fast it developed.

I noticed that sometimes when a RNA entered a cell with DNA, there was a splitting of the DNA, which ended up forming three individuals or more of RNAs restructuring the newly formed DNAs, which in turn, would enter more cells splitting and becoming a single-stranded encased celled form that came from the template of the strand of the original RNA. Each cell played a part in how they attach to one another. Some finally connected, and we watched as the fluid from one entered the other, as the shell was very soft. The exchange of chemicals started to form into a strand. The cells then split with the combination of both combinations, forming a new strand combination within the cell, alike but different than the original because of the links from both strands. One became the template with new combinations.

This was the first step of life, as the very first one-celled virus had its beginning. Not sure whether they lived off other cells or they just needed the lukewarm water to survive having had just formed in front of us.

"This is it, Jescan. This is it," I said, noticing that the RNA's were way more abundant than the DNA's at this stage.

Watching with total amazement as the new one-celled virus joined with another, then with additional ones, second generations started within hours of the initial stimulation. Within the first ten hours, little one-celled viruses began to dominate the screen, mixed with a few DNA celled microbes.

"This is unbelievable, remarkable, amazing!" Jescan said, watching so intently that he didn't even realize that he moved his lips and mouthed the words.

Surprised at hearing the words instead of through the mind, it was a pleasant feeling, as I realized that he never had used that form of communication before. "Glad to see that you are able to talk through the voice as well as through the mind."

Jescan looked at me, embarrassed at what had just happened. "It is a response that I did not even expect. I am sorry."

"I find it nice to hear a voice again."

"My people do not use their voices very often except to exercise their limited underdeveloped voice box. I rarely use my voice except for the exercise. This is a very remarkable event. Maybe it was meant to be spoken and not thought."

"When did your people learn to communicate telepathically?"

"Our historians suggest that we have always had the ability. At one time in our history, the leaders adopted telepathic communication as a means of ritual communication with the common people. The people, revering their leaders, did not use telepathic communication except to communicate with them. Our ancestors really never used it, except for rituals although there were several occasions that couples would occasionally use telepathic communication in their courtships, and in their personal relationships, and eventually became a regular way of life. Thus our voice box never developed to the extent of your people.

On a regular basis, it never came to be a regular everyday usage until we started into our technical period, especially to the start of our space program. At this point, we learned that we could communicate better than any machine could do. We actually heard the thoughts, and then like an echo, the microphones actually made communication jumbled and confusing.

Although over long distances, we still rely on machines. Although we have devised a method of transferring our thoughts not our voice, through the communicator, problems of being out of contact were alleviated. With the exception of over vast areas, were we used our communicators.

Our people did in the beginning practice its use, of course in ritualistic format. Now the children are taught from the moment of inception and use it all their life. Rarely do we use verbal communication, as once we could understand the language of many living things, we are able to communicate with all forms of living entities in several forms of communication or any language.

As long as the creatures are capable of a form of communication and can understand, we are able to reach and understand a wide variety of animals and including some plants. There are very few barriers that interfere with our form of communication."

"I hear you. It is a great gift." Suddenly, I realized that I too, held the power to communicate telepathically long before my joining with the sixth plane. "Is there any way to block out thoughts?" I questioned.

"Yes, you only transmit what you want to be heard. Same as verbal language, the thoughts of another is their own. Although to break into someone's inner thoughts can still be done, it is very hard to expedite it for an extended period, as it requires a lot of practice as well as an enormous drain of energy."

"Are you able to limit communication with one person only and not another if they are in the same room?"

"Yes, although again requires a lot of energy but is easy enough to do."

"Then if a person doesn't know about your telepathy, then all their thoughts are relayed to you?"

"We do have that advantage over some types of animals and plants, but there are certain things that I, or anyone cannot penetrate.

That is your subconscious mind. You are private to your own thoughts, and your expression is of your own accord. Although you are implying for the purpose of private thoughts, and if I really wanted to yes, I could really read every thought you have. This is similar to a psychic probe, although the person must have an open enough mind allowing me to enter. We as a people, do not like to intrude into someone's personal innermost thoughts. Ethically, there would have to be a good reason to do so."

"How do you communicate with plants?" I inquired.

"Plants are unique in that they do communicate with other plants, for plants in soil, it is through a fungi that sends out communication to other plants through their roots sending out vibrations and it passes along to any plants around them. With plants communication is extremely slow and with limited information. With plants that are floating, they send out a vibration to communicate, again it is this vibration that is what is used to communicate, although information is again like slow motion, but information can be obtained. Kind of like watching them grow, on the other side their information can be useful. Not used very often, I have never had an instance to use it, except for them to grow. Used mostly for that purpose." replied Jescan.

"I too acquired the knowledge necessary to understand the basic ability, which I had already possessed before my joining, but did not realize that it had always been there. I would have called it a gift before, but now I realize how easy it is to form a thought and transfer it through telepathy to another. The thought waves are quite remarkable as they are received. It is as clear as a bell, yet sometimes I hear thoughts that I know are your own private thoughts.

I am surprised at what I hear and yet when I answer, you have responded every time. I just had to know some of the limits," I said, contemplating the complexity of the thought processes. "Hum . . . interesting."

"You Adam are in all respects, the teacher. I have been very curious as to how you communicate with the sixth plane. I can tell when you are communicating, but I hear absolutely nothing. Is it subconscious?"

"I suppose, in a way it is. I hear a type of music, music that is the start of all language with a beat, a rhythm, a tone in the right key. It is all part of it. I can as you say hear and interpret it, allowing me to understand it. It is in a way a form of language . . . It is based loosely on a mathematical language. I know exactly what it is telling me." My thoughts focused on the last communication and the pleasant prospect of traveling to all the most significant times in Earth's history, all from the beginning." I commented. Does the RNA always dominate in the beginning, and what happens when the first DNA replicates itself to form the foundation of life, allowing the unique diversity of every species? *I thought to myself.*

Changing the conversation, we went back to the combining of the RNA's, which was in a way a hostile takeover of the cell it was attacking, forming replicas of itself then splitting sending out replicas of itself.

With the DNA's it, with the help of the telomeres, duplicated two strands, separating within the cell then dividing the cell to form two cells. At the start of the helix shape forming in front of us, the two strands as in most viruses only had one strand, usually absorb the other forming several single-stranded RNA's which in turn, disperse into other cells that they come into contact with.

Although, it was inevitable that the single strands would combine, and to be the first to witness the first formation was as interesting as the viruses themselves. This particular joining was unique in the fact that all the strands stayed within the shell.

Upon touching another virus, instead of transferring its single strand it absorbed the virus, breaking the strand down and the formation of a single strand formed first, then it built from the telomere which was first formed, then causing and directing the forming of a double helix. It rebuilt a new strand of itself by splitting down the middle, but as it split, it reconnected itself with the chemical strands of the available other RNA strand, forming two identically double strands. This was when the two new strands separated within the newly formed harder cell. Each side separated themselves and formed a small membrane between the two sides. The cell then sort of shrunk or grew thinner in the middle, breaking away from the parent cell, leaving only two identical cells instead of several copies of the parent, as was the case of most viruses.

As we watched the next encounter, it was two strands combining with two strands. As the strands split the configuration of both was changed as the telomeres grew in length, and not matching either of the parents but a completely different life form. We watched as the mitochondria started to duplicate itself again without having contact with another virus.

As we watched the next encounter, it was two strands combining with two strands. As the strands split, the configuration of both was changed, not matching either of the parents but a completely different life form. We watched as the mitochondria started to duplicate itself again without having contact with another virus. The splitting continued, and within a relatively short time frame, absorbing elements and atoms within the water, and surrounding elements had polarized itself, pushing exact replica strands to opposite sides of the cell. The cell then started to form a thin membrane between the two strands. As the membrane formed it created two separate walls and with polarization repelled from each other, separating forming the first one-celled life form to replicate a copy of itself, then separated to repeat the process all over again once the elements were absorbed.

The nutrients were absorbed though the thicker wall of the cell as it enveloped itself around another cell, taking only the chemicals that it needed, rejecting the leftover chemicals that it did not require. Noting that it enveloped viruses containing RNA as well as DNA cells, the first predator was just born.

Several times, this process happened, and although it came into contact with other viruses, it repelled the contact although not in every case. Occasionally, a collision caused an exchange of fluid, but the two-stranded cell reconfigured itself with the help of the telomeres, splitting the strands and exchanging the half with the other half from the other single-celled life form, forming two new exactly alike strands. These in turn polarized and separated, transpiring the replication of itself, now with the ability to accept both means of reproduction, polarization, or transference of the DNA strand. In one case there was a collision and there was no transference, the

DNA strand though transferred completely. Not splitting completely, although breaking the bonds, it started to add to the strand forming a much longer strand. The result was division of bonds that were linked together, yet when they started to split, they made two cells but stayed together. Now for the first time it had formed a multi-celled life form.

My interest was fixed on this new life form, as it wrapped around other viruses and not transferring the RNA but digesting the chemicals and rejecting the shell of the now dead virus. This was the very first microscopic animal or ameaba to have arrived on the planet.

The first bacteria had also arrived using only the sun and moisture to reproduce.

To actually be an eyewitness to the absolute beginning of life, it in itself an accelerating event, although action-wise it was rather mundane, and to have the ability to observe the remarkable events excited me, striking me in a very profound way, that I could not believe. My pulse quickened, a flush of excitement as adrenaline surged through my veins, and I tingled all over as my nerve endings were crackling with the energy that emulated from each and every synapse throughout my body.

This experience with the small viruses forming the first double helix life form was as exhilarating, almost but not quite as much as the connection with the sixth plane. We had witnessed the beginning of life, and not only witnessed the beginning but also the start of the first life form that perpetuated itself. This was the answer to my first question.

Turning to Jescan, I suggested, "Let's travel ahead in time to the next major occurrence."

Touching the control button, the buzzing sound alerted us to our arrival.

We looked out at the same area but were surprised to discover very little change in the landscape. The flowing of the molten lava was still part of the land, although it had grown daily in size, significant as the increase was, it would in time become a substantial landmass.

The ocean had receded some ten miles and was now a part of the landscape off in the horizon, although we had an impaired view of the landscape, as the land was almost over the top of the *Genesis*. "Let me see now," I said as I made some minor adjustments, "We should have a better view now." The *Genesis* was now sitting on top of the land instead of being partially buried.

"The land does not look different, although it has changed because of the volcano's oozing hot red rivers, and volcanic ash is still covering everything, which was expanding in size as well as the buildup of dust and debris started to become thicker in depth. Mind you, look at how bluish green the ocean is. The water had changed from a grayish black to an amazing reflection of blue but had a hint of green. We must be imagining the change. Is it possible that the life had multiplied to such an extent as to change the vast oceans of water? Could it be the storm that caused the initial formation of life, enough to change the color of the water from ten years earlier?

"These have to be the effects of chloroform-producing plant life or possibly animal life. Possibly both could actually be changing the water in a way almost purifying or recycling the water, as the isolated molecules of water were recycling remarkably fast. With the explosion of such vivid bluish-green colors, it could be possible."

"Let's take a look at the overall planet. There is obviously bound to be some major changes," I said, manoeuvring the *Genesis* in a westerly direction. "Computer, start taking samples in same pattern as previously. Store in same order for an accurate comparison. Itemize changes of each sample in comparison to the first sample."

"Look, there is a green slime on the coastline," said Jescan as he pointed to the green jellylike substance on the beach.

"You are quite right. This is interesting, as it has never been determined at which point in history that life, plant or animal had ventured onto land," I said, pausing to study the green substance. It could have just washed ashore. "Computer, please analyze. Emphasis if this life is actually surviving out of the water, and I would like a breakdown of the structure to the smallest combinations of atoms, special attention to the building of the DNA if any. Report as soon as data is available."

"Look at the green mass in the water. It is massive." Jescan pointed to the ocean.

The computer interrupted, "The analysis of the first sample is in. Others will be possessed momentarily from several locations. There are several types of Cyanophyceae and Euglenophyta. The first group is referred to commonly as algae, which is the simplest form of one-celled plant. Some are referred to as a form that carries on the process of photosynthesis. Cell division is the only means of reproduction known as fission. These plants have asexual bodies that are usually formed under adverse conditions and that are very resistant to heat, cold, and dryness. They flourish in fresh water and yet can survive in very toxic water as well.

The second class is the flagellates and dinoflagellates. These creatures are many different colors or can be colorless. They are the earliest forms of animals that ingest solid food, such as one-celled algae. At this point, it is not sure how to categorize them, are they a plant or an animal as they have characteristics that meet the criteria of both plants as well animals because they also have the ability of photosynthesis. These forms of flagellates and algae have been divided into several different and unique forms. In the samples that have analyzed, there are 2,415 species so far recorded by the ships computer, status to change as more samples are taken. It is highly probable that this number will increase."

After the samples have been taken, my thoughts wandered, as it was so logical, that the moment one cell was absorbed by another, the nutrients from one could sustain another. "Let's follow this through. Let's see if the history of this one-celled creature could be the foundation of all the animals, evolving into a multi-celled more complex animal which would appear on Earth from this day forward."

I sat back and looked at the earth as the red lava looking like rivers running down the sides of the volcanoes and the dust that was filtering though the layers of the atmosphere, several layers deep.

"All that I have read and learned about this remarkable journey does not excite me as much as actually experiencing them for myself. It is a dream come true," stated Jescan. I could see the excitement in his body language.

As the data from the samples were finalizing the information gathered on the computer, I said, "Let's proceed to our next historical event."

You have another important task that must be completed, first came the voice in a very clear musical way. *Your next stop is one that is critical to yours, and the third plane, none of the others will be affected, as it is only your two planes that will be affected. Your task is in the future, about fifteen thousand years to solve an eminent problem quite unique in the sense that it could affect the planet that you refer to as Mars. It is something that will affect life on Earth if it is not diverted.*

You are able to return to your quest after this has been corrected. A cloudy vision of a massive storm appeared. As it came into focus, it would dominate the entire planet. One of such velocity, that everything will be left continually and constantly changing with extreme speed, mountains will be worn down in a matter of weeks, the planet is left in constant carouse for eternity. The vision passed over to an ice planet that would be suitable to accept the storm without affecting life within this quadrant, the other is the sun.

"We have a short detour, Jescan," I said as I pushed the control, and the buzzing sound announced our arrival.

We were suspended in space just above the equator on the planet Mars. The atmosphere was normal. There was no noticeable changes in climatic conditions. What would cause the radical changes, such as in the vision in the condition of the planet during my conversation with the other planes?

"Nothing seems out of place. What are we looking for?" Jescan said as he observed the planet from the viewing screen.

"There is a storm that is forming or on its way that will destroy the planet, causing a continuous shifting of the terrain, a storm that will carry on for an eternity. In the third plane, there are life forms that exist on the planet." I was interrupted by a strange object just entering our solar system. Resembling a comet, although it was oscillating as it approached, it almost looked alive as it pulsed in a simplistic rhythmic motion, almost casual. "Computer, monitor and record this moment of discovery and record the redirection of the solar storm destined to change the ambiance of this solar system if not diverted."

"The solar storm is in a direct collision course with the planet Mars. The storm will make first contact in thirty-six hours eleven minutes," announced the computer.

"Now we know the time but . . . but how will we protect the planet?" stated Jescan as he turned from the viewing screen and looked deeply into my eyes, searching for any information.

"This is an interesting situation. The gravity is pulling the storm toward the planet. The storm is so intense and massive that it would envelope the entire planet in a perpetual motion, and in a millennium, the planet will be torn apart into a never-ending ball of particles of the broken-up planet. All atoms will be absorbed within the particles.

Our task is to deflect this storm and protect the life in the third plane as well, the life that will someday be an important landmark in this plane. Let's land.

"I have some equipment that I need to situate in three strategic points. Hopefully, I will cause a shield that will protect this planet, deflecting the storm." Manoeuvring the ship, I took a long pondering look at the other planets that possibly could be a target for the storm.

It would be ideal to divert the storm directly into the sun, which could absorb the storm with only extra fuel for the sun. The alignment of the different plant angles could possibly work to our favor, although the planets that lie between Mars and the sun could be affected if the angles were out even a fraction of a degree. The ship came to a stop as we landed at the first point." I commented.

"Can we go outside?" questioned Jescan as he looked at the atmospheric readings. "It seems okay."

"The atmosphere is very light. Oxygen levels are adequate. Nitrogen and carbon dioxide levels are in acceptable ranges. Strong recommendation is required. Your movements should be controlled and not hurried, as you will experience a feeling of light-headedness, as the oxygen levels are lower than your body is used to. Temperature is within acceptable limits. At present, you have no anomalies that would show signs of danger. You have thirty-five hours fifty-five minutes till the planet is completely consumed in the storm," stated the computer.

"This, although several millions of years from now, shall have a significant role to play in relation to man's quest to explore. Although this incident is a critical moment in time, we are very safe, as this can and will be diverted. This will someday be a thriving vital part of our civilized life, as from this day forward, it will become a reserve for mankind, allowing it to expand the area required for growth, and the first step to our survival in space to start mankind on its journey into the rest of eternity. It will be a sterile environment that will be completely molded into another planet that will be the envy of all planets, inhabited with similar earth-like conditions, hopefully, a completely unpolluted habitat that will become a complete priority. It is a remarkable planet, as it contains all the chemicals that allow for a completely self-perpetuating environment."

"Computer, can we safely leave the ship without any protective gear?" Jescan asked as he turned from looking at the various screens on the console, facing me.

"You are safe to leave the ship as you are. This is an M-class planet capable to sustain life. Atmosphere is a lot thinner than that of Earth or Edan but adequately meets all requirements to sustain life," stated the computer.

"Yes, we will go out but first, I need some materials that I think can be replicated. Computer, replicate three carbon 57 based stones . . . precisely 2,222 carrots each. Scan the planet for gold, enough to make three separate candlesticks with three prongs to hold the three pointed stones. Point out and in direct line down the center of the candleholder, a hole 2.2 centimeters to a length of 22 centimeters.

On the opposite end to the stone, around circular cage of bars, 2 centimeters wide forms the circle, exactly 10 centimeters wide on the inside." Turning to Jescan, I said, "I think we should have a hat to protect us from the sun's UV rays, as the planet does have a thinner atmosphere."

"Computer, transport candles to my location on my command."

Heading to the door, I said, "Let's see what Mars is like," as I placed a sterile field around Jescan and myself.

Opening the door, the fresh, light, clean air hit our bodies, coming as a complete surprise to us, as we had not had the chance to breathe fresh air from a planet for some time. We both looked at each other, pleasantly pleased at the sensation of the fresh moving air. Stepping out onto the reddish-brown soil, I could feel myself sort of spring as

I walked with a light bouncing motion although strange, as it was quite a different sensation. The gravity is noticeably less than that of earth, and the adjustment as Jescan was lightly springing five feet in a single bounce. It was like bouncing on an air-filled mattress. Looking around, it was desolate yet very breathtaking, as the majestic view of the red color of the rocks, the soil and even the red mountain range was looming in the background. It was awe-inspiring to say the least.

There was a river slowly winding its way across a vast barren plain, which was dotted with small lakes and finally to a large lake or a small ocean off into the distance.

"Look at this view," stated Jescan. "This is like a place on our planet named Rotan. Our planet is limited in water in certain areas too. Is that not a form of algae along the riverbank?" he asked, pointing to the river in the valley below us.

"I really don't know. I think that this needs to be investigated further. It could be . . . it could be something that looks similar, although it looks alive, imagination, Mars having life on it, thinking of the last time we were here. The only way is to go and check it out personally."

As we walked down to the river, the signs of life were very prevalent, as there was a moss type of fungus growing in areas spotting the landscape, camouflaged, almost invisible, as the color took on the natural colors of the planet almost identical to that of the soil. As we approached the riverbank, it was obvious the sludge was a type of algae. The alga was similar to what was on Earth, but yet it looked somewhat different somehow I couldn't put my finger on what was wrong. "It doesn't feel right Jescan, just doesn't feel right."

Looking down to the soil, there was a definite sign of a minuscule wormlike creature. I could sense the chemical makeup of several other small bacteria-like animals.

"What . . . what's wrong?" Jescan asked as he turned and looked intently into my face, showing definite concern as he almost jumped back from the water as if he was about to be swallowed by the slow running water.

"I'm not sure, but something is wrong with this. It is as though everything is dying. Let's get some samples from the soil and some of the algae." Bending, I took a handful of soil, and reaching over, I took some of the fungus.

Jescan reached into his pockets and pulled out some vials, bent taking a sample of the water in one and in the other, a sample of the algae floating along the bank.

Smiling, I was surprised at how prepared Jescan had become.

"How did you know you would need to take samples?"

"As I had mentioned to you, I had read a lot about myself. Even though I did not know it was me, I read that Jescan never went anywhere without his sample bottles. Here are some for your samples," he said as he reached inside his suit and pulled out two sample bottles and held them out to me.

"Thanks," I said as I took the bottles and placed the samples inside my jacket. "We should carry on, as I have to make it to the top of those hills."

Prodding uphill to the top of the hills to the north, the land was so immense and barren yet strikingly beautiful. The land was so deserted.

I could feel the eerie sensation of loneliness complete and absolute.

The rock was loose under my feet as we made the final ascent. As the summit was reached, we had a spectacular view of the landscape.

The land stretched, red shale rock being the dominant color of the hills and mountains, through brown shades in the low-lying valleys and coulees, worn away by the rainstorms that covered the land with a surprising vengeance at times. It was barren as far as the eye could see.

Jescan turned, looking from all the different angles from this lofty perch. "This is so impressive. Nothing like Rotan because there is life in Rotan but yet there are similarities, like the air is light and the heat is as unbearable, as the temperature was well above forty degrees Celsius."

"This is a unique landscape, all right," I said as I reached for my communicator. "*Genesis* create a removable foam covering around the candles and beam the candles to my location."

As three boxes appeared, I opened the first one and carefully carried it to a small open space. Scraping a small indentation in the red soil, I set the large ball into the ground. I then proceeded to the second box and then the third, repeating the process each time. When I had completed the last one, the three stood almost in a direct line straight up out of the ground. Although they looked straight up, each was pointing with a slight angle in, focused straight up into space in readiness for the approaching storm. I stood to inspect the triangle I had made, nodding my approval as I knew that the angles were correct. As the light from the sun passed through the crystals, it started to pulse, causing a beam that shot out into space. The land started to tremble as the beam intensified.

"Let's go back to the ship now."

Jescan followed as he glanced back at the strange magnificent candles sitting on a high point of land, looking extremely out of place in this barren sterile planet. Noticing that his steps started to become lighter and lighter, each stride allowing more distance between strides, he asked, "What is happening? I am able to jump as high as the clouds."

Opening the door to the *Genesis*, I turned to Jescan and said, "The gravity is being drained from the planet, displacing the actual weight, allowing the storm to be drawn into a false gravitational pull. The beam will project all the gravity of the planet. In a way, it is similar to a hologram, and on the same level as a transporter. The difference is that no matter is being transported."

Pausing as I looked out over the landscape, although no communication with the other planes had occurred, I could sense something that was not sitting right with me. "There was always speculation but no proof in every textbook as well as all the data from space encounters, and knowing the limitations of the technology there was no life on this planet. Could this fungus be from some rogue comet, or could it actually be the start of life from a natural occurrence? Here on the surface of Mars, I still think that there is something wrong with the life on the planet. It still bothers me. Let's find out what the samples tell us."

Jescan pulled out the samples from his pocket as he entered the ship, moving directly to the analyzer. "Computer, analyze samples. Purpose, to determine whether life is natural or alien in origin."

"We have to move into space now," I said as I sat down to the console. "Our task will be to cause enough of a pull away from the planet yet not affecting any of the other planets if possible."

"The samples have been analyzed," announced the computer.

"Let's hear what results you have come up with, computer," I said as I moved the ship up and through the atmosphere.

"This is of alien introduction, but natural materials in the chemical makeup of the organisms now on screen. As you can see, they are a carbon-based life form. Genus not previously recorded, but is of the fungus family. This form of fungus comes from the planet Earth. Estimated year of arrival, three thousand years ago or in the year 4.53 billion years BC. In the period of the Earth's collision with an asteroid forming the satellite known as the moon, fragments landed in the central and northern areas.

The plants disperse themselves through the movement of air as the parent dies, and intern becomes the food source for the next generation. The soil samples indicate that they contain only spores from the fungus, but no deviation is present as to any change in the chemical makeup of the fungi, and they are not capable of changing to climatic conditions. As the planet is starting into its first cooling down of its crust, they are not able to survive the lower temperatures.

This species, although able to change its structure, is not capable of producing chlorophyll, which is a key link to the survival of a planet's life form. It does display the ability to adapt as indicated from the different forms that it has developed. It has also not developed the ability to live in lower temperature.

"The soil samples indicate small invertebrates, which will survive till the fungus expires. Estimated time of expiration of organisms is seven hundred earth years, as the planet has already cooled to a temperature that new spores are not able to grow. The survival of this form of fungi is due to the high temperature needed to germinate. No other life forms are present in any of the samples. End of analysis."

"This fungus is not capable of adapting to the temperature changes. Most species mutate in order to survive. This doesn't seem normal, does it?" asked Jescan.

"No, I would guess that this species was the only one capable of surviving the entry. Although it did cause the start of microscopic organisms, life should be able to survive. The fungi possibly germinated with the high temperature of the entry into the atmosphere. Since that is the dominant characteristic of the plant, it didn't have a reason to change until now at the start of the cooling phase of the planet. Earth had the advantage of so many varieties and intermingling of the gene pool that when one died, another replaced its link in the overall niche."

The thought still lingered. *Could we have caused this?*

I watched the planet pull farther away as the *Genesis* moved farther out in space. We soon arrived at our position, allowing enough space to be able to create enough gravity to attract the approaching storm. "It is now time to incorporate the 'protect and preserve Mars' portion of the trip," I said, holding my position deep in space.

"Computer, create an inter-sonic beam linked to the candles, start with a level two, and increase amplification every fifteen minutes till gravity is completely transferred to our position. Notify when gravity on Mars is zero. Oh, almost forgot, increase stabilizers."

As the silent inter-sonic waves increased, both of us could feel the pressure increase as the ship increased in density. "Computer, isolate control room and decrease pressure. Maintain at normal pressure levels," I said, almost instantly finding relieve, as the pressure decreased to normal.

"My head felt like it was ready to explode!" exclaimed Jescan as he sank relaxing into the chair, expelling air as his body returned to normal.

"The gravity has completed its transfer," reported the computer.

"Computer, display plotted map of the approaching storm and give new estimated direction of storm on monitor," I said as a map of the storm showed on the screen.

The map revealed that the direction although altered, was still too close to the planet. "Increase gravity to level five . . . Come on," I said, trying to coach the storm over a little farther. "Pull the storm closer to us."

As we both watched the storm slowly move closer to us, the impression of how massive this storm was coming into perspective. The storm swirled, kind of like a satellite picture of a low-pressure area or a hurricane moving across the surface of a planet, making a definite eye in the middle. Although this was in space, I was amazed at the speed and velocity of the storm as the screen showed the slow undulating pulse of it.

"Look, the storm is coming into visual range! Computer, magnify and monitor," explained Jescan as he stood and moved from the monitor to the window, looking at the now visual massive storm, watching the particles of rocks, ice, and debris moving so fast it almost looked solid; yet areas gave away the millions of particles of debris that were moving in a clockwise motion, black with light reflected from the sun, glimmering off the solid particles. Even though the dark areas were intermittent, they gave a good perspective of how massive this storm really was. "I have heard about such storms, but to actually see one is very impressive . . . very impressive indeed."

We checked the speed and velocity recorded on a graph inserted on the monitor.

"I can now understand why the sixth plane was so concerned about this storm. If this had not been redirected, the whole planet would have been dissolved by this monster and could possibly have carried the mutilated planet out of orbit, readjusting all the planets in this sector from all indications straight toward the next largest planet, that being Earth," I said as I too stood and went to the window to watch the strange phenomena unfold in front of us.

The storm in all its glory swirled and churned. The storm came closer, and it passed ever so slowly, undulating almost like exotic dancers, dancing ballerinas, then turning to a stampeding wild herd of buffalo, then into a rolling tumbling avalanche, back to a very serene, peacefully soft object that looked very gentle in a strange way.

Taking a long look at the monitor, I said, "Well, it is moving in the right direction, away from the planet."

"On the monitor, it looks large, but to actually see it gives it a different perspective, the dimensions exceeding anything I have ever read about. It's heading straight toward the sun. Will it not affect the sun?" inquired Jescan.

Noting a serious concern in the tone of Jescan's voice and indications of his body language, I was prompted to explain. "The sun will attract the storm and suck it into its depths. Swallow would be more accurate. It will increase the mass by a minimal .0025 percent, and the size of the storm could possibly cause minor solar flares.

At least that is what I think will happen." Then I added, changing my mind, "That is what will happen, although the flares cause their own consequences . . . Could be wrong, but now we might not see anything that significant, as the sun will simply increase its fuel source, maybe even without a hiccup. Let's find out, as there is no time like the present." Computer turn off the candles and let the gravity return in increments every fifteen minutes, till it returns to normal. Let me know when it is complete.

The computer replied. "Completed."

The storm moved with what seemed a snail's pace, and although it took three days for the tail to finally pass by, and the head started to dissolve almost like burning a plastic bag into a fire, it simply evaporated as it touched the licking mass of exploding gases. As the storm touched the sun, the storm seemed almost to suck into the flames extremely fast with little or no remarkable significance.

"Well, let's go back to Mars first then to Earth," I said as I pushed the control and sat back as the buzzing sounded our arrival.

The music started in the back of my head, it was the third plane.

The planet has been touched by a small offshoot from the storm, that is what was needed to set things in motion for our plane, one fragment kept going even though you moved all the rest of it, that will change the ability of life to actually renew itself, and no other plane is affected except ours.

Computer check all anomalies, and any changes to the planet, as we proceeded toward the candles.

"There is an area just south of the equator that has an electric storm very small but it covered several thousands of miles across the planet, sensors indicate that it has rejuvenated some of the fungi stimulating the carbon atoms. Everything is doing fine, no problems will be caused because of this mutation which has now begun." announced the computer

"Ok, proceed to the site of the candles."

Picking up the candles, we proceeded on to Earth.

CHAPTER FOUR

The light could be seen touching the earth in beams dancing across the landscape as it found its way through the thick rain clouds, placing a sterile field around both Jescan and myself. The redness of the setting sun gave a spectacular picturesque view. As we opened the door, the humidity of the late afternoon enveloped the entire room. We took a deep breath and relished in the remarkably humid oxygen-laden air. It was only about four hundred years from when life had begun. I was excited to see any changes that had happened.

"This planet is waiting to be explored for the first time. The humid air was remarkable. Breathing was so easy, as the moisture was filling every pore." I could sense the purity of the air, the land and above all the chemical reactions that living organisms give off, just by being alive.

Walking out Jescan stopped about three feet from the door, his arms stretched outward as though he was about to fall. "The ground . . . the ground is like it is jiggling!" he exclaimed, looking at me for an explanation.

"The land is solid, although it is still very thin. It in a way, is still floating on the magma. The crust is still very thin. Even though it is safe enough to walk on, it still will sort of wave as it releases more magma in the nearby volcanoes. Rest assured that it is not yourself that is causing the movement," I said, reassuring Jescan that it was safe.

The barren land covered with volcano ash did feel like a floating dock on a lake. The newly formed crust was black and firm almost like a skating rink under the muddy white-grayish ash, giving an even more uneasy feeling, as there were several uneven layers that caused us to slip and slid over in many cases, siding into crevices almost buried in ash in the newly formed land.

This was not as fun as I thought it would be, as there was absolutely nothing but shaking trembling lava rock and ash with nothing but the same ahead, including all around us.

I proceeded toward the sea, as I wanted to physically see the water with the possible new life forms becoming visible. With the sea only about five hundred yards from the ship, I was surprised at how long it took to reach the edge.

The water was lapping against the black lava rocks and really was not any different, look wise from four hundred years earlier. The animals and plants were still very microscopic in size, and I could sense the chemicals of the microorganisms, but could not see anything that would give me an indication that anything was changed in the water.

Jescan reached into his pocket and pulled out a vile and took a sample of the water, looking disappointed in the fact that there was nothing that was noticeable in the container.

Turning toward Jescan, I said with a little disappointment in my voice, "This is really unexciting, isn't it? Let's head back to the ship, as there must be something a little more interesting in the future."

"Yes, I too am a little disappointed, as I would have thought that there might have been more to see. It is not at all what I would have expected. Even though I know that there is life present in the vile, there is nothing that can be seen by the naked eye," he said as he turned toward the ship.

As we walked back, I noticed clumps rising out of the swampy wetlands. They looked odd.

"Let's take a closer look. They do not look like they were natural formed," I said. Moving closer, I sensed something alive. Approaching the closest one, I said, "Jescan, take a sample. I believe this is something unique."

Well still disappointed, we both walked back to the *Genesis*.

Entering the *Genesis* both of us were disappointed in that there was not really anything that could be noticed in the planet's overall look.

"Computer, let's take a trip around the planet to see if there are any changes that are noteworthy, and analyze the samples that Jescan brought back," I said, sitting at the console.

"Analysis complete," the computer reported.

"Report, please."

"There are single-celled animals in two samples. The third sample contains chlorophyll-based fungi."

Jumping up, I said, "Let me see the sample magnified."

Looking at Jescan, I added, "I think we have just discovered the start of plants, the start of the production of oxygen. That is why there was so much oxygen in the atmosphere."

"Yes, we have known of this fungi, but did not realize that it was this old. If I am not mistaken, it was the very beginning of the oxygen producing plants," replied Jescan.

"This is the start of the time when all the iron, because of the oxygen is or should I say was, separated from most of the waters, though out the world's oceans and lakes and swamps, it is one of the major de-emulsification layers of iron throughout the entire world," reported Jescan.

This is the reason why animals could begin to live on the land—an amazing start.

"If there is nothing else that is significant after a survey of the planet, then take us to the next important time in the future," I said as I touched the controls, watching the outside window.

The ship scanned over the barren lifeless swamp-like land, and close to the equator, it came to a stop. "This is the first life form that appears to be growing on the land," replied the computer. "There is also an invertebrate animal present in the mud. It has spread over most of the valley."

Out at a swampy low-lying area was small fern like tuffs of green. This plant had started in the swamp yet was starting to adapt, slowly changing from a rooted water plant to a plant that was utilizing the muddy layer of ash to send its roots out in all directions, covering the sides of the swampy banks. The muddy ash was moist enough to sustain the plant, although the roots were still attached to the main plants under the water, which still supported the main bulk of the water supply. The plant was not yet very tall, although it was spreading outward, enough to cause a green patch just above the water level that could be seen from the ship.

I noticed that there wasn't any other green patches in other areas of the valley, at least not that I could see. "Computer, is there any other root-based plant life that is growing in the water?" I questioned.

"There are several other plants growing in the water. Most are still one-celled plants, although there are a few of these that have started to attach themselves to the rocks and mud at the bottom in the shallower water areas, mostly in the swampy parts. The data is not yet complete, as some areas have not been scanned. I will proceed." Replied the computer.

"Yes, carry on," I said as I realized that this stop was not completely a waste, as we now had discovered a plant that was inhabiting the banks as well as an animal that was similar to a segmented earthworm or in many ways, like a tapeworm. These were the simple foundation blocks of life, as they would evolve over time into what I knew would someday become a complete biosphere. Although it was in a sense a complete biosphere now, it was just more limited in the number of species.

I watched as the land and sea passed by the window as the *Genesis* gathered data, finally ending up where we had begun.

Pictures of different plants and animals that had started to develop showed on the monitor as the computer sifted through the now millions of distinct animals and plants, most still microscopic in size.

One small little animal caught my attention, as it had formed what looked like eyes.

"Computer, is that the formation of eyes on that species? Go back through the list . . . Yes, there, that's the animal," I said, leaning forward to study it closer. "I would say that this animal is the very first animal to have developed a brain."

"Pardon me," Jescan stated. "Why would you say a brain when I see the formation of a set of eyes?"

"The eyes are one of the sensors that animals developed in order to perceive their surroundings and to be able to get or avoid, their prey.

The brain is actually the processing center of the eye, not as we humans think that the more intelligent we became, because of our brain size, although there is a lot of truth to that too. In the beginning, it was simply a sensor developed to visualize what was going on around them.

The intelligence in a way, is a by-product of our visual capabilities as it is in most animals."

"Our people have measured the intelligence of a species by the size of their brains," stated Jescan.

"In a way that is true. The size does have a bearing on the intelligence of a species, but all the species have had eyes. The ability to understand the messages obtained from the eyes, which can be analyzed in many different ways, actually is the perception of intelligence. It comes down to how the species perceives the information, and how it reacts to the different stimuli obtained from the eye, as well as how it decides what to do with the information.

Intelligent species tend to analyze the information, forming different opinions of what the information means, often reacting differently from another of the same species. Generally speaking, it allowed or gave the predatory life forms an advantage whereby they could see their prey. Keep in mind that there are organisms, in the future have eyes but their brains are very limited, but enough for them to survive."

"This causes differences of opinion among many different individuals," commented Jescan as he studied the small wormlike invertebrate, probably the first in a line of fish to inhabit the seas. "Is this the only species that has developed eyes?"

The computer answered, "The analysis of the species on this planet indicates that it is the first, although several other animals are in the process of developing such organs. There is no real link between each one, as the mutations have separated each species, although the common link is the omeba ancestor that feeds on other plants and animals. It is a common code developed in the DNA that is present in all the animals that feed off another species."

"Is there anything else that is significant in this time?" I asked the computer, impressed with the data retrieved from this period.

"All significant data has been recorded. The next significant time occurs about four thousand years from this time," answered the computer.

Touching the controls, the *Genesis* blinked as it passed from one time to another.

Looking out at the land, it in many ways resembled the last stop, yet there were significant changes to the overall landscape.

"This has really changed," I noted. "Let's take a walk and see the changes, as it is only a little over four thousand years from when life had first arrived on the planet and we last left Earth. The planet was now covered in small thick clumps of green, as the stubby long strands of a plant resembling what would become ferns seemed to have popped up everywhere. A small shrub-type plant could be seen growing in little pockets in the crevices of the hills. These I suspected would be the very first pine trees. They resembled a sea plant that had very long stem like branches. No real leaves or pines as yet, only green was on the ends of the branches. They could be seen in the many swamps and crevices along the sides of the large volcanic mountains that dominated the landscape as deep valleys formed between the looming volcanic mountain ranges.

The red rivers of lava still flowed aimlessly across the land, and the ground still rumbled, as the volcanoes were still actively erupting and spewing large mushroom clouds. Large smoke rings could be seen in the open cloudless spaces along the horizon as the volcanoes erupted.

The humidity was still as overwhelming as it was in the beginning, but the solitude somehow seemed very distant knowing that life was evolving all around me, and the simple pleasure of a swaying fernlike plant was very relaxing.

As we approached the edge of the water, we could see little creatures, white in color and in the oddest shapes, spindly crustacean creatures with segmented bodies and protruding eyes from delicately fragile-looking heads, and some but not all had shells to protect themselves. These looked like creatures out of an old movie, and although they were very small, if enlarged they would have easily fit into a movie scene, which portrayed the ugliest creatures meant to scare the watchers, if only they could see these delicate little animals.

In their own way they were very personable in both their appearance as well as their aggressive attitudes, some unsure as we approached hiding timidly behind and underneath things, some quite indignant and aggressively put up a grand show of defending their ground or their territory.

It was very strange, it seemed that no two looked alike, yet on the other hand they were very similar in that you could tell that they where definitely of the same species.

Jescan bent gently, reverently almost as he collected samples of these creatures. There was such a diversity of the same species that he ultimately picked ones that gave a good cross section of the diversity of looks that these creatures in all their mutational exotic forms displayed, each of their young was similar yet slightly different from the parents, they did not seem to care what their mate looked like. Watching them try to mate, some could and some just could not physically mate. It must have been the mating season because they all seemed to be hunting to find a mate.

Looking around, I realized that this was not the case as some were laying young as well as looking to mate, some not even finishing laying their mounds of small egg pouches at the waters edges, they were being bothered by another male, as if this was all that their life were meant to accomplish, after they had laid several nests of eggs. Throughout their seemingly short, although fertile life from my observation, it looked as though the oldest survived maybe six or seven months some maybe a year old. If they showed any weakness or could not breed they were eaten, as they were cannibalistic in nature.

The young that were emerging from their egg clusters, seemed to look for contact with other young. Although some would be eaten large swarms of the little larva congregated in the shallow pools near the shore. The shells developed on some and others didn't even have a shell, which confined them to the water. Some had partial shells.

This I could tell was caused from the fluctuating acidity of the water.

Some not even able to maneuver on land stayed in the water, seeming not to affect their intent for sexual activity as within weeks of being hatched, they were reproducing young. I realized that not all the animals were only from the same species noting some had mutated, separating the species as I could see little waterspouts from what was a small clam-like creature, in the black sandy coastline. On closer examination rather than a clam, it was more like a large bulging worm that although the shape was like a clam, the future evolution of a shell was not yet developed. Although a crude protective shell was forming along the back of the flat soft body, although no eyes were apparent it seemed it was a totally blind animal. It seemed to filter its food through its almost transparent body.

"This is nothing like I expected," Jescan stated as he turned to look at me.

"This is not what I had expected. I thought the animals that first came onto land were mudskippers. These are more like snails and slug like animals, although they somehow make more sense than just a fishlike animal as I was taught in school. Let's have the *Genesis* analyze each species, although I think we will find that they are still so close in their evolution that they could all be the same species."

There were still clumps of fungi along most of the swampy areas. There were now more plants to help in the production of oxygen.

We wandered further up the black volcanic sides of the rolling hillside gorges, that made us walk slow and careful up and down the edges. The land was so vast and empty, yet the land also held a very serene peaceful open area that masses of volcanic ash lay as a gray fertile soil waiting patiently until life itself drew closer and eventually inhabits the open spaces. Though the land looked vast and was very impressive, the green of the fungi had already reached and started to intrude the landscape.

Some had even started to take on the look of ferns, yet the color of green was not there as it would in the future, but a multicolored landscape was starting to appear, dotting the landscape. Life was on its trek toward the growth and multiplication of the planet. The first to arrive on the land were the plants soon to be followed by the animals.

Looking down to the ocean from the top of a cliff-like escarpment, the land disappeared as I looked out onto the ocean in all its glory and majesty. It would not be long before large creatures with an unlimited growth environment would arrive, and at present no predators could be seen swimming in large schools. Small creatures seemed to be abounding in a frenzy disrupting the ocean surface, as the water seemed to bubble as they broke the water's surface in extremely large schools. It is true that the oceans did abound before the land. There will be creatures of such large proportions, that the body would start with a head of what resembled a large reptile and with a body that followed for seventy to a hundred feet behind it. The body looked like a small island and looked as solid as the land we were standing on. Premonition was what is to come, not yet but soon.

This revelation gave me comfort in knowing that what I had been taught was true in the future. As the planet evolved starting in the oceans as there was a multitude of new species in the seas, now it was the time for the land to vegetate on its own. The urge to delve even further into history intrigued me even more. The ideas regarding the evolution of this planet which was developing slowly, surprisingly the evolution was moving along remarkably fast, faster than I ever thought is should have although no one knew how it progressed, so it was totally new to me as much as it would be to the scientists of the future.

The earth trembled as a volcano erupted several kilometers to the north of us, and the ground shook with a vengeance and disturbed the ground so much that it threw Jescan over the escarpment.

As the vibrations grew worse, I too started to fall off the cliff. As I was falling, I suddenly realized that I could save both Jescan and myself; and I stretched my arm out sending an energy flow from the palms of my hand and cushioned Jescan's fall, and he came to a complete stop several feet above the jagged rocks, kind of like he was standing on an invisible piece of ground. This remarkable feeling came over me as I started to hear the voice musically in my head, saying,

You have just experienced your first levitation, and you did it easily. The powers that you are not aware of are arriving, as you need them. You will, in the near future, have others revealed to you that will as this has been a reflex action, but there are others that must be made known to you as you learn about the limitations of these abilities.

As the images left my mind, I slowly floated down to Jescan, and looking into a shocked but relieved face, he asked, "How are you doing this? This is unbelievable."

"Not as surprised as I am. I am learning as I go along, so I am told. Shall we go back to the ship?" I asked as we floated safely to the ground. "This is a weird sensation though, isn't it?"

Nodding, Jescan studied me as we turned to go back to the ship and never said a word. Although I could sense admiration in his body language, his deepest thoughts were one of wonderment, and a warm sensation of accomplishment overtook his thoughts as he wondered what might occur next.

In the distance, the volcano was still erupting, and the ground was still shaking although it didn't cause us any problem in walking, as I still maintained the levitation. As I looked down, I noticed that we still had air between the ground and us.

Ahead of us I could see that the *Genesis* was slowly being buried in a river of molten lava. A sudden panic overtook me, as I could see the *Genesis* leaving us stranded. We could never enter the ship covered under a river of molten lava soon to solidify.

Stopping in mid stride, I raised my hand and could feel the energy emanating from the palms of my hand, and it was like a tunnel opened up in front of Jescan and I. The reddish-black river simply stopped, diverted like a damn had suddenly appeared. Although invisible it started to continue flowing past on the other side of the ship.

Amazed, Jescan placed his arms up to his face to protect it from the unbelievable heat and walked out in front of me, and entered the ship first as the door closed behind me. The red river of lava could be seen filling in the space that I had created to allow us to walk to the ship as I was now suppressing my released energy flow.

"Let's get above the lava flow and then start recording the life on the land, the seas and the little ponds," I said as I touched the controls. "This is very exhilarating. I almost know what is coming next, yet I do not know what is coming and how I am going to react to the situation. It feels very strange."

Jescan looked deeply, penetratingly into my eyes looking for some explanation of what was happening to me. Unknown to him, his thoughts were clearly understood by me. *How does he do these things and not know how he does them? He, from the readings accomplishes so much from these powers. This must be his learning stage. This is where he takes time to discover who he is, and I am here to witness the events as they unfold before him, and me as a lone witness.*

Jescan never looked away only observed silently as I directed the ship to scan and analyze and take specimens, as new genies and species came into range. Smiling, I turned and looked at Jescan. "Do you know all the things that I am going to go through? It might not be a bad idea if I read what you have written, or do I go through my experiences on my own, never reading your stories?"

"I don't think that you read them because you do not want to know what is going to happen till it happens and besides I haven't written them yet."

"Good answer. I understand why it would not be beneficial to know the future, yet I am the future and in that respect I think that

I will read it later when the time is right and not before it happens, or for that matter written."

Jescan never looked away, just shifted his eyes from my eyes to focus on my face. "As far as I know you never read my writings and possibly, you never will because you know everything that is in it, and you never concern yourself with what has already happened, except to right what was wrong."

"Yes . . . makes sense to me," I said, and I knew he was right that I would probably never read them nor have the desire to. "You are becoming a great friend."

"Thank you. You too are a good friend," he said as he finally turned to look out the observation window.

The variations in the plant and wildlife were very surprising. They somewhat resembled some of the plants and the animals that were removed when the moon was formed, and the plants although different had similar looks and characteristics. These plants and animals although did look weird with different shapes and sizes, there was no question that these animals and plants evolved into the species that I on my maiden voyage, removed and protected in the *Genesis*.

As the collection and the documentation of the species class, and the genus were being completed by the computer the different lines as the different places that the species evolved, could be seen in a very clear and chronological order showing up in the slow evolution of the different species. The new life forms were definitely starting to mutate on a very regular, yet a somehow consistent pattern. The differences that the mutations caused were sometimes remarkable changes that changed the looks and the characteristics of both the plants and the animals.

The changes caused some of the weirdest-looking animals even though they didn't always survive in regeneration or passing on the new looks, there was a definite direction that the animals were taking. The largest animals seemed to grow very large simply because of the increase of oxygen in the air and the large surplus of food for them, both vegetarian as well as carnivores, and the smaller animals although they seemed to multiply faster and with larger numbers there was still a well-maintained balance. In the oceans though, it seemed that the animals multiplied so rapidly and had so much space and food that it had little territories that were not occupied. The planet was in such a remarkable balanced harmony.

The urge to discover my new abilities took over my thoughts, and I started practicing my newly discovered levitating, I was wondering how the powers worked in principle and what the limits were that the sixth plane had mentioned. There didn't seem to be any limits to the length of time or the limits of energy that were being sent out from my body. It dawned on me that one of the limitations was that I had to physically see the thing that I wanted to levitate and found that once it was levitating, I could go into another part of the ship and it would stay levitating, but to levitate something in the other room, it didn't levitate till I physically saw the object.

I was so engrossed with the new power, that I actually sleep levitating and had other things levitating at the same time and found that when I woke up, I was unbelievably exhausted to the point that as soon as I set everything down, I lay down on one of the lounge chairs in the console room falling asleep almost instantly.

I woke and found Jescan at the console going over data that had been gathered and could tell that he was totally submersed in the screen of the monitor. "Find anything interesting?" I asked as I stretched, well I sat up fully refreshed with the sleep that I had just had.

Jumping with a start, Jescan smiled and took a deep breath, said "I guess I was studying the monitor too closely. It is so interesting what has taken place in a span of ten thousand years. I also didn't know how long you were going to sleep, as you have just passed the seventy-two hour mark. Are you all right?"

"I feel great, but I didn't realize that I had slept that long. Amazing . . . seventy-two hours. The energy certainly must have drained me more than I thought," I said as the time I had slept seemed to have been only a short catnap. Considering my extraordinary length of sleep, I now knew some of the limitations of the power of levitating.

It felt odd in a way. The time I lost seemed totally irrelevant, as this was obviously something that I had to learn, and time suddenly had no significant importance, as I somehow knew this was to be, I would be able to recoup the time somewhere in the future.

"What would you say after breakfast, we take a look at the next significant time in Earth's evolution?"

"The computer indicates that the next significant change is when you take all the life off the planet, and the moon is formed. Let's travel a little farther, say sixteen thousand years."

"Done, but first, let's eat," I said, as I felt the pangs of an empty stomach. It suddenly was a priority that made my mouth water, thinking of the different ways to make eggs.

CHAPTER FIVE

Touching the control, we landed with the now familiar ring of our arrival.

The view outside was that of lush green fields and bushes and unique trees, something that I realized I had not seen for quite a while.

"Let's take a walk, as I set the computer to start analyzing the plants and animals in this time. As we let the ship cover the planet, we can maybe go camping. What do you think? I would like to get some fresh air. Let's get some gear and stay out for a day or two. Well the specimens are being collected and we can really see this land, not just observe it."

"Sounds good to me," Jescan said as he turned. He thought for a minute then immediately started giving the computer a list of different things that he wanted.

Sitting back, I was amazed at how long the list was that Jescan was requesting. It seemed that there wasn't anything that he didn't have, and when I thought he was done, he thought of something else. "Do I need anything, or do you have everything?"

"I don't think that I have forgotten anything," Jescan stated with a concerned look as though he had forgotten something.

"Just kidding. Did you put a fishing rod in?"

"No, I didn't think about that. I have never fished before."

"Then take two. I'll show you what it's all about," I said as I walked to the door. "Let's find a spot, and the ship can transport them down to our location. Shall we go?" I asked as the door opened to the humid fresh air.

It was early morning, and the sun had just crested the horizon, and the ground was moist with the morning dew.

The fern and pine-like bushes crunched beneath my feet as I stepped out of the ship, followed by Jescan. Inhaling the air it was exhilarating as the smell of life was everywhere. The volcanoes still erupted in the distance, but they were diminishing as the mantle was thickening and was cooling compared to the earlier history, and several had even gone dormant since the earth had come to a somewhat of an equilibrium of land and water; although there was still the struggle of the land against the water, it had settled into a steady ebb and flow. The water washed the soil from the land through the rains, which filled the vast rivers that streamed steadily toward the lakes and oceans, from where the water once again evaporated, and the process started over again.

Walking to a ridge overlooking the ocean I realized that we had landed as we usually did in the same spot, although I had made the proper adjustments to land on top of the land and was not buried, noting that we were several hundred feet higher, and the sea had been pushed several miles out as it could barely be seen in the distance. The smell of the salt air though was still very prevalent.

Animals seemed to be everywhere, the plant species of such varieties as I had never seen nor ever heard of. Most of the plants had developed from single organisms that had developed the ability of photosynthesis, allowing it to transform light into sugars which could sustain its life, as it also used the carbon dioxide from the air, expelling oxygen.

Still there were no large deciduous trees, although there were large plants similar in many ways to the trees that I was used to seeing.

These plants were mostly made up of different variations of ferns, probably due to the constant rains with no need for larger leaves, although there was the occasional small plant with needles as leaves, indicating that the pine trees were just starting to arrive. The dominant large plants were of the fern variety, as ferns of all different sizes and shapes, for that matter colors as the vivid shades of green were dominant. There were indications of white as well as hint of red along the edges of some plant stems, especially near the seed-producing areas. Some were with somewhat bizarre stamens coming in odd shapes and sizes that produced the seeds after being fertilized, usually by pollen that was carried by the wind.

The diversity of the single lineage plant was remarkable, as it ranged from a triangular semi-tapered leaf to a sharp needle like leaf. *Fascinating*, I thought, as these plants were the dominant plant life. They were the foundation of all the plants in the future. Could it possibly be that all the plants that existed in the future were descended from this fernlike plant? It would seem so.

The animals strange as they were, odd would be a way to describe them. Some were with spines all over their bodies, protruding in such odd locations that it would be almost impossible to discover a motive for most of the artistic design of the animals. Some were with semi segmented bodies almost comparable in ways to the insects, except that the ones I was observing definitely had a different agenda, as these creatures would someday, if my hunch was right become the foundation of the dinosaurs.

Most of the wildlife had developed protection that was so elaborate, some with tails, some with body parts that didn't look like they should fit together, although they were actually living breathing animals.

Most of the animals had shells protecting their soft vulnerable bodies, which inasmuch as I could see had not developed a bone structure yet and relied on cartilage almost like crayfish, where the segmented body parts allowed for movement from one location to another, also allowing the fluids within the body to stay constant.

They carried these elaborate shells to protect their body, some with the main bodies becoming quite large, as the shells seemed to continually grow around the segmented body parts. Some had developed lighter cartilage-based protection shells, segmented almost like scales on fish, which allowed more freedom from the heavier shells that some sported. These animals were much more active, and the mobility gave them a great advantage, as they could move quickly to capture their food.

The thought occurred to me that these lighter, yet bulky bodied animals could be the primitive version of the reptiles. Some with the heavier shells almost resembled tortoises, although overall these species looked nothing like a tortoise, as the lighter shelled animals did not resemble reptiles, either.

One particular animal that caught my eye had a hard shell with razor-sharp edges from its sides and had a slug like action about it since the shell was almost pointed at the top and flared out to edges that came to a jagged sharp turn up with layers of cartilage lines added or grown on an ongoing basis as the animal grew. This could possibly indicate the age of the strange slug like animal, as each ring was like the rings of a tree with the outside ring being of a softer cartilage, which was not yet as hard as the rest of the shell but was taking the same shape as the rest of the shell. Although the animal looked like a slug, it moved more like a centipede sort of wiggling along the ground, with little segmented legs helping to push or pull itself. The rest of the body that was not protected by the shell had a hard layer of scales, similar to fish scales common to the other species of animals that wandered across the grayish, now mostly composted to the darker lava soil.

Looking at a diverse unique animal life was a thrill in itself, but because of warm temperature, not one animal to date had developed fur or feathers. All the land animals were wormlike with lots of variations ranging from a slug up to a recent new lineage, which was more reptile like, yet the little creatures that we were observing had come a long way over several thousands of years evolving to the animals of the same likeness in many ways as was in the *Genesis,* that we had transported.

They were very localized at this time in history, possibly the area that they started was the start of a major migration, as the animals in many ways were resembling their parents. Some species were dominating the local animal kingdom in large territories, as the food chain was a very natural evolution. The larger animals were feeding on the smaller animals.

Making our way up to a volcanic mountain where it was evident that the lava had flowed over itself several times, I could make out a bubble-like cave along the upper hardened lava flow, which had cooled down but had left a cavity in the side, possibly exposed by erosion, but from the looks, possibly from lightning strikes indicated by the jagged scorched edges. There was a natural release of negative ions from the large deposits of carbonate elements, causing an electrical attraction with a large number of atoms wanting to attract elements that gave off a positive charge.

I could sense large amounts of nitrogen, as the lightning strikes leaves behind nitrogen deposits, something that plant life required to grow. It was an odd feeling, as I could sense the ions around me, not necessarily the elements but the atoms and their chemical charges of negative or positive. I realized the chemical makeup of all the things around me. Possibly, it was a logical explanation for my ability to create energy from the chemicals around me as well as from within.

"I say that this looks promising as a campsite. What do you think?" I said, knowing that to be in an area that generated a lot of negative ions was very healthy.

Jescan looked out over the hillside, and the ocean could be seen in the distance. "Looks like a great spot, great view, semi-protected from the weather," he said as he started up the hill. "Let's see if any animals have inhabited it."

Making our way up the steep slope, the landscape could be seen for miles from several directions as the *Genesis* could be seen off in the distance becoming very small as we climbed higher and higher. The land sort of leveled off as we came closer to the cave. There were no trees or bushes, but there was a moss type of growth in little crevices lining the smooth sides of the hill, where the deposits of nitrogen had been formed by many lightning strikes.

Approaching the mouth of the cave, the cavern went deeper than we thought. The opening looked small but opened into a very large area that circled like a large ballroom, not a cave. It had amazingly smooth sides and the floor, although covered with lava dust, was as smooth as the sides, yet toward the back, jagged rocklike structures could be seen. It was obvious that it was where the side of another bubble had formed. Possibly they had formed together. Either way, it made the cave massive. From all indications there seemed to be nothing living in the cave as far as we could tell. Nothing but the dust from the volcanic ash was all that was in the cave. Not even any tracks could be seen as we walked to the back toward the other cave, kind of like a cave in a cave. It was so dark, and it was not possible to see how large or small it was, as the light from outside was limited by the small opening of the entrance.

"I say that it looks pretty good to me. How about you?" Jescan turned to look at me.

"This is the spot," I said as I let the *Genesis* know to transport our stuff to this location. "I hope that you have a flashlight in with all the stuff that you arranged."

The supplies arrived, and I was amazed at how much stuff Jescan had brought. Shaking my head, I smilingly said, "You didn't forget to bring the kitchen sink."

"Oh, of course I brought a wash basin," he said, not realizing the humor of the situation.

Smiling and then snickering a small laugh, I found myself starting to feel little bursts of laughter definitely catching the giggles, realizing the complete humorous bewilderment of Jescan.

Smiling as he realized what he had just said, he slowly started to laugh out loud and then as the full realization of the situation hit, burst into a loud laugh that echoed off the walls of the cave.

"Well, let's set up the kitchen sink," I said, fighting the urge to laugh.

"Here are the flashlights and the lantern," I commented as I reached down to pick a long tube like object and pushed a switch that lit up the cave.

Looking around, it was obvious that this room was the inside of an air bubble caught within a lava flow, as everything was smooth, and the back bubble could be seen now and was a little bigger than the room that we were in. It was also lower than the cave we were in.

At the back of the second cave, there was an indication of some water in a pool, possibly trickled in from the entrance. As we approached, the water was not flat and smooth as I expected but had ripples in it. "Let's check this out. The water in here could be an underground river fed from the run off rain trapped in the crevices formed by many volcanoes in this area."

As I approached the water, I was correct it was a river and was flowing slowly across the back side of the cave. "Fresh water as well. There must be a lake nearby . . . This cave was made to be lived in."

As we proceeded to set up camp, a cloudburst started to pour rain in a flurry of flurries. It was as if the rain could not come down fast enough. The protection of the cave was unscathed, and even though we couldn't see out of the mouth of the cave, because of the slope of the hill, the rain ran off and away from our shelter. This, indeed, was an excellent spot for camping.

The rain proceeded for about two hours nonstop, and just as fast as it had started, it abruptly stopped, and the sun was again shining into the mouth of the cave.

Walking to the entrance, the cloudburst could be seen off in the distance and was heading out to sea. It was remarkable how much rain had fallen. I would have guessed six or seven inches at least, although that was hard to tell because the water was still rushing down the sides of the cliffs and the sloping land in front of our cave. Yet the land seemed to take the storm in stride, not even noticing that it had just had a remarkable bath. With a rain like that one, the erosion would have to have some effect on the land. Although from the looks of it, it seemed unconcerned, and animals could be seen moving in the open areas below and seemed to just carry on as though nothing had happened.

Watching the animals, they seemed to move slowly on their way, not even noticing other animals around them as they moved. One animal was eating the plants, as it was moving and seemed not to notice a larger animal that turned and noticed it was there. It simply turned and proceeded to kill and eat the passerby. The intelligence of these prehistoric creatures was still very limited as was demonstrated by the two that I had just witnessed.

Another group seemed to move together, and as they moved, they seemed to travel in a set path for anything that moved and could be seen starting after one thing and then changing direction and moving after another. This process seemed to be a very slow and agonizing one, yet animals seemed to walk straight into them, and some with built-in protection survived, but others simply were devoured.

Jescan came out of the cave and said, "Camp is now set up. Look at this country. How is it, that from the information that I gathered from the *Genesis*, this is the only major landmass other than small volcanic islands dotting the eminent stretches of ocean?" he asked as he turned to face me.

Looking down to the smooth rolling hills caused by the lava flows of thousands of years, I answered, "It stands to reason that since this land is the only one large as it is it was the area that first erupted through the cracks in the mantle, releasing the pressure of the shrinking earth, and due to the rotational turning of the planet, the overall flow took on a westerly movement with the same logic as water takes the easiest route, so did the magma from the interior of the earth.

With the cooling of the mantel and the land cooled by the water falling from the atmosphere returning to earth, slowly over millions of years was cooling the earth enough, causing yet another release of pressure as the earth started its slow shrinking, as more liquid turned to a solid forming small mountain ranges of volcanoes, the heavier the land and because this landmass seemed to be floating on a molten sea of magma.

The water eventually cooled everything down slowly as time goes, and around the edges were the easiest points to expel the pressure from within. So soon the massive island will as the earth gets cooler, obtain a massive crack that will eventually cause this land to sink, someday becoming the water-covered area, and the edges soon will in turn spew out the excess inner mantle and become the dominating landmass rising above the heavier established land since the heavier part will eventually sink, as the pressure of the core is released on the edges of the existing land, allowing for the flow of new magma to become exposed from the large cracks as the new land becomes heavier in density and area. The earth as it is cooling is becoming smaller, and the crust is becoming thicker, causing collisions of landmasses.

Usually moving from one side of the planet to the other, this process will continue till it is cooled down so much that an equilibrium is reached and it cannot shrink anymore, overlapping and growing thicker as time progresses."

"This land that we are walking on will someday become the bottom of the ocean . . . Awesome. This has happened on our planet, and as on many of the planets that we have studied. We knew that the earth had gone through such changes, as we had documented the melting of the ice caps as well some of the ice ages, although we have not seen the reversal of land to sea other than islands . . .

Nature is amazing, isn't it? I am so privileged that I will be able to experience them with you," Jescan commented. "Let's walk through this remarkable new garden."

"Just what I was thinking," I said, smiling as I started walking down the slope. "It's still early morning, isn't it? We still have a lot of day left."

Looking at the fungus growing in the crevices, it was a multicolored variety that seemed to cling like it was still in the ocean, yet it had developed such a spongy body that the rains sustained it enough to survive and obviously flourished.

Jescan took out a bottle and pulled some out of a crevice and placed it in the tube. "The plant life is definitely becoming more diverse and also more complex," he commented.

Walking further down the hill, the grass had started to take hold, and although it looked more like a mossy fern like growth than grass as we were used to, it was cushioning our steps and felt great. The start of the bushes also increased, as the fern like plants had a darker brown stem and grew very tall. In some cases, it would grow from a crude large stamen, as it grew the leaves opened up, leaving the stamen exposed, and the new leaves stayed on the top as the leaves below dies or were broken or eaten. The stamen got larger and taller. Some were already ten to twenty feet high and still growing, almost like a palm tree except its leaves shoot straight up instead of opening out.

Some trees were growing in a similar way, except the leaves grow out from the old growth, and the bush continued to grow. It was at least ten feet wide at the top and spread out in a pear-like shape, reaching a huge width of maybe fifteen or twenty feet wide at the base, using the dead branches and leaves as its own compost supply, and relying only on the nutrients absorbed by the rain and on the sun to sustain itself.

Some of the smaller versions of the first trees, presently more like bushes, were little fernlike plants that covered the landscape with a chlorophyll-based leaf causing the deep green colors that dominated this area and was never ending in the pursuit of more territory to dominate. The small green plants with a perfect climate and weather conditions grew from very small to enormous. I estimated that some of the larger plants could possibly be several thousand years old.

Looking closely at the plants, different little bacteria and fungi seemed to flourish within the cracks of the plants and under the leaves. Usually, damage would occur to the main plant yet very little destruction seemed to be occurring. With little concern of the plants, it was more a means to cover more territory. The plants allowed the necessary support that they required with little or no restrictions to the bountiful rich volcanic soil and with humidity that would have allowed even the most delicate or fragile plants to survive, slowly converting the gray-black soil to a deep blackish-brown compost, allowing tube-type animals wormlike, eating and causing composting to happen very rapidly as things died and things rotted.

Although they decomposed, the molecular and animal remains, well cellulite remained for the fungus to breakdown. This I noticed, would follow through to future centuries with other animals decomposing the biological life forms.

With the constant rains that seemed to continually come and go, there was little struggle to find a space in which to grow. These plants slowly and methodically moved ever inland.

I noticed some of the seeds, seeds of such unique shapes including spores. Some of the seeds were nothing like what we would call seeds, as they were more like projectiles from a machine gun, shooting from the different plants at different times, as we cautiously walked through this unique forest, sometimes the seeds coming slow and far between, and sometimes it was like dodging balls from a batting cage machine.

Some though simply relied on the wind, and yet others had a sticky substance allowing for animal transport, and others had little burrs or thorns that also relied on animal transportation.

One of the fern like trees, as we walked by, caught my interest as on a closer inspection. It had a little small segmented millipede like animal that move in and out of the leaves and stems. This animal didn't seem to be destroying the plant, but seemed to be attracted to the liquid produced by the stamen. This little animal was extremely abundant, covering most of the plant, and was almost as small as a little aphid, but since there were no winged insects to compete with, the little creature seemed to enjoy a drink from the juices at the center of the flowers and its body, in turn became soaked with the liquid thus became covered with pollen. Then a strange journey began as I watched one travel down the stem to a leaf that was touching the first plant. Traveling to the other plant, it then proceeded to search out the nectar of next flower that it came across, passing the pollen directly to the other stamen as it passed through the narrow opening, fertilizing the different plant as well, satisfying its need to collect the nectar. As it collected the nectar, it deposited the nectar into a communal nest at the bottom of the plants then traveled to the next plant. I could not help but notice that the pollen was light and could just as well be carried by the wind, but this little animal spent a continual ritual of traveling from one plant to another, visiting each stamen as they came across them.

The fascination of these minuet insects new to the earth held my curiosity for several hours, which passed so fast that I realized that Jescan had left on his own to explore other things in this fascinating spot, and was now just coming back from his walk in the thick rich foliage of plants, and to my surprise was carrying a little animal.

It had a hard divided shell similar to an accordion. Its head was small, almost delicate with an extended segmented eye sockets containing large eyes. It had ears that stood rigidly straight forward.

It had segmented body parts typical of several of the animals, my immediate impression was that it was similar to an armored armadillo, except this animal was the size of a week-old kitten or a pup.

"What do you have there?" I asked as he approached.

"I just rescued this little guy. He fell into a hole as I was passing. I guess he was surprised by me as I approached. The rocky hole was too deep for it to get out, as he was trying desperately to scramble up the sides. He would not have had a hope of getting out and as I picked the little guy, he took to me right away as he nuzzled into my hand and was so cuddly, I thought I would bring him back for you to see, and besides we should think about lunch. It is time to leave the plants and insects alone for a while since it will be raining soon," he said, noticing the little animals, then he pointed to a very large dark rain cloud that would be arriving in a short time. "Look at this little guy," he said, holding him out with pride, wanting me to hold him.

As I reached out, the delicate little head smelled my hands as I took hold of it. It sort of rubbed its body against my hand, closing its eyes as if anticipating the transfer. It nuzzled into my sleeve as I drew it close to my body. It was so friendly it was as though it had been a pet for years, although I could tell it was a younger animal, possibly just on its own within the last few months. It surprisingly did not show any reservations or fear, although it could be the heat of our body that gave it warmth as it was held by us.

"He is an attractive little guy, and is he ever making himself at home," I said, smiling as it curled up in a ball and proceeded to fall asleep.

"He is a friendly little thing, isn't he?" Jescan said, smiling as he reached out and gently rubbed the little creature's armored back. "Can we take him back with us to our camp?"

"I suppose so, as long as you return him to where you found him before we leave in the morning," I said, realizing that the *Genesis* should have completed the survey and should be waiting at the campsite. I would like to take a quick observation trip around the planet this afternoon." Beaming a smile, as Jescan took the little creature back, disturbing his sleep. He quickly cuddled him close to his chest.

"What do you think he eats? He looks like he would eat plants. What do you think?"

"It looks like it is a vegetarian, but we will have to wait till he wakes up and eats something before we will know for sure," I said, smiling as

I watched the great care Jescan took not to disturb the little guy as we walked back to camp. "Let's find out what you have planned for lunch."

Approaching camp, the little creature could be heard making a little squeaking sound as it moved into a more comfortable position in Jescan's cradled hands.

Walking inside the cave, he sat on a cot that he had brought and laid the little creature down upon the taunt blanket that was neatly made to conform to army-like standards.

As soon as the little guy was set down, it started to move around, checking out the top of the cot and running back and forth and nuzzling into the blankets and almost playing like a cat might play, although the look of surprise and complete innocence as it proceeded to urinate all over the pillow made Jescan jump to catch the little guy before he did any more damages, but was already too late.

I laughed out loud at the performance of the two as the dribble went from the center of the pillow and was on a sure pathway to the blankets below, and the pillow was successfully removed just in time, as the quick-moving Jescan snatched it away.

Looking up, almost perplexed he started to smile followed by a laugh, as he realized the situation was quite humorous. "I guess this is to be expected. Just haven't had time to house-train him yet," he said as he started to laugh even louder.

"I think our friend can sleep on the ground," he added as he picked up the pillow and went back to the river to wash the pillow out.

The little animal ran after him and as he walked, kept knocking the back of Jescan's legs with his small paws, thinking this was great fun.

Walking over to the ship, I entered the *Genesis* and started to compile all the information that was surprisingly diverse. Overall the lineage of several animals had made several distinct separations and were still changing to meet the local conditions. Overall, the animals were becoming more diverse, and some were growing to unprecedented sizes. Although they were not the immense sizes of some of the future dinosaurs, the links or similarities were starting to emerge. In the oceans, large creatures dominated the waters and came in several different shapes and sizes.

The computer gave some pretty bizarre indications that certain kinds of fish because of the cooling of the earth were developing a method of controlling the wide fluctuations of temperatures, and were developing a method, by which the temperature of the inner core was isolated with a layer of fat, something that would become a major factor in future animals. This allowed the movement of these new species to travel large areas without slowing down in the colder areas, and still be able to travel through the hotter equator waters, with little change in performance.

I set the controls to continue to geographically pinpoint these new animals, both on the land and sea, to later see how they distributed though out the territory, or within the oceans as well as on the land.

This was the first sign or start of warm-blooded traits in animals, at least the start of an internal heat-saving mechanism that would later be utilized by several animals. I was surprised, as I thought that the warm-blooded characteristics would be discovered on the land, and not in the water first, although browsing more of the information in the files, they showed that warm-blooded characteristics were appearing all over, in both water and land, at about the same time.

Jescan entered the ship and reported that supper had been prepared, and I should join him by the fire before it got cold.

After the meal that Jescan had prepared, and the dishes had been cleaned and put away, we decided to sit out and watch the sun set in this little utopian paradise.

Jescan gave the little guy some lettuce, and he was eating it as fast as he could get it into his mouth. Not wanting it to be left behind he pulled the leaf of lettuce with him, and followed us as we set up our chairs, and poured ourselves a drink. Sitting with our drink in hand, we watched the sun slowly sinking into the ocean horizon. The red color was remarkable, as it lit up all the clouds, which looked like a picture of mountains off in the distance, and images of valleys and the white tops of the mountains could be visualized, although to date, none existed yet on Earth, just in the clouds. It was remarkable, as

I realized that nowhere, except the highest volcanic mountains, had snow ever fallen because of the thinner cooler atmosphere, and I wondered when the cooling of the north and south poles would create a climate that would allow the first snowfall to arrive, blanketing the southern and northern areas of land. It could be several millions of years maybe. We'll have to wait and see.

As night advanced, different new sounds also arrived. The sound of the nocturnal animals, which was like the security of the night, started to become active. The other animals that were present during the light of the day, were finding protected areas to rest for the night, kind of like the changing of the guards, as the light grew dimmer.

The strange eerie sounds from the nocturnal animals started, one in particular was loud, yet in a way softer almost a seducing sound, as the sound floated over the land and carried by the wind, which made the little guy scurry to hide between Jescan's feet.

"What is that sound?" asked Jescan as he picked up and soothed the little guy.

From the lack of tracks, this place had not been visited by animals, there would seem to be no reason for the animals to climb this high.

I realized that there had been no reason for any animal to climb here until now. "It was our scent . . . we left a trail or sign as large as you could get from their perspective, and we could have company tonight, as they are following our scent."

Jescan jumped and said, "Should I get something to protect us, or will a fire keep them away? Let's build a fire before it gets too dark. Are we going to be all right with just a fire?"

The musical lyric of the sixth plane started in the lower part of my brain and resonated between my ears, equalizing in the center of my forehead, close to the front of my head. *You will be able to radiate a protective control area that will allow you to be protected. This is but another power that you have at your control. Use it, learn it, and enjoy its benefits, as this will become very valuable in many situations.*

As the music slowly disappeared, my attention was again reminded of Jescan's last statement. "Relax, Jescan," I said, realizing that he knew that I had been communicating with another plane. "First, we'll hear them coming, and second, as I have been informed, they wouldn't hurt us when they do come, as I have learned something new that will make sure that if any are hostile, the animals will become docile as little lambs. As well, there are probably no animal that is large enough to do us any harm, at this stage in Earth time line."

Settling back down in his chair, Jescan sighed a breath of relieve.

"I keep forgetting I am with you. I will hopefully, someday get used to this."

"I do sense the presence of a larger animal, possibly a carnivore. It is following our scent and should be starting up the slope within a couple of minutes. That is the soft throaty sound that we and little guy had heard and have been hearing for the last hour or so. Listen . . ."

Jescan sat up straining to hear, when off in the distance the sound of soft shuffling steps could be heard. "What is it? Do you know?"

"It is a larger animal, very strong. It is not very smart, but it survives by its sheer size, keeping in mind that the largest animal was like an average-sized smaller dog. I really don't know what it is called, no one named it yet, but it is now going to come up the last little rise, to the flat area in front of us." As I spoke, we could see the head of the creature. As well, we could hear the low throaty sound as it released a breath of air. It too had spotted us, stopping to study our very strange looks. Its head was long and pointed at the top. Its eyes were placed at the widest part, about two thirds of the way down. Down the face, it was pointed almost like a beak shape with the nostrils flaring out slightly, relatively small for the size of the animal. The narrow mouth, almost pointed, had several small narrow sharp teeth lining the sides at both the top and the bottom. The neck was slender and came from just behind the eyes that moved independently, from the top of the pointed beak-like nose, came to a slender chest with small slender legs that were much smaller than the back legs that maybe was twice the size of the front legs. The animal looked very heavy in the back, but was very light in the front. It had claws or talons on the front legs, and the back legs were larger and more like an elephant's foot with little claws coming from the front and sides of the main pad. The back was ridged with spikes running the full length of the body, including the long tail that had three spikes dominating the end of the tail. The animal was possibly three feet in length, standing a good foot to foot and a half high, a very formidable, dominant presence indeed for the life on this planet. The look in the eyes, and his body language, told us that the animal was ready to charge, very admiral for the size of him and the size of us, which would be the largest living thing it would have ever seen. It sort of raised on its hind legs as it started toward us and came thundering across the flat area in front of us. I could see

Jescan held the little guy closer to his chest, holding his breath. He looked like he was going to bolt himself. Throwing a glance at me, I saw him relax a little, as he remembered he was safe.

The animal came full bore till it reached the fifty-foot boundary and almost looked like it was put into slow motion as it slowed to a complete stop, approximately twenty feet from us. Getting up, I beckoned Jescan to follow me.

I approached the large reptile like creature, sort of like approaching a large turkey. I put my hand out and let it smell my hand, then I moved my hand up the nose, to between the eyes, and scratched it between the eyes, and I could feel the dry, scaly soft reptile like skin, although it was still more like fish scales than skin. The animal acted like a pet horse that would press into the soft scratching, which I did firmly but gently. I moved to scratch it under the jawbone and along the neck. The animal was massive, yet it was remarkably very light-boned, as it was a cartilage-structured animal, although it was forming a strong almost like bone structure. The animal was starting to generate its own heat and was definitely not completely cold-blooded as it looked like it would be, but was remarkably well on its way to becoming warm blooded.

The massive size of the animal was probably generating its own heat although, if it stayed still for some time it would slow down like the reptiles. The overly hot days and nights as it was still in the high thirties or forties on the Celsius scale even when it rained, could be the reason that it could function as a nocturnal animal.

The night animals could very well be the start of warm-blooded lineage of animals, having more moderate temperatures in the mid-to-high twenty degrees Celsius, including the mammals that still had not arrived in the evolutionary line.

Jescan also moved close enough to touch its shoulder and rubbed it softly, almost like he would injure it if he petted it any harder, but almost immediately relaxed and started rubbing the animal in a massaging motion. "This animal only thinks of the most rudimentary instinctual thoughts. In its basic form it only eats because it is hungry, nothing more, nothing less. I gather from it that it usually travels in a herd. During the daytime, it stays in a cool darker area. It must mean a cave. Closest comparison would be underground. Its communicative capacity is very limited. It is having a very hard time understanding that there is a way to communicate to another creature since it has never had any reason to communicate with anything else. I get from it, that it has the capacity to understand things for a short period, then because it is not necessary to sustain their living, and is quickly forgotten, as the brain size is extremely limited, although it seems to end up in the same place every morning, sort of like a homing device, to avoid the heat of the day. I get the impression that they sleep with their heads all facing out, with their tails as well, as their young in the center."

"I forgot that you can communicate with all kinds of animals.

That's fascinating, as I also was listening to them communicate," I said as I examined the structure of the animal, realizing that this animal would branch off into possibly the *T-rex* as well as or possibly the raptors or both.

"This is fascinating. Just think this poor animal will forget us by tomorrow morning," stated Jescan.

Well, we were engrossed in the creature we didn't realize that several other animals had followed our scent and were walking up to us to smell us, and basically see what was going on.

As the night proceeded, it was as if a steady stream of animals traveled up the hill, which had never been climbed or attempted before. I guess our scent was very strong of course being unusually different was extremely unique, drawing all the animals whether they were carnivores or vegetarian. On top of the fact that so many animal scents were all heading in the same direction, we found that we had attracted several animals that had crossed the path that we had walked on during the day, and since it had not rained since the morning, the scent stayed strong and long lasting, also the traveling scent of the other animals following our scent made it torturously painful not to follow their noses, as there were so many scents since the animals each left their own scent.

We, although very interested became very tired as the evening dragged into the late night. It was like no camping trip I had ever been on before, as nothing else in my new life was like it was. This was an important learning, one that could control the wildest of beasts, subduing them to the same level as a friendly pet.

The animals seemed to slow down about three-thirty in the morning, just after a rain burst hit, lasting for several hours and the animals that had arrived seemed to file down the hill oddly in a single file, as they were still very docile simply followed the animal in front of it. Then another downpour of rain started, which would wash away the scents.

Since the scent had finally been washed away, peace finally came to our little campsite on the side of a mountain. We could finally get some sleep, and sleep we did. Not until midmorning did we get awakened by the little guy, running and jumping onto the cots since it was all alone, and didn't have anyone to play with. As soon as we woke up, it lost interest and wandered down the hill to forage for food. We both watched, as it toddled its way back to whence it came. We would never forget the little guy.

The new day had started with its humid warmth and a clear blue sky with no clouds. The night before was an exhilarating experience that I had never had before, which I would not forget being my first encounter with the animals of Earth. My thoughts were of all the strange animals, large and small. Each animal that I had meet was mostly carnivores, as the herbivores because the desire for hunting was not in their nature, mostly were asleep as everything was happening, and their food source was within the grassy areas where we had not been.

"Let's check out some of the day animals and especially the herbivores."

"Yes, that is an excellent idea, maybe I can collect some food for our meal this evening," Jescan said as he grabbed a knapsack and a small shovel that fit into a pouch on the knapsack.

Heading out down the flat slope in front of the cave, I used my levitating ability, to levitate us over the ground so that the scent could not be followed and we landed close to the bushes, past the flat grassy area between the cave, and on the edge of the forest.

Looking around, it was in an area that was densely covered with a white leaf like flower with green tips, and the leaf like flowers completely covered the plant, which gave it a ghostly white contrast against the multicolored background of the forest. The plants varied in size from plants a couple of inches off the ground to plants that maybe rose six feet up into the air, displaying the small delicate white leaf like flowers.

The flowering plant was localized in this little remote area, as it could not be found even on the other hills. It so far was confined to this little gully or coulee. This plant was the only colored flower that I had seen so far.

"Let's take a closer look at this flower, since I haven't seen any other flowers in my other wanderings. Have you?"

"You know, I don't believe I have," Jescan answered, rubbing his forehead in thought. "Interesting."

Moving close to one I bent over to inspect the flower, sort of like a rolled leaf in a little bell shape. It had a very strong nice scent and I marveled at how colorful the brilliant white was. "Here we are. Look at this," I said as I pointed to a little creature that was jumping all over the plant.

"I see . . . It's an insect!" exclaimed Jescan, somewhat surprised.

"Yes, although I think it is possibly the start of the insects that we know about. Look at its body."

It had a head that looked too big for its neck and a semi-segmented body, but the interesting thing was it had back legs that pushed it high into the air. It was small maybe the size of an aphid or a large flea.

When it jumped, it could jump maybe three feet in one leap. The little creature was doing very well and was obviously thriving, as there were several in and around the flowers.

Jescan took out one of the little tubes that he carried with him and after several attempts and some unique acrobatics, laughing as he seemed to be falling all over the place, finally placed the tube down inside a flower and waited till one finally went inside and, with a quick motion, slipped the lid over the tube and finally caught one to take back to the ship.

Standing back smiling as I watched, I realized that the insect on the flowers as was the one studied yesterday was the start of the insects, although the one yesterday was not yet a true insect. It was the start of a form of insect. This on the other hand, was probably one of the first true insects again probably one of the reasons for our arrival, as the *Genesis* was programmed to stop at the most important or significant points in the earth's development.

This was the start of the first insect-like creature that would sustain its life on the nectar of a flowering plant as well as on its leaves. Eventually, it would dominate the earth probably eventually develop wings. As more plants develop possibly an offspring of this, the first of the truly colorful flowering plant shall sustain several kinds of insects, unique since the insect almost arrived at the same time as the flower.

Looking over the surroundings, I spotted a single animal limping along as it grazed under the shade of a large fan-shaped fern. Looking closely I could see that it had been badly hurt on its front leg.

Walking over to it generating a docile field, I had no trouble walking up to the poor female. I could see that she had a nest of eggs that she was guarding, I knew if it didn't have some kind of help it would probably die before the little ones were even born.

I gently picked its leg up. It was as if she knew I was there to help her. She cooperated completely. The female had somehow stepped onto a fragment of cartilage, possibly part of the remains of another animal's kill and a splinter, a good-sized splinter was sticking deep into the space between the pads of her foot. It was so lodged that it never would have come out, I squeezed my finger and thumb between the pads and finally got a good grip on the splinter with a good jerk, managed to remove the splinter and as I did so the blood from the wound oozed out.

I massaged the foot till enough blood had passed through the wound to clean the wound. I realized that there was no infection present, since airborne viruses probably had not become mobile yet or possibly didn't exist yet, although I would check the findings with the computer. I felt confident that it would heal fine. I let her put the foot down and almost immediately she walked on the bad leg with no limping at all. As she walked back to her nest, she turned almost like she was saying thank you although I knew she was just curious probably amazed at this creature that just cured her leg, allowing her to walk again.

Jescan's voice was saying, "Look, look."

Turning, I could see Jescan gazing into the sky and quickly looked up to see a burning ball of a meteor streaking by us and landing with a huge bang, shaking the ground and a large cloud of volcanic dust rose and continued to rise into a mushroom-shaped cloud. The meteor was obviously a very large one and had landed maybe twenty kilometers away. Almost immediately the ground started to shake, and the earth cracked and groaned, as several earthquakes started as the thin crust had been violated, allowing the mantle a free flow area.

Levitating both of us, the earth thundered as the new cracks opened a direct flow of the lava to spill out of the ground and shoot straight up, in the distance lava shot up maybe a couple of hundred feet into the air, which came crashing down everywhere.

Realizing the danger, I rose both of us into the air and set us down safely by our campsite. Since the cracks were several miles away from the campsite, the overall picture could be observed without lava flowing or falling everywhere around us.

The ground was still shaking and the lava was still falling from the skies as the red rivers of lava started flowing in and around all the cracks in the earth. The lava flows gushed in every direction as it oozed from the center of the earth. The lava boiled in the ocean, we could see the lava way out in the sea shooting high and in turn the earth shook with new growing pains. The land felt like being on a boat on a very rough sea, which waved back and forth as the land swayed from the violent surge of lava flowing from the bowels of the earth, noticing that the area of the flowering plants had been completely covered in flowing magma totally destroying the little coulee.

Slowly, the shaking subsided as if it were back to normal, then it would start to wave and shake again with the aftershocks till it finally settled down.

By the time it had calmed down it was late afternoon, although the shock waves would happen for weeks to come. We could see a thick cloud coming in our direction with all the new volcanic ash falling everywhere. I surmised that it would make a very thick soup.

"Let's go into the cave before the cloudburst hits," suggested Jescan as he looked at the disappearing landscape, as the rain blocked the view of everything behind it somewhat like a curtain being pulled across the land.

"That might be a good idea. The increase in the volcanic activity may increase the rainfall as it travels across the land. The steam is rising as fast as the cloud could release the rain. I believe the name is called verge, as the rain was falling but was pushed back up before it hit the ground. Looks like we could be in here longer than we thought. I didn't tell you before, the ship is not going to be back till tomorrow night possibly the next day, because of the increase in the amount of wildlife and plant life. I set it out to do a complete survey of all species."

"Life has increased so much that it is going to be recording that long, at least?"

"If we needed the ship, it could be back right away, but it is collecting each different variety of plant and animal, which I forgot to tell you about. Sorry, I just thought about it now. I wanted to spend some time fishing, maybe some later time," I said, apologizing as we entered the cave. Turning to look at the advancing thunderstorm the thunder and flashes grew in intensity, and soon the landscape was gone and the rains hit with an unbelievable suddenness as a sheet of gray mud seemed to gush all around the opening of the cave.

"I think this is going to settle in for a good long one. We may as well get comfortable."

I could hear Jescan starting to laugh. Turning, I could see the little guy curled up on top of Jescan's pillow. "Look who came for dinner," he said as he bent and gently petted him on the little nose that stuck out from his armor.

Groggily, the little guy moved its head slowly back and forth in a swaying motion as it reached out to sniff, licking Jescan's hand. As soon as the little guy woke up, he was kind of like a little dog and started wagging its body and then jumping to the ground, started to tear around the cave, every circle he would go between Jescan's legs, and to one side of him and then the to the other side.

The laughter of Jescan seemed to brighten up the cave, and I sat to watch the two of them play this game of circles.

As the night went on, so did the rain. The next day, the rains carried on in unbelievably heavy torrents, even into the evening till the next morning when it started to slow down to a drizzle, enough that we could see the trees in the hills below us. The volcanic ash was washed away, and the place looked as though there had never been such a violent occurrence two days before. The drizzle still continued, occasionally picking up in velocity but remaining for the most part a drizzle for most of the remaining day. The *Genesis* arrived, still the rain stayed.

"Just another day in the life of this time . . .," Jescan stated as he stood by the entrance. "Look, I can't see the ocean anymore. It's all volcanoes now. This period increases the land even more. Was this meant to be?"

"I would have been alerted if there had been a problem, so it is obvious that this was the way it naturally was. This is a natural process that happened because of the lighter atmosphere. The meteors didn't burn as much as they do later on in Earth's history. Let's check out the next significant period," I said as I turned from looking out over the land and headed toward the *Genesis*.

Jescan pondered what I had said and soon turned and followed me to the *Genesis*.

CHAPTER SIX

As the buzzer announced that we had arrived, I turned and looked out the window, casually commenting, "Doesn't look any different, does it? More ferns though and look at the trees . . . Let's take a walk." I could sense that there was very little change. The important event was already here. This event somehow was significant, in the respects to the planet, but little in respect to the significant or evolutionary changes to life on this planet.

Opening the door, Jescan and I walked out to an unbelievably beautiful, sunny, clear day. The cave that we had camped in was still there, although the sea could no longer be seen, the ferns and the foliage had made its way up to the mouth of the cave. The trees now stood where the fungi used to be, although some of the fungi were still present, slowly being pushed out by other plants.

The area was more scenic than it was before because of the green vegetation that had reached the higher ground. I noticed that there was definite animal droppings all around. It was obvious that there were animals inhabiting the cave. Although the land was very familiar the change was little other than the plant life now extending further inland, and the presence of plants meant that the animals, in turn were also further inland.

As we were making a general survey of the immediate area an animal came out of the cave. Although changed slightly in size and shape, it was similar to the size of a large porcupine. The animal was the same lineage as the little guy, as the distinctive armor plates were moving like an accordion. We were definitely looking at the descendants of the little guy. Several thousands of years later, his genes had survived in these, his descendants. The little guy probably had made the cave his home after we had left. Obviously, he had enticed a charming lady friend to join him, raising a family in this area. It was obvious from the tracks that several were living here.

The little guy's offspring was remarkably similar to the little species and although this animal was not as young as the little guy was when we first encountered him, there were the obvious larger body and a slender head that had filled out more, in that the eyes were not as segmented or separated from the head as before, in a way almost resembling more closely the armadillo of modern day, yet it still had quite a ways to go before it would resemble the modern-day armadillo.

Although the size was larger, possibly because of the vast food supply in the area, allowing for the larger size this being several millions of generations later, overall the species had not evolved that much.

As we watched the larger animal, Jescan was the first to notice about four little ones running and playing in the mouth of the cave.

"Look, she has young," he said, beaming as he turned to look at me.

"That one there looks like the little guy. Is it safe to go up to them?"

"Yes, it is safe," I said as I generated a protective zone, approximately a radius of about two hundred feet, encompassing the entire cave as well as the surrounding terrace, comfortable in knowing that Jescan would be safe, for he would be preoccupied with the young animals.

Jescan slowly walked up to the little animals and started to pet the little ones. He looking into the cavernous cave, he noticed about forty other animals of different ages. "There is a whole herd of them in here."

Not surprised, as these little creatures were a very social animal that unlike a lot of animals, looked after their young, teaching them until they could look after themselves, at about six to ten weeks.

Although they would be capable of looking after themselves, they tended to stay with the group, learning their position within the group as well as finding protection with larger numbers.

I took a walk in the other direction and walked down to the flat area and practiced my levitation, as I wanted to see the general area, and I came across the little ravine where the flowers had first arrived.

The ravine was completely buried, but the hills must have had some of the seeds, as they were green, and the plants had moved all over the hills. The bright white flowers, some with hints of a reddish tone, where starting to appear in the center of some of the plants.

One thing that did surprise me as I passed overhead was a flower that looked like a new species of plant; and although it looked like a different plant, with brilliant red flowers also starting to appear, mixing among the prehistoric white color, which was the first flower color or combination of as the light spectrum goes, all the colors in the light spectrum being white, the first to exist in the flowering plant kingdom, and the red color was the next step in the evolutionary progression, which could be seen dotting the landscape, standing out among the stark white of the other flowers.

Landing near the flowering plants, I checked out the little insect that we had seen the last time. Taking a closer look at the plant, I saw a little insect, similar to what I had seen the last stop and was surprised to see it still jumped. It really hadn't changed that much, if at all.

It was as though the evolution of a species was not changing as fast as it did in the beginning. Possibly, there had not been enough time or reason to evolve as of yet.

I wondered what significant occurrence was going to take place, or had taken place as my senses revealed very little change. Realizing that the data that the ship would be gathering would not gain much more information, I decided that it was time to head back to the ship and have a general check on the overall populations of the plants and animals, as my overall interest was with the living plants and animals.

Going back to the cave, I could see that the land was still new with growth, and the advancements were more in distribution than radical changes as we had seen in the past.

Jescan was in his glory, as he was playing with the young animals.

As I came near, he said, "I don't see much difference in the animal life, and the only difference is that the plant life and animal life are now more selective with their partners. They seem to be breeding with species of their own kind, unlike before where they breed with anything that was compatible. They seem to be attracted to animals that are like themselves. The last time we were here was probably the dividing of lines, and species were beginning to be selective in their breeding mates."

"I too have come to the same conclusion. I thought it might not be a bad idea to have a once over, with the data gathered by the *Genesis, to* check on the changes. Would you like to come with me, or do you want to stay here and play with the little guys? I get the feeling I won't be long."

"I think that I would like to go with you. It is neat to see these creatures again, but it is not what I would like to do now," he said as he walked toward the ship. "I am more curious, as to how much more land is above the water table. The ocean is no longer in view as it was when we left the last period, but I am still curious."

As we found out, the land had increased a lot in some areas and not so much in other areas, and although there were some species that had changed slightly, some animals in localized areas still had some rapid changes, but for the most part, the planet's landmass was still largely uninhabited.

The wind was still the main reason for the plants migrating so much faster than the animal life, yet I was surprised at how many were transported by animals that migrated steadily inland. Overall, there were very few changes, and we decided that we should go to a different time. The computer interrupted our thoughts, informing us that the landmass had reach its equilibrium, and land and water would stay relatively constant from this day forward.

"This is the important event, in that from this day forward, the land has reached its maximum mass that will, throughout time, stay relatively the same. The water still covered most of the planet, and although it would fluctuate depending on the ice, as it melts and freezes at the poles, overall the land-to-water ratio would be consistent," I commented.

The computer then calculated that the next major change would take place about one hundred fifty thousand years from the present time. Jescan and I decided that we should check out one hundred thousand years first. Setting the controls of the *Genesis,* off we went.

The buzzing sounded our arrival, and looking out the window, we decided to use the ship to survey the land. The landscape was remarkable, as the vegetation was now everywhere.

The animals could be seen dotting the plains and hillsides. I was glad that we decided to see the land from the ship, as we floated around and checked out the landscape. There were still several active volcanoes, but many were dormant and signs of life were encroaching along their perimeters, including the insides of the craters where a multitude of different types of fauna and pine-like ferns were starting to turn the black lava soil to a lush green.

The computer scanned for any major changes, although nothing major were found. The diverse society was leveling out with a normal amount of mutations, showing up in each new generation as the genetics had also reached an equilibrium, separating the species and locking in the DNA. Several species were now separated enough that several lines were incapable of interbreeding with another species. The species were now separate classes of their own. Within each class, the animals would now start to evolve from these distinct classes of plants and animals. It was interesting to see the differences, as the numbers were increasing in each of the lines. Animals were overall becoming very biologically distinct. The animals still did have the ability to breed within their own related genetic lines. That was still not too far evolutionary-wise and was still close enough in the lineage line that it would occasionally happen, where a situation that allowed the interbreeding of the different animals. Although, they tended to avoid one another in some instances if interbreeding occurred, the breeding pairs tended to remain together forming a new lineage of animal. This occurred rarely, usually because of migrating to a different area where mates were limited and the similarities were enough to attract one another. These occurred rarely overall but did play enough of a role as to redefine several of the lineages.

The different terrain spawned the need for different looks and characteristics unique to their area, but the changes were not yet significant enough to place them into a distinct species within their class. Eventually, they would become quite different and would be classed differently someday.

Each animal would fill in the niche within the environment that
it is in either, carnivore or herbivore and fit into the pecking order that
all life brought.

Overall, we decided to go ahead fifty thousand years to check out
the next major change.

Arriving at the next time era we looked out the window and was
surprised to see the land and the animals looking the same.

"It would not be recommended to leave the ship" came the
computer's voice.

"Why not?" asked Jescan.

"The earth is about to have a major seismic change in catastrophic
proportions, and the exact time cannot be determined, as it is
extremely unstable, because of the cooling of the outer layer of the
planet. It has reached the point when it is about to start collapsing or
folding in on itself, although this will not happen on its own, as there
is a shower of meteorites, that is about to collide with the earth in
twenty-one minutes nine seconds," informed the computer.

"Let's take the ship up and watch," I said as the ship pulled up into
the air, giving us an overall look at the massive landmass.

Looking out the window off in the horizon, burning meteorites
could be seen streaking through the sky and could be seen crashing
into the ocean, causing the water to boil momentarily first and then
more entered the Earth's atmosphere, about ten very large meteorites
with smaller ones mixed in although those were all that could be seen.
Possibly more but because of our position we may not have seen all of
them. Some streaked by us and landed in several parts of the land.

Some struck the earth with the same catastrophic effects as the
Hiroshima bomb, only five up to twenty times more powerful. At this
range, it looked like the ocean in the horizon was starting to bubble
violently and volcanoes were starting to erupt everywhere. Even the
land was starting to crack from the impact. As the land heaved and
swayed, it suddenly seemed to collapse or crumble sort of in slow
motion.

Moving closer to the open sea to watch the volcanoes spewing lava
everywhere, the tidal waves rose to heights of maybe one hundred,
maybe up to three hundred feet high every minute or so another

came as the water crashed onto the land, and still more meteorites came whizzing by as the waves crashed into the land, washing several hundreds of miles into the landmass.

The volcanoes in the ocean seemed to explode everywhere, as the whole earth heaved as if this was what was needed to release the pressure built up over millions of years. The landmass seemed to dip on the left side and was immediately covered in water like a sinking ship, the land staying mostly intact with the large waves moving westward, as the earth seemed to spew out more and more lava along the edges of the ocean, and the land that was slowly being washed under the rush of the water, the land from the depths of the seas started to wave, causing it to slip over the top of the existing land, forcing the existing land to slide under the existing floor of the ocean.

This was the start of the plates that would continue to slide under one another for all time, until such time as the planet was so cooled, that it became a solid mass, unable to shrink anymore.

The volcanoes shot lava two or three hundred feet in places, and the ocean became a moving red and black mass moving and shifting as it grew larger and larger, blocking out our aerial view from all the releasing of volcanic gasses, and ash started to rise filling the skies with large gray billowing clouds.

Parts of the land were submersed underwater, as they were moving at an alarming rate. The waves moved across the land as they claimed more of the existing land, staying as another wave was right behind it and kept moving, seemingly eating away at the earth. Parts of the seafloor seemed to float to the surface and were carried slowly, like a surfboard riding a wave overriding the present landmass. The start of a massive ridge of mountains formed, as the existing land was forced under the ocean floor, working like a bulldozer as the rough edges were bunched and pushed together.

The movements seemed to be traveling in slow motion, yet on the planet, things were happening so fast that entire populations of plants as well as animals were completely extinct within a short hour or two.

Jescan was so astonished he was talking out loud as he moaned and gasped at the sights unfolding before him. "Think of all the animals that have been destroyed. Shouldn't we have done something?"

As he was speaking, the musical sounds of the sixth plane reassured me that I was to do nothing, as this was the natural course of nature and that most of the existing life does survived. *Lots died, but it was just the way that it was. The earth will go through more events in its history similar, in many ways to this one, but nature following basic physics will sustain and maintain life.*

Turning to Jescan, pausing as I started shaking my head in disbelief, in all respects humbled at the amazing phenomenon developing before me, and said, "This . . . this is the way it is supposed to be, and I cannot change its history." The devastation was mindboggling.

I had said that this would happen, but as it was happening in front of me, my thoughts could not get the plants and animals that would be destroyed in a single swoop out of my mind.

It again brought the reality, that this planet was letting me know once again of how small and fragile the earth really was. The land that "was" was simply sinking to become the bottom of the sea, and the bottom of the sea was now being pushed out becoming the land, and the animals and the plants would remarkably somehow survive.

Overall, the earth was settling down and was simply going through the increase of mass, causing huge growing pains. It was going through the equalizing pains of growing as the crust of the earth was becoming thicker, and the lava was churning and sliding under the new terrain.

Massive amount of solid ground was starting to liquefy, as it became exposed or buried in the molten magma from the core of the earth.

The ocean was very rough but overall was settling down, and even though the land was continually expanding, grinding shaking the earth it sank slowly then heaving, and the animals would have the time to stay on the high and drier ground. The ferns and the pine like trees would survive because of the seeds that they produced. The overall general population will be able to migrate comfortably.

The land settled down as the exchange of the landmass had suddenly changed as the amount or close to it exchanged the mass of one landmass with another landmass that was rising, exposing the lush aged soil that life needed to produce and multiply within the new soil of the fertile land. The older land was slowly sinking, and the waves started to settle down starting to run over the land, rather than crashing into the land. The first of the titanic plates, that will from this day forward will decide the rest of the history and direction of all the land which in turn became predictable, from this period in time. This was the earth's way of recycling itself, slowly liquefying the old and spewing out the new.

The musical sound came again. *The land will settle slowly and will not be complete for the next three hundred thousand years. At that point, most of all the land that was, will be under the sea, and the parts that were the sea will now be the dominant land, now becoming the land that life will exist. The wet rich seabed is starting to slide over the existing land, forcing the existing land to melt back into magma within the womb of the planet. The soil from under the sea is extremely rich, and life will flourish very rapidly in most areas. The life will, even in some areas, restart from small microscopic life contained in the water. There are indications that the chunks of frozen water from the asteroid had also started forming new organisms. Overall, there are representatives of almost all the life forms that will survive and will migrate to the new land, as there will be a direct route from the west to the east, where the new land will continue to rise. The water shall continue to move east, and the majority of animals will continue to keep ahead of the water.*

Document as much as you can at different times over a period of four hundred thousand years. Every one hundred thousand years is adequate enough to gather the important information. This is of importance to your plane as well as mine. You are learning more than you realize. And the voice disappeared.

"Let's start documenting the plants and animals, and see how many did survive, as the gene pool must stay intact," I said, looking at the earth to find a high point, or perch with a view of all below. "Yes, that is the highest point. An old volcano filled in by thousands of years of sitting on the bottom of the ocean. It was located about the middle of the equator and a little south.

"All the animals shall eventually end up in this area, and most of the land can be seen from up here," I said as the buzzing sounded our landing.

Jescan opened the door, and although more than unusually humid, the air was still refreshing.

Looking around, some plants that had once been on the bottom of the sea were surprisingly surviving, and animals from the sea were everywhere, caught in pools of water, yet there were carcasses strewn all over the land. Those were animals that got caught in the undergrowth, or animals that were attached to the rocks, and the other crawling animals like the snails and such, although several, had floated within the waves of water, carrying them to their new homes.

Sending the *Genesis* to collect and document all the surviving species, including the terminated life forms, I turned to take a walk, and Jescan followed.

The way down, although steep in places was not a difficult one, and as we wound our way through the debris the lingering stifling odor of dead fish was everywhere. The smell was very prevalent, and the plants that were so colorfully beautiful under the sea lay composting, already starting to decompose and were very smelly like the fish still an overpowering potent smell. The smell of death was everywhere. Knowing that even after their bodies had decomposed, they would be leaving only the skeletons and the remaining oil that will be leftover, especially from some of the sizeable animals that will lie in pools. Although, other than the strong fish smell, it was somewhat overbearing especially in the heat of the day. Although, I could tell there was not as much volcanic activity producing volcanic ash, as I thought there would have been.

The seafloor was soft and rolling in areas and rough and treacherous in others, and I couldn't get over how black and rich the soil was. The hard coarse fern like grasses from the almost barren land of volcanic ash were sliding under this rich seabed. Although the land had been rich in minerals, it was no match for the fertile land that was exposed on this day. Things will grow very rapidly as several seeds had already been deposited as the water had dispersed to the lower regions.

I did notice that a lot of the plants, even though there was no water, were still living and some even were standing, as though there was still water to support them. As long as the water stays including the torrents of rain that soaked the land at least once if not more during an average day, for some of them they will survive adapting to the new environment especially where there were pools of water that they were living in.

Lakes had formed everywhere, and the sound of running water was everywhere. The saturated soil relinquished itself to the pull of gravity, the trickles of water that would eventually be rivers started to form, and salt was starting to whiten the drying soil as I observed the drying soil on the tips of the uneven clumps of dirt.

Some crustaceans were scurrying out of the way as we walked on the flat rolling area below the mountain. Because of soft deep soil, I caused us to levitate. "We need to travel to the west where the animals will soon be arriving. We should see the unfolding situation from the original landmass as well as from this area."

Returning to the ship we traveled to the west landing on the area of land that was still sinking, sliding under the new higher land.

The land could not really be seen moving, and seemed stable enough, although the ground was constantly rumbling and shaking sometimes very loudly, as the ground slowly was grinding its way under the old seafloor.

Some animals were bruised and hurt, especially the ones that had been closest to the meteorites, as the sound waves were so strong that for a radius of maybe a thousand to two thousand miles most every animal was knocked unconscious some not able to withstand the shock waves. A lot died, but a few regained consciousness several hours later. Others that seemed totally unaffected simply wandered around as though nothing had happened, overall there were few that were killed. Although, the animals on the west coastline probably had perished, coincidentally nature had somehow arranged that there were little major life forms on the west coast. There were still some that lived there but were insignificant in the overall scope of life, as a small portion of the main lineages had migrated toward the west coastline. The animals seemed to sense that they had to move to higher safer ground.

All were heading away from the grinding rising mountain range. Their instincts told them to move away from the loud noise coming from the west, yet the water forced them to travel ever eastward toward the ever growing higher ground. As the migration carried on they simply went where the food was, as the aroma of the sea animals waffled through the entire atmosphere.

The *Genesis* arrived, and we went inside to find out how many species were lost. Checking the logs, there was little life actually lost.

The species that were lost had similar or the same species on a safe part of the land so, all in all there were very few species that were actually lost, as it turned out animals that liked the harsh sulfur-producing vents of the volcanoes under the water, were actually increasing in numbers as the ocean was dotted with vents.

Touching the control, we advanced one hundred thousand years and again took a walk as the *Genesis* surveyed the planet to report any changes on its return.

The land had quite a different look quite a change, as new sprouts of fern like grasses were starting to carpet the ground with an amazing green hue. Plant seeds that traveled by air were starting to sprout up.

The animals seemed to be spread out inhabiting the valleys and the hills of this new land which although sparse now was able to sustain the wandering animals.

The majority though really had not moved that much, staying above the rising water. The animals stayed within the reliable food source, moving as the water slowly took over the land and really had moved little from the ocean side as the plants had weathered the storm quite well, and started to produce even more seeds from the plants. In turn, new seeds would soon be covering more of the land. The earth still had several trimmers, making it known that it still had some wounds, that it was getting over.

There were plants already starting on the hills that had once been under the ocean. Several trees that boar seeds, had spread with the combination of water, air and fire. Plants that relied on fire to germinate their seeds had, through the unbelievable hot temperatures of the new volcanoes caused the burning of the brush sending new seeds, some floating in the water washing up on the new beaches some landing on new solid ground.

There were little bushes starting all over the land. Some trees that spread from their roots system, similar to the modern bamboo trees, were trenching their way up the riverbanks and starting to build around lakes and following the streams. Although they stayed relatively to the lowlands, some had made it up to some higher altitude lakes.

Some of the creatures that had somehow lived through the tidal waves and had landed in remote areas had no problems as they lived off the dead sea growth, till the new seeds germinated, or if they were meat eating, they lived off the dead sea animals, or the ones caught in the pockets of water throughout the land as the holes disappeared and dried up. There were a lot of sea animals mostly crustaceans, and a good food source for a lot of the animals.

The majority of the land was under a constant rain, mixed with the ash of the volcanoes, including the sulfuric acid diluted with the constant rain and humidity rising, restocking the clouds. The clouds were slowly cleaning out the floating debris left in the sky, and the lighter atmosphere allowed the particles to fall a lot easier, and the winds that were at the higher levels were still drawn into as well as pushed away from the high-pressure areas and drawn toward the low pressure areas. They guaranteed that the most of the land, was always experiencing a mixture of weather, another natural occurrence that would never end, until man intervenes millions of years from now.

The skies cleared in streaks, as the volcanic ash slowed their vigorous belching of magma, slowing to a steady flow. The rains continued, and skies from all indications would be clear once again, probably within the year to a year and half. The constant rains washed away the salt in the soil slowly but surely. The lakes too slowly lost their saltiness, gaining new sources as water flowed from the higher land eventually flowing back to the sea. Some animals adapted and could live in the less salty conditions without dying, as some did. The rains also moved and eroded large areas of the earth causing deep gullies that in turn, formed the gigantic rivers and streams. This allowed a lot of creatures a route back to the sea.

Others simply found a lake that was compatible, and stayed in the sometimes deep salty lakes.

There was still no definite seasons, although at certain times of the year there was less rain or more rain in certain areas, and although the north and south poles were starting to cool faster than the rest of the earth there were no dramatic temperature changes. The north and south pole were maybe two to five degrees different from the equator, although the decrease in temperature slowly evolves over the next few million years but for now it was the same as the rest of the young

Earth, heated by the closeness of the molten core being so close to the surface. The atmosphere because of its thinness let a lot of heat escape into space. Although an ever-thickening layer of ozone was starting to play its role in the planet's history, even now the atmosphere was starting to build a reflective barrier that reflected some of the heat back to earth, including from the sun. All in all, the earth was rather warm from within as well as externally. The earth though being warm almost like an incubator, was also extremely humid to the four corners. It is the perfect place for life to exist and flourish.

Jescan bent over to pick a small snail like animal and starting to examine it, he said, "It is quite different from the beginning when we only had one or two species to look at. It seems to be going so fast.

Although I know that it has been millions of years since the beginning. Life still seems so uncomplicated so simple at this stage of Earth's growth."

"Yes, it doesn't take long for things to change and adapt yet stay surprisingly simple and uncomplicated. I would say that this is probably the least complicated the earth will ever be," I said as I walked toward a river that was remarkably wild and turbulent.

The river was black and murky. Surprisingly, the amount of soil that was being removed was astonishing, as chunks of Earth were washed away with very little to stop it as it rushed toward the open sea. Large quantities would continue to gorge the once soft seabed and would be transformed into a large wide valley, forming a river that would survive possibly to modern day.

The *Genesis* returned and upon entering the ship, I was anxious to find out any major changes. Although few changes were found, there were a few species that were too fragile. Possibly a better way to put it was that they were destined to become extinct as they depleted their food supply as well as were not intelligent enough to move with the moving food supply. They had become too limited in their way of life. Without the ability to change, they simply died off or were eaten.

Survival of the fittest was playing out its part in the grand scheme of things.

Touching the controls, the *Genesis*'s buzzing sounded our arrival one hundred thousand years more.

Opening the door, I took a walk outside to a land that was green in most places, baring the sides of the steepest hills and mountains.

The land was now almost completely covered by fern like grass and moss. The bamboo and mango type trees were still young but starting to show their presence multiplying as they moved up the rivers and streams. I noted. that something new was starting to take a hold still on the moist banks, but actually out of the water as the trees similar to willow trees or bushes of all kinds and types from ferns to small seed-bearing trees from pines of various types to spruce-type trees, to some of the newly arrived willow type and fern types growing the fastest as they mostly grew from the main plants that had been anchored in the soil sending off shouts, growing ten feet in only the last year.

The animals were migrating and spreading out over the massive land, each finding an area that suited their needs. The herbivores traveled first as the plants sprung up in great abundance, thriving in the rich black soil. The hunters were following as the populations were increasing, not only with a bountiful food supply, but also with nutritional value of this newly introduced soil exceeded anything that had occurred on Earth before, with remarkably healthy and fertile offspring. Multiplying at a remarkable rate with few predators and an almost unlimited food supply was the fastest growth of land populations that happened at that time on Earth, and had ever experienced. Although the population was exploding, the predators were soon to follow. They too found the abundance of animals that they hunted, allowing the animals to spend more leisure and relaxing time, which had again never occurred on Earth, as it had been a continual struggle to etch out a survival technique that worked and setting up their own territories. The population of each species was exploding as more food became or was available.

The top of the mountain became a great observation point. The animals were starting to reach the base of the mountains, surrounding the territories all around in every direction.

The coastline on the east was still oozing lava, which was underwater now, increasing the coastline, and pushing the water ever farther west, as the rotation of the earth was playing a major role in the movement of both land and sea. Very little life could survive in the harshness of the lava flows and although very inhospitable there was as the saying goes, an exception to the rule, as the little white oddly shaped creatures that lived and liked the higher sulfuric water and air very similar to and genetically traceable to the first creatures that developed from the beginning of life with the DNA rather than the one-stranded RNA or virus type of creatures. I was fully expecting that they in turn would develop new species in a manor such as they did in the beginning. Oddly my thoughts knew that they would not be the major contributors of as many new life forms as would the existing life already well established in this new planet. The ships computer would be able to verify my suspicions.

Walking to the edge of the sharp cliff side I sat hanging my feet over the edge watching the animals wandering here and there, still very comical as they carried on in a very haphazard way almost bumping into their enemy or prey. Some looked like they were in a hurry. Well the largest portion of the animals plodded along ever so slowly.

Jescan came and sat beside me and pulled out his binoculars as we watched the antics below laughing at some just observing others.

"This is so peaceful. The land so new, and the animals peacefully doing their own thing. It looks so uncluttered. Is this the time when the species start to reproduce at an accelerated rate . . ., or is this increase just natural?"

"This is the time when the populations increase so fast that in three hundred thousand to four hundred thousand more years, the animals will be spread out everywhere. The animals have started to have offspring some related yet most interbreeding with a mate that was compatible. Some still mated with several species as it would first try to mate with the animal it approached and if unsuccessful, would kill and eat the other, sometimes the reverse. It was surprising that genetically different animals from a different lineage, yet evolutionary still so closely related enough that in a high percentage of cases, the conception took place. Although the offspring definitely showed the combined characteristics of the parents, most did not look like the parents again causing major changes in the direction of the species, as the mated pair would generally stay together, sometimes for their life, and similar species did stay building several herds that would eventually cover the land with the richness of the land, would accelerate massive herds even more," I said, wondering what the next hundred thousand years would bring.

"Do you realize that we have traveled to four times in a half a normal day?"

"I really never thought about it, but yes we have, and covered three hundred thousand years of time, since the asteroids had started the transformation. Do you want to stay here for a while, or do you want to go to where the sixth plane suggested and go to the—four hundred thousandth year today? The *Genesis* has been back for a while now."

"Well, I think we should let the situation decide how fast we should go. I still can't get over the fact that we are the only people to witness firsthand the beginning, the first people to see the life as we are able to witness seeing it as it occurs. I know that as we experience it, history is still in our time no further ahead because of our experiences. Our experiences and knowledge of where we are right now will not be allowed to be known, as mankind must and will discover the information slowly piecing together the small fragments of the past, yet still relating it to the future of the planet as pieces must be worked to discover the wonders of how we became what we are, in time they will know.

"We are on our way to the point in time when all the knowledge of the universe is at my fingertips. I know now, that the more you know the less you know. Such as the subtle small things seem to have a profound effect on the direction of the planet's life. To think of all the knowledge that the archaeologists and paleontologists would give to have a fraction of the information that we have, or to spend even one hour at any location that we have been visiting, the information that our computer contains will help all the future civilizations at a future time when it becomes important to the planet. Things that go on now are things that could never be completely verified. We now can verify all the major events as well as where we came from and where we are going, and how we got there with the information in between. There is little that we can do at this time. All the animals are doing very fine. Let's move ahead in time and see what the next hundred thousand years shall bring."

Opening the door, we walked out to an ideal paradise. The land was amazingly rugged and fertile. The animals were still in a very unlimited growth environment growing to enormous sizes, creatures of all different sizes and description. Most animals were multiplying at a very unprecedented rate. The young per female was for the large, two to four per year as there were still no noticeable seasons weather wise, and the animals continually mated although the multiple births did play a very important factor as most still laid eggs, although live births were starting to show up in some of the species especially the midsized to small-sized animals.

Midsized animals started producing up to thirty per year. The small produced hundreds and sometimes thousands per year. The microscopic phytoplankton and zooplankton never stopped, generally they split every two minutes. This amazing spurt in the regeneration of such a diverse group of different types of varieties was a natural occurrence.

The animals were growing in numbers, almost as fast as the plants could grow, and grow they did as the land was bursting with plants of all sizes and descriptions. In the last two hundred thousand years, some had grown a hundred to two hundred feet high, resembling somewhat the young jungle it would become in the future. The most perfect conditions were with lots of water and sun in several intervals throughout the long days and warm nights.

Looking over the land, it was lush and bursting from every corner. The animals in four hundred thousand years had grown in size as well. The largest animals were merely miniature babies as eventually they would become creatures of maybe twenty feet long, and some with necks that reached a height of thirty feet tall. Some were just large, with large bulging bulky bodies. Most of the animals carried their large heavy armor with them, sort of a reformed shell that kept growing. The animals in turn grew with such bulkiness that a lot simply could not move fast enough. As they were carrying several times their own weight in a shell, most often they would sit logged between rocks or brush, simply becoming a meal for another meat eating animal, were devoured and literally torn to shreds by some of the large carnivorous animals, that was large and strong enough to flip the massive weight of the armor exposing the substantially large fleshy underbelly of the main body.

The expert in this was an animal that had developed extremely large hind legs with the physical ability to allow it to apply tremendous pressure and strength with smaller strong forearms that could hook the armor, and with a gigantic shove it could flip the animal over. The large animal could then enjoy as much as it could eat, then it would leave finding a place to relax and sleep digesting the massive meal. The other animals, smaller and more agile could then move in having their fill.

This particular animal fed several animals because of its size, another remarkable aspect was that this animal reproduced at an alarming rate, of close to one hundred per year, ultimately an extremely large food supply for many of the large meat eating animals.

The animal also grew extremely fast. From hatching to one year it had reach almost full growth, and started reproducing as soon as it reached about five to six months old, reproducing approximately a hundred eggs every other week. Some produced faster and some slower, but they continued to reproduce, generating an important link in the food chain.

As several animals realized a ready food supply, and these herbivore large slow-moving animals would be eaten rarely did they die a natural death, rather killed with an average life expectancy mostly always killed within one to five and a half years of age, reproducing very young and many at a time.

There still were some that did live a natural life although so rare, as the animals that had adapted to this food source also reproduced reasonably fast.

The herbivores grew strong because of the lush rapid growth of the different types of plants and bushes contributed to unlimited constant eating and growing. Rarely was an animal able to die because of old age. It generally died at the mercy of another hungry animal. It was the norm that most animals became victims, with the exception of the largest and strongest animals the top of the food chain which usually died from injuries or in mortal combat with another carnivore.

The population explosion on all levels, especially the lower smaller life forms, gave the food chain an excellent opportunity for all animals to populate in turn. This new land was large still there were vast areas of land that had none or very few animals even though the plants flourished at remarkable rates and heights.

The *Genesis* disappeared documenting all the changes that had taken place in this period. As we walked, the animals seemed to rally around us not to attack us, but to follow us letting us pet them. It was remarkable how such large creatures became docile and gentle.

Rarely was there a disagreement among the animals. Deadly animals that would ordinarily have killed one another, walked side by side and gave no notice to one another.

Animals surprisingly never ran away from us as we walked.

It was as though they were like old pets that had been raised by us accepting our presence, just as anything that was familiar around them, accepting us unconditionally.

The *Genesis* returned and landed close to us. As we walked toward the ship to check the logs, it occurred to me that there was one animal that was especially friendly not to me, but to Jescan. It was a young animal the same lineage as the little guy with Jescan having a peculiar interest in this strange young little animal was egging it along. Playing in a very subtle quiet way was enticing him as we entered the ship, this little guy ran in front of Jescan and hid behind the console, playing a hide-and-seek game with Jescan.

Smiling, I let on that I hadn't seen him as I walked into the *Genesis,* around the console reaching out about to touch the controls.

Jescan intervened, "Look, this little guy must have followed us in.

We had better let him go, or . . . could we bring it along? He is very cute."

"You must upon our arrival release him, and you cannot keep him, as he will get to big." Correcting myself as I took a closer look, I said, "I mean, she will get too big."

Jescan was smiling and very happy to have this time to play with this new little female. "Thanks. I know that she could never stay with us, but this animal is really fun to play with. They have a great temperament, and they overall are a neat animal," he said, picking up the young little female.

Looking at the monitor, I could see that the first form of insect had finally started a crude form of a wing more like a gliding appendage than a wing. "Let's look at something that is very interesting before we go to the next period."

Opening the door Jescan followed behind with his new friend in his arms. On route to a little valley was a short walk to the east, we soon overlooked a valley with several colors of white and red blossoms from some very large plants, which in three hundred thousand years had grown into a sizable garden of remarkable growth.

The seeds were constantly being spread, as the plant was continually producing flowers similar to the modern myrtle plant. On one plant you could find flowers that had gone to seed, as well as young buds ready to open in the next day or so.

Looking closely at the plants the little bug-like creature was buzzing all over the plant and although it still jumped, it was starting to develop a part of their anatomy that was in some animals would or was a part of the gills, and since the animal had no more use for a pair of gills this layer of scale like material could be flared out as it jumped from flower to flower, leaving its segmented legs unencumbered. For now it was only used to glide, not yet to flying. It did manipulate the air currents by increasing the glide from about three to four feet up to a distance of maybe ten to twenty feet. It was remarkable as this little creature was the first to take advantage of the segmented parts, forming the first insect-like animal that had finally devised a method of traveling from one flower to another, without having to land on the ground. Studying this creature, we were amazed at the shape. It looked like it should not even be able to jump, let alone glide through the air.

Evolution as well as a natural change from the radiation of the sun that mutating genes produced things out of the ordinary, still over time kept improving on what it already had.

The little creatures sailed from the top of a plant to a flower ten feet away was learning to control the currents of air in between.

The first creature too actually, although crude, actually flew. The Wright brothers would be proud.

Jescan watched with interest as I reached down picking one so that I might show him the first insect that will fly someday. For now though, the first gliding insect.

"Now we can go to the next time frame," I said, pleased that finally I knew how insects got their wings. "Finally, I have the answer to a puzzle that has had people guessing for several millenniums," I added, observing the total fascination Jescan had for this little insect, as he did for most of the animals.

Heading back to the ship I noticed that Jescan had let the little girl go. As we walked to the ship, I knew that he would have felt guilty if he had taken the little one from her mother.

Entering the ship I stepped around to the console and pushed the control to take us to the next stop, which would take us one hundred thousand more years. The buzzer sounded our arrival.

Just as the sixth plane had said, the sea now covered most of the land that once was the home to the start of life.

The trees were starting to become quite thick in areas, as they broke the landscape into picturesque forests. I noticed that as they crowded close together because of the roots and seeds scattered in a confined space starting new plants the trees started to grow thinner and taller, reaching some two hundred feet. This in only three hundred thousand years, it was remarkable. The trees although confined in small pockets were taking over a good portion of the land, some trees were starting to produce an abundance of fruit. I could tell that the only areas that they would not be covered in by trees, were the areas that the animals grazed keeping the trees from growing as they ate the young shouts.

As we walked down the path from the mountain, I noticed that trees were even starting to grow on the sides of the mountain. I also noticed that some of the trees that produced fruit were also producing small colored flowers and checking the trees, discovered that the gliding insect was also found on the leaves and fruit of the trees.

The insect though was not just flaring the crude wings but was also occasionally flapping them, giving them some extra lift if the target was just a little farther than they expected. Although the flapping didn't make much difference as they generally fell short when the distance was farther than they planned, I could see them practicing flapping the scale like wings knew that this little creature was in time, going to cover the world with creatures that could actually fly to any destination they wanted to go. I also noticed that they not only liked the nectar but also as I watched them, as one could be seen eating a millipede type of creature, showing that they could live off many different things.

Another, although slightly different in appearance was actually eating the fruit and leaves of the plants and didn't even pay any attention to the flowers.

As the years had gone by, each generation of offspring in many cases where still slightly different from its parent, and several generations could be produced within a year. This creature had somehow reactivated the same gene that mutated from one generation to another and the offspring might look like the parents, others had variations within the same clutch of eggs. This change could have been caused by the need for change as much as the external effects, such as the sun's effect on the exposed eggs.

Walking further into the woods animals were everywhere, some climbing the trees some using the trees as shelter, and some of the larger creatures using the trees as protection from the blistering sun.

Others just found them a good food source, simply found them convenient to stay in the general area where the food was plentiful.

Little creatures that scurried along the ground could be seen, I was noticing that they too were creatures that had not been around in the past, they in their funny fast way of moving were animals that dug into the ground making their homes underground.

These were still cold-blooded animals as most of the creatures were except for the very large reptile like animals, which because of their mere size generated their own energy were the start of the first forms of what would become warm-blooded animals. These little creatures were small and long with very short legs. They had a long reptile like tail, and they had a small very pointed nose. These small creatures lived off grasses, leaves, seeds, and fruits, and were relatively harmless.

The uniqueness of this animal was the fact that it burrowed underground similar to the animals of the ocean that hide under the silt. Up till three hundred thousand years ago, the hard lava flows didn't have much depth to the soil with some of the rains there was little that could dig in the hard black rock. Never before had an animal thought of going underground, although this animal was the first.

This was the start of the treed areas becoming the home of new animals as well as the birthplace of many new animals, sort of a melting pot of the animal kingdom, the start of new life formed almost daily.

A little sound came from the top of a tree, and being that it was unusual, it caught Jescan's attention as well. The sound came from a small lizard-like animal that, in some respects, was like a small dilophosaurus. It had claws on the back legs as well as the remains of the gills and the forearms had formed a growth that allowed the two to mesh together with the floppy skin held firm with the spreading of the fingers that made it look so out of place, yet this animal with a short fanlike tail extended to a point. This was the first creature to have formed a web between its fingers, and used the skin from the now useless arms, allowing a rhythmic beat, as it could move its arms, and not think about the movement. Completely automatic muscle control allowed the animal, to beat its arms as easy as breathing.

Although I didn't really know how the first wings came to be, and here in front of me was a genetically mutated lizard-type animal which still had cold-blooded characteristics yet because of the muscles, moving when needed, with the same likeness as the heart or the lungs it was starting to generate its own heat was well on its way to becoming warm-blooded.

Watching us, this little creature decided that it would like to visit with us, as most every animal did. It jumped off the limb and landed on my shoulder with a swishing sound. It landed on two back feet and, although not very steady used its skin-covered arms to give it a little support as it rested comfortably on my shoulder, with its little hook at the end of the wing hooked to my shirt.

The wings reminded me more of a bat's wings than a bird's wing, but the weight was light, and I could tell that the bones were hollow and very fragile.

I could see that it had a nest in one of the thorny cactus-like trees, and I could sense that it was a mother. "Let's see if this animal has any young yet."

Jescan followed me, as we moved toward the nest and inside, we could see six small spotted eggs. They haven't hatched yet, so we will have to wait for the young to hatch. I could sense that it would not be long, as one of the eggs moved slightly, as the layer of soft dried grasses lining the nest moved slightly as the egg resettled into its former position. The new bird jumped from my shoulder, and was proud to show me the nest that it had spent a long time building. It also had soft moss from the trees lining the sides, and moss and grass mixed together to make the bottom.

I noticed that the moss had not really died, when it had been used as nesting material. I supposed because of the humid air, and it reattached to the wood and was growing although slowly. It still was extremely soft and with a greenish look blended into the tree as if it were part of it, a great food source for the young after the eggs hatched as the new bird was a vegetarian although the plants would be regurgitated from the plants that the parents retrieved, leaving the new growth of the lichen-like moss for later when the young was able to digest its own food.

The sound of a little creature crawling in and out of the grass and moss on the ground, caught our attention as it almost chirped. The small creature was broad and flat, pointed at both ends. Its body had four layers of thin skin that was across its back, and the skin was split down the middle.

To make the sound of a chirp as it rubbed the hard skin across its ridged body.

Jescan reached to pick one up surprised when it jumped and flapping its skin like wings, it landed on his shoulder. "Another flying creature.

Each could not possibly be related to the other different species all gaining the ability to fly?"

"All the animals started out with a similar gene pool. The changes from parent to young are still changing. These creatures have not yet isolated themselves in their breeding, yet again if two of the same looking species breed, the offspring from them generate the same like babies and they interbreed among themselves generating offspring, that generation usually becomes the dominant characteristic. As long as they breed among themselves, they in turn become a new lineage or species."

"So that is how different species develop similar type of characteristics, yet are nowhere close to looking alike. Are there large animals that are developing wings then?"

"Possibly, but the larger animals tend to have developed a method of walking with all limbs, although some of the cartilage structures are rapidly changing and it could be very possible that large creatures also needed the protective ability to fly, raising their young in very inaccessible places like the tops of trees and cliffs. This is one that natural selection is the determining factor. The *Genesis* will determine how many are developing. We have come across three . . . It is possible to find more."

The walk to the river was refreshing, as a slight wispy wind puffed softly against our faces. The terrain around the river was rough with huge balls of dirt the size of small hills reaching twenty to twenty-five feet high. In the middle of the river it looked like someone had a giant mud ball fight. Moss were growing along the bottom and sides with grass growing from the top and the sides, making it look like little grass shacks as we came closer to the water. The wildlife, was amazing, as the creatures were all individually different yet strange-looking some very small some larger, but still no larger than three feet high.

One of the creatures that came up to us had a very round head, thin neck and body, with long segmented legs. It had a segmented curled tail. It stood approximately ten inches in height. With the tail curled out it may have been fifteen inches high, a very formidable animal in that it had such an aggressive attitude. The head was followed by the curled tail which rose as it approached making it looked like it was growing as it came closer. The creature was definitely a meat-eater as the egg-shaped head had large teeth that were visible as it opened its mouth as it stretched its nose out to smell us.

Small animals that were more like huge slugs also came out of the muddy ground, and moving very slowly made their way to the lush grass to eat as they moved.

Little creatures seemed everywhere swimming in the lukewarm water, fish of all sizes and lengths could be seen.

Climbing to the top of a dirt mound, a clear view of the rushing water could be seen in its entirety. The washing effects of the dirt caused the large balls that rolled along the banks some stayed but some breaking up into wet mud disappearing into the raging currents.

Turning to Jescan, I said, "I think that it is time to call the *Genesis*. It has been back for several hours."

The buzzing sounded our arrival as we landed. Since the land had been transformed, three hundred thousand years had passed.

Looking out the window, the land had changed even more. The ocean had advanced swallowing the enormous volcanic countryside, in turn replacing it with this rich land. The continental shelf was starting to be formed, although several large hills and mountains could still be seen as the land was continually sinking, with a grinding that shook the earth from time to time as the rush of the displaced water was causing the ground to seem rubbery and elastic. Although the land was relatively stable, the motion of the seabed falling to settle below the new land caused an uneasy feeling, as the ground seemed to rock and shake occasionally.

Walking outside the humid air was filled with animal sounds coming from all directions. The animals were all settled into a natural routine set out by each of their positions in the food chain, and the land, oh . . . the remarkable land was teaming with wildlife of every description.

The little bird that we had visited one hundred thousand years ago was at the point of spreading to the several groves of trees dotting the bush-filled valleys and hills. The young could be seen sailing almost flying across the sky, landing on the trees and high rocky ledges.

The flying insects had also arrived, with their crude wings helping them to spread to several new areas which previously would have taken them several years to migrate that far.

The creatures were starting to stabilize into separate species again, although there were several new species born almost daily. The rapid rate was starting to level out even decrease, from forty to fifty a day to below thirty a day.

The large animals seemed to be growing to gigantic proportions, as was the plant life because of the overabundance of oxygen in the air.

With the unlimited food supply both took on the race of the bigger the less danger of getting eaten, right out to sea as the animals were swimming in a virtually endless supply of food. Simply by swimming with their mouth opened they could feed, quite different yet similar in ways to the animals inland that had to hunt, chase and kill their prey, food sources which were increasing with each day.

Overall, I could tell that the populations would not yet be radically changed for now, the species would start to change only when the need to change was needed and mutations would become the common means of change, as well internally the structure allowed organs that where no longer necessary for survival to become unused organs.

Although most would still carry those unused organs some over time would genetically gradually delete them, or in the case of the flying animals utilize them in different and under observation, unthinkably new ways. Other characteristics that become more important to that individual species would then develop their more important traits that sustained them in the role they were living, sometimes completely changing over time.

The species that developed on this new continent will over time develop different types of animals with similar characteristics within their own genetic makeup but looking and acting different, yet of the same lineage. Every plant and animal had and will continue to have mutations that allow organs to lie dormant, until such a time when it is required. Some lay dormant were never required, but at this stage almost all the organs were functional as well as useable, serving the purpose that they were intended for. Certain animals placed in different settings, utilized different physical requirements.

These changes utilized within the same species caused unique differences that over time, develop differently. They in their own right became separate creatures, living even off different food sources.

These animals, although spread across all corners of the continent were separated from their family trees, producing different genetic information from that of their related ancestors, eventually not even looking alike physically.

This separation was already prevalent, as animals found their own niche to live and raise their young. The landscape was quite diverse and once an animal crossed over a river, or a mountain range the connections to their past most often would be lost.

There were few isolated areas left, as the rich soil allowed fern like grasses to spread their seeds by the wind including animal droppings, or the root system grew continually gobbling up any space available. After the first year the grasses started the animals soon followed, and at this time grasses had three hundred thousand years of development and were everywhere. Even little isolated areas along the rim of mountains or valleys where animals may have fallen into and could not get out, or rivers that carried them to a remote area maybe isolated by lakes and old volcanoes. Thus animals ended up in very unusual areas without any means to return to their own kind. Oddly enough it seemed in most instances the animals found mates that were compatible. Quite often more than one of the same species somehow found each other, although there were rogue animals and loners, but rarely was there an isolated individual that didn't find a mate. Females quite often may have been fertilized, before they were carried away, and it was very common seeing several stranded females raising their young without the protection of the main group or mate.

There was almost very little or no diseases to be observed being that the air and water were pure the cleanest of any period on Earth. If an animal was injured it rarely went too long before it healed, or the animal fell prey to the hunters.

From the computer information, there were few that died from old age, although the life expectancy was usually short as the land supported life, but it also took life. Smaller animals and some insects whose purpose was to only reproduce lay their eggs and then die shortly after. On the whole though animals were tending to live a longer life, some being capable of living several hundred years the average though living less such as twenty to thirty years. Each species usually having its own destiny inevitably was hunted and died a fast death at the mercy of a predator.

Several because of inexperience, tended to die young. Some species never reached their full maturity as they were easy prey. These types of animals tended to reproduce at an early age, they usually produced several offspring at a time to try and keep ahead of the predators.

Jescan and I sat on the mountain watching the animals move about in their own particular manor and uniqueness. It occurred to me that we had not stopped for nearly thirty hours in real time. It was time to rest and get something to eat. "How about stopping here for something to eat and maybe some sleep before we travel anywhere else?"

"Yes, I am a little hungry," stated Jescan as he rubbed his stomach.

"The *Genesis* is on its last area. It should be arriving back shortly, then we will have a good meal before we proceed."

"It is remarkable. The changes from volcanoes and lava flows to what it is today, with everything alive and thriving," Jescan commented as he saw the *Genesis* appear.

Sitting as we ate, we contemplated and watched the animals as they played and carried on.

When they were on the hunt it was generally a swift fast kill with little work involved, as game was everywhere. The animals were generally well fed and usually spent most of its day lazing in the sun.

Some of the smaller animals were peacefully eating grasses or plants. Some of the larger carnivores animals spent time dining or guarding their last kill.

Scavengers, as a necessary part of the food chain were everywhere, but there was always food left over from an animal's kill as the predators usually ate their fill, leaving the remains. The scavengers although numerous were spread over the land only immediate family units seemed to travel together, most only approached after the kill had been surrendered, so because of numbers rarely would a scavenger rush an animal away from its kill. It would not be long before something would be surrendered.

The sounds were remarkable, from the small insect type to the deep bellows of the large animals. Everything was very close to being in perfect harmony. The animals even played with animals that they if hungry would think nothing of killing them. Although the submissive animals would be desperately trying to get away, it was as though the smaller animal knew that it was not going to be lunch.

The air the plants and the animals all living together with nothing more than survival on their agenda. This comfortable lifestyle would last for millions of years.

Through all the years the animals would evolve adapting and changing as the situation requires, but with all the changes the animals all find their niche, the harmony would stay relatively constant.

Jescan took his plate into the ship, and as he started out of the ship he grabbed the latest printout. "The data is almost the same as it was a hundred thousand years ago. Does this mean that it has leveled out like it was before the new land formed?"

"There are still going to be changes, but they will slow down to a normal rate now at least as far as I know," I said, looking up to Jescan. "There could be things that I am not aware of till they happen.

There are similar things that happen in the other planes that directly influence this plane, although I am not sure of what they are or when they will happen."

"As I recall, there were four that concerns Earth. They happened with very long intervals in between although in the future, past the initial contact there is nothing written so there may be many more that I do not know about," Jescan said as he contemplated the book that he had been reading before this remarkable journey.

"You may be right but I do get the feeling the growth rates of new species are slowing down," I said getting up, I turned to Jescan.

"Shall we carry on, or maybe get some sleep before going on?" I asked, motioning to the ship.

The buzzer sounded our stop on our quest for more knowledge, and this last of the one hundred thousand year stopped as this was the five hundred thousand years this time would tell us if my premonition of the slowing down of the new species was right.

In this five hundred thousand year there was little that was changed except that the trees had even grown taller, I could sense that there was little change from one hundred thousand years prior.

The new birds were flourishing as they could raise their young in very safe place atop the high cliffs, and more insects because of their ability to reproduce so abundantly, but all in all there was little change.

"The trees have really grown," stated Jescan. "Look at the trees along the side of the mountain. They have grown to such heights and diversity covering most of the land in an amazing forest. The trees had grown so much and covered so much of the land that they even produced their own rain, something even in the future still produce their own rain or weather."

"It is remarkable what perfect growing conditions will do for plants.

Look at the animals, they too are growing in size." I said. Looking out on the plains I could see large bulky animals that looked somewhat animated as they moved ponderously because of their large size.

The changes, though were not in the large animals but I could sense that the major changes were in the small insects. Looking down the side of the mountain, there were swarms of insects that all flew, and I started down the hill to investigate further.

Getting close to the insects I could see that these little insects were not swarming around the plants, but they were swarming around the animals. Checking out the animals the insects were eating away at the animal and welted areas of their small bites could be seen all over the animal's body.

"Oh . . . the first form of a mosquito had arrived." Although it was similar to modern-day mosquito it still was not like a mosquito yet. It had a segmented body and wings. It had a jaw that was fairly large for its size. The head seemed too large for its body because of the size of the razor-sharp teeth. "From this day forward, there will be that cursed of all pests with little relaxation for the animals of the earth."

"Can we not go back and get rid of it?" Jescan asked, knowing the answer before I answer it.

"As loathsome as this creature is it is a vital link in the food chain. Regrettable as it is there is no way that I can just get rid of it. We might not like the replacement animal that would sooner or later take its place if I did stop the mosquito, which I wouldn't."

Oh, how I wanted to as I remembered the annoying pests ruining evenings outside but like a kid with his hand in the cookie jar, I knew I couldn't change what already was.

"You mean that for millions upon millions of years this little pest will torture all the animals?"

"Yes, I guess so, painful as it sounds."

Looking up into the trees I could see a snakelike creature winding its way down to the ground. "This is very interesting. Look another addition, a new predator," I said, pointing out the young small animal winding its way down the branches.

"This is when snakes arrived from the wormlike creatures. As the birds became more abundant a method of controlling their numbers was needed, as well it could also control the animals that burrowed underground," Jescan said, understanding the role of this new predator. "Now that I think about it, I would have thought that they would have arrived earlier yet there was no purpose for it before now."

"This is unexpected but it is here now, where it must have developed closer to water and worked its way into the woods, or did it come from a land animal instead? We will have to verify our findings when the *Genesis* returns," I said as I pondered the possibilities.

Moving further out into the flat rolling terrain, life was similar as several predator animals were having their fill of a fresh kill. Coming closer these animals were animals that obviously traveled in a group and were very agile. As we came closer I could see that they had long pointed heads as did several of the animals, but these animals were ones that came from the sky as the animals clawed out large chunks of meat. A layer of skin was webbed from the clawed tip to the center of the back almost to their tail, and their bodies were fairly long with a tail that looked like a regular tail till the end where it had a half a saucer-shaped bone with spikes coming out at both sides and one in the middle.

Standing back, we watched as the animals tear the flesh from the carcass, they barely chewed their food as they gulped it down.

Their movements were very fast and they left very little for any other scavengers that might have come along. One had, had enough and started running with surprisingly strong legs strange looking for the shortness of them. Running it spread its arms and a full wing of skin caught the wind slowly the animal became airborne and flapped its arms fairly fast at the beginning, and then slower as it gained more height. It soon was heading toward some cliffs overlooking the flat land below. The others decided it was time to go as well and they all headed straight into the wind lifting off, heading toward the cliffs too.

"Again, an animal that doesn't look like it would ever be able to fly . . . is," said Jescan as he shook his head in wonderment.

"We must have assumed that this creature could not fly a hundred thousand years ago and possibly it couldn't as a young animal, but as it gets older it certainly can. I remember looking at that animal and didn't associate the skin growth with a wing. I guess I better check the data closer next time," I said, realizing I had simply not looked close enough at the animal.

Jescan was amazed at the remains of the carcass. It was almost completely gone except for the guts that were left lying under the skeleton. "These animals mean business. Nothing is left but the bones and the intestines. Even the skull is crushed and eaten, leaving only the shattered bones."

Looking out across the forested area it seemed very active, another animal was being killed to feed another. Moments later the sound of the screaming victim could be heard as it came to a swift death. Soon after the regular forest sounds again went back to normal.

"Watching from up on the mountain, it doesn't seem so bad, but as I hear it at a close range, it is very unnerving," stated Jescan.

"In five hundred thousand years, the creatures have come from small reptile like animals to a diverse civilization that now has insects, snakes, and animals that can fly, a lot of changes over the remarkable five hundred thousand years." I found myself contemplating. *Killing is necessary to sustain life, the law of the jungle. To use an old statement, survival of the fittest.*

Walking further my thoughts raced as I contemplated the new continent. The east side of the continent was still alive with volcanoes adding more land, as it moved the landmass farther west. The land to the west was slowed to a minimal movement. The newly formed plates far out in the ocean had cracked, and were now flowing outward from the crack in both directions instead of sliding over top as was the case five hundred thousand years ago.

Life on the planet flourished and seemed endless to the extent it could reach. With plenty of food with an abundance of water causing the rich humid air with little temperature change the plants and animals grew to unimaginable sizes and because of these three conditions, there were population explosions that would rival any found in the history of the planet. As one animal multiplied, nature provided a check of another species to control the other species.

Nature was remarkable as in the seemingly endless land, and the only limitations were the natural barriers and isolation. The animals changed as the need arose, and the evolution of the mutating genes caused new species to spring up in an endless number of sizes and shapes.

"What would you say to checking the next important point in time?" I asked as I summoned the *Genesis*.

"The earth is still so young, yet the plants and animals have come so far from a microscopic virus, to small prolific abundant microscopic phytoplankton consisting of both plants and animals to a very diverse and formidable population," commented Jescan as he followed me to the ship.

"Life has gone through remarkable changes in the last four hundred thousand years. When did humans appear? I have somehow forgotten the dates," questioned Jescan.

I tried to remember the date that we were at now in relation to the date when the first human arrived. "Give or take a million . . . about sixty million years from now, man will be walking on the earth," I commented as I touched the control to jump us to the next significant period.

CHAPTER SEVEN

Exiting the Genesis, Jescan was about to say something, when he started sneezing as the bright sun hit his face, most uncommon for his people catching him off guard, and then I too could feel a sneeze coming on because of the rapid adjustment of the cornea of my eye, tickling my sinuses. Starting to laugh we both sneezed several times.

Still laughing more giggling, we stepped out of the *Genesis* turning away from each other, as the look of the other person's face struck us as funny so that we could stop laughing, and finally had an opportunity to suppress the giggles, and finally could take a look around.

The air was a little drier although still very humid, off in the distance a thunderhead cloud was releasing its fury with thunder ringing in our ears. Seconds after the lightning struck the ground, revealing that the storm was heading away from our location.

The grass and the bushes were freshly washed, and were still wet in spots. I realized that the storm had passed this spot within the last hour giving the great fresh smell after a good rain.

The pungent forest smells dominated the air and the view was breathtaking, covering most every part of the continent. Lakes could be seen dotting areas everywhere, and large rivers winding their way to the sea.

"What a spectacular site." Jescan sighed as he walked to the edge of the mountain. Life was abounding everywhere. Birds could be seen flying between the trees. Trees had grown considerably higher. Several had survived for more than several thousand years. "I can say that I have never seen a view so breathtaking as this . . . Unbelievable." He slowly breathed out.

"Yes . . . I agree," I said soaking in the view. Then sensing something was different, I added, "But the air, something is different.

It . . . it is not as humid as it was the last time." I rolled my head in contemplation. "Why does it seem so different?"

Jescan turned and looked at me and said, "You are right . . . It's not as humid. Is there something wrong? The temperature is cooler, I think . . . Wouldn't you say?"

"That's it. You are right," I said, smiling as I suddenly realized what was causing the difference in the humidity. It was the temperature that brought forth the reality of the situation. "Everything is all right. The air is drying out and the temperature drop means that the north and south poles have over time because of the cooling down of the earth which ultimately cooled enough, allowing for the slow buildup of an accumulation of ice and snow. When the *Genesis* comes back, we'll maybe go and take a look."

"Right. The movement of the earth allowed the poles to become cooler, because they are spinning faster than the rest of the planet.

Also the static electric field it causes, attracts the moisture in the air to flow in an orderly manner which for a number of reasons, causes caps of ice to form on both poles."

"I could not have explained it any better. Makes sense to me. How did you know this information?" I questioned, somehow knowing he was drawing from information that he already knew.

"Actually . . . I believe it came from one of the papers I worked on in my junior level at the educational institution, if I'm not mistaken," he answered, as he strolled toward the path leading down the mountain beaming with pride. "Shall we take a walk?"

Smiling, I followed him as we walked down the mountain. The many varieties of trees were now all over the mountain and had developed from little fernlike twigs, which still were springing from the rich soil covering the sides of the mountains and valleys ranging from full deciduous trees in the lower levels, to pine and spruce trees at the higher alpine levels. Looking at the size of the gigantic trunks, again was an indication of how old they were being there for several centuries completely undisturbed, although there had been signs of areas that had been burned. The peat built up indicated that several generations of trees had lived and died, as mushrooms and fungi matted the floor of the forest as we proceeded down the hill. I noticed that a bird flew by and landed on a stump beside Jescan.

The outstanding aspect was it had developed a coat of feathers, unlike the first primitive birds, that had a thin layer of skin covered with a hollow, thin armor-like shafts similar to a crude rudimentary hair follicle.

Insects were everywhere and although slightly different under inspection, a fly-like insect had arrived. This species was very small as they swarmed around a pile of manure droppings from a reasonable large animal, and were eating and laying their eggs in the large mound.

As we walked down the side of the mountain, the animals started to catch our scent as they started to come out of the woods, checking us out.

Animals of all sizes unlike the last period where most of the larger animals, had soft bodies supported by a cartilage skeleton usually in the form of armor-like protection.

Cartilage was changing in the tissue now. Calcium forming into bones, incorporated and strengthened the basic structure of the animal, in some ways restricting the growth. Animals were limited by their bone structure not by the food supply, which had allowed the animals of the past to develop gigantic unrestricted sizes. Although cartilage was still prevalent the animals had simply developed a bone-like armor to replace the cartilage-like armor, most covered with a soft lizard-like leather or skin. Like the past where the animals' armor never stopped growing this armor grew with the animal and stopped usually at death. The spikes of cartilage was now calcium-based bone, and from the look of them they never stopped growing as some had gigantic horns and spikes. The spikes and horns looked like they were constantly being rubbed to keep them somewhat sharp and from growing too much, as the local trees showed the scars. As well the rocks attested to the constant rubbing with most of the rough edges worn smooth.

Some of the animals resembled monsters conjured up from gargoyle legends. Movie producers would have had a hay day with the specimens presently in front of us. Others though were so remarkably beautiful with the colors of the rainbow reflecting from their gleaming skin. Skin similar to a snake's scales yet smooth, not so segmented as a snake's, more like a soft, smooth leather.

From the grass came a creature that surprised both of us as we watched this turtle-like creature. Unlike the turtle, this creature was faster moving and to our surprise, it had young following it. As it came closer we both were astonished that there was hair on the legs and head. Although the back was still of cartilage-type material it was obvious that it was much lighter than the turtle's heavy shell. The smaller creature was about eight and a half inches long with a large round pointed tail and as it came directly in front of us it stopped, sitting on its hind legs and used the tail as a support, licking an itchy spot on its leg. Nuzzling and pushing lightly with its head as the young arrived it started cuddling its young.

Jescan stopped. Watching with great interest, he said, "Look at that . . . It's suckling its young. This definitely is one of the first mammals we've seen."

"Let's take a look. It certainly looks more like a reptile than a warm-blooded animal," I suggested. Walking closer the visible breasts surrounded by fur became clearer. "This is a milk-feeding almost turtle-like animal . . . It is a mammal," I said, looking at the unusual animal. I bent to pet its young as it innocently leaned forward to smell my outstretched hand. From the warmth generated from its breath, I could tell that this reptile like animal, was a live-bearer of young. It was definitely warm-blooded as the young sucking away on the breasts of this remarkable beast.

"It doesn't look like it should be able to feed being so bulky in the body. How would a creature like this happen to be a mammal?" questioned Jescan as he too petted the young that was sucking.

"The mammals did develop from the reptile like animals. Usually, it was the sheer bulk of the larger reptiles that necessitated the need to release excess heat, but also in turn burning more calories unlike the reptile that speeds up when there is a lot of warmth or heat. Because of the size of the animals they developed a method of retaining the heat simply by the movement of their bodies, when temperature would drop. It still had to have a means to release the excess heat on hotter or warmer days developing pores releasing excess heat generated as the muscles contracted and retracted, especially on hot days. The animal moved around to stay warm finding that it could keep its body temperature constantly warm, thus requiring an insulation that could not only hold in heat but also release heat when required.

The creature discovered that moving could keep their body warm without sunning themselves in order to warm their internal circulation. These crude warm-blooded animals had the ability to stay warm, due to the development of fat cells even when other animals were still slow moving from the cooler nights or temperatures. The animal adapted to the constantly changing temperature rather than the restrictions of the cold-blooded animals which slowed as it became cooler. Bodies that required outside heat to stimulate the normal movements held so many restrictions. The warm-blooded animals, on the other hand could stay active all the time, any time if necessary giving them a great advantage with several taking advantage of the cooler evenings, many developing into night hunters.

"Picking up one of the little animals, it was playful alert and covered with a fuzzy fur almost the color of the ground, camouflaged from the air so that the giant dragonflies and birds had a hard time spotting them. They would from the air still looked like a rock, and serving a dual purpose from the ground again would look like an odd-shaped rock. This little animal is one of the first mammals we had encountered on this planet, although I expect that there are more mammals arriving with each new generation.

Some of the creatures have finally evolved the ability to have live births, carrying their young eggs to the hatching stage ingeniously inventing a method of holding the eggs in the safest mobile location, inside themselves. This on the other hand limited the number of eggs that the animal ovulated, restricting its numbers ingeniously starting a social network necessitated for survival reasons, rather than laying eggs by most species where hundreds even over their lifetime millions of eggs would be laid reassuring their survival by sheer numbers.

"This is the period when the mammals start to arrive. This, as I recall, is also the period that fish start developing bone skeletons. Also, there is a decline in the soft-bodied animals like . . . that animal," pointing down to a small animal that was somewhat similar to a salamander, "except that its structure was closer to a slug in looks and

unless there was a lot of moisture, the animals simply dried up or stuck
to the rock that it had crawled up onto well sunning itself."

Jescan was stroking the mother's hairy chin. "I wonder if the little
guy has survived as well."

I realized that Jescan was thinking of the little animal that he liked
so much, the little animal I knew would evolve into the armadillo,
realizing that now was the time to let him know. "Jescan, you will be
pleased to know that the little guy although has and will go through
several changes develops into a much smaller animal like it was when
it first developed and was or is a very distant ancestor of the armadillo.
The same genes run through the little modern armadillo."

This I just knew although after the first encounter I had confirmed
my suspicions through the computer on the *Genesis*.

"That is great," Jescan said, smiling. "I was hoping that he would
be one of the animals, that survived the changes. Do you think it
would be all right if we checked up on them as we go through time?"

"That can become your project, as we will be able to see all the
progress. You will become the resident expert. I have a good feeling
you will enjoy that task."

Jescan was beaming in his own peculiar way and his mind was
saying, "It did survive . . . The little guy did survive. Way to go! I can
follow his ancestors throughout their life . . . Way to go. He survived."

Smiling, I said, "Why don't you take some time now, to look for
the descendants of the little guy. I'll meet you in a while. I would like
to investigate this remarkable animal," I said as I motioned for him to
go. Jumping at the opportunity, he was off in a shot.

Laughing, I turned my attention to one of the first mammals that
we had just discovered noticing a small cave. The small creature was
a gentle creature by nature, a herbivore but could simply tuck up into
a ball underneath its bone shell covering. The young were born alive.

Their soft small shell-like skeleton and almost completely naked
bodies resembled a small blind mouse more than the adult. It had
developed a gland that produced a white life-giving substance. This
gland with stimulation of nursing would allow antibodies combined
with nutrients, later to develop into milk to be generated by glands
along the sides of the abdomen and the animal could feed in a
standing position, with the young suckling from each side, or it could

support itself with its tail and stand like it was right now in a sitting position or lie down on its back with the young on top. In a short week the look of the adult started to become dominant in the babies. It was turtle-like in appearance as its skeleton started to fill out hardening each day. It slowly transformed from a helpless blind little creature to not only becoming aware of its surroundings, but also growing remarkably fast and was able to follow its mother within the first week of being born, if necessary. The mother generally had a sheltered nest dug underground.

She would protect her nest from other animals for at least a week, longer if possible as the reserve fatty layer supplied enough nutrients to the mother as well as the young, till the young were more able to travel and had their eyes open. About the fifth day the young were able to comically wattle behind their mother. Usually, unless danger threatened they would stay in the den or nest, following their mother more and more as they matured, generally very short trips in the beginning. The young usually did not leave their protective hole or den under the ground till they were about four to five weeks.

At this point like their parents, had between three to six weeks they started to eat more solid food, they lost their teeth for sucking usually between the same period. They wandered usually in company of an adult, or as they became bolder and more independent they would wander out with another sibling to graze on the lush tall grass as their dependency on milk gradually diminished till they would be completely weaned at about seven weeks.

As I studied the animal, which later I found out was called a Glyptodont, I was so fascinated with seeing the first mammal for the first time, it was a pleasantly humbling experience.

Walking farther some of the other animals came up curiously smelled my clothes and my hands. It was like Jescan had said. The soft bodied animals were not as prevalent. The animals that had an internal skeleton were becoming the more dominant animal.

The reptiles were starting to dominate, controlling most of the territories. Well some other reptile like creatures were starting to develop fur a lot would eventually become carnivores, but several were in the beginning herbivores'. Although, some had not yet developed to the stage of giving live births yet because of survival necessity, they would start to delay laying their eggs producing a slowdown in their reproduction, in turn produced an animal that was more physically mature as well more able to protect itself earlier than the eggs that were laid by the general reptilian society.

The adaptations of these animals, were the ingenious start of a whole new kind of animal, within a few centuries of several thousands of generations would start bearing live young as their internal organs were becoming more sophisticated, or should I suggest more adapted.

Some of the creatures that generated their own body heat were developing the similar characteristics of mammals, and were starting to have live births but still didn't have the capacity to nurse. They fed their young characteristically similar to that of a bird or a dog or a cat where the young fed off the regurgitated food of the parent.

The young generally stimulated the parent by playing with the soft lips of the mother stimulating the stomach muscles which in turn, allowed the animal to bring up what the parent had just eaten. One benefit was that both parents could share in the rearing of the young.

The bonding would start with them stimulating their sides of their mouths. Although most of the females could feel a stimulation in their developing mammary glands they would generally rest the young on their swollen mammary glands relieving momentarily the hard swollen glands. Although not yet developed enough to generate milk, some though did ooze slightly. This in a simplistic analogy, was the start of the production of milk. Most times though not enough, but it was a start. The young at least benefited somewhat by the antibodies of the mother's body giving the young a small head start although because of the immature mammary glands, the production of this not yet milk substance was short-lived, the female usually dried up within the first day, some possibly because they had never been suckled deprived their young of this nourishing liquid. The young females sometimes lost their first litters, but as the females gave birth to more litters more milk was produced, and most discovered the relief achieved by allowing the young to suck. It was all these changes that were coming into its own, or it could be said the beginning of a new evolutionary age.

On the whole the mammals developed from smaller agile or fast moving animals although some midsized animals started to develop similar features to the smaller mammals, possibly through generations the heat from within the body warming the blood so that it flowed faster through their body. As they developed so did the changes toward an animal that could move freely without having to guard their nest for weeks before the young hatched, the phenomena of live births arrives.

Even the reptilian life forms were developing a means of delivering live young, some with a metabolism that developed enough so that the young could be left, on their own at birth. In the beginning of life the splitting of the single cell forming two separate entities each able to survive on its own, in a way had somewhat gone in a complete circle. Although the animals were much more complicated internally the basic result was similar. Live births started developing as a need for a safer hatching time allowing a longer developing time with more growth happening inside the females, and internal organs were changing to accommodate the need for the longer incubation time inside of the mother.

There were still many animals that produced eggs, so much so that animals were filling the niche of egg eating to an ultimate. These specialized animals were fast with larger hind legs and shorter forelimbs. Although the forelimbs were capable of grasping things, their jaws were toothless as the need for teeth was not necessary. The need for a jaw that could apply a lot of pressure was. These animals including snakes did survive many millions of years as the time line goes although limited, there were still millions of eggs eaten every year.

Animals of the reptile families were bearing live babies, such as the snakes that left the young to survive on their own as soon as they had their young. Many perished simply because they were not protected and were so young, and most passing local predators took advantage of such a windfall. There were generally several born at one time and the mother protected them only as long as she was giving birth, leaving them within an hour or so. The majority of reptiles still laid eggs, with only a small percentage of the unbelievable diverse populations tending to have live young. They also tended to abandon their young very quickly.

The animals that looked after their young developed stronger bonds and they tended to stay as a family unit, and massive herds of animals became more common around this time more than ever before. The larger the herds, the less likely that they would all perish, similar to the large schools of fish swimming in the ocean, each developing a unique defense setup.

The animals that were light framed and quicker on their feet, developed more mammal-like qualities. With each new generation the dominant males that carried more and more the mammal-like characteristics were selected as the new leaders, which were generally faster as well as stronger. With the new males genes passing on to the offspring, the new warm-blooded mammals developed. Although, throwbacks could be born from some of the females the herd overall changed quite rapidly.

The bonding directly caused from the nursing of the young caused social changes, whereby the parents could spend a longer time teaching and training the young. As the mammal-like qualities developed, so did the functions of their developing brains, as they became larger than that of animals that slowed down as the temperature dropped, these new animals started to out of necessity as well the brain was beginning to be utilized other than for sight, smell and touch, and taste producing a longer memory function, and teaching characteristics started to develop.

The young in several of these little groups started learning through watching rather than from personal experience which was passed on to each new generation.

Because of the formation of social groups, the young learned not only from the parents but also from other members of the group. The experiences of the group as a whole also played an important factor of what was taught to the new offspring.

Off in the distance I could see Jescan and was happy to see him with a mature female version of the little guy. Off in the distance I could see the rest of the herd. He was stroking the animal behind the ears and was rubbing its head with his other hand. I could sense as well as see that he was very happy. As I approached he spotted me. "This is one of the little guys, but it is changing. It is not getting smaller. I would say they are getting larger," he said as he pointed to the larger animal.

"You might be right, but do you think it might be because of the condition that the animal is in?"

Looking at me very strangely, he asked, "What do you mean?"

Then he looked back to the animal.

"I can't be sure, but I would say that there may be some additions very soon," I said as I noticed the tightening of the abdomen, indicating a contraction. "You're going to get a firsthand experience in the birth of an ancestor of the armadillo."

"Oh," said Jescan, embarrassed that he had not noticed that the size was mostly in the abdomen area. Smiling, wide-eyed he watched as the animal's water broke. "Looks like sooner than later."

The female was in a little gully semi hidden under some trees and had probably been there for a while before Jescan came along. The female started to contract at regular intervals, and the female set her head down as a very strong contraction waved over her body. A small head appeared, and almost immediately the main body started to show seconds later a newborn was lying on the ground covered with a thin membrane. The mother quickly turned and started to clean the young little armadillo as she was cleaning the first, the contractions came again stopping her from cleaning the first, which was already struggling to get on its shaky little feet.

"They have started having live births as well," stated Jescan, surprised, because he still thought of them back, some three million years ago when they still laid eggs.

"The armadillo is one of the strangest mammals, that had survived for millions of years looking similar to its prehistoric ancestors.

Although it through time will become smaller, it will retain the armor-like appearance due mostly to the fact that the armor was a very reliable safety mechanism."

"Look at the newest one. It looks so much like the little guy more than the first one. This is why they survived. They evolved and started to have live babies. They were large enough that they generated their own body heat. Look, the females breasts are oozing milk. They have developed into a mammal."

"This is quite a change from the beginning when they were all cold-blooded. In the beginning there was no need to stay warm because the planet stayed constantly warm, hot in most places. There was in that period little need to generate the heat required to stay warm, even in the evenings. Today the air and the climate have changed, where in certain areas especially the north and south poles, it actually gets cold dropping to well below freezing in some of these areas."

Watching intently as she had a litter of five in total, Jescan was like an excited father, cleaning each one and helped them find the nipples.

After she was finished delivering the last one, a small female he helped it to suckle.

Looking over the little ridge, I spotted several other armadillos, grazing in a little clearing in the forest, had moved closer to us.

They had developed a very close social group, with several females probably all related. The young males stayed with the females until they wander off to mate with another group of females, winning the battle necessary to win the right to mate usually when they came into their prime at about three to four years. The dominant male was very vigilant as he kept the young males at an acceptable distance from the group. The male was the closest to us, and was already in the clearing slowly making his way toward us.

Jescan looked up at me as I walked to the ridge to get a better look at the little meadow surrounded by thick undergrowth and as it moved back into the ancient forest, the undergrowth thinned out because of the lack of light being blocked out by the gigantic trees.

Jescan was curious as he saw the other armadillos starting toward the meadow.

Watching the group, the herd would not move too far away from the female and the dominant male stayed close enough as to protect the female well having her young. The group had picked a very natural way of protecting the new family since the main group would have attracted the hunters thus protecting the female that wandered a short distance away almost circling her area but not too far. Jescan had just come over the rise when the group was alerted to a hunter, a large reptile that I recognized as the Tyrannosaurus Rex. The large creature boldly came into the clearing and went for a small female.

The dominant male moved to protect the female. Seeing that there was absolutely no contest, the animal was not going to win, raising my hand I let the energy flow from my hand. All three of the animals suddenly were passive. The large reptile turned and wandered off into the woods. The male was very proud of himself acting like he had scared the giant off, strutted around the females shaking his head in a victory display of his dominates.

Jescan turned to me and said, "You said that killing was a natural thing, the law of the jungle, yet you saved this animal."

"The reptile will find another meal and the male didn't need to die right now," I said, defending my actions. "To let him live a little longer is not changing the realm of things. If I had not been here the male would surely have died. I would prefer that there never was any killing, although that would not work as nature has developed a very simple method of control. Would you have wanted him to kill the male?" I realized that there were exceptions for everything.

"No . . . Thank you for saving the leader. It would, as you say turned out differently if you had not been here and the law of the jungle would have reigned supreme. The male shall have the honor of living another day. I think that I understand how this law of the jungle works. It is nice to help the underdog once in a while," he said, realizing that if possible an animal could or should be saved as long as it is not interfering with the natural scheme of things.

"Look, the female is wandering back to the group. They will wander back into the protection of the forest soon and again have the safety of the forest to protect themselves," I said recognizing that

Jescan was right, but also realized that although death was a natural event it was possible to be altered occasionally without changing the natural progression of things. I was more thinking of the possibility of changing the course of history which I knew was not going to be the case in this instance.

Well watching the group as they slowly wandered into the woods, we decided to wander over to a lake that could be seen in the distance from the ridge, partially visible through the tall trees.

The forest surprised us as it was like walking into a building, the canopy of leaves and branches blocking the light, covering the remarkable canopy over the jungle. This was a jungle, a true rain forest in the truest sense of the word as creatures of all sizes and shapes existed and etched their food and shelter from this very busy area.

Small and large ants were everywhere, some with wings some without, working diligently for the good of the colony.

Giant dragonflies, although becoming smaller in size, flew aimlessly throughout the trees, snakes and reptiles of every description. Plants too were so different from what I had ever seen.

The new varieties were springing up everywhere arriving as fast as the animal populations were multiplying. The forest with its humidity so high generated its own rain causing cloudbursts. Several times throughout the day we would have a saturating mist of water falling as the humidity reached its maximum. I was amazed at the creatures small and large that seemed to be crawling, climbing, and flying everywhere.

Breaking out of the forest cover the land had berry bushes and small ferns, flowers everywhere of all different colors. Foxtail grasses, intermingled with prairie-like grasses intertwined with ferns of all shapes and sizes. The land rolled gently down to the edge of the large lake, clear turquoise-blue water reflecting the majestic landscape that surrounded it. Since the water was so clear, the animal life and the plant life could be seen even to the bottom of the deep lake, giving the illusion that the bottom was close enough to touch.

The different species of fish was remarkable, as was the colors. The rainbow colors of the fish with a backdrop of vivid greens and reds intermingled with different shades of browns and yellows, were almost indescribable in the sheer beauty and purity a most impressive sight.

Jescan finally let his breath out. "This is the most scenic, spectacular spot I have ever seen. Look you can see the fish as if they were just under the layer of water, as if you could reach out and touch them. This part of the lake must be very deep. Look at the way a valley has formed from the two massive rocks jutting out of the water one who's edge we were on, rising some two hundred feet behind us and possibly a quarter of a mile away on the other side. Yet, it is so very pure and clear," he said as he bent and put his hand into the tepid water, realizing that the slope was quite steep from the bank to the bottom.

"I have to agree this is probably the nicest place that I have ever seen. Is the water warm?" I questioned Jescan.

"It's reasonably warm," answered Jescan, surprised at the question.

Starting to remove my clothes, I said, "Let's go swimming." We raced to get our clothes off and jumped into the warm water and was pleasantly surprised that the temperature was refreshingly comfortable, and the acceleration of the great scenery and the fresh water was all that mattered at that moment.

We swam and laughed, and swam some more acting like little kids. We spent most of the afternoon indulging in the pleasures of relaxation, rigging up a makeshift fishing pole well soaking up the sun and the landscape.

The *Genesis* arrived and we were still not ready to give up this pleasant adventure discovering all sorts of different creatures, reptiles as well as fish.

Worn out from swimming, we decided that it was time to return to the *Genesis*, as it was late afternoon, and the sun was threatening to disappear behind the mountains. The changes present in this period should be interesting, and although somewhat tedious would be interesting to go over the visual data.

The earth had changed. It had thousands of species, that were not known in any fossil collections. No literature could imagine the diverse and unlimited types of animals and plants, that were present on Earth at this bountiful period. The animals ranged from the microscopic one-celled animals and plants, to huge animals that would soon dominate the earth to the smaller mammals to the birds, all the building blocks of modern-day life. Our surprisingly relaxing afternoon gave us a new outlook of the wonders of this remarkable planet. It was as though we had just been reborn and everything was fresh and new once more.

Although I could sense the change, the *Genesis* confirmed that the planet was also developing ice caps. Although small now I knew that they would eventually grow with a vengeance but on the other hand, they would also recede.

As it had always been, something that seemed so unrelated would cause major changes here on Earth, like when the sun goes through its own growing pains and would have massive disturbances on its surface, sending out solar flares that would have an effect on the polar ends of all the planets that surrounded it. On this planet it would cause ice ages every so many million years or so. It would at times cover most of the northern hemisphere and to a smaller degree the southern hemisphere. One such advancement of the ice was in progress now although it would take several thousands of years to advance to its maximum before retreating which also would take several thousands of years to completely retreat. This was the start of Earth's first ice age.

"This needs more investigation, I think," I said as I turned to Jescan. Reaching for the controls, the *Genesis* started to move north, and the land seen from the air was remarkable, as the continent was massive.

Looking at the continent, I said, "We could see the mountain ranges to the west and a smaller range closer to the middle of the continent, although it was anything but straight. The mountain range in the middle seemed to be growing, yet it was almost like it was coming from a line that seemed to be pushing the land out from it, as the lava flows were still prevalent in some areas of the continent, the indications that this could be the collision of the plates, more so than the eruption of the crust as in the past.

"The earth is starting to split pushing all or most of the land to one of the earth's sides. This must be close to when the continents start to separate, and move against the plates," I added, contemplating the impact of this discovery. "The crack in the continent is the start of the division forming North and South America, splitting away from the main continent. Although the crack could be seen from the air, the most noticeable area was from the southern region where two cracks were present."

This crack was formed from the collision of another landmass colliding with the main body of land, although the actual division would take millions of years to separate completely. As well knowing what it would someday look like the lines were present, even this early in its evolution. The rubbing and collision of the plates was the cause of the pulling apart of the land, as well as giving the Earth an area to release the pressure of the landmasses that were thickening on an ongoing basis compared to the earth in its infancy allowing the lava to flow freely from the core, as the floating landmass cooled and became heavier, exerting even more pressure. The radical eruptions of the earlier periods where volcanoes were the normal landscape, this was now being substituted by solid ever-cooling land. Volcanoes still erupted in many parts of Earth, but for some reason such as a thinning of the land forming a buckle in the crust, or a slight crack could cause a series of volcanoes some in a line and several solitude ones but overall, there were less volcanoes and several active volcanoes were actually slowly going dormant.

The north was starting to be covered with a massive ice sheet that in turn also enhanced the splitting of the continents, as the heavy massive ice flows seemed to follow this crack down moving farther south. The land was constantly moving to the west due to the rotation of the earth which started and continued the movement of the land to the west was overriding the movable shifting plates underneath the continent of land.

The land had split and had time to collide several times over the millions of years. This constant collision of the continents meant that several times the landmass was one, and then the land again would through a crack such as a fault line would split and again move west.

This movement of the land, which took millions of years to complete, ended up in somewhat the same starting position that it originally started from centuries prior.

This also would explain the change in the humidity as the moisture was being deposited at both the poles in extremely large quantities. Something that was a surprise to both of us, although traveling through time I realized that we were only seeing fractions of time that between visits sometimes millions of years had passed.

The soft cartilage animals were changing at a remarkable rate transforming and developing bones. Several of the soft-boned animals unable to change simply disappeared and were never to be seen again.

Although from these species that disappeared, their genes were present in other branches of their family lineage, was a natural extinction. The animals were changing rapidly, in a way similar to the first animals that changed from generation to generation. Today the mammals and marsupials were evolving at a steady rate although most were developing where there were temperature fluctuations, but they were also developing in areas around the equator, although less prevalent in and around the equator, as well as the southern hemisphere.

One mammal that I didn't expect was a swimming bird like creature possibly the ancestor of the modern penguins which had started developing mammal-like qualities as well as the ancestors of the whales and dolphins which had not yet even appeared, although there were indications of several air-breathing animals that spent some time on land but still utilized the oceans as its means of food as well as for safety measures, would return to the sea where it could outmaneuver most animals. These animals were starting to develop a fur. In a way they could be the ancestors of the seals or the walruses. Although quite different in appearances, they showed similar characteristics to the dolphins and whales and as with other mammals that were arriving, these animals were developing the internal organs that would allow them to give birth to live young.

This period was a remarkable time. The dinosaurs were the major dominant life were the creatures that came in all sizes and shapes, odd as they looked with their armored plates huge sizes in some cases.

It was surprising the animals that were developing unique internal organs generated its own heat and energy. With the complex changes that their bodies were transforming from simple animals to a complex species, most of these animals would not leave any fossil remains, and would never be found or recorded. Some of course, left remains that would be discovered as their bodies would be covered with silt or layers of sand. The amazing thing was that we were actually here to be witnesses to the events, as they really were.

We had witnessed all the present significant changes that this period was experiencing. Knowing full well that these changes played a significant role in our past, and we were not able to spend as much time as we would like, maybe I will return to this period sometime in the future. Touching the control, we jumped ahead in time as the buzzer rang our arrival.

Looking out the window I could see nothing but the tops of trees and a very cloudy stormy day. Pondering the look of the clouds and the wind as it whipped relentlessly at the tops of the trees it was the day that you would like to crawl back into bed and sleep the day away . . . not a pleasant day.

"Let's take a walk," I suggested as I opened the door to a rainy drizzly sort of day. It was midmorning, and the clouds were thick overhead. The weather was somewhat colder than we had felt in a long time and even though we were just north of the equator, the air had a chill that reminded me of winter.

"I think that we should get some warm waterproof jackets," said Jescan as he had two suits replicated and brought one over to me. "It looks cold out there."

"Yes, you're right. It does look really cold. This doesn't seem right, especially since the equator is not that far south. Let's see what is going on," I said as I stepped out into a luxurious forest.

There were signs that the plants had been hit with a frost. Several leaves had black rolled edges. It looked so out of place for these tropical type of plants to be exposed to weather conditions, that were more common in the northern regions or the very far southern areas.

The bushy pine trees had developed spreading out covering an extremely wide territory, as well as spruce and cedar trees were emitting the wonderful smells of the forest. These smells had not been as present or as dominant in any other past period and it smelled like the forests that I was used to wandering in as a child.

The temperature was colder but not unreasonable and we found that the jackets although useful were a little warm, and we opened the front of them to let the cooler air in. The air was strangely different. I could smell snow, which was strange with all the smells of the forest. This must be the height of one of the ice ages, although I had always thought that it occurred much later in time. I wished now, that I had checked the date. We must have traveled several millions of years. I thought to myself.

Walking to the ledge at the edge of the thick forest growth overlooking the land, the sheets of ice could be seen in the distance to the north. The animals to my surprise were doing very well and most seemed to be unaffected by the cold arctic-like winds that were coming off the ice fields. I realized that the ice had reached its pinnacle, as the temperature in this zone stayed above freezing, at least most of the time, as I looked at the black rolled-up leaves, although it was the top of a fairly high mountain, the plants below suffered little or no frost as the warm winds could be felt coming from the southern areas.

It was remarkable that the dinosaurs although most were groggily wandering around seemed healthy and from my first impression, were living a very productive life. The awe-inspiring dinosaurs were definitely the dominant life form and could be seen as their heads reached over the tops of the trees keeping an eye on movements of other animals. Herds of animals could be seen grazing in the massive plains were the large herbivores had cleared the land as they uprooted the large trees, allowing the grasses to overtake the land. This process allowed the much richer grasses to become the mainstay of their diet.

It was as though they intentionally cleared the land so that they would have a more bountiful food supply, as the trees tended to shelter the growth allowing very little vegetation to live under the canopy of the trees. In areas where the larger animals had left for another area the trees and underbrush were once again starting to grow back. Trees all of the same approximate age were slowly springing up, would someday become the thick forest like we were starting to enter in this time frame.

As we started into the forest a strong wind whipped across the tops of the trees and a pelting of rain came in a gust. Looking up at the unbelievably heavy clouds it was mainly raining, but there was a mix of sleet occasionally whipping across the land melting as it landed, then it would turn to snow then back to sleet and rain once again. Although the clouds were heavy we could see that they soon would pass as the clouds were starting to break up and spots in the cloud allowed patches of light to streak to the ground, showing off the beautiful colors of the rainbows as several could be seen across the land. The heat of the sun's rays conflicted with the weather as it was very warm almost instantly sending up a bog-like mist, as the wet ground released the saturated ground moisture. It was such a radical change it seemed so out of place in this tropical rain forest.

"From the looks of this, the ice age was pretty dominant. Wouldn't you say?" queried Jescan "I never knew that the ice came this far south."

"I thought the same," I answered, contemplating the weather, "But this is the way that it was, or I would have been told or informed of something being wrong. Even the mammals were curling up in a warm, dry place as the winds blew, and they could be seen in hollow logs and standing under a sheltering of trees."

Walking the land below the animals I could see were in turmoil, as the cold never had reached this far south. In the distance the mountains of ice could be seen. Although they were thousands of miles to the north, the effects were devastating. Even from here it was obvious that the northern half of the continent was almost completely encased in miles deep with ice and snow. From the looks of it the snow was still coming down as the clouds hung over the ice almost like a fog.

To the south there was no ice advancing now, and the ice age was as I suspected was mostly from the north. I would double-check my suspicions when the *Genesis* returned with the new data. Somehow I could sense that the south, was simply covering the immediate areas around the south pole, and not fluctuating much as the north did.

I heard the music in my head, and the explanation was suddenly clear to me. *With life, there is an exchange of chemical reactions, and this reaction is not caused by the natural occurrences here on Earth but from the disturbances caused by the sun.*

These have a direct bearing on the planet, and although it affects the other planets, it is not as obvious as it is on this planet, because of the existence of the plentiful life presently here. These radical storms on the sun have started up once again, starting to become more prevalent once more, as they were somewhat dormant for the last few centuries, as the sun was relatively undisturbed from outside influences over this period, meaning that the ice age is now on the decline, and the earth will recover over the next several thousands of years, as it will take that long for the ice caps to completely return to a normal level.

This is the longest stretch of time that the sun goes somewhat dormant. Although it is not the last, the sun storms will not subside, for as long a stretch as this period. The sun will over the next several million years or so fluctuate only fractional. Although the earth will go through several ice ages the most violent of storms that the sun will experience will be about three hundred million years, and the earth will experience another wet and humid climate after the fourth ice age, and although they will happen again they will not be as intense as this, the first one.

With the earth cooling down, over the last few hundred million centuries, calumniated with a period where the debris for the solar system are at a low collision period, have compounded this particular ice period as well as the natural cooling, the sun will return to normal with storm

activities, as well as debris once again making their way back to this sector
of the galaxy.

"The humidity will again return to normal conditions, as the
snowstorms are starting to slow down. The low-pressure areas that cause
the clouds, laden with moisture, to be attracted to these cold areas have
now started to diminish, and are returning to normal patterns, allowing
the high-pressure areas to take hold for longer periods once again, clearing
the skies and allowing the sun to once again melt the newly formed ice
fields. This is a natural occurrence and this being the first and most severe
of any that will follow." The musical sounds subsided.

I was surprised at the complexity of the situation, it made me stop
and marvel at the simplicity of the situation, and how minor things
affected things in such a drastic way.

My thoughts once again returned to what I was seeing around
me. Looking at the animals the large reptiles especially, which still
relied on the reproduction by eggs were found guarding over eggs
that although fertilized and would normally hatch but because of the
colder temperatures, the embryos would only develop males as the
chemicals required to produce the female hormones was blocked as
heat or warmth was required to trigger the female hormones. Several of
the eggs would not hatch as well because in many cases, there was not
even enough heat to allow the eggs to mature, and they would simply
rot, as the embryos in a way were slowed down causing a similar
reaction as hibernation, slowing or stopping the basic functions since
they were not frozen they simply died and rotted. The animals were
slow and awkward as their metabolisms could not withstand the lower
temperatures. A lot of the animals simply did not lay eggs as all urges
to reproduce were not there. The animals that had no concept of what
was wrong with them simply slowed down and in a way went into a
form of hibernation, only semiconscious leaving themselves wide open
for attacks from the carnivores.

Changes in the temperature, also affected several of the tropical
oriented plant species, although with the return of the warm
temperatures, the seeds would once again come back. Several plants
had turned brown and withered and died. For this year I knew that
they would start again from the roots and grow back although they

left the land sickly looking with the frost arriving occasionally just
before the sun rose in the early morning. This was to last for another
twenty years, some years better than other years with less frost in the
later months as well as the early months of new year, definitely the full
scope of seasons. Each year that passed would become warmer. Even
though the sheets of ice would not fully recede for a thousand or so
years each year the temperatures as well as the plant life would slowly
return to normal.

As we walked around we noticed several changes that were taking
place as the animals that generated their own heat were the animals
that were on the move and never missing an opportunity to eat taking
advantage of the slower metabolized creatures, which at certain cooler
periods of the day were so easily killed. This was the period where the
warm-blooded animals start increasing rapidly as food sources were
readily available and the food chain was slowly becoming replaced
with mammalian competitors in this changing population.

The largest dinosaurs although were warm-blooded, stopped
laying eggs because of the cooler weather, and although had a faster
metabolic circulation than other reptile lineages their systems were still
much slower and more cumbersome. A lot of the regular functions
like disposing of body waste were slowed down considerably thus the
combination of colder weather, the dulling of their senses as well as the
slowdown of their bodily functions. They were suffering severely as the
temperature fluctuated returning their regular functions momentarily
sometimes for a month or two at a time, but again as the colder rainy
months caused them to go into a semi-hibernation mode in some cases
full hibernation, some never woke up. As we were walking the *Genesis*
arrived, alerting us that danger was eminent, and we must return
immediately.

Once inside the *Genesis* the computer stated, "There is a meteorite
that is about to crash into the planet."

"Let's go out into space and observe what is happening. This could
verify the meteor disaster that scientists have been talking about as a
possible answer to the extinction of the dinosaurs." Stopping to think
of all that we had seen and flashing through my mind, I said, "But
it really wasn't just the meteor as we have just seen. Although the

animals would or could have survived this ice age, had nothing else happened."

The large meteor was not just one but several fragmented particles, all in a cluster. They were heading directly toward Earth, and were beginning to be attracted by the gravitational pull, starting to glow red as they entered. One after another the massive rocks started melting but they were so massive that close to two thirds of the rocks crashed into the earth and clouds of dirt and debris clouded into the atmosphere. The most dominant pounding of the earth lasted for three days diminishing over the next five days. Watching the spectacular sight was horrifying, as I thought of all the animals that would be obliterated.

The musical conversation stimulated my brain, as the sixth plane started to explain. *This is a natural occurrence and is not to be changed.*

The creatures that will become extinct are meant to be. This catastrophic incident is absolutely necessary in the second and third plane, as this will initiate the changes, needed in life of these two planes, and it will not affect the other planes, in that it will not radically alter the life as it is supposed to be. The arrival of these meteorites was fragments of the collision of the earth that caused the moon to break away, and the fragments will not cause as much damage, although it will take several years to completely recover. Life will carry on though, and the planet will again return to normal.

There is another factor that does cause mostly the dinosaurs to become extinct, which is that because of the distress and lowered immunity, overall most will become very sick from viruses that infect almost all of them.

The other factor is where these meteorites land in, is a very high level of sulfur, which also has an effect on the animals. as it causes sulfuric acid to rain down on earth.

Jescan was sitting at the console and was patiently waiting an explanation to why we were simply watching, and not changing anything or stopping anything. "Sorry, I could tell that you were just in communication with the other planes, I assume. What do they say?"

"This is necessary. Two other planes require this occurrence to start a change in life in their planes. They seem to be running behind us by a few million years. Then again, it may just cause the changes to the life forms there to develop into the forms that they are supposed to be.

He really was quite casual and projected very little images. Just that life on the earth will survive enough to allow this catastrophic incident to happen without major long-term disaster to most of the wildlife.

Although some species will be completely changed forever, the life of the animal and plant populations will take a new direction."

"I think that, that was the answer to my lingering question. I could not believe that we would stand and watch the life on this planet be allowed to all disappear and have to start over again. I now know they will survive . . . Just look at the clouds of debris that these meteorites are causing. The last one is just entering the atmosphere now."

We looked at the last meteorite to enter the atmosphere and disappear in the cloud of dust and particles, which was so thick that we could not see the collision as it hit the earth. Moving to the console, I said, "Let's help the survivors." I touched the control to land the *Genesis*.

Upon landing the window was clouded like looking through a dust storm. The debris was still falling, as it had been thrown up to the highest layer of the atmosphere and was now pounding the earth with large debris as well as small fine powder debris. In most cases, the debris was as hot as the meteor itself when it landed. Fires were lighting the landscape as the debris landed.

We watched the particles small and large, land all around us as we sat witnessing the remarkable shower of dirt and rocks, some of which had been thrown several hundreds of miles from their original spots.

The shower slowly settled down as the small particles were the only things that were still floating in the air, the landscape was like a red Mars-like wasteland. The dust was already several inches thick, as it blanketed the land. The water was also covered with the fine dust that floated like a huge carpet, slowly sinking as it absorbed the water.

"Let's see what damage is done," I said as I opened the door and walked out into a red world, where there was once a green world. The plants were weighed down with the dust, and some were cracking, as the weight of the thick dust became too much. Although the trees were still standing, branches could be heard snapping, as the weight grew with each hour that passed.

The sun was completely cut off, although you could still tell that it was daytime and not night, although it was dark enough that you would have thought it was a cloudy evening around dusk. The fires were burning out of control all over the land even the grassy meadows. There were very little areas that were not affected. It was the forests that lit up the land. The huge old-growth trees burned with a furious vengeance, as it quickly reached the combustion temperature, covering thousands of hectors of land. The land was fractured splitting down the fault lines, and lava was slowly pushing the land apart at the heaviest areas of ice, melting the ice as well as causing major flooding as the forest was raging as the skies were even blacker with the added smoke.

Animals were fleeing some so disorientated not knowing where to go. I found myself totally caught up in the plight of the animals, redirecting all the animals that were going in the wrong way with energy surging from my body in turn surging through my hands. I helped as many animals as possible and set them down by the rivers and the lakes and by the seas, the little and the large wherever I could spot them, but even as I tried to help thousands perhaps millions were suffocated from the thick smoke or burned as there was no way to reach them in time.

As the forests burned out of control I realized that the only way to stop the fires was with water. Mustering all my attention to the clouds pulling the moisture clouds from the ice caps and from over the oceans, forming a massive thunderhead, although it blended into the already black sky I pulled together as many as was available. Although it was a little premature as it would have happened on its own within a day or two at most, the rains started as the massive cloud formation started to release its humidity.

Still desperately in need of help, I again started to help the animals get to safety and was surprised at the number still coming from every direction. By the time night came most of the fires had slowed patchy areas had even been extinguished, and the animals huddled in little groups all along the river's the lakes and the oceans. Even with the rains the old wood in some areas were still burning, but overall, the majority of the woods were steaming with dampened smoke. The burned smell permeated everything and I found that I was physically exhausted and mentally depleted.

Jescan was carrying a young animal, finding a safe sheltered area for it setting it down. It stood on all four legs trembling not knowing what to do, but shortly lay down and was sound asleep within moments in this protected little shelter of an old fallen tree.

Taking a closer look, I noticed that it was a small mammal having small split hooves. It was a short stocky animal with an oddly familiar look. Because of my exhaustion or probably because of mental fatigue, I could not figure out why it looked so familiar. I later checked its gene pool and discovered that it was the ancestor of the modern horse and hippopotamuses.

Jescan too was physically exhausted, as he jerked himself awake as he was resting against the tree. "Let's consider getting some sleep. We will be able to see better when there is some light."

Knowing he was right, we headed toward the *Genesis*. Each of us headed straight to our separate rooms not even saying a word. I finally found my bed. I fell asleep almost as I was falling onto the mattress.

I awoke with a start as I recalled the day before. Sitting up I said, "Computer, lights on." Looking at the clock beside my bed, I knew that it was early morning. Getting up I walked to the control room and was again surprised that the window was like looking out into a stormy night scene, although it was possible to make out images of the landscape.

Opening the door, I walked out into a reddish-black world, steaming with the rain still landing on the hot coals of the burning logs. The area with smoke billowing from the remains of the old forest. The land was totally in shock.

Walking down to the flat land, the smoldering of the wood was like walking into the smoke from a campfire, and the smoke from the trees lingered everywhere. Animals were starting to wander from the rivers and the lakes, and although there had been fires before, the habitats of most of the animals had been destroyed. The herbivores found little patches of grass saved from the rain and areas that the fires had somehow missed.

The red dust was still filtering out of the atmosphere, covering everything, making it look similar to the landscape of Mars rather than that of Earth. Trees, blackened from the fire, lay where they had fallen, and several still stood, tall and black, and there was such a pile of burned lumber, several hundred feet deep, as the trees had been toppled over onto one another. As I surveyed the devastation of the land, I suddenly realized that this was the start of the coal and oil deposits, as layers of dust still filtered down and over top of the chard wood. In some of the valleys, the fallen timber made them look flat, as the trees had fallen into the valley floor although wet from the rain, would smolder for months. Animals had stampeded into the valleys and low-lying areas. To their demise they not only trampled one another, but was also buried in a mound of animals.

The earth in its majestic way of cleaning itself continued to rain for months, this also caused a problem, as the sulfur had mixed with the rain and it was literally raining sulfuric acid, very devastating as it covered everything only occasionally breaking.

The dust and the smoke would last for some time as the debris had been deposited into every layer of the atmosphere. It was like a mud walk as the rain gathered the dust particles forming little dirt droplets as it landed. The light was rarely seen and for months this would be the norm, and the temperature dropped significantly, adding to the stress on the animals.

Jescan could be seen coming out of the *Genesis* finding a path over to where I was. It was slow walking as he picked the easiest route through the smoldering, charred remains of the fire, making his way to join me.

Animals needing medical attention were everywhere I wandering from animal to animal I chose a direction toward Jescan, and I was treating them as I came upon them or as they came to me, some with severe burns others badly injured limbs some came just for assurance. I found that I could help each animal that was injured, some in a small way while others requiring more received more.

The energy coming from my hands seemed unlimited as well as unbelievable. Yet I somehow was able to control the power, a power I realized that I must understand better as I was aware of all the physics involved but yet how and where was the power coming from. The long progression of animals left healthy even the severely disabled. Jescan, on his arrival helped some of the animals by carrying them as they were unable to make it on their own.

Several days went by, as the animals that couldn't get to us, we went to them. We were surprised that such a large number of species had indeed survived uninjured and able to carry on with their life almost unfettered, yet completely changed forever.

When we had felt comfortable that we had done as much as possible we decided to travel one year ahead to see how the world was recovering.

The door opened and although the days were brighter the dust particles still blocked a good portion of the light as the thick ozone atmosphere held and retained a large number of the fine particles.

In some respects it was like it was a thick cloudy day except that it was every day slowly diminishing over the next ten years. There were thin ribbons of clear sky that could be seen allowing patches of light in and the sun could be seen breaking through the atmosphere, allowing ribbons of light to enter into the atmosphere, although there were intermittent clear skies and occasionally a wide beam of light would make its way across the landscape, covering most of the planet occasionally with enough light to allow the plant life to survive.

The green colors from plants were slowly breaking through the thick layers of red iron-laden soil the remains of the meteorites, and although the layers were thick in some areas the new shoots were coming alive once again.

Most animals were fairing all right, although because of the colder climate the lack of direct sunlight to warm the planet, most of the egg-laying animals were still not hatching their young; and as the dinosaurs' metabolisms had not recovered from the colder ice age, they produced none of the hormones necessary to stimulate the breeding urge.

Due to the varying temperatures most of the dinosaurs wandered around trying to find warm spots, which some did find but most went into a form of slow bodily functions again similar to that of hibernation, except they did not completely fall asleep, which in turn left them wide open to attacks from the predators and within the first year several species had gone extinct never to return. The dinosaurs that where in groups often huddled together and died with hundreds of them in the same valley or coulee, this was wide spread all over the world groups all over were found from the computers information.

The slow cleansing process of the rains took their time, as the temperature was not conducive to humid rainstorms and snow usually was the outcome. Some areas more in the southern hemisphere had more rain, allowing the animals to survive much better than the wildlife in the northern hemisphere. Although the humidity did rise and fall, it tended not to be warm enough to cause a lot of rapid evaporation the rain clouds took a long time to build up enough moisture allowing it to rain forming large areas that had drought conditions for several decades, although in a lot of cases the colder temperatures bringing with it snow caused even more losses, allowing several species of animals as well as plants to perish. Death was usually from hypothermia as well as from the lack of food for the animals.

Well, the plants generally froze destroying the non germinated seeds necessary to replenish the species.

On the other hand, the rapid metabolism of the mammals allowed them to flourish even in the dismal surroundings. Birds also could be seen landing on chard burned stumps and nesting in the blackened tree stands.

There were patches of forest in some areas both in the south as well as the north, and although set back the equator still maintained the largest stand of trees that did survive although there was little sunlight, and the dust weighed down every branch, some areas had not been burned, having escaped the devastation although red soil covered most of the plants with four or five feet of the thick powder soil mixed with the sulfuric acid had caused severe damage all over many parts of the planet. Although it was thick it did contain lots of nutrients useable by the local vegetation and new shoots were sprouting through the red soil. As well leaves were seen on most limbs of the older trees.

The new seedlings had started to spring up between and around throughout the burned areas as well similar to what happened after a natural fire starting off with a covering of hardy weed-like plants and bushes a lot were growing from roots still left from the burned trees and plants, and certain insects and animals survived quite well in the hardest hit areas.

Some of the animals that had found suitable places to hibernate had somehow allowed several of them to survive. Although several species simply exhausted their excess layers of fat because of the length of time never woke from their sleep and being unaware as well as not being able to wake from their groggy state, simply starved themselves to death.

There were animals that had lived in groups, which had found shelter in valleys and coulees in combination of the events that had taken place with their hurried unnatural hibernation. As the animals huddled sleepily together several layers of dust built up and buried them under several feet of this red dust. Compounded with snow on top they never survived the first year. All in all the species that survived had the chemical makeup that allowed for the changes, even such harsh ones as this.

We took our time and, recording the events over several decades found that over the next century there was a complete rebirth, adapting and yet continually changing.

The animals that survived were rapidly adapting to the changes remarkably well and although changing their habits didn't always change the looks. The armadillo for example survived and was steadily growing in numbers but with each generation because the large size was not as necessary as it was in the past. Each generation was slightly smaller as the females picked the smaller males to take as mates, yet the looks stayed very close to the original.

The saber-toothed tiger had also started its slow evolution changing from an animal that resembled a small bearlike animal to a wiry vicious predator changing in the opposite direction, as it grew to gigantic sizes with the plentiful game and no major competition for the top of the food chain.

A similar growth spurt was happening with the small ancestor of the woolly mammals as the grassy plains that had been cleared by the ice and covered vast expanses allowing a very healthy environment and large herds which grew in size as well as stature.

The land was now changed in that the forests would grow again but because of the decreased number of larger grazing animals, which ate most of the young shoots, allowed the forests to grow slowly, well maintaining large areas with very few trees, this did over time maintain herds of grazing animals on the open plains.

These boundaries were also influenced as the ice caps expanded and receded. Certain animals flourished in the remarkably abundant steps bordering the mountains of ice. This included plants as well as animals that lived within the range of the ice caps making a very diverse population which allowed animals to cover large areas or territories each year.

Animals in the southern hemisphere were not so influenced by the radical temperature fluctuations, as the earth still could maintain a reasonably higher temperature allowing several slower-moving species to survive the enormous changes. Animals of large stature tended to revert to a more refined smaller version although as in most things there were exceptions. As the populations grew the need for such large bodies was not as important in the protection of themselves. Agility coupled with warm-blooded attributes seemed to be the norm. Faster smaller animals seemed to flourish better than some of the larger animals and the overall sizes diminished rather than increasing in size.

One animal, a small mammal was of great interest to us. The animal was a descendant of an animal similar in appearance to the modern lemur, although slightly smaller this lineage had evolved into a very interesting mammal, as its paws took on a hand like appearance rather than a claw like appearance like most of the mammals.

It was a mammal that was located in the southern hemisphere just south of the equator. The effects of the radical temperature changes seemed to have little or no effect on the life of this little animal. It was a creature that had adapted to living in the jungles of the southern continent and most often found refuge and safety by climbing into the trees. This little ape like animal would gather food on the ground but flee to a nearby tree if danger came close, overall was starting to adapt to living on the ground as well as the trees. This I was sure was the ancestor of the modern apes including the human race.

Although they started from this one species they were extremely adaptable little creatures and soon over time developed several different distinct lines each having different looks and although looking different had very similar abilities, with similarities in the structure of the skeleton. They mostly were all about three and a half feet tall when they stood on their hind legs.

We both knew the generalizations concerning the development of man with the help of the analyses from the *Genesis* confirmed we were studying the beginning roots of mankind.

This would now allow us to confirm the beliefs as well as the misinformation. Impressed by the opportunity to be able to observe the little creature, a better explanation would be "creatures," as the different looks were remarkable with each separate and distinct lineage that had developed from this one small creature. My recollection of what the scientists knew was the development of the species was generally under the impression that man originated from this general area although there was not a large population, surprisingly spread over a very limited territory and growing in little groups in an isolated territory spreading out from a specific geographical area.

Food although disrupted temporarily, was abounding within months as the temporary colder air being completely back to normal in the area from just north of the equator to the area which would become the continent of Africa.

Life was rather simplistic idyllic almost because of the rain formed from the plants themselves. The atmosphere in the rain forest was purifying and recycling itself somewhat faster than the rest of planet. With little disruption the plant and animal life was relatively undisturbed. The accessibility of food in the bountiful rain forest allowed for limited travel in order to acquire whatever was required to live grow and multiply. The group did split into different groups as genetically they were the same, but looked different from the normal group. Some of the groups became isolated and because new areas demanded that new characteristics developed. As with all living forms of life there were changes that occur from a molecular level which in turn caused some major physical changes, like the loss of the tail. These mutating genes often meant that the offspring was quite different in looks from the parents.

If the situation arose where two animals were isolated being from different lineages it was still possible for them to be interbreed although depending on how far from the lineage tree, their separation was determined by their ability to interbreed. In some cases it would be like crossing a horse with a donkey. They could raise offspring but the offspring was usually infertile allowing for only one generation to be produced. The same occurred in the little apelike mammals. After several thousands of years the ability to interbreed became less likely but not completely as there were some that interbreed and worked well.

As these creatures became more aware, as the size of their brains increased, they began to place certain members of their group in the lowest level because they looked different. In some cases, these different-looking offspring were cast out if they looked and acted differently from the rest of the group that caused them to band together which caused a different branch in the family tree.

One difference was the color of the fur. As a good example, generally if a black to black furred animal interbreed one in so many would be an albino or with the lack of pigment in the hair or skin.

Some would have partial pigment and would come out a gray or black with gray patches. If not expelled from the group if their young was born with lighter fur including reddish colored fur in some cases at the most convenient possible time it was sent away, usually not by the mother but by the group. These individuals that where cast out of the social groups would in most cases band together with another outcast. This caused several offshoots of the same species each having their own looks and characteristics. Nature can only say why several similar-looking animals all from different colored parents started to appear, and still the banning of the animals after being cast out of the main group, formed their own groups.

CHAPTER EIGHT

Landing every hundred thousand years was our standard that we had decided on because of the rapid changes that the animals were going through landing on the mountain where we usually landed approximately a hundred thousand years from the meteor shower that had devastated the earth.

I opened the door, well the *Genesis* surveyed and documented all the changes. We took our usual walk.

The trees and vegetation were growing in great abundance, the animals sensing our presence through our scent came out of the woods and meadows to investigate us as we walked. Generally we would take a wide sweeping route to cover most of the surrounding area. Although something was quite different with the animals on this visit they seemed to almost be afraid as we approached, which was most unusual.

Jescan also noticed the mistrust of the animals. "Why are the animals acting like this? They have never reacted to our presence like this before. Have we done something wrong?"

"I really don't know," I said stopping and watching the animals some cowering along and behind the protection of the tree lines, never taking their eyes off us. One of the mammals was very similar to a modern deer probably I thought maybe an ancestor of the modern deer, using the same technique that Jescan had explained to me was one of communication with almost any form of animal that was capable of thought. Approaching the animal I was able to start to communicate drawing some information from the timid creature.

The animal in a very simple way gave images of a creature apelike in appearance that lived in the caves that could release their limbs that made the animals drop as they approached. They then would walk up to and carry off the carcasses. Visions of fire also were indicated as these creatures stayed close to and used fire to keep the animals at bay.

"I can't believe that there are creatures that can control fire as well as have weapons. This doesn't make sense," I said as I turned to Jescan.

Jescan hesitated and after a long pause he looked at me. "Our people have been visiting your planet for a long time this could be the first ship that was sent to this galaxy. A small scouting ship of twenty-four was assumed that it crashed and was never recovered.

According to the information, they had no way of tracing the ship, and as far as we knew according to the books there was, with no substantiation almost like on your planet a legend suggesting that there was only one survivor. The reality is that the story that I am referring to comes from the documents that I will be writing in the future. They suggested there were indications that somehow that this civilization had originated from that man. So we as children were told now it would seem was true." Jescan looked in the direction of the caves overlooking the valley that the animal had indicated. "Could it be him?"

"Let's see what is going on," I said as we walked in the direction of the caves.

Approaching the valley, smoke was rising from the caves high up in the cliffs. The walk was a steep one with indications of being used on a regular basis. The prints indicated bare feet and was definitely humanoid. Other signs of habitation such as bones from animals had been thrown over the edge and littered the side and bottom of the valley.

As we came closer everything seemed to go quiet the animals even were quiet, kind of like the silence just before a tornado hits. No tornado was about to hit but I could sense that we had definitely been spotted.

We approached very cautiously not making any sudden movements. We came to the clearing were obvious signs of a camp was set up with a fire still burning in a crude rock fireplace. I could sense that we were surrounded and one was just in the shadow of the cave hiding behind the rocks on the side. Raising my hands I said, "We come in peace."

With careful uncertainty a creature definitely humanoid stepped out into the light. He of a small barrel-shaped build was clad in furs and was sporting a wooden pole sharpened at one end poised and ready to throw. Lowering my arms I held my arms straight out with my palms opened and facing up.

The male approached cautiously smelling the air as he approached.

I stood still as he came close enough to smell my hand. He was maybe three feet high and although had characteristics such as standing on two legs very apelike similar to a chimpanzee was definitely different from any monkey I had ever seen. This male with black fine hair covering most of his body with the exception of his hands, feet and face, although he did have a thick, matted beard and mustache. In most parts of the body the lighter skin could be seen through the fine hair that softly moved in the slight breeze. I believe that the first thing that struck me as unusual was his hands with the ability and control to hold onto the stick ready to hit at any moment if threatened.

His eyes were unusually large lighter brown eyes with a small pupil that dilated as they adjusted to the light. He growled deep from within his throat as he approached. Then as his eyes adjusted he studied me. Then his attention was focused on Jescan. He was totally awed, and walked several times around Jescan showing a complete surprise yet more in reverence, then the strangest gesture catching both of us off guard. Looking into Jescan's eyes he held his hand to the uppermost portion of his forehead. Slowly and deliberately he telepathically said, "We are your children to serve as we can." This unique humanoid that was nowhere close to resembling his kind talked as clearly as a fellow Edan with exactness to the accent and definition of the words with no clear change in diction.

Using telepathy Jescan said, "We come in peace. We are travelers and we have come to visit." As he watched the surprised look as he understood what Jescan was saying.

"We were drawn by your smoke and have come to visit. I am with the caretaker of the land, animals, and plants."

"We will welcome you to our fire caretakers of the land, animals, and plants," he replied. "I am Jarid, leader of my people son of Seth. Come tell us where have you come from? Is it the mountains or from the heavens as where our Adam came? We have waited for this meeting as we have been foretold of your coming and have waited many generations for your arrival. We have thought it to be conjecture or a legend some not believing in the stories of the ancient ones."

"We have come from the mountains over there," I said as I pointed to the mountain where we had landed.

"We have never seen you in these areas before," he said, deliberately testing us as he rubbed his head pondering the possibility of us living in another area. "You have strange furs," he added, smelling us as he circled around me and Jescan. Placing himself in front of us he said, "You talk through the mind like our ancestors and our forefathers like we do in our rituals. Are your ancestors from the heavens too like our ancient one? My people as I am is a direct descendant to Adam from the heavens our father."

I paused as this remarkable story unfolding before us, was totally unexpected. "Yes, could be the same. You mentioned your ancestor came from the heavens. How long ago?" I asked, looking at the small older man, older than any of the others in this little clan, guessing him to be in his early thirties.

"Our ancestor came from the heavens. They came so many many rains ago long forgotten. I carry the knowledge of our people as did my father and his father's father passing the knowledge from generation to generation from father to son."

Turning to Jescan, I asked, "How long ago did they arrive?"

Jescan spoke so that the man could also hear. "They would have arrived maybe a 350 possibly 400 years ago. They were all males."

He looked very reverent almost like he was seeing the answers to all that he had wandered about in his eyes as well as his mannerism yet it was evident that he did not completely understand. He cautiously planned his moves as well as his jesters both word-wise as well as physically.

"Yes . . . I would like to know what is years. Is that like the heavy rain time? There was one our leader our common father who talked of the day that a strange people would come and we would be able to communicate with them they will be our savior our future," he said sounding excited as though he just found a lost family member. The little man grunted guttural sounds and the bushes started to rustle as people from all directions came into the clearing. Most of them were carrying spears and some were carrying fist-sized stones.

The strange group of about a hundred people was all of similar stature and similar looks although some had features with slight variations in the coloring. The faces of the men were hairless except that they had hair growing on them in the form of a beard. The larger cranium was set low, yet of all the animals that we had studied on the planet, they showed the largest of the brains of all the existing animals. The average height was about three feet, some maybe three feet four inches.

They were quite bowlegged and walked with a swaying motion. I got an eerie feeling as I looked into their eyes. It was like looking into an ancient orb. It was like all the information present and past was maintained somehow in the very essence of their being.

Jescan was only about a foot taller and although there were many differences, comparing the smaller features like the larger eyes and the smaller formed hands and feet but similar in one of the most important aspects the ability to communicate telepathically and the ability to understand it, the evidence meant it was possible that these people however it happened came from his people's genes.

This primitive class of people talked with guttural sounds because of the voice box, not being as developed as it will eventually become.

As I was observing the crowd I noticed that there were no women in the group. Setting aside my obvious question of no women being present, although possibly they had hidden them for safety reasons instead I asked, "How do you pass the knowledge from generation to generation? Is it written?"

Jarid looked strangely at me and answered, "The knowledge is only known to the leaders and the shaman, which is passed by the leader to his eldest son from him to his eldest son. The holders of the tablets are the leaders of our people as it is explained in the tablet. I would be honored to show you, but first a feast in your honor a great celebration this day brings. Come, I have the women prepare feast."

Turning he uttered a guttural sound that carried deep into the cave. Pondering for a moment he turned again through a guttural sound and gestures he soon had everyone hustling about making preparations for the feast.

The camp came alive and not only women scurried from within the cave but also children hustled about. Two of the ladies brought out a large log, which when placed on the ground removed the loose top piece. Dipping leather pouches into the inside of the hollowed-out log they offered a drink to Jescan and I then to Jarid followed by the other males that had stayed obviously of important rank within the clan were still huddled in a small group behind us each taking their turn as their position of rank demanded.

Accepting the drink a dark red in color, I turned to Jarid, smiled and said, "My companion and I accept your hospitality and await the appropriate time to be able to view these important tablets, and possibly to answer the questions that you are looking for."

Jescan, although concerned about his people's possible involvement, was so curious about the people, realizing that Jarid was not about to be rushed. Looking at the crowd that was gathering as their tasks were completed, he picked out one of the men holding a spear. "How are these used?" he asked as he pointed to the spears trying to start a conversation with the clan people.

The man that was holding the spear beamed with pride proud that he had asked him to show off his spear which with every movement was obviously something that he prized very much. As the man took Jescan to a stand of trees near the entrance the men gathered behind as the man that called himself Kaa proceeded to demonstrate his expert throwing.

The aroma of meat cooking in the cave filtered out and around the campsite. In the back of the cave I could make out the scurrying of feet on the dirt ground. I adjusted my eyes to see better in the darkness of the cave and several women and children were preparing the food.

They were using a bone sharpened on one side to remove meat from the carcass that was lying on the ground. Others were pounding something on a large flat stone, and others were standing around watching us as we were given a demonstration of the techniques of throwing a spear.

Listening to their thoughts it surprised me to find out that they had never had any visitors before. This group must have over the centuries stayed together. It seemed odd that no one had left the group. I could feel the anticipation and excitement building as the feast was being prepared. They watched and gestured at our height and our clothes. This was a first . . . Never had they seen anything like us.

One of the men took my hand and placed a spear into it. It was my turn to be shown how to stand and to hold my arm at just the right angle. Setting my feet, I calculated how far the distance was taking a step, I sent it flying through the air hitting the target dead center to the amazement of the onlookers. A great roar of approval echoed from the walls of the caves. The men were jumping in sheer delight.

Jescan was smiling and said, "You don't have to show off."

As the day proceeded and the people opened up partially from the aged wine as much as the slow acceptance of us, they started to tell us stories. Jarid stepped forward slightly inebriated yet fully in control and started the story of how the leader arrived from heaven and made his home in the very caves that we were sitting, the great deeds that he had done, and the spectacular hunts that had taken place. The others pantomimed each part as Jarid told the story. Each character was portrayed with great care and was very graphic in the great fight with the saber-toothed tiger. The great tooth was the trophy. Jarid pulled it out of a pouch that had been set beside his seat proudly paraded it around so that everyone could see and touch the large fang.

The women brought out the food appropriately as the story had ended and the men started to eat of fresh roasted meat that had been boiled in a stew-like mixture with different roots and herbs.

There were different platters with different types of meats served in large quantities, platters of nuts, as well as platters of fruits mixed with freshly picked berries and roots ranging from wild pig weed to wild turnips and wild garlic. The meal was eaten out of a main bowl made out of a burned-out log. Hands were all that were used except for the drinking pouches, and the large chunks of food was dug out and eaten. A fermented blackberry wine was also served seemingly endless as when one container was emptied another one was brought to replace it.

As I watched the men eat, one of the men two down from me started to choke on a piece of meat. One of the guys sitting beside him started hitting him on the back. The longer the man choked the more the man hit him. Rising I moved behind him and, raising my arms placed them around the man and squeezed with a jerk. The man coughed out the chunk of meat. Choking and sputtering the man regaining the color to his face, looked up at me and started to thank me profusely. He then bowed feeling totally embarrassed.

As the evening proceeded the men got drunker, and the women came out sitting in the background and eating as they sat holding the children so they wouldn't interrupt the men as the stories started and at this point everyone was allowed to watch and participate if they decided, including the women although few did. The drunker they got the more they wanted to be the next one up, and some of them really had a hard time standing let alone telling a story. As the night wore on it was obvious that it was going to be a very long night, but I decided it was time for Jarid to show me the tablets. "The meal was the best I have ever had, and the stories were grand indeed. My interest is the completion of the story of the beginning and the great tablets that have been handed down . . . I was wondering about the tablets that have been the center of all the stories."

"Enjoy. There will be time in the morning," he said. He was still a little apprehensive of showing the tablets and although willing to show the tablets he was enjoying the celebration, as they had never had visitors before. He wanted this to last as long as possible.

I could sense the reluctance and I decided that I should not push it, as it was a good time, since we had not been around people for what seemed such a long time. We had little choice but to spend the night and one by one they fell asleep, and soon there was only Jarid whose obligation was to be the last one up.

The leader directed two of the women to show Jescan and I where our sleeping furs were, leaving our slightly inebriated host.

I awoke to the movement of the women preparing the morning meal. The fire had been guarded all night and the smell of the reheated meal of the night before, was reason to get up.

Walking up to the fire I noticed a girl in the background, one that I had not seen yesterday. She was dragging herself across the floor.

"What has happened to you, my child?" I questioned, as she a young girl probably no more than twelve had a severely deformed leg. Then I recognized that it was a definite broken leg as it stuck out in an odd direction, it was in such a direction causing unimaginable pain realizing that it was possibly a week old.

Stopping, she was startled that I talked to her, as deformed people were avoided basically isolated from the rest of the people.

Cautiously she began the story. "I was being chased by an animal, as I was running the side of the cliff came loose and my footing gave way and I fell. The animal was killed by Gaan, but as the rocks started to fall, the rocks fell all around me one falling on my hand and one on my leg. The men came as quickly as they could, but my leg was hurt very badly."

Knowing that I could help this poor girl, I walked over to her picked her up and carried her to her bed of furs.

As I set her onto the bed of furs I asked her to close her eyes and that there may be pain but I will try not to hurt her too much.

Using the energy from my hand I gently positioned the leg with a large crack followed by two other cracks that echoed off the walls of the cave confident that it was in proper place as the energy flowed I could visualize the damaged bone and muscles the sensitive nerve endings and the damaged veins. Slowly, I healed the wounded leg and pulling on the leg adjusted the hip with a pop sounded once more throughout the cave. Holding the crushed broken hand, I could once again see deep into the damaged flesh, and again drew from the energy within as I healed the hand.

"Open your eyes little one. You are better now, you can now walk, you have the use of your hand," I said, stepping back to allow her to get up.

She opened her eyes and first looked at her hand, realizing that there was no longer any pain, and then at her leg that was completely regenerated and healthy. She started to cry as she stood. "No pain, no pain," she sobbed with joyful tears.

The people had gathered around amazed as they watched with disbelieve as the girl stood to her feet. Guttural sounds were being made as they gazed almost afraid of what they had just witnessing as the cracking sound of the bones had attracted all the people.

Jarid, the leader came from the back of the cave where he had been watching the events as they unfolded before him. His face had a blank look as he walked to the girl and touched her leg not believing what he was feeling. The leader turned slowly his mouth partially open. His eyes were filled with a grateful look as he started using telepathy as did most of the people and said, "You have saved my girl child. What can I do to repay you?"

"I do not need any payment. I heal things that are in pain. We . . .," pointing at Jescan, "we are here to look after the planet including all things contained within its domain. It is my purpose to protect all things as they arrive before me. I had to help the suffering and pain she was in. We as you are destined to be keepers of the Mother Earth to protect to nurture and to look after the plants and the animals taking only what you can use, so there will always be plenty for our children and their children's children."

The leader was about to say something and was interrupted by a mother carrying a young boy. He was very sickly looking. He was skinny and weak. "Help boy child?" she said as she laid him on the ground at my feet.

I could sense the boy had been born with a small hole in his heart, and as he grew older he could do less and less. The boy was going to die in a matter of months without help. He was maybe six years old although loved very much, was a very large burden to his family.

The boy was also malnourished and because of that, he was losing the sight in one of his eyes, the other was not far behind.

Laying my hand onto his chest the energy was flowing from the palms of my hands. As the vision of the muscles within the heart flooded my mind I carefully repaired his heart. I also knew because of the poor food he had been eating, he had some lung, kidney, and liver problems, and then I moved my hand over his eyes and repaired and cleared them. The boy was surprised as he took, for the first time in his life a deep breath, and looked at me as he rose to his feet.

"You must eat lots of fruit, berries, and plants with your meat."

The mother, weeping and sobbing from joy pulled her son to her chest. Not knowing how to thank me she simply sat there sobbing, the tears running down her low-set cheekbones dripping onto her hair, thinly covering her bare chest.

Several people started to gather around as others ran to bring their sick and injured. Such excitement was caused, as several of them ran to their caves to gather their sick and disabled. One at a time was brought and helped. Each person, young and old, was inspected by the people as they left my side. The excitement swelled in everyone.

This small group of 250 people, the only humanoid people on the planet and the only witnesses to the healing power generating from my hands, all were now healthy directly changing the course of their lives.

One woman the one who brought the young boy to me, held a pelt that she had chewed and labored on, working it till it was soft and pliable. It was as her mind told me her most prized possession, as she held it out to me. When I did not take it right away as I was overwhelmed by the importance of the gift as her subconscious mind gave the complete story and the pride involved in the making and completion and the desire that others had shown toward the fine fur large enough to make several articles of clothing, or an extra large blanket she then started to set it on the ground at my feet.

Taking her hand as our eyes met I reached down and picked the fine fur and placed it in my other hand and said, "I accept your gift. This is such a precious gift. You have honored me in the highest fashion. This is my gift to the one who should have this, "I said as I walked over to her boy sitting on the straw bed that she had made for him. "This is my gift and would hope that it will keep him warm at night and so that he will always remember this day throughout his life."

Jarid came forward and said, "I too have something for you. I would like to show what we have left from as the great one, our father Adam called it. The Garden of Eden. Come, follow me." He walked to the back of the cave.

Following him I motioned for Jescan to follow me. At the back of the cave was a neatly stacked pile of rocks. Jarid placed his torch in the hole in the wall and started to remove each stone very carefully, stacking them on the side. He finally revealed a large wood box. It was a log about two and a half feet wide set on its end and about three feet high. As he lifted the lid off the table-sized stump I could see clearly the inside had been hollowed out by burning then had been chipped out with a sharp stone, removing the charred layer from within. Inside were stone tablets of shale, which had been split from the same stone to form thin sheets, which could be easily stacked.

Jarid turned and faced me hesitated, then pointed to sit on the floor waiting for Jescan and I to sit. He proceeded with his story. "Several rains ago before I was born my father, and his father's father to the beginning of our people, way out where the sun and the moon and came upon this land, from a far-off land which he came to affectionately call Earth. As he landed there was a big fire that he caused, and he knew he could not ever leave.

"He found plenty of food and water and a suitable cave for shelter.

Several rains came and went till he happened to come across a female that he took as a mate. The first child was born and was called Cain, and the second was Abel. The father nurtured and fed and clothed and taught the sons to hunt and look after the family under their care.

"This knowledge he declared, shall be carried from the firstborn male child to his firstborn male from one generation to the next generation, and on the arrival of his people they who can communicate through the mind and can interpret these pages, shall be introduced to our destiny in the scheme of this land and theirs. Thus, it is written to save our people. On that day, our people will be united with their brothers and sisters from which our roots have come from, as we are made in his likeness."

Reaching into the wooden box, Jarid pulled the first slate out. He handed it to me with great care and I got to look at the inscriptions scratched deep into the rock.

Jescan looking at the slab said, "This is his journal, describing the important events as each event happened. This first paragraph is when they crashed on the planet. He after several arduous days found that he was to be the only survivor. It states that the ship was destroyed and was beyond repair. This is what happens in the first year although this section here is a part of the second year."

Jarid pulled out one at a time and handed them to us.

Reading each tablet, it gave the story of each of the important dates. This is the finding of a compatible mate, now the second mate, outlining how the family was started.

"This is his first child, then his second. It records all the births. Here is the first of his children's children. Full detailed records of the offspring and something of each of their story.

"He regrets never being able to teach them to read or write, although he tried but found that they just could not comprehend the concept, but he knew that his people would someday come and they would now know how everything happened, bizarre as it seems. This was a direct quote."

Jarid handed the last one to me and when we were done, he started to gently place them back in the box sorting from last to first, taking great care not to damage the slates of stone.

"I thank you for allowing us to view these remarkable documents. You must continue to guard these documents as they are a testament of your heritage. You and your people have from this day forward inherited this land and seas and all the creatures that inhabit this Earth. You are now the protector of this planet, and you are the caretakers of all that lives, plants and animals alike. Live in harmony with all the creatures on this planet, and in return they will provide for you and for the generations that follow. You will from this day forward be master of all the creatures of this land, and they will serve you and your needs. Your people are now master as every living thing is for your use." Turning to Jescan, I said, "I now think it is time for us to go."

Jescan nodded and we started to leave the cave, proceeding toward the path leading down the mountain.

As we approached the path we were stopped by the woman who was Jarid's mate, and she warmly hugged me as she thanked me for helping her firstborn girl child.

Knowing as well as feeling that I should say something, I paused before I said, "Tell and teach your people to look after the wildlife and plants. Take and use only what you need and can use. Live a long and happy life."

Taking our leave, we walked down the path. Looking up, the small clan gathered at the edge of the cliff watching as we walked into the woods. When in complete isolation I summoned the *Genesis* to come.

Entering the *Genesis* Jescan said, "This group of people is all from the lone survivor. That's amazing."

"I would like to know for sure. Let's see what happened," I said as I sat at the console and touched the control, sending us back in time to the estimated year of his arrival.

The buzzing sounded our arrival. Jescan was first out of the ship, excitement in his actions. I followed him, a little more reserved as we walked up the same hill we had just come down.

Being very careful not to let our presence be known we stayed behind trees and bushes as we climbed to a place that we could observe without being seen.

Looking out from the bush line we could see the man. I used my telepathy powers to gain access to his mind and started to sift through the information of his mind carefully so as he was not aware, finding a vantage point that we could observe without being seen.

The man was huddled around a fire as the late afternoon was drawing near, placing us downwind from him. The food cooking on the open fire floated throughout the light breeze. Occasionally we were able to catch a whiff of the stew-like mixture cooking in one of his pots that he had been able to salvage from the destroyed ship.

The man was healthy-looking and to our surprise a mature female distant member of the chimpanzee tree lineage which had broken away from main lineage about eight hundred years earlier. This relatively new strain of apelike with chimpanzee attributes was sitting beside him as he was tenderly feeding the female, as he feed himself.

The man occasionally stroked and petted the animal tenderly the man talking telepathically to the female, and both laughed occasionally.

The female was relaxed and obviously part of the conversation as they talked back and forth between themselves.

Turning to Jescan, I said, "The female is very pregnant and remarkably healthy. This man has taken her for his mate. She was separated from her group and was rescued from a predator that was stocking her. The man killed the animal and nursed her many chest wounds mostly broken ribs, as the animal had stepped on her right side of her chest, as it turned to fight this new attacker the man called Adam.

"He cared for her in the beginning as one would look after a pet, but through telepathic means he was able to learn the thought waves of her mind and they started to begin communicating. He to his surprise found that she was quite intelligent for the intelligence found on the earth at this time.

"They have been together for three years, intimate for almost two years now. She is very comfortable with communicating with him as he talks. Oddly, the relationship is genuine love. Friendship between the two has grown, and true love exists.

"The man was shocked as well as elated when he realized that the female was pregnant. He in his wildest dreams never thought it could be possible, especially since his DNA was alien. He thought there was no possibility that they could produce offspring. He could with some of the wreckage be able to check the DNA strand of this animal, and found that taking an egg he could manipulate the DNA so that he could start the combination of his and her DNA to procreate. After which he placed it inside her hoping that it would develop. After two years of disappointments and some progress, after several rejections as well as several miscarriages this was one that actually had matured. His hopes where very optimistic in that this species could actually be genetically changed.

"This unexpected occurrence gave him a new outlook as well as a new purpose on this new planet, and although he hoped that he would be found by his people this unexpected twist to his life not only made him proud but also in a way he deep down secretly hoped that he would never be found, although as each year passed his hopes diminished knowing that there was no possible way that his people could know of his whereabouts.

"With Eve, as he called her, now pregnant with his child he was now content. Though it was extraordinary he was totally excited and very proud in a fatherly way."

"Remarkable . . . Yes, she is going to have his baby," Jescan said as he studied her large abdomen as she scooped out more stew from the pot over the fire, a look of total disgust showing in his eyes. "And several more, according to his journal. In another year he will take another female. In his life he takes several but five is all he is able to impregnate. He knew that the different females' offspring would be able to breed without too many complications of interbreeding.

"When our people finally came to explore this planet, it was about a thousand earth years or so later, long after you and I visited this area and came across the small clan of people. Our people had been studying other galaxies that we thought had more potential and had not been interested in this sector being that it was so far out of our way as well as all sensors had indicated no potential planets of any interest.

We had started in this side of the galaxy that you call the Milky Way but had concentrated in other sectors closer to us not realizing that as the spiral-shaped galaxy turned, we would find a planet with life on it so close to the outskirts of the system.

When we finally discovered this system that had been so far from our search area but was now coming closer we once again came back to this sector. We through exhaustive study had come to the conclusion that the humans had evolved naturally the way that they were found.

"Genetically all indications were that they had developed from the natural species on Earth. Although complicated DNA tests were run, it had never shown anything abnormal. It never crossed our mind that the DNA was so similar to our own. Again the genetics of this type of ape was similar to the other ape like groups all were classified as humans that had been discovered, there were five similar but separate looks. Our scientists concluded that the inhabitants were of natural evolution."

"You are saying that the apes would have evolved naturally to the human stage without the influence of this man. The introduction of these new genes from this man must have played a very important role, a role that should have been easy to detect," I commented.

Jescan's eyes sparked. "You are very right, although according to our modern scientists, it would take the apes, the closest being the off shoot of the chimpanzee, several millions of years to develop. The possibility of the genetics being accelerated by the introduction of one of our people was not considered especially since the disappearance of our people was in a sector millions of light-years away and was assumed that it was a separate hominoid with not thinking or that we had any influence on this planet.

"Although the evolutionary process was on track, the slight changes could have occurred at any time without question, was not an unusual results for such a diversified planet as yours was and is.

Our scientists studied this planet. Multiple books and theories were written none even indicating that my people inadvertently, through this man were the building blocks of your civilization."

I pondered on what Jescan had just said. "This changes all the history of our culture . . . our very essence. This includes your culture as well. This is amazing," I said, contemplating the implications.

"It was never anything more than a passing speculation on the possibility of alien influence. How could this not have been a . . ." I paused, realizing that the human race was not accepting of anything that could possibly suggest that aliens could be an influence in our development. I had a strange awakening as the realization hit home.

"It was this discovery and your interjection that we were presented with a dilemma. Your society was not ready for the information that you presented to us, as we did not even conceive that we had had any influence on your culture that you have just uncovered. Although we had thought possibly that some other civilization that lived in this area of our galaxy may have had an influence, we had no idea that it was us.

"Our people knew that the culture was not capable of understanding how we unknowingly influenced their existence and although somewhat advanced was nowhere close to being ready for the technology that we had as they were so primitive as of yet. So we decided that we would wait till the time was right to introduce ourselves.

"Several times throughout history we have tried to introduce ourselves, but it turned out that it was not the right time to reveal the truth. Even as you grew up, it was not yet time to introduce ourselves.

"We have been monitoring your growth for nearly two hundred and fifty million years. If you change the natural history of events, and you interfere and help this man by taking him back you in turn, will cease to exist or at least not exist at the level that you are now. Your people would still be in the Stone Age which in turn would rewrite the earth's history."

The musical images began to appear in my mind. *The other planes began to show me the images of what it would look like. The timing of this accident was coincidental, but it was really destiny as it was supposed to be. If altered, the changes on Earth would be doomed to a stifled existence, and in time the Edan people would arrive. There would be no humans as per say, only the evolution of the apes. The Edan people did not know that there would be interventions of other civilizations that would also be an influence as well, and would eventually set up stations on the planet, changing the history as it was now with several interventions, which was the true history of humanity. If changed, at this point, it would forever change the destiny of the universe. Their genes would eventually be intermingled with this separated lineage of chimpanzees, and man would arrive but under strict supervision, limiting the growth of a new society.*

The images slowly dwindled away.

I paused as I pondered what I was just told, knowing that I could not change this event. "This is and was a somewhat unusual occurrence. The sequence of events did in real time happen. This is in fact what really happened. I don't think that I would or should change it," I said, contemplating this new development of evolutionary significance.

Jescan turned toward me and said, "If this event did not happen, I wonder what would happen to the evolution of Earth had this Edan man not landed on the planet. Would your people have evolved to the same level, or would the society have gone extinct like the dinosaurs? A question for philosophers, I suppose."

"Our civilization would still come about, although it would be a society repressed by many outside influences. The way it has happen is the way that it will stay. This incident has allowed the civilizations to develop without the several influences from your people as well as the other civilizations, which neither knew about the other interventions nor manipulations that took place," I said, now questioning all that I had been taught.

"Our greatest scientists have worked out the scenarios after your appearance, and most of the possibilities suggest that the planet would still be in the Stone Age. Again, this is only a speculation."

Directing my concentration on the man again, I said, "He believes he will never be discovered because of the drifting of his damaged ship, setting them down in an uncharted planet millions of light-years from where they were supposed to be.

He was in human terms homesick and was very lonely. In his mind he for a very long time was longing for a companion, someone to keep him company to be able to communicate with. This was beyond anything he had ever expected."

Jescan knew what I was doing and could not do it himself without total exhaustion within minutes. He looked at me with envy and admiration at the length of time I could last without becoming totally exhausted. "How long before the baby is born?" he questioned.

"I think she has one, no maybe two days to go," I answered, trying to draw information from the female. "She is starting to feel very mild contractions now, but yes she has a little longer to go. She barely notices the contractions. She thinks it is just the movement that is causing the discomfort."

Suddenly I could sense her picking up on my telepathic influence, although she looked around as though she was looking for someone. She assumed that it was just the man's thoughts and was contented with her conclusion.

"Do you remember the rock by the entrance?" Jescan was pondering with an idea.

"Yes, the fairly big rock. Why? Oh . . . I see. Let's do it," I said as we turned and quietly walked through the bushes to the *Genesis*.

Once inside the *Genesis* we set about setting the *Genesis*'s controls to exactly match the size and shape of the large stone setting the controls to absorb the stone as we landed. I touched the control and the buzzer sounded our arrival. Looking out I could see both the inside of the cave as well as the terrace in front of the cave.

"This is like watching a television on a big screen or an IMAX picture. The only difference is that we get to watch it live and in vivid color." I smiled and chuckled, thinking it had been a long time since I watched television. "Would you like some popcorn and a Coke?"

Jescan looked at me like I had gone crazy. "What are you talking about? What is this popcorn?"

"Don't tell me you have never had any popcorn before." I jested then realized that he was serious.

"No, what is it?"

"I'll do better than that. Computer, I would like some popcorn, buttered and lightly salted in two big bowls and two Cokes."

The room filled with the aroma of popcorn as it arrived, and I grabbed the two bowls handing one to Jescan. I then reached for the Cokes handing one to the puzzled Jescan.

"What do you do with this white stuff?" he asked, looking as though he didn't like it before he even tasted it.

"Go ahead. You eat it. Live a little," I said as I grabbed a handful and sat at the control table.

Jescan took one inspecting it closely and finally put it into his mouth. He pulled his head back and was surprised that it was good. "It is almost like eating nothing yet it does have a good texture almost a taste with the butter and the salt. Not bad this popcorn."

Looking out the window, night had come and the fire was the only thing that light up the cave and the flat terrace in front, and the two were getting ready to retire.

The man put extra wood on the fire and lined them up so that he would still have some coals by morning, although he was used to getting up and putting more on in the middle of the night to keep the animals away.

He had set up a very functional cave, as it had a layer of grasses that he had laid down and a large fur from a large sheep-like animal, forming a cushion with a fur similar to a sheep's wool stuffed with grass, and on top he had a soft deer skin.

He had set up a storage area for his food and was well stocked with different dried and fresh fruits, wild onions, and meat from his last kill and herbs and spices from the surrounding area.

"Computer notify us if the female has contractions consistently at six minutes apart." Turning to face Jescan, I said, "We could be called in the middle of the night or early in the morning. So we may as well call it a night too." Looking at the nearly empty bowl, I smiled as I looked at Jescan. "Looks like you liked the popcorn. See you in the morning."

"The contractions are now six minutes apart," reported the computer.

Sitting up in the bed, I scratched my arm and started to wake up, stretching as I yawned. I realized the importance of the day being that the first human was to be born this day. Rushing I dressed and was out to the console room and at the window within moments.

Jescan came from his room moments later and we both stood watching.

The female was in the farthest corner of the cave, her water was just breaking and she as most apes squatted well giving birth.

The man was actually still sleeping, just had not heard or noticed that she was up out of bed and having her baby. She would lie down and then after a contraction she would get back up and nothing happened, so she would lie back down. This was when the man realized that she was up and ready to deliver. This went on for quite some time and finally she squatted, and the head was starting to crest.

She started to breathe heavier, as she knew something unbelievable was happening. The great moment came fast and uneventful. The little boy looked more like the father than the mother, and it cried a healthy cry, and the female made it obvious that the man was not to come near as her primitive instincts were at their highest. She cleaned herself and the little boy and placed the infant to her breast.

The man quietly went out and put some wood on the fire, his face was beaming as he was now a father. Listening to the sounds of a newborn he couldn't sleep and he sat by the fire waiting to be allowed to see the little boy.

The dawn came and the heat of the morning was starting to send heat waves rippling, blurring and distorting the vision of the landscape. The female finally came out to the now small fire and sat on the opposite side of the fire pit still not wanting to have the man close.

The man talking all the time slowly moved his way around the fire to look at his offspring. She finally allowed him to touch the baby not for too long, but the acknowledgment of his presence as the father was a large step coming from a primitive beast yet the communication of the two made it so much easier for her to understand, and him to understand.

I could read the satisfied fulfilled persona that this Edan man was going through. He was completely elated although now the possibility of his people coming to rescue him loomed before him a concern that would never be realized. "Let's see how things are going in one year," I said as I touched the controls.

We looked out the window and could see a very pregnant female caring for the little toddler, which was just starting to walk and was much slower to walk than most apes. She was a very devoted mother taking each step as it came never rushing things as she too was completely comfortable with this arrangement. Both protection and food were well provided and she was prepared to die for this man whom she had devoted so much of her life too.

The changes that she had gone through were so subtle and gradual that she was not even thinking like her wild counterparts. She really was not sure what the normal amount was since she had never had any babies before, and she had no others to learn from except from her upbringing that she had almost had no recognition except little flashes that she consciously was not even aware that they were part of her past.

She was caring for the young boy tenderly and with great motherly love. The man was just returning from a hunt, and he was dragging a good-sized roe deer. There was also another young female that had been found stressed and nearly dead because of the loss of her mother recently and at just over two to three years. The first female looked after this one too.

Not known by him yet, he would someday take her to be his second mate artificially inseminating her as well. Although the usual mating time was about five to seven years before they start gestation, so the man although not consciously considering it now would over the years, grow to love this female almost as much, yet not quite as much as his first mate.

I got the impression that he was still totally amazed that he was compatible with the female as he watched his son hanging onto his mother amazed that the genes could be mixed as these females completely of a different species were in fact, wild uncivilized animals.

Through telepathy he was able to talk and to his amazement, be understood as well as in time would start to listen to their directions with their concepts influencing his direction.

The children were the ones whom he would have the greatest influence over, and he ruled with complete authority although he was extremely fair and just. The females were used to a dominant male so his rule was never contested. He could tell he was starting to change the natural instincts of the females as they became more aware of the things that he was doing as they were imitators, imitating the actions of this new male and becoming very competent in the understanding similar to a parent teaching their young how to use a twig to get termites out of a termite hill which took them years to accomplish.

With the communication used and the explanation that the man gave them it was quickly learned and adopted as a way of life. In turn they became quite civilized in human terms in a very short span.

They in turn looked after the cave and the surrounding mountain as their designated territory set out by their dominant male. This was true as the group never wandered very far from this territory up to the point of five hundred years in the future.

At which point over the years, several of the males actually mated with the wild populations, impregnating several females. As well, the odd female had mated with a wild male making the gene pool more varied than what we had thought. I realized that the man would live for probably four to five hundred years more the average life expectancy of an Edan person, although Adam only made it to approximately four hundred years. This man was a very good provider, protecting this strange little group from any predators that came into his territory.

One major significant event that he had no comprehension of the importance of such knowledge, one that he did not even think was important was the very use of fire, keeping the fires going setting a regimented schedule not allowing the fire to go out.

The females learned very fast as a few burn marks scarred their bodies, usually their hands but the first female had a burn scar on her left leg as she had tried to grab a burning branch with her hand like foot burning her leg and foot. She taught each of her children as well as any of the new arrivals that they would know the power of the fire. She would also use it to keep away unwanted animals. She had discovered the third weapon of the human race next to a stick, which inflicted pain and was usually enough to chase away most predators and of course rocks being the second, but if possible she would use fire as the weapon of preference.

Once taught the female was able to do the basics of preparing the meals and eventually she became very competent in simple meals, spending extra time on special meals that she knew he liked. She would watch him with great care as he would carefully explain what he was doing, and she would practice it until he was satisfied.

He too was not averse to trying different plants that she was used to eating, and although limited by the territory he had set out it was amazing how complete their diet was, although they tended to eat meat as a mainstay. Plants were an afterthought and sometimes were missed completely. He spent hours explaining things to her in the beginning, and then to them as the group grew. Although slow to grasp some of the concepts, the females were slowly beginning to become educated.

The older female was also in turn educating the young and new females. Although she remained the main and dominant female even to her last days she would attempt to cook something that he liked. She lived with him for forty-six years, a most unheard of milestone for her kind especially since life was harsh and very unforgiving.

This man was a very loving and devoted mate as well as a father, and the children grew up to immolate his life, both in actions as well as in the structure that he had lived his life. He was the hunter and the provider. She was the gatherer and the person who looked after the cave, the sick and who raised the children. This way of life was a natural process that met the needs of their way of life as it evolved. Unknowingly, he was to set out a pattern that would endure throughout the existence of mankind.

One thing that was unique, putting aside their compatibility, was that as the children grew up the males were trained to hunt for the group. As well they were encouraged to mate with a female from another mother other than their own mother. Once a mate was taken, only when the male was able to look after her through his hunting that he was responsible for any offspring that she produced.

This alien man did not however, although attempted several times, to teach them of the results of sexual intimacy, and the process involved with a child growing inside the female and to some extent it was beyond their understanding. Promiscuity was a very dominant factor as the group grew in size, a size that was very difficult to control over a long period, and although interbreeding was sever in nature few abnormalities existed in the children at least none in his life, and he did try to match children of different mothers. One thing that did happen was that the children all looked very similar to one another as the dominant look of dark hair and low brows as well as a taller straighter stature. Although slight bowlegged was prevalent, it was quite different from the chimpanzee-like posture.

The last female that the man took as a mate was the last link with the offshoot of the apes, and no connection with the apes occurred after she joined his group. Although the females lived to produce several of his offspring most of them died at a fairly young age, usually within the twenty—to thirty-year range, most in their early twenties. The first female was his true mate to the very end of her life and he never looked or was interested in another mate after she passed on.

He then devoted the remainder of his life to teaching his children and their children. He died an old nearly blind man, with all his children attending to him. He never lost hope that he would someday look up and see a ship from his planet coming to take him back to his home planet.

Thus, the legends of coming from the sky, although very real were not something that these people could understand, and through word of mouth the stories that were told from generation to generation lost the main story and over time, began to take on its own life being embellished as it was handed from one generation to another. The tablets although very well looked after, did eventually crumble with the continual handling. As well as the fights that these tablets caused as to whom was to be in possession of them, and eventually were completely destroyed by a disgruntled mob that smashed the tablets out of revenge not realizing there value to future people. The use of a written language would not come into use for millions of years later.

This was the humble beginning of one man, crashed on a distant planet to a small clan of humans which throughout several disasters and many setbacks, would someday dominate the earth.

We watched the second child being born. Again the mother had a relatively easy birth laboring for a short four hours, again was very definite that she did not want the father to come near her as her maternal instincts came into play, reaching its maximum height as the child was born.

The newborn was strong and healthy as it cried loudly announcing its presence till the female held the newborn to her breast, and there was an almost instant silence. Adam took his time as the female cleaned herself and the child and again after a few hours, was ready to introduce her new addition to their family. The man again talking all the time as he worked himself to the point where he was able to see and touch the new arrival.

The child definitely resembled the mother more than the father this time. The man seeing his second born, looked disappointed for two reasons. Firstly he was hoping for a girl, and secondly he would have liked the infant to look more like himself. But he was satisfied that other than the extra hair on its body the child did resemble his people in many respects, although his face was characteristic of the offshoot of the chimpanzee. He was satisfied that this little boy child was carrying his genes and although the features of the mother were more dominant, the hands and the feet were similar to his, the eyes were large but a lot closer to the females.

Perhaps he will change as the first son had, as the first had a lower brow but had less hair on his body, whereas the second had a lot of body hair something that the Edan people lacked. One thing that he was thankful for was this child was healthy as well and again there were no complications in the pregnancy.

Leaping ahead again two years this time, the first was three years old and was learning to do several tasks around the cave and helping with the little brother with the help of the other female. There was another addition to the harem, a little older around six, was busy doing things around the cave and seemed very comfortable to be looked after by the strange male that she was able to talk to and learn from.

I noticed that not only the first female was pregnant, this would be her third, but also the new female the youngest one who was still not old enough.

The eldest boy was doing remarkably well and was very intelligent as was the second, although the second was slightly slower learning things. Overall, I could see that he was going to be all right.

We tried to be there for every birth, and although the births were almost continuous around the fourteenth year the first couple was mated, the firstborn male and the daughter of the third female now nine years of age.

They had their first child within the first year. Although in human terms it seemed very young, in chimpanzee terms most females were mated any time after their fifth or sixth year.

The family group was not without problems, as the raw animal instincts caused conflicts that ended in the first death. The murder shocked every member of the group and it was the first judgment that was passed on a member of its own.

This out of necessity, was the first time that rules were set up for conduct of the group. The head of the group the eldest, passed the judgment on his own second child, although never questioned it was a decision that the group agreed with completely.

The lifelong sentence was to be banished from the group. In their eyes he was from that point on dead, as they turned away not looking at him ignoring him till he finally left. It was made clear to him that he was never to come in the same territory and if found in the same territory, he was to be killed like an animal to be hunted.

This man left and never returned. He traveled several miles a day and after several days came upon a valley where outcasts similar to his mother lived. Within a few years because of the superior intelligence combined with his cruel ways he outwitted even the largest dominant males giving him the right to be the dominant male.

He overall was a very cruel leader, generating two generations of human descendants. That in time started a fraction group that was to cause several problems in the far future.

Long after the cruel original male had died, generations later the now old leader was killed in a battle for the leadership by one of the great grandsons of the banished man. The new leader, having a wandering instinct moved them farther north and they became wanderers, mostly following herds of animals never settling in one spot for very long. This was very unusual for a territorial animal.

Surprisingly, the rest of the group adapted to the continuous traveling, as this became a normal way of life.

The following leader still ruled as he was raised with cruelty, and for generations the strictness and cruelty continued for thousands of years. The two groups would not come across each other for several centuries long after the man was expelled from their confined territory.

The introduction of the alien's blood had complicated the entire evolution of life, combined with the split of the exiled lone male, which in a very short time had started his own group.

Touching the control, I decided I would visit the second ship to arrive from Jescan's people. "Let's visit with the first party, after the first crashed ship that landed on Earth from your planet."

Looking out the window, it was midmorning, and the heat was rising in waves. Opening the doors, the heat hit us like a ton of bricks.

The dinosaurs except in very remote areas were isolated many where not fertile, and in geological terms, were completely gone allowing the mammals who were definitely the dominant group next to the insects, which were an understatement as there were millions of insects covering the entire planet but as for dominating the land, mammals at this time had no equal.

Jescan looked at the scanners tracking the ship that was about to land. They had no idea that their lives were about to be changed as we watched the ship hovering over the land.

As the ship casually moved from one area to another, they suddenly discovered the humans living in the cliffs above the valley.

They hovered quietly above the little group getting as much data as their ship was capable of, then they sent out a pulsing beam of energy. Immediately, the small people froze almost like the aliens had paralyzed the people placing them in an almost hypnotic state.

Landing they proceeded to come up and touch the little unsuspecting humans. They started to take them one by one to the ship where they took samples of their blood and started a series of tests that they ran on the humans one after another, after another as they seem very excited as they tested the individuals for everything.

They had completed their studies several hours later and we watched as they took one of the young females into the ship, I could see that they were about to keep her as they traveled back to their planet to be able to study this remarkable life form that they had discovered.

Turning to Jescan, I asked, "Are they going to take that girl back to your planet?"

"Yes they are going to take and study her, as she is a new species that shows intelligence. She will be treated quite well as she undergoes several tests."

Checking the monitor on the control panel I studied the future history of the female, rerunning it if I never intervened. "I think that this is the time that I will make a visit to your ancestors. Let's head back to the ship and visit your planet."

Jescan knew that this was going to be the first time his people would meet me, and I could sense that he was controlling his mind so as not to influence me.

Setting the controls, I made the ship look like a large rectangle box with a door in it. I touched the controls and off we went, the buzzing sound announced that we had arrived.

Looking out, we could see a very shocked man, as he was on his way to the door when I opened the door and stood in front of him.

"Please, I am not here to harm you. I am here to straighten out a problem that has happened on my planet. There is a ship that will be arriving and will have a young human female that must be returned unharmed."

A surprise look came over his face as he saw Jescan came out of the ship. The look, was that of surprise and total confusion as he realized that Jescan was one of his own kind. He stopped trying to get to the door and said telepathically, "Who are you? What is going on here?"

"We have come to return a girl to her people on Earth unharmed.

We have come here to discuss the situation as friendly as possible, as there are several things that are involved."

The man sat back at his desk, feeling he didn't have much choice in the matter. "How did you get into here? What quadrant are we talking about?" he asked, pondering this situation as he studied the both of us.

Jescan sat, and I leaned against the table. Jescan started to give him an explanation of why we were here and then gave him the quadrant.

The man raised his hand. "You are talking of the edge of a spiral galaxy and traveling to this area is a very long trip. We have not been in that area of the universe for quite some time as we have spent most of our time in different sectors." He paused, reaching inside a draw of his desk and pulled out a schedule of all the ships out of their immediate sector, looking up the schedules of each ship that was in that area.

"Several years ago, we sent a ship out to study that area, as the spirals of the galaxy have moved enough to warrant another survey.

This ship could be in the area that you are talking about, although if they are already there, they are well ahead of their schedule. Our sensors have detected no unusual readings from that area," he said correcting himself. "We had no way of knowing that there was an advanced intelligent life that existed in that quadrant. I can assure you that we do not harm any specimens. How do you know that we have this person?"

"We have just come from the planet and we watched them take one of the females from the group of people on the planet. We know that your policy is that if intelligent life is discovered, you take a specimen and study them."

"This is information known only by the council and the captains in charge of a crew. This policy is only on planets where special situations have happened and not a regular situation."

"We believe that this is one of those situations." Looking at the man I could tell he was genuinely interested. "This little group has developed a small group of about six hundred people. The species is not required to be studied, as all the information is contained in my computer. I will give you all the information that you require or need."

"Is this true?" he asked as he looked untrustingly at Jescan for a supporting nod considering the implications, wondering how one of his kind was involved with this strange humanoid.

"Yes, there was intelligent life, but we too have a dilemma. The genes from this woman influence the future human population. We cannot change the world's history by removing the female who is an important link in the history of the planet's human population.

"This population has developed for a thousand years. The population has developed and made their mark on the society of the planet. This cannot be changed, but this female is one who mothers the future leader of the group and becomes a very important leader," Jescan stated.

"You keep talking about the future. How do you know this?" inquired the man, puzzled by the conversation.

"We have the technology to be able to see the future. The information is accurate and you will have them return the female." I caught myself giving him an ultimatum.

"I will see what I can do," he said as he reached for the intercom.

Reading his mind, I knew that he had no intention of helping us. I reached out and took hold of his hand. "I think you will come with us," I said as I took him almost lifting him toward the *Genesis*. Opening the door I almost pushed him in. Jescan followed and the door closed.

He looked around, and looked at me, then looked around not even paying any attention to Jescan. "How is this possible? This room is bigger than my office," he said, looking like he had seen a ghost or having illusions as if in a dream. "What is this? How is this possible?"

"We will communicate from this ship. Jescan, you can open a channel with the ship."

"If the ship is close to home their fuel will be close to being empty. They could not return the female without first refueling," the man objected.

"We will make certain that they have enough fuel," I said. Looking at Jescan he had a line open and communication was ready. "You will tell the ship that they will be met by a ship called the *Genesis* and they are to transfer the alien to the other ship."

"I will on one condition. You will let me know how this is done."

"I cannot do that but rest assured your people will have the information in the future," I said, smiling at Jescan as I took him over to the console.

"No, I would like the information before I agree to do this."

"Jescan, inform the ship that they are to expect a load to be transported to their ship. Inform them that the emissary will be aboard," I said, looking at the man "You will be able to talk to them in person." I readjusted the controls.

"That is impossible. They have to be one hundred and fifty thousand light-years away."

Waiting for Jescan to finish the message, I touched the control and landed in the ship's hold. The buzzer announced our arrival. "Well, we are here. You can talk to them yourself."

"We haven't gone anywhere. What kind of a joke are you pulling here?"

"This is no joke, and we are on the ship. Let's go see the crew," I said, directing him to the door.

As we walked to the door I opened the entrance, and we exited the *Genesis* into the ship's hull. As we left the ship and closed the door, the man was beside himself.

"We are here on the ship just like you said. I don't believe this. We are really here, or is this an illusion?"

Coming into the cargo bay the captain studied the three new passengers. "How is this possible, and where did this . . .," he said, correcting himself as he recognized the looks of the leader. "This is true then. How is it possible, emissary? Where did you transport from?

Is this a new device that allows you to transport over such distances?" He stopped, as the leader raised his hand.

"I don't know. We came from Edan," he said, looking strangely at me as he studied my face. "You are a strange man."

"We have come for the female human. She must be returned to the planet. You can take the emissary back with you," I said, facing the captain of the ship.

"The specimen is in stases. We need to study the female and check out the genetic makeup."

"I will give you all the genetic information, including a history or family tree, as I will allow you access to this information so that her life will not be disrupted."

"Is this true? We are to turn over the specimen?" asked the captain, raising his laser gun toward me.

"This man has broken into my office, took me into his ship and we have ended up here." said the emissary. "Arrest these men."

"I would not do that if I were you," I said as I calmly raised my arms, followed by Jescan. "We have a lot more to explain to you," I said as I looked at the captain then to the emissary. "You will be quite amazed at what you will learn and hear. Your people will become much the wiser for the information that you are about to receive."

"I think that we will have to have a judgment on this. When we return, we will have the decision agreed upon and then we will return her. Let's go to the stasis room and take a look at this specimen."

"If you decide to take this course of action, your entire crew including the emissary here from this day forward, shall be suspended in space for a long enough period that you shall grow old and die in space, possibly starve to death never reaching your home planet."

Over the intercom, a voice said, "Captain, the engines are unresponsive. This is impossible, but all the stars have vanished. The ship seems to be suspended in space. It is like we are in a vacuum with all our bearing stars gone."

Moving to the port cargo window he stood staring into empty space. A concerned look swept over his face as well as the emissaries as they looked at each other. "What strange power is this that you can control the very universe?"

"This must be an illusion like the ship that we came out of, the ship that came into my office, and then appeared on this ship. This cannot be possible!" the emissary said, looking totally bewildered. He stepped toward the captain and grabbed the laser gun. "This has to be a bad dream, and it will end now." He pushed the button, releasing the laser beam, striking me in the chest.

To my surprise, the beam was completely absorbed by my body, not even the smell of a laser burn, although it was set for stun it did not have any effect on me.

"Now I know that this is a dream. The beam didn't even touch you!" He was totally stunned as he took a second look.

Totally disbelieving his eyes he reached out and took the laser gun and examined it in total amazement. "This has been fully discharged. Totally impossible." He paused as he shook his head. "This is impossible. I can see that we are in a situation that defies all known laws of the universe. Is this really happening?" questioned the captain.

"I am the caretaker of all the universe. I look after all that is in this universe. As well, I can control everything that is in the universe. This is Jescan. He is a liaison with your people and me, although he is from your future, I am from all time."

Contemplating the words that I spoke as well as observing the void of space that they were in, he let out a sigh. "You leave us no alternative. Okay, we will return the female. Please release the ship."

Jescan left the cargo hold and entered the *Genesis*, transferring the female as he touched the controls. "I have transferred the female to the *Genesis*."

The emissary turned to me and said, "You could have transferred the female without our knowledge. Who are you? Why the games?"

"I have the information of Earth's history as well as the information on your planet. You will change your mandate from this day forward. Your mandate will be that of an observer, a protector of planets and of galaxies. "You shall play an important role, as societies and civilizations will appreciate the information that you will gather and record for all life present and future.

"Your mandate will be vitally important to all life on all the planets that you are in contact with. The recording of the events, small as well as grand, shall become your task, you shall become one of the key factors in the whole realm of things to be, present and future."

"Come with me," I said as I opened the door to the *Genesis*.

The emissary took a walk around the box and looked inside and then outside as if he could figure out how such a large room could be in such a small space.

"This as you know, is Jescan. He has helped me document and catalog information that will become very important to your society as well as mine. Your purpose will be to collect specimens to be held in stasis within guidelines set out in a disk that I shall give you.

The information of each species will in time give you the answers that everyone will be questioning in the future as they do today. The questions shall be for any and all to see and know of what really happened in the past. For that, knowledge is what you will collect, and catalog all this information and your task will help explain several questions that each society reaches at some point or another."

The captain looked and watched in pure disbelief as he touched and pondered as to the capabilities of such equipment. "Will you be helping us?" he asked, more of a thought than a question.

"I will help when I can be of assistance. Our paths shall cross several times." Sitting down I paused, thinking about what information I could give them. "Your society will grow and more and more knowledge shall be accumulated over the years, and as you need me, I shall be there. The information that I will give you will start you onto a very interesting road of discovery."

Looking at the information in the computer, I isolated the information that was important to this period and had the computer make a copy of the information, storing it on a disc that I knew was compatible for their technology. "This will transfer the information to your computers," I said, taking the disc out and handing it to the emissary. "Put your best people on this new project and have them sift through the information on the disc. After they have understood the information, your society will excel in many fields."

Trying to read my mind, the emissary looked at me, studying me. "You surprise me. Our people have been searching for minerals as well as planets to inhabit. Why should we change our strategy to what you think we should?"

"Jescan is from your future, and he will be able to help you understand what you become." Jescan knew the importance of limiting the information to things that were important to them and to limit the knowledge that they will acquire over the years, and he stayed with generalizations more than specific facts.

I watched as Jescan explained to the emissary and the captain as to what they have in store and what they become having studied their involvement. I knew that each of the men was an important factor in the changes that would occur. I smiled at the expressions on their faces as they heard what was going to happen to their people in the future.

Adjusting the controls to return the emissary, I waited till they had completed their conversation.

Jescan had finished, and the captain and the emissary were looking at each other in sheer disbelief. "Come, follow me. I have something that you need to see."

Taking them to the room where we stored and collected all the specimens, I said, "You will build a building that can contain all these specimens. As soon as you have completed the building, I shall transfer this collection into your care for safekeeping."

"This is amazing. How did you obtain all these specimens?" the Captain asked, shaking his head. He was definitely believing what we had told him.

"The information is contained in the disc, and your people will be studying the information for several years. The information on the size of the structure is also contained on the disc," I said, directing them back to the console room. "It is time I return you to your planet. This will allow you to start immediately."

Turning to the captain, I said, "You will now have your ship back, as I have released the ship."

Showing the captain out of the *Genesis*, I could see him shaking his head as he turned and looked into the room he had just left, which was larger than any room that he had on his ship. Nodding a good-bye, I closed the door and returned to my console.

Touching the control, the buzzer sounded our arrival.

"You are now back on your planet. The information that you have in this disc will bring your story to a believable reality your emissary, so please, let them know that you are changing the agenda. Handing him a communicator, you will be able to contact me when everything is ready. Let the disc talk for you. Also, the promise of the specimens will be of great interest to your scientists. I believe that you will be very interested in the information on the disc."

Returning to the planet Earth, we arranged our timing so as we arrived moments before the ship was to take off. Landing, absorbing the rock as the *Genesis* stopped in the center of the camp, we transported the female to the location that she had been, just before she had been abducted, releasing the stasis as the ship took off at the same time as the others. All things were back as they should be.

I was amazed at how the people carried on as though nothing had happened. They didn't even realize that they had lost about six hours, part of the conditioning that the aliens did as they left, although the girl, because she had not been left with the hypnotic suggestion, paused, looked around and couldn't figure out why things were not quite right, although it was momentary, as she placed it in the back of her mind. She looked around and shrugged it off, as she was the only one to have noticed any of the time that seemed to have vanished. I felt confident that we could leave, as she would hold it inside for her entire life, not able to fully come to an answer, passing it off as one of those things.

CHAPTER NINE

Setting the controls, we traveled to the next period after we knew the girl was all right.

Upon opening the door, we walked out to a glorious day. The sun beat down on a fresh clear land. The temperature was moderate. The sky was azure blue, and not a cloud was present, as a high-pressure area was dominating most of the continent. The clear day was also a perfect day for a swim maybe. "Let's walk," I suggested.

Jescan was very quiet and followed without saying anything. He was in deep thought and was deciding whether he should tell me all the things that were to come or to hold his thoughts. I did not pry because I knew he would in time, reveal all in his own time. In a way, I wasn't sure I wanted to know at this time, as I was discovering I had a lot of time.

As we walked, the plants were starting to take on the similarities of the plants that I was used to. Although they in some ways looked similar, they still had a long evolution to go, but the basic look was starting to appear. I could see smoke curling up from campfires, dotting the landscape. The humans had spread over a larger area now, as more separated and or broke away from the main groups.

Coming around a bend, in a hilly part of the country, there was a small group of hunters, tracking a giant sloth type of animal. Although it had the characteristics of a modern sloth, it was big and would walk slowly from place to place but if cornered, had the same brute strength as a giant rhinoceros. This was a formidable hunt.

The men spread out to form a circle. The sloth was sensing danger and was starting to walk faster to find cover and where it could defend itself. The animal was no match for the fast-footed men as they came from all sides, and the poor animal had little chance of defending itself. The first man ran at the beast. Running with a spear, he landed a great blow to the ribs, trying to puncher the heart. It went deep and yet not enough to puncher the heart. It did though puncher the lung, the animal turned and with its great claws, sliced the man's stomach splitting his guts open exposing most of the major organs. Grabbing and holding his wound, the man fell back. Another man ran from the front, and another ran from the other side, and the fourth came from the rear, and all rammed a sharp stick into the beast.

The sloth's lungs were so full of blood now that the animal was suffocating slowly, almost like slow motion. It sank to the ground. All its muscles relaxed totally, and it fell in a pile to the ground.

The other men ran to the older man of about thirty years, obviously their father. As they ran to his side one placed his hand on the stomach pulling his hand away to find it covered in blood. One of the others grabbed his head, his eyes as big as possible tears almost forming into his eyes.

Not able to watch anymore, I hurried down to the men huddled around the injured man. Two of the men started to grab their spears from the beast. The boy holding the older man's head his eyes full of water was suddenly more frightened at seeing me than he was feeling sad.

As I walked toward the man I held my hands in a cup shape extended outward showing no attack was intended. Bending over the man, I laid my hands onto the man's stomach and started to place the organs in the proper place, repairing anything that was damaged, stopping the bleeding as I pulled his skin together, closing the gap and mending the skin as I pushed the skin together.

Realizing that Jescan would be looked upon as so different, I gave him the suggestion to pull his hood over his head down low, covering his eyes, giving the illusion of a human-looking head.

I looked up at the terrified boy of about fifteen years. The other two stared at me with the widest eyes, almost looking like Jescan with the huge eyes.

I spoke softly out loud. "This man can now eat the meat he has killed."

One of the men of about twelve jumped when I spoke, surprised at the sound of my voice. The others simply stood there, not knowing whether to smile or to run. I used my telepathic voice. "My friend and I are travelers, and we have come across this accident and could not let this man die. I am able to heal people and your father shall be able to hunt tomorrow. We shall bid our leave now."

Turning to walk away, the healed man lying on the ground stood and grunted some soft guttural sounds. He walked up to me extending his hand as I turned toward him. The gesture was one of peace and thank you wrapped up in one. Holding his stomach the minuscule scar was still covered in bright-red blood still drying on his lap and his legs. His hands were still red almost a crusty black from the exposure to the oxygen. Using guttural sounds as well as telepathy he said to me, "Please eat at our fire tonight. We will have a feast of all feasts. I will show you the way."

He signaled with his hands to the other men to take and prepare the sloth and to follow gesturing to Jescan to follow as well, waited till Jescan came down to the group.

Turning, he started to walk toward their camp a short mile or so, we came to a slight hill with large trees surrounding the hill, making the hill seem smaller than it really was.

Approaching the campsite a fireplace smoldered lazily in the calm day, rising almost straight up with rocks placed in a circle within the fireplace to form a cooking spot tended by three women and one older man and a small girl of about two, maybe three. It was the older man who noticed our group approaching, announcing our arrival.

The rest of the group came running to welcome the hunters back, stopping as they spotted Jescan and I freezing like a deer or a coyote, motionless not even breathing, ready to bolt at the first sign of danger.

They realized that the men were happy and showed no danger signs instead they showed friendly excited signs, and as we came closer they started explaining our presence and the curing of their father and elder, the extended family unit showing and taking great care to be courteous in every way.

These people were extremely observant and absolutely respectful of whatever we needed even before we needed it, as they were always anticipating what we would like, want or need. They were extremely superstitious as everything had a meaning, and to them most things meant more than it actually was. Politeness was a fact of life, everything was done with meticulous care and respect.

The men started telling their story as they carried the animal to the fire and dropped the beast. The village all wanted to look at the scar and touch the blood and listened intently as the man told the story, overly embellished by the youngest hunter who was beaming as he was telling the unbelievable story. The other two also mentioned as much as they could to the story, most often talking all at once. The man walked over to me and he took my hands and laid them on his stomach, smiling and thanking me.

The women listened to the men as they started to skin and started to cut up the carcass for the feast that the men had ordered. They started to stoke up the fire, and gathered the storage of vegetables and roots, and a group of younger kids gathered large leather pouches to collect fruit, which grew in abundance all around the village. The women started to cook the large sloth, more than could ever be eaten by the small group in this camp.

The men gathered around large wooden logs that had been hollowed out by burning and then filled with a multitude of fruit. The fermented fruits gave a strong alcoholic smell as they removed the lid.

Burned-out, cup-looking like coconut shells were handed first to me then to Jescan, and the rest were handed out. The men all gathered around and made sure that I and then Jescan were the first to dip our cups into the strong liquor drink.

As the men gathered all with their cups in hand, they raised their cups in my honor. The females were all rushing around, making sure that nothing was forgotten. Some of the runners were returning, as they were inviting the other camps. The men really had nothing to do in the preparation of the meal since they had brought the meat and invited the guests, and they sat starting to get mildly drunk.

Watching the women working away, I could see how they were placing dried plants, an assortment of different spices, that gave off a great aroma as they started pots of wild legumes and wild roots. The roasts were starting to get a thin black layer, and the women turned them occasionally.

Other groups started to arrive, some with the runners who had stayed to help them get ready and came with them. There were within a very short time about seventy to a hundred people, which would grow to three hundred to four hundred people by the time the feast would start. All brought a special gift of food, or furs, or spears, each one showing their appreciation for the honor of attending.

Several gifts were a thing that was a prized possession or an object like a shiny rock that was interesting to look at. Material things were things that were given, as the accumulation of things was not a part of the society, built on making another happy.

The people gathered around ready to start the feast. As everyone waited for us to begin, one of the women wheeled a large sharp flint stone that cut through the meat, placing it into a burned-out bowl, filling up the bowl with the remaining plentiful amount of food. We sat around the huge fire and drank and ate till we couldn't eat anymore.

The story was told over and over. Finally, an older woman in her late thirties and was slouched over from hard work approached me politely, not raising her eyes as a woman was not allowed to look at a man well, asking a favor. "I have great pain in my hands. Could you look at them to see if you could take the pain away?" she asked, humbly waiting for an answer.

I looked down at her arthritic hands all knotted and twisted. Looking at her feet her toes were twisted as well. "Hold my hands," I directed her. She had trouble lifting her arms as the arthritis was in almost every joint. The pain must have been unbearable. Leaning down slightly taking her hands into mine, I released my inner energy.

"You can get up, and get me a cup of wine."

The woman, not looking up, started to get up in the same manner that she had gotten used to. Realizing that the pain in all her joints was gone, and looking down at her hands that were straight, and bending over, she could feel no pain in her feet and hips and back, she looked at my chest smiling, and bent to pick the drinking bowl.

"Thank you, thank you," she said as she straightened up and walked like she was young again and probably felt like she was a little kid again. Bringing the bowl back she knelt hugging my legs.

Hurrying back to her mate, she ran her hand over his arm, showing off her new feeling body. Turning she showed the woman beside her, the woman looked not believing what she was seeing.

Soon, others approached me and I healed each one as they came.

As soon as the crowd had settled down, and no one was approaching me a young boy of about eight approached me. Looking down he asked if I might be able to help his mother as she was so sick that she could not come to the camp.

Holding the boy's hand, I said, "Take me to your mother now, please." He started walking to a camp several miles away. Looking at the people, I said, "I will be back as soon as I am done."

The man who bore the scar on the abdomen grabbed a spear, he was about to make certain that no animal would get the boy and me. Stopping him, I insisted that he stay here and we would return safely.

Jescan said that he would try to keep him at the fire till I returned to the group as he was pleasantly drunk and was not too hard to convince that they should stay by the fire.

The boy walked with me across several rolling hills. The boy jumped as the animals would all come out of the forest and get rubbed or scratched by me. The boy just looked up at me and was not paying attention as he stumbled on a large stones that caused him to fall this happening more than once.

Approaching his cave the fire was still going, and was tended by an older woman maybe in her middle to late twenties. She groped for a log and placed it onto the fire and then slumped back to the ground, clearly knowing that she was of no use to the tribe. She was deciding as to what to do. Should she wander out into the jungle to be attacked by animals, or should she walk to the high cliffs and throw herself over the high cliffs? She had lots of time to ponder because the group would not be back till the next day.

I knew that she was thinking of a way to ease the burden she had become to her people. I could read her mind as I approached and could sense the deep depression she was in.

The young boy started talking as he approached telling her about a man who has come to help her. She was very surprised thinking that she would be alone till the next day at least, wanting to be gone by the time the group returned. Her heart was very low, concerned that another opportunity may not come again for a long time since she was rarely left alone.

I approached her noticing that she had been blinded from being scalded as her face was covered with burn scars. The scars covered most of the front of her body including her one arm, which was almost rendered completely useless as it had taken a lot of the burn.

Most of her skin on her arm was burned off and the muscles were withered, and bone was exposed.

"Tell me what happened to you," I said as I placed my hand on her shoulder.

She started to explain that she had been rendering the fat gathered from animals that had been hunted, as she was rendering the large abalone shell slipped and splashed the hot grease all over her, mostly on her face and arm. The grease had burned her eyes and cooked them causing her to lose site in both eyes and the loss of smell, as the grease had burned her mouth and nostrils.

Lifting the lady I walked down to the creek that ran at the bottom of the hill telling her to close her eyes and hold her breath, as I was going to dunk her into the stream. I walked out to my waist.

I held and comforted her placing her into the water and completely submerging her body letting the energy from my hands start to mend her arm and her eyes. The scars started to disappear, as the water was rushing over her body. Lifting her out, I started to walk back to the shore. "Open your eyes and behold, your son awaits."

She opened her eyes and could see her son who was excitedly bouncing as he waited for them to reach the shore. She turned and looked at me and was surprised that I did not meet what she expected, since I didn't look like anyone whom she had ever seen. Smiling, she hugged me as we approached the shore.

"Your son wanted you to come to the feast," I said, setting her down in front of the son. "I am certain you would like to show him the way."

The woman leaned over, hugging her son as he hugged her. The boy and she inspected her arms and legs as well touching her body and face. Both turned and again hugged me giving their thanks.

The boy started telling her about the remarkable way that I had with animals and the way that they came up, not to attack but to be petted, as we walked on our way back to the large group. She walked beside me holding my hand, and the boy holding hers.

The animals did come from the dense jungle and they did want to be petted, they petted the beasts as they came close. They had never been so close to a live animal as the only animals they had been close to where carcasses of the last kill. There was a preconditioned fear of these wild animals. "You will in time, be able to control a lot of these animals but you must be very patient with wild animals, be careful not to do this alone," I warned.

Approaching the group, the boy ran ahead to tell everyone of the magic that he had witnessed and the help that had cured his mother. The people gathered around quiet and mystified, as she and I approached.

A man came running up to her and hugged her with tears in his eyes. He was her mate who had given up on the fact that she would ever be able to do anything except tend the fire.

Motioning to Jescan, I knew that it was time for us to go. Again, I turned to the group. "Look after the land and the animals so there will always be enough to feed your families. Take only what you need from the land, and do not waste any life unless it is necessary." Turning, Jescan followed as we walked along the path that we had arrived on.

The *Genesis* had returned several hours before and had completed the analysis of the planet and was still cataloging the records of all the new animals and plants. Although there were less new animals and plants, as most were evolving from existing plants and animals. It was the age of evolution. The only dinosaurs that remained were the reptiles and birds and some small animals that had been lucky enough to have been in an area that was warm enough to exist. Several still survived in the oceans, although they were slowly diminishing, as other animals started to dominate the seas. Animals that were in competition for the food started to overtake their territories, replacing them in the food chain. Most animals including plants, on land as well as the seas were evolving, changing as needed occasionally mutating into a more modern form of animal. This of course included the plants.

Jescan was glued to the monitor as he studied the changes, major as well as minor that the flora and fauna were slowly transforming into. "The first fraction of land that had been cracked away millions of years ago was starting to push on the east side of the continent, and the land that was split shortly after was now almost out of site from the west side. If you didn't know it was there, you would almost think it was part of the horizon or part of the sea," Jescan commented, looking at me. "Some of the animals in the separated landmasses are evolving slower and looking totally different from other parts of the main massive continent."

"The splitting of the continents does cause a separation of the species, and each changes to meet their own territory and climatic conditions. Some will stay similar and evolve slower as well as the changes tend to be less dramatic as compared to other areas of the earth. Similar occurrences happens on every planet that holds life. It also occurred on your planet. Someday we will have to check out your planet and check out the evolution of Edan."

"Yes, that would be interesting, although you do in the future, according to our texts." As Jescan thought of his ancestors, he said,

"Let's find out the secrets of this planet first. This is part of the history of my people in a sense."

"True, and we will trace your history in time as you have said I already have but first, let's see what we have at the next important period." Touching the controls, the buzzer sounded our arrival.

The day was a cloudy, rainy kind of a day with rain falling lightly in scattered showers, covering most of the land. Walking out the air was cool, as the winds were blowing over the ice flows that had advanced once more. The land was radically changed. The plants were more like the modern plants that I grew up knowing. The animals were still massive. The mammoths in the northern areas wandered in large herds, the saber-toothed tiger in a more spread-out area and the ancestor of the bear covering almost all the landmasses. Dragonflies were still huge, due to the oxygen levels being so high, spanning a good ten to twelve feet in length, as these were dominant hunters.

The ancestors of the buffalo with huge horns traveled in herds, so numerous that one herd covered thousands of acres as they traveled across the land. In the south, large giraffe camels wandered throughout the arid areas of the land. The elk were huge, standing fifteen feet high at the shoulders, wandering throughout the forests because of the plentiful plants. Most of the animals grew to massive sizes in a way almost paralleling the massive size of the dinosaurs, only more sophisticated internally as well as more adaptable and agile.

The humans also had grown. There were changes that they were going through as well. The different groups were starting to spread to all areas of the continent. They had even spread into the North American continent where they had not been before, because of the ice bridge attaching the Bering Strait and the European continent.

There were different cultures developing. Some were staying where they could collect wild crops and started to harvest the wild crops yearly staying in local areas, although the largest majority of people still wandered and spent most of their time hunting, though they did have areas that they visited each year to collect certain berries, fruits, wild onions, roots, and peas. The groups although spread out, traveled in smaller family and extended families. It was not uncommon to come across travelers, as many people wandered from place to place.

Wandering throughout the land, there was a group of humans that had obviously, I could sense developed to a modified slightly changed line of humans, as the humans had larger skulls, not having the dominant low brow and extended chin. This human had a modern type of skull and a chin that was not as pronounced as in the past.

These slightly larger yet physically weaker humans walked a little taller, and although some still had the bowlegged look, they were noticeably straighter, giving a different type of walk to this human, not sure from which alien linage was causing this, realizing that it could be the Blue Avian's, possibly the Annunaki, or the taller blue people that in many ways looked like the greys but not sure which. The arms were not as long and thick as the others.

Setting aside the physical changes from the hunter gatherers these new people were more inquisitive much more adventuresome, leaving their family unit a lot easier than the other more regimented groups.

They did things that no other human had done such as starting to trade or barter for things. They also had acquired the ability to start speech, as they found that communication was easier, when trading.

Before if you needed something you simply asked for it, although at times it was like they were little children and wouldn't share but usually if asked rarely were they ever turned down. This type of modern man did specialize more than the others as one man might specialize in the making of spearheads and another specialized in making pots or baskets. They wandered around, trying to find a group that needed what they made. With something to trade it became a natural course of evolution, as groups with surpluses in one thing found that it was just as easy to find some group or person that had more than they could use of another thing or object. Although in most cases, the concept was easily accepted. Some clans gave not expecting to receive anything in return. Overall though it was an acceptable practice.

Several would trade for the typical things, such as food and furs, but some would trade for objects that had no serious value in their present economy but were good for looking at rather than for practical purpose. Flint and stones were always big trading items, especially shiny stones, but unique things such as a skin of a different color or a nice looking seashell became very "in demand" items. The items ranged and were as wide as the individuals' likes and/or dislikes.

These people also started to have a different outlook on animals, not as their elders who feared the animals as their elders taught them.

The first domesticated dogs were starting to appear as well as some of the larger herd-type animals like the buffalo, deer, mammoths, and the wild horse. Although they were not tamed as they were herded into canyons or run over cliffs. The clans followed certain herds of animals.

Some even found they could chase them into a boxed canyon and the animals would in a sense be restricted enough that a ready supply of meat was always available. In many cases the animals needed more pasture, and they would leave the canyon not returning till the next year. This was something that this modern man could figure out that they had the capabilities to restrict a small group of animals rather than a large group.

Generally though the largest groups of people still following a herd of animals which became the easiest, as it was discovered that the animals tended to migrate to warmer areas in the winter and cooler areas in the summer.

The invention of threading two pieces of leather together started to appear, although the needle was not used at this time. This newer man was becoming more self-aware questioning many things like why the sun appear every day and the moon every night and why the tides moved in and out on a regular time.

These were the first people because of the superstitions that in most cases had no real bases, although individual experiences were the bases of the first start to an organized or ritualized religion. Small groups started to worship the sun and the moon, adding to their main god, the little statue of a pregnant female called a doni. This little statue had a simple form with no face but a representation of a short female definitely pregnant with the rounded tummy being the most important feature. This statue was made to represent the Mother Earth and was the most common object of possession and was carried by several shamans. Many individuals who received them from a shaman revered them and only brought them out on special times, or if they had a special question or problems. There were many other smaller gods that was prayed to as well, but none was more revered like the Mother Earth called Donii.

The people found that because they had surpluses as well as things that they had collected, they were able to live in one place and people started to come to them. The start of a marketplace appeared.

As we walked we came across several different groups. One thing that was very noticeable was that the humans who still had the same characteristics as the original humans isolated themselves and rarely did they wander very far from the herds that moved across the land, although most stayed in one location and hunted in a territory that they had designated for themselves, hunting and gathering food within that region.

The only time they really traveled far, was when they had a summer meeting place that drew people of the same family lineage from all over the region. Each year they would meet and tell stories and the young looked to find mates, the older members would visit with friends and relatives who had migrated to another territory.

It was a great meeting with the elders controlling the pace of the gathering and each year there was a set sequence of events. These events never changed from year to year rarely if ever changing, like the people not willing or not able to accept the changes that were taking place around them. Generally, they stayed within their own isolated territory segregating their group.

The newer humans lived within the same territories and rarely bothered each other almost avoiding each other but tolerant of each other if encountered. During the gatherings the newer humans avoided their area. They did from a distance observe them and studied their strange rituals. They also held their own gatherings and were generally at about the same time. Usually they started later or earlier than the older humans and they each had the opportunity to study each other. I noticed that the new humans had more interest in the old ways where the older humans tried to avoid the newer people's ways, probably out of fear of the gods becoming mad at them for doing something new or different.

Jescan and I wandered from camp to camp helping out the injured and the crippled the people humbly making offerings of food, rocks, shells, or almost anything that they held in high esteem. Each time, we declined.

Walking into a gathering of the newer humans I found that they did not communicate by telepathy as the others did. They relied on verbal conversation. They could be communicated to by telepathic means, but they seemed afraid of it and they would back away avoiding the conversation. This presented a problem for both Jescan and myself as we found ourselves trying to mimic their language, which was nothing like what we had ever heard before. One advantage that we had was that we could understand their intentions through reading their minds, and associating the sound to the actions they were looking for.

Without this ability we would not have been able to communicate, and although we held our conversation to a minimum we still found out several interesting concepts that they had developed. They had developed the concept of spirits, and when I healed someone they insisted that I was a good spirit. I was welcomed with great reverence and no matter what I did to play down my possession of spirits the people spread the word even before I came upon them. I was most often greeted with great reverence. People who were desperately seeking help came looking for me if I had been seen. People even walked for miles to see me.

Jescan and I tried to get to every continent and look in on every group of humans as they became our most significant interest. We noticed that even on the isolated continents the people were changing, and a more inquisitive structurally different group of people was starting to become the dominant people. This change gave me an uneasy feeling as we came across more and more of these people.

Back at the *Genesis* I started to look at the areas that these changes occurred and all indications were that it was happening all over the world. I was just about to accept that it was a natural occurrence when looking over the pictures of the land and a close up of the land, I noticed a valley with modern-type building, much different from anything else we had witnessed.

The people from Edan had inhabited this area. They had set up an airport with the usual three landing strips to take advantage of the wind from any direction. These strips were forming a rectangular shape on the top of high mountains and they were able to fly to all parts of the earth. Looking at other areas I found a total of three airports with the triangle-shaped runways.

"Jescan, what is going on here?" I asked touching the control and landing in the middle of the isolated valley in the southern continent being on the west side of the main continent.

This area had very few human inhabitants, as most of them were in the northern continents. I was to find out later that the local people called this the valley of the blue people. It was obvious that they had been here for quite a while, as some of the buildings showed that they had been there for some time.

"Your people look like they are interfering with the natural evolution once again," I said, turning to Jescan.

Looking away he said, "I was not sure if I should have told you that this was going to happen. This is not my people. This is the Annunaki and Blue Avian people who have set up an outpost here so that they could study and observe how things were progressing on this planet. There is something else that you should know . . . that is, Annunaki and the Blue Avian people have been artificially inseminating some of the females in isolated groups in all regions, especially groups that are secluded. There is really no missing link from the modern man to the first primitive man. The missing link is our people and these people. They have supply ships that only come every one thousand years because of the distance to be traveled and to make the trip takes with the technology as it is at this time, about two thousand earth years to reach and return to their home planet. In one expedition of twelve ships they brought supplies and equipment to build these buildings and they never exchanged the crews for they live a very long time compared to our people and they used their ships to depart. This place has been abandoned here for about eight hundred years now. The modern man, was from the scientists well examining them, have inseminated them with sperm from their sperm banks.

"This had been done because of the improvement of the population as a whole and the faster the advancement, the faster the introduction of them and our people to your planet. Their people had been living with the people on this planet for almost a thousand years. The life on this planet has grown in the last eight hundred years."

"You mean that all along that, these people have been here and again interbreeding with the local people?"

"To a certain extent, yes," he said, turning toward me, "but not totally true, but there was other alien species that was also doing the same thing, us included, that again changed the DNA of your species.

Your race is a mixture of several different species from different areas within the universe. Our people have in most cases lived with and have been a part of the different clans. They have been in love. As well, they have hunted beside their families. Most started out as celibate, but over the years there grew relationships and with relationships grew love. The average life span is thirty years. Our people live an average life span of three to six hundred of your earth years . . . some more.

"The first people who became involved with the humans have all since died and the council has decided seven hundred years ago that no replacements will be allowed to walk among the people. The council has taken the observation of the planet to be restricted from the air. We did look after the people . . . medically if necessary mostly to make sure that they are well taken care of, and the day-to-day things are of their own choice with no influence."

"How much do your people think is enough . . . and other species having also been an influence?" I asked as I felt the blood start to boil in my veins. "This is not how it should be."

"This is how it happened in the history as I know it and the history as we have been educated. Is it your intention that you would like to change it?"

The music came into my head. *This is your history and should not be tampered with. This is how they and the other species have influenced the history of your plane. It is as it is and as it was. The influence all throughout the different galaxies in your plane has something to contend with this form of being. All the humanoid life in almost all the planets have their roots, in some way involve the aliens, including the people from Edan, blue avian, Annunaki the blues, and the ant like people, and the list goes on about nine to eleven different aliens maybe more as history will tell that we know of making them all somewhat protective of this planet.*

That is the link with all the six planes. They develop in the future with our help, the knowledge to carry on to such a level that they exceed all their expectations of themselves. They are the first to evolve into what all the humanoids will eventually attain.

They will though not be able to travel in time, although they will be able to reach future times, with very limited ability in the past, because of the ability to reach the speed of light as well as the use of portals and will be restricted mostly to their future, but that is thousands of years in the future.

This is the inevitable outcome of all our species.

This is all because of the connection between you and the five of us. We will attain uniqueness as does the four other planes that we will eventually connect with, and we shall intertwine as one, as we are but one, even now.

This though, is our learning stage. We will learn as much as we can first about our own planes, then we will study the other planes in due time.

The changes that are occurring in this time, are as they are suppose to be and they will become part of history. We like you, are learning, it is a controlled development, yet we are capable of extraordinarily unique capabilities. Each of us shall become an expert in our own plane and together we shall nurture the civilizations to expand their capabilities to such a level that the universe becomes as complex and diverse as the different planes, in that we exist. This is your task to improve what is, and to expand what is. If changes are not to be you will be able to adjust the situations as they are in time. We become the keepers of time.

Sitting back and going over the conversation as though it was just being said, I found myself wondering what was to happen next.

This was everything that was against what I had ever thought as the information was accumulating. It seemed harder to piece the whole picture together yet the more I found out the easier it became to figure out the order that it was to fall into, and things did have their place in the history of all things. This was worse than any cramming for any school exam I had ever experienced, and although the same neurons were needed, the experiences of the crashing or colliding of these ideas all had to come together in a logical manner.

Some of the things that were going on did make sense in a manner of speaking, even though I disagreed with it. I was capable of understanding as mad as I was about it. I could still communicate without sounding mad. At this moment I thought it would be nice to be back when life was just beginning. I thought of myself as a very level-headed person. Now I am finding that everything that I thought was a natural evolving society was now a manipulated society.

In a manner of speaking they were meeting their main goal, adding genetic pools that would guarantee their species striving through any possible means, and any unseen catastrophes through their genes would not prevent them from becoming immortal in their own way.

This is not how I envisioned things were to be even when I had the helmet on and gained knowledge beyond anything I had ever thought possible. Now, I was like a baby being reborn and the discovering had just started, I was still no way ready to understand, or appreciate the bigger picture. This was a day that I should have stayed in bed, nothing seemed to be right.

Yet again calmness set in, and reality overtook my mind. It was not as I saw it as I grew up but as I was seeing it now, no judgments to be made, just facts to be collected. The things were as they were now and as they were but nothing seemed right . . . yet they were.

Jescan became my guide to the steps that happened as they happened, and nothing more nothing less. I should and will not tamper with the steps that have occurred before I was born as well as the things that happened up till I was connected with the other planes.

What would I find out about my whole culture my every belief that would be shattered as it was today on a small piece of history that was the reason for the future, yet will affect the future?

Jescan was watching me quietly and soberly, not knowing how I would react. He knew that this among other times was the time that he was supposed to be here to relay as much of the knowledge that he could to me, to help me cope with and understand how it really happened.

Looking at Jescan I said, "I had no idea that the influence was to this scale. Taking into consideration all the things that I have known or believed although important in the overall picture, it is a shock to sit here and not be shocked at the unbelievable things that others and your people are doing.

"The people as primitive as they are, know that there is a greater being that is and has been, but they do not have the luxury of knowing how and why," I said feeling that I had just given birth to a new planet, one not like the one I had been told about but one of the real planet with a different history. My mind was taxed to the maximum, yet not completely.

I started to relax as I knew the overall information was still to come, not from this conversation but from the experiences yet to come. It felt like . . . no, it was an abrupt awakening of reality.

Jescan's eyes even grew larger, as he realized I understood the effect that his and other alien people had had on the unsuspecting innocent people, although genetically manipulated humans.

"We are not bad. We have as your ship is named, planted our genes all over the universe. We, our people are in most cases subtly genetically linked to all humanoid life forms throughout the universe.

Although this planet did have life and did have intelligence it was our mandate or task to elevate this form of life to achieve the potential of the then unattainable, to now accomplish more than ever conceived."

"Your people including the other aliens have manipulated, although well intended, the genetic makeup of the entire humanoid makeup.

Although the term "observers" is very true in the real world, the manipulation of the main population is anything but observing."

"Our people are the seeds that have seeded every sector of the universe. Your people will in turn spread their seeds on other planets in time," stated Jescan, almost as a defense to his situation and his people.

"You mean that your prodigies are going to in turn, spread to other planets since the background is definitely your people. I am a direct descendant of your people's and other alien's interference. In the long run it will work out all right, yes, but how do you accept the manipulation of different life forms and not feel a little regret in that you may come across an equal to your own without genetically altering their DNA?

The manipulation of the genetic codes although speeding up the evolution guarantees your species will in some way survive anything that could possibly happen in the different sectors of the universe. With me here, the manipulation is no longer necessary."

"This is before you were even thought of. At a certain point in time the species can no longer be influenced and at that point, we introduce ourselves and our technology. The introduction of the genes is a protection mechanism which is inherent in all living things to reproduce and to be able to outlive the individual through offspring, is and has been our legacy. Since I too am from the future I have as my people debated the philosophical discussion that we presently are having. We are a witness to all that has been.

"You have the capability to change it but in our past it was our belief that we as well as other species should multiply the universe with as many descendants as possible.

"The civilizations are such that we do not know all their potentials, and even when we left Edan different descendants of our species are achieving things that we did not know or would not have envisioned or conceived things that we as a people will never be able to achieve.

This legacy as you put it has surpassed us in leaps and bounds in some cases."

Looking at Jescan I realized that no matter how we sit and argue over the ethics of the situation, there was no possible way that it can be changed simply because the civilization was what it became because of the influences that were directly linked to the people from Edan and different aliens from other planets.

At the stage that the humans were right now, they had just started to develop a language that was not telepathic and nothing written as of yet, they were just starting to draw primitive depictions of events.

"Your people though, are not initiating any education or methods of influence other than the genetic introductions of their DNA . . . Why?"

Jescan, taking a deep breath, said, "Not totally true. When we lived with your people we taught them some chemistry and mathematics and biology. It is our belief that each civilization has its own means of acquiring knowledge that, as the society grows and has a need for such things they come up with their own solutions. In many ways, they come to better solutions than what we could suggest. The perpetuation is the main purpose of our involvement. The decisions or directions they take are decisions of their own choice, although there are other societies that have taught them other higher skills, as we know from the history and their documentation."

"This installation is just an observatory, even though they are still genetically changing the population?"

"This is the most economical means of observation on yours or any other planet. The genetic infiltration has slowed down now and is basically halted. I am not sure of the exact reason but at this stage of your Earth's history, the introduction of any more direct DNA would result in your species resembling us, or the other aliens, and not the humans that you do become. Remember, they have no idea as to what you evolve to or become."

Realizing that what Jescan was saying was true, I found myself almost accepting the reality of what he was saying. The revelations of the conversation were activating feelings that threw away all the beliefs of my childhood and adult life. Everything that I believed in, took on such a revolutionary change, that restructuring my concepts and beliefs happened almost instantly.

I found myself questioning everything that I believed in. I looked to the ground in a contemplating look, not really seeing anything and not looking for anything, reflecting on everything. I almost felt like I had the helmet on once again, as my mind was exploding with the new information.

Jescan realizing that I needed the time to ponder all that had been said stared off at the console, waiting for me to say something.

"Let me understand this. Your people introduce their genetic influences, then allow that new species to develop without any guidance from your people. Correction, a person is introduced into a planet and it is their task to reproduce as many offspring as possible after an average of six hundred-year life span. Then the population is allowed to survive with no guidance after the transplanted alien passes on. Only the information that the first alien introduces is the legacy of the people who follow.

Yet in the case of Earth, you introduced one man. He multiplied and then you introduced a second genetic transfer by placing several aliens in different locations. Again, you leave the people to fend for themselves. How many times do you inseminate the people of Earth?"

"There are according to the literature only isolated introductions from this period on. The other species have and still will have influence over the general populations. Your people develop their own culture and societies. This is the time when I feel I must tell you more about our people because it will influence what happens later on."

Pausing and taking a deep breath, releasing it slowly, he picked the words slowly and deliberately. "Our people, in my time, have advanced to such an extent that our females are not capable of carrying our children. We have to rely on females of other species to carry our children. Your people are very good mothers, although they never are allowed to see the baby from our people. The women who are usually picked, are women of healthy childbearing age. Some but not all are already pregnant. At a certain stage the fetus can be placed into an artificial womb. The longer the time in a natural womb the better. In some cases the child is able to be left longer if the female is already pregnant, and before full term our people remove the planted baby that is then placed into incubators to be brought to full term. The mother has her baby with usually no side effects.

"At this stage of our history, we are just discovering that our females are starting to have birthing problems. As the generations pass it will become more and more of a problem. In the future in my time all the fertilized eggs are raised by surrogate mothers."

Watching Jescan painfully explain the plight of his people I understood that this was not just the means to populate the universe, but it was also a survival of their species. "Your people must rely on other species to reproduce. Have they not come up with an artificial womb?"

"In my time we are still trying to artificially create a womb that will stimulate our offspring in the same manner as our young need to grow, but it is not yet possible."

This new information placed a new light on the plight of a desperate very scientifically intelligent society, which will be completely dependent of other species to reproduce. I could understand now why they were the way they were, considered observers in some areas of the universe, but the plight of these intelligent people was not known by the people who were sustaining them directly bearing their children without their knowledge.

"During this time though your people could still have children on their own, yet you still genetically were changing the life forms to produce possible surrogate mothers, even though at this time your people were just more interested in reproducing the universe."

"Yes . . . in a way, I suppose that we were," answered Jescan, looking down at the ground, understanding the consequences of what his people were doing.

I looked out to the compound where they had used the air as an economically efficient means of transportation. To perpetuate their own species as much as protect the new humanoids, they developed.

"Let's take a walk."

The compound was on a high mountain that was beyond the ability of the inhabitants of the planet to reach. Even if they did, they could not have known what it was unless it could have been seen from the air. This airstrip was not to be discovered till long after humans could fly. Overall it was as secure as anyone could want. The buildings were now falling apart as the people had not used the runways for several centuries. "Why have they abandoned this station?"

Jescan was behind me and came up beside me. "About three hundred years ago our people had developed a means of traveling through the atmosphere of planets without causing the warping of the metal and tile plates which caused serious damage to our ships. This advancement now allows us to stop in midair or move in any direction desired without serious heating problems.

"This also allowed us to observe the inhabitants without drawing attention to ourselves, such as an air vehicle does. This new technology is very manoeuvrable and can land if needed or can stay in one spot if the inhabitants happen to notice us. At this stage of our technology, we had the capability of entering the atmosphere and leaving the atmosphere very easily with little problems. Our ships also used less fuel than did the air transportation although at this period, it was not an important factor."

The information was an important factor, and the reality was that the events that were taking place were exactly as it had happened. I also realized that only the connection of the five planes had given me the ability to travel in time, one thing that had up until the point of connection with the planes, never been possible before.

The events should not be changed. The events were as it did happen and if changed, would or could cause irreparable damage.

I was caught in a situation that I neither agreed with nor condoned. Life had all of a sudden become very complicated but overall, probably not the last I suspected.

These buildings had been abandoned about from my estimation seven centuries. The buildings would eventually rot and over time, nothing except the ruins would be left to bear witness to the inhabitants that once were here. One thing that bothered me was they were not hiding anything. It was as if they wanted to leave their signature.

"Jescan, why would they leave a full airport out in plain view where man will someday find it?"

"This is true, although at this period it was inconceivable that these humans would ever be able to fly, let alone travel into space. We found ourselves at a stage after the second landing of our people for what would be forty million Earth years give or take. Man developed over the centuries, and at each stage they came closer to becoming self-aware and realizing that the earth was a small planet that was a bountiful planet. The realization is that there could be other life out in the universe. With the information that you have it will help both of our people and yours to know how we evolved as like the information of your life, the little atoms that combined together. Billions of years ago life started long before we ever arrived. This is how our two planets have evolved. We have in the future made some very serious mistakes yet it is how it has evolved. We have looked out for your planet for only a short time. It did very well on its own.

Our intention was that someday we would be able to meet without fear or misunderstanding. We too are looking for any information that can verify how we came to be as we did evolve from somewhere. Although our history is only from the time that fossils and relics can be found, our history is unknown as were most of yours. It was based on theories and artifacts that could be dug up.

As you know, your link was the last of the planes. We are verifying all that has happened things that we did not even know.

We are finding out. Like you, we have had little true accounts of what really happened. When the second ship arrived, you showed us that your people are the product of our people. We at that time had no idea that life would evolve to the extent as to show up on our planet as technically advanced as that.

It was something that must be protected, nurtured yet allowed to grow alone. We have found no other planet that has advanced as rapidly as this planet. Others that we have started, have begun to show the same tendencies. Your unique arrival made us realize that we were watching a very special new species growing to such an extent to be more technically advanced than we were. They also realized that we were together, meaning that we were to meet in the future and be working together. The revelation was almost similar to the turmoil you have just went through, realizing what your presence had started was a bond that was inevitable.

"There was only the report or the disc that you left, data that took a long time to completely go through then suddenly a building was erected, and the plants and animals from millions of years arrived.

The information was mind-boggling. In the years to come, the studies from the disc took centuries to complete. There was always the possibility that the disc had been placed by the government, causing many rumors and most civilians did not really believe all they heard, as the decoding of the disc which because of the amount of time, was questioned constantly.

The information was finally figured out thanks to you, and until your sudden arrival to Edan, the information was not really understood until then. As you told them they started to take samples of every living thing that was on the planet including other planets, for preservation as well as the knowledge of each species for all to be able to see and appreciate. This is how it all happened. This was what they had to do as you had directed them.

As we shall in the next period get an accurate account of the events that take place as they really happened. In this period we stopped all introduction of our genes as soon as we reached the planet.

By that time all is as it is right now." Jescan slowly exhaled as the truth had finally started to be released. Even though all had not been said, it was a start.

"Hmmm . . . Even though there are several millions of years to go to reach the period when I was born, I have to admit that it is definitely an eye-opener," I said, looking intently at Jescan as with all the new information that was inundating my mind. "I believe that it is time to visit the next period. Let's find out what really happens," I said, starting back to the *Genesis*.

CHAPTER TEN

The buzzer sounded our arrival, and looking out the window, the rain was lightly landing on the window, allowing droplets to run down the pane. We had arrived three million years later. I decided that we should take a trip around the planet before taking our usual walk. Touching the controls we traveled slowly across the land observing the landscape as it went by.

The land was dotted with the signs of man as fires dotted the landscape and could be seen from the air. The people had spread out over most of the continents and checking the northern areas first, we could see that the ice flows had started to retreat and were almost to the northernmost parts exposing vast landmasses barren and treeless.

As the ice had receded the grasses had taken the land as fast as the ice gave it up, forming massive plains that were even more prevalent from the sky, which were covered with large herds of buffalo, muskoxen, yaks, mammoths, deer, and elk. The other animals seemed to be lost in the vastness of the huge herds. Predators were present and of course man although man was very low in overall population of predators.

They were dispersed over the continent quite disconnected from the other people. In places it was common for thousands of miles to separate different units. Each unit or clan usually consisted of extended families with additional people joining as they were on their way to somewhere or was incorporated into the family unit by marriage.

I slowed the *Genesis* down so that we could watch a tribe of hunters stampeding a fraction of the massive buffalo herd that they had separated and were running the animals toward large cliff near a fast-flowing river. The people worked in the same pattern as a pack of wolves which they had studied, having people placed at the right points along the route that the animals were being chased.

As the animals stampeded by, they jumped, waving furs at the animals scaring them even more and changing the direction a little to keep them going in the right direction forming a sort of a funnel formation. The unsuspecting animals now worked into a panic, ran in the direction that was directly determined and allowed by the men.

The stampeding herd ran straight toward the drop. The final men were hiding behind rocks, in the middle of the stampeding herd, waiting till the herd had past, and jumped out at the last animals, causing them to run even faster, pushing the animals in front of them.

The men also were hidden in the grass, well out of the way of the stampede but necessary in case the animals deviated from the path that they wanted them go. Even though they were far enough away from the thundering pounding hooves, they were still remarkably close as I could sense the nervous feelings of the men.

The animals following the lead animals, ran one after another over the cliffs most of them being killed instantly as they fell, snapping their necks or their backs as they fell a good sixty to a hundred feet to the bottom of the cliff.

At the bottom of the cliffs were the women and the children. Most of the women and older children were carrying spears, bone knives and stones just in case the animals that survived the fall, charging them.

As the pile increased, the last few of the animals had some cushioning from the turmoil at the bottom, and surprisingly several survived, continuing to run over the carcasses of their now deceased herd.

The confusion was remarkable, and in all the confusion, the women moved in as soon as all the animals had landed. They rushed to the animals, cutting their throats with pieces of sharp stones and spears especially if they were still alive. All the women carried leather pouches in which they gathered the blood in large leather sacks, as it was part of the ritual that would start the feast that would be held tonight. The men gathered on the top of the cliff watching as the women and children started to skin the animals after they had cut their throats to let the blood drain out.

The tribe's camp was set up along the river the makeshift shelters spread out over several acres along the shore of the river.

The *Genesis* calculated the population number of the tribe, which consisted of 37,612 people. Looking at the monitor, I was impressed at the size of the tribe, as most tribes split up when they reached a large size, splitting and claiming a new area. Some of these splits could be due to disagreements, but most were due to a shortage of food.

Obviously they didn't have either of those problems, probably because of the abundance of food. The tribe had the resources, enabling them to stay in a larger group. As well, they were with the large group able to acquire large stores of food and skins.

Landing the *Genesis* on the top to the cliff, disguised as a large rock, we could watch as they methodically skinned and hauled the carcasses back to the camp. Using poles with leather stretched between the poles, set up in a traverse fashion, pulling them as they held the poles some cut the carcasses into smaller pieces and carried them back to camp usually on their shoulders or in handbags. The organization was remarkable, and the people knew exactly what to do showing that they had done this many times before.

Watching the remarkable speed and skill that the people used, coupled with the large number of people as everyone participated, they had removed all the animals within hours, and the meat was being carefully shredded and hung on the drying racks.

The people were a gentle caring people with the philosophy that if someone was in need if you had it you gave it to them because they needed it more than you at that time. It worked remarkably well as not one person was out for personal gain and if fortunate enough to obtain good fortune their status was increased, as they could give it to those who needed it more than they did. In their own way the more they could give away the more prestige they acquired.

Touching the controls we passed over the different continents one after another usually zigzagging across the land. Watching the people as they went about their business we noticed several larger groups or villages.

These groups obviously had control over certain territories that they patrolled regularly, especially when there were animals or other clans within their territory.

One group south of the equator we could see was about to be invaded. The one group was surrounding the smaller clan with a remarkably large cave. Obviously, they had missed these secluded hidden caves. The newly arrived smaller clan was definitely claiming a smaller territory, but this newly claimed area was strategically placed in the larger clan's hunting grounds.

This would be beneficial to the larger group to overtake the smaller group reclaiming their hunting lands as well as the large caves that they had not realized were there. The men kept sneaking closer and closer as they got to the fringe of the campsite they came running with such loud screams brandishing their spears and rocks.

The little group was obviously new to the territory possibly a fragment group that had separated from another group as it had all the indications that they had just recently set up the camp.

The camp was not old enough with the hearth being newly constructed and had been used for only a short time. They obviously had several scouts watching which had obviously reported what they had seen. The little party of approximately forty or so consisting of four main extended families with the largest being mostly young men had joined the wandering group. This group also included two female elders, eight childbearing aged females and some very young females.

This small well-organized group charged back with torches, spears, and rocks. The battle was fast and very brutal. The oncoming group was met with such a flurry of rocks and logs that were strategically placed, able to form little avalanches as well as bombarding unwanted animals and intruders such as this group, which caused several to die almost instantly at the beginning of the fight the little group striking down the larger group one after another and although they had been outnumbered three to one was dominating the fight.

They triumphed in a surprisingly short time and the leader declared that the captives were to be tied to poles like the animals that they hunted and proceeded to head to their captives' now defeated camp.

Most of the men being dragged and banged against every rock that they passed heading back to their camp several miles away moaned and screamed agonizingly, as their bodies were dragged over the rough terrain.

As the victors marched in to the surprised camp and with all the adrenaline still running in their veins, they killed anyone who showed a weapon or any defensive or aggressive move. They then rounded up all the women and the children, choosing whom should be given to whom, as the victors in an unchallenged proclamation accepted by all the local clans inherited all the spoils that at the top of the priorities were in this case the women and female children.

Next all the men and boys were crowded into a corner of the cave and guarded intently as the women and girls were selected.

The selection of the women was fast and with little bickering or disagreements, as most were jokingly whispered to another warrior or commented across the circle to a younger warrior. Although the joking was mostly in fun the warriors seriously studied the potential females, as they smelled them between their legs. Most of them were stripped down to get a better look at the newly won property. The priority was the selection of young potential mates.

The men knew full well that too many females could become a handful, as they would be responsible for feeding and clothing as well as supporting the siblings that would come. It was not in any way a joking matter as they let it seem.

After the women had been selected and standing in little groups with the new master standing in front the time had come for the men to be given to the victors to serve as their slaves and apprentices. The older men knew that they would most likely be spared as they could do tasks around the camp. As well elders were respected even if they were from a captive clan.

The warriors would mostly be banded or exiled as everyone knew that it was hard to control and dominate a strong-headed man that had been set in their ways. This was a common conscientious although some could if they were young enough be useful for hunting, as well as if taught in the art of making tools would become a very helpful addition indeed. Several talents which the men were trained in could be the determining factor of life or being expelled.

The men who had been the defeated captives which were kept as their slaves, were given a choice to become a member of the winning tribe. Unless someone insisted that they wanted the individual to be their slave he was accepted by the new tribe unconditionally as one of the clan. The individual's status in the new clan was very low in the hierarchy although was above their previous owners.

The warriors would be set into the group of men that were of no use to the new victors and would later be banished or sentenced to death.

After the long selection of women and slaves had been selected to serve the winning warriors, they rounded up the warriors and abandoned their captives' cave. Pelts and articles of importance had been gathered and wrapped in carrying furs. They assembled long lines with the victors leading their own little groups, with the last groups having the victors following their defeated group to stop any runaways from escaping. Although this was rare to be alone in the wild was almost sure death as there were so many predatory animals ready to attack a lone human, especially one who had no weapons to defend themselves.

With all the new fortune in pelts, spears, bone knives, pots, and other articles of use, they piled the possessions on the backs of the slaves, forcing them, sometimes very painfully beaten if they fell from the heavy loads. They herded them back to their cave which was large enough to support the large increase in population and were met with cheers and excited jumping from the group that had remained to guard the camp. The surviving warriors were ceremoniously lined up for public display.

The feast had been prepared for the returning victors. Well the men had collected their new booty from the defeated clan's cave. The special preparations had been started by the excited women who knew that their cave would soon have many more people joining them for the victory celebration.

Before any food would be served the captive warriors would be forced to run a gauntlet, either to freedom of the wild dangerous land or to be beaten to death along the brutal gauntlet which was usually the latter as few could withstand the unbelievable brutal beating.

They were stripped of every belonging before being allowed to run naked, being beaten on their way out of the camp. The humility was more than one of the men could handle and he walked slowly, finally standing still in the middle of the gauntlet as the beatings overwhelmed him, withstanding the rocks and sticks finally being struck down with an amazingly heavy blow to the head, shattering his skull.

He, a short few hours ago had been the leader of his people, now defeated could not have lived with the knowing he had been beaten and let his tribe suffer such humiliation.

The tribe beat him dancing around him as his body glistened with his blood as he lay in a crumpled pile staining the ground red, turning black as the air oxidized the fresh blood.

One of the men stepped forward and with a flint knife, cut an incision along the rib line exposing the man's internal organs as he reached in and pulled and cut out his heart. Holding up the still pumping heart he walked around, proudly displaying the prized possession believed to hold all the spirits and contras of the defeated leader and was presented to the leader to eat, which he did. Without a second thought he devoured the organ as he gestured his new spirits that he now possessed.

The people danced and hollered each reaching down with a cupped hand and scooping up the blood from the open cavity drinking it as they danced, as their leader stood in the center beside the fallen leader's mutilated body for all to examine his new spiritually improved body.

The next man who ran the gauntlet died halfway through the line and surprisingly five badly beaten men survived the viscous brutal beating as the men in the gauntlet hollered and jeered at the naked men fleeing for their lives, having survived the gauntlet and disappeared into the trees and underbrush, never to return or enter this newly claimed territory again.

If they were lucky enough to survive the wilds without any protection, most would likely parish. Some surprisingly rare though would be able to survive the harsh wild open country, the lucky ones sometimes coming across a group of outcasts or a fractured group that would accept them into their clan. The five men gathered together several miles from the cave and headed south, out of the territory of the new victors.

In our travels across the continents, we found more people in larger groups on the continent that would become China, Europe, and Russia. They seemed to be the most territorial as well as the most aggressive, and vast lands were dominated by a handful of rulers that controlled the land with a strong rule. The people were still very primitive and unbelievably superstitious. Generally their life was hard and although short as the average life expectancy was usually to their mid to late twenties, the very old was in their thirties overall life was in most cases, a fulfilling good life. They hunted where the animals were plentiful and foraged for plants that grew in abundance.

The hard life was in many cases self-inflicted as they could have made life easier but because of the possibility of displeasing the gods, the way that they had been taught or the way their father had done it was the way it would be done and was as their children would be taught.

The higher the statues of the elite rulers, the softer their life became with unbelievable privileges limited to a very elite few, the self proclaimed monarchs. These men wanted to control more land and more people. They in their own right created their own dynasties, and some gained land that they never even traveled to yet bequeathed to their sons, as the firstborn son was prepared and groomed to control all the areas and to become the self-crowned kings or monarchs, which they preferred with complete and total rule over their dynasty, including their brothers who had been sent to distant areas to uphold the territory in the name of their king.

The people were strong dedicated people very concerned not to anger the gods, as earthquakes were commonplace and followed their leaders sometimes blindly as they won territories in the name of their masters, or switched sides when they lost their leader by death or their lands being conquered to another tribe or clan. It was a localized continental way of life with each continent having their own individual habits and cultures, not that the life was completely decided by ruling a territory, but life in the larger northern continents was that of territories and control.

Traveling to the southern continents life was calmer than the northern colder areas. Life was simpler with minor conflicts but rarely was there the massive rush for power like in the northern areas. The tribes were more laid back and much more casual although usually, their punishment for crimes was harsher than other continents. For the most part life was more rapped up with the spirits that caused the sun to rise and the moon to follow each night, and the time of year making sure that the rains came to guarantee a bountiful food supply. These people, in some ways, spent more time contemplating than working to survive as everything was so readily accessible. They uniquely discovered the importance of their looks to improving their sexual qualities, as they spent a lot of their leisure time improving their looks.

Cutting their hair was one aspect that became common practice and eventually would become common all over the inhabited continents but was just being experimented with here where life was so relaxed and uncomplicated, food was within close proximity and water was plentiful, as the rain forests surrounded the areas.

As we traveled farther west, we came across what was a small piece of land that had recently split from Africa and was the fragmented remnants of South America. It was almost as large as the British Isles that was as of yet not completely separated, although water filled the fault line and was starting to become quite noticeable. The island was just west of Northern Africa near the equator along or about the thirty-sixth parallel. Taking a closer look the island was a remarkably luxurious island with lush tropical plants, fruit trees and palm trees.

What caught my eye on the southern area of the island was a remarkably beautiful pyramid. Looking closer, I spotted ten more, spread out over the island.

"Jescan what is this? Is this some of your people?" I accused.

Jescan looked at me rocking his head, a little uncertain of our location. "I'm not sure. Let me check the computer . . . Yes, this is what is known in modern time as Atlantis."

"Atlantis? It really did exist . . . Amazing . . .," I said, looking down upon a city to rival any in the modern world. The streets were even cobblestoned. This I could not resist. Touching the control, I landed just outside the city.

This place was remarkable. As we looked out the window, I said.

"Fill me in on what you know of this place."

Jescan could sense my keen interest. "This land was once part of Africa as well as South America. Summarizing the details, it was left behind from South America. Although it fragmented and is basically caught in the center of the tectonic plates and is presently a floating island although it is solid to the mantle. It is located on the center of the continental tectonic plates the fault line created between the largest two mass of continents.

"This island though, is situated just above the lowest sea level in the history of the planet. As the ice from the ice cap starts melting it will raise the levels of the seas. The island is imminently going to be completely flooded.

"One of the original men from my planet a very intelligent man, started a family on this island which was at that time still in sight of Africa. The younger man according to the reports made by the crew that discovered the inhabitants several years after the Edanian had expired, was surmised to be very devoted to his offspring, and it was a natural thing for him to teach his family but he went against everything that our people have been told not to do. He over hundreds of years taught his children about engineering and art. He taught them to read. He explained to them that they were isolated on an island, and that they were on a planet that was much larger.

He and his family unit built this beautiful city. Because he was so isolated by the time we discovered his island, he had left a socially educated, democratic society with an educational program with everything from mathematics to sciences.

He wrote down things he had observed, things he had known and his love and interest was in physics. Several of his students, his children or prodigies so to speak with the carefully controlled interbreeding, mentally as well as physically developed at a very rapid rate. Faster than was expected, he even selected the mates, keeping complete records of each birth. His people studied the planets although he knew they should not leave the island. He had them working on all sorts of different projects. Because of the large deposit of crystals on the island it was inevitable that he taught them to use them as a means of barter. They had boats that they traveled to the mainland and traded with several coastal groups.

This was when they also started to study the light given off by the crystals. He eventually came up with a crude form and use of lasers, and they did several things with the technology.

Although his technology was limited when he arrived, toward the end of his life his ten most promising sons set about learning the properties of the crystals and the use of light to be used as a heating source as well as keys to unlock hiding places. Two of the ten died. Their firstborn son inherited their position, their sons following and had been completely trained in the ways of their father, realizing that he would die soon, he divided the island equally between the ten. Their work was carried on by their children and they because of the educational program that he set out surpassed his every expectation.

"He also had a fascination for the marine life and he did experiments on several fish inseminating several that would take. He had mostly misses, but he did have luck with three species. One was the subtle transformation of the mammal known as the dolphin and the other was the whale, also a creature, genetically linked to humans referred to as mermaids or merpeople as he called them. He spent years with the dolphins and merpeople, as it was his favorite. The whale was much more difficult to work with and to contain them was a task in itself.

"From our people's point of view, once a life is started it cannot be changed. The sea animals seemed insignificant compared to the unacceptable educating of the people, his offspring. We have always believed that each species should learn on their own and at their own rate. Because he was so isolated everything he did was watched and learned by his children. As he did so many different things, so the children did emulating him.

"He did live a longer than usual life, even for our people. He lived close to fourteen centuries or Earth years. This island was believed to be uninhabited or simply overlooked, and inhabitants really were not discovered till approximately three thousand of your years before our people took an unprecedented first look at the educated, democratically governed society.

"The inhabitants of the island started to figure out a way to travel in the water and fished the open seas. Eventually, they built seaworthy ships that could travel the open seas, allowing for exploration and the discovery of other people in other lands. They are believed to be the ancestors or the rulers of a group of people called Minoan. They controlled a lot of the surrounding areas through an island called Crete."

"This man sounds like quite a man. Let's take a walk."

The humid tropical air overpoweringly caught our breath as the door opened, and the smell of tropical flowers emulated the room as we walked outside. It was a strikingly beautiful place. The animal sounds came from all parts of the island, and the birds flew all around, this was a paradise of paradises.

Walking from the jungle rain forest like terrain, we came out to a city of cities as modern a city as any in the twentieth century or twenty-first century for that matter.

The marble cobblestoned roads were remarkable and the buildings more beautiful than I could ever verbally describe. The lawns and gardens were amazing as we stared at the beauty of this remarkable place.

I could sense that no one had yet noticed us as we came upon the real Atlantis Island bustling with people. There were spacious pastures for the animals tended by young boys. There were fields of wheat, legumes similar to our peas and beans, root plants similar to our modern potatoes and carrots, vineyards, orchards, flocks of birds similar to wild chickens and geese whose wings had been clipped and were being tended too, close to the shelters built to house them at night, as well as wild birds landing and flying all over the island.

A common meat bird was the dodo bird which was very prolific and was a bird that was hunted and not tamed as they covered a lot of the island.

Animals that resembled water buffalo and the relatively new giraffe camels were roaming in herds as well as sheep all tended by young kids. This was an island that would be the envy of any world.

Unlike the purposes of the later pyramids on the African continent and the pyramids built in South America that were all built for the purpose of a burial tomb, this pyramid on the other hand, was the civic building, and was the center of the community where all the decisions were made as well as a meeting place. Only he knew, because of the shape it also generated power which is a little known fact about pyramids and was never revealed to his people, but when he passed away the people decided it would become his burial spot and eventually they enshrined his remains within the pyramid.

Houses surrounded the pyramid and meeting places, markets, and parks. The people had worked on buildings made of marble with spectacular statues, and water ponds were everywhere. Stone canals were connecting the natural springs that fed ponds, which ran in a direct root surrounding the city, the water finally forming a unique moat, encircling the pyramid.

There were fountains surrounding the pyramid as the water was controlled from a fresh water spring that was well above the valley, enough to have fountains in the ponds and baths all over the city.

Fresh running water was also piped through bamboo tubes to each home. Looking closer, I realized that the pyramid as well as the homes were made from mostly the same material, not built but carved out of a small solid marble mountain. Looking at the overall landscape the small mountain was a rock formation that rose about two hundred feet above the solid marble base. It uniquely had occurred in the middle of a valley as the huge hard marble rock had survived the rolling crushing effects of a meteorite, over time been pushed even higher because of the mountains in the background and as the land that had been torn apart from the medium-sized meteorite some hundred million years ago. As well, water had, over time, eroded the now older mountain, actually eroding faster, as all the rain was drained from the higher areas, passing over as well as around the smaller mountain formation. The valley ran from the high mountains in a direct route to the sea past the small rock formation.

This was the most remarkable place I had ever seen, the beautiful city surrounded by larger mountains, giving the people a means by which they were able to control the water, demonstrating their fascinating engineering skills.

The people wandered about their business, in no way hurried. The people in the marketplace could be seen walking around, looking at what was available. A man walking with a giraffe camel loaded with baskets stopped and unloaded his goods. People came over to check out his goods.

There were community baths everywhere, as people could be seen bathing in the remarkably well-sculpted fresh spring feed water pools.

Children accompanied by an adult, were on an excursion to one of the fields. Another group of older children was sitting on a knoll under the shade of a large tree, intently paying attention to the only adult as he talked with several hand gestures.

The afternoon was such as what you would have ordered if you could ever order a perfect day. The gentle breeze was blowing over the countryside. The humans and the animals were both comfortably living in remarkable harmony. The humans were at the top of the food chain with no predators of any danger or consequence to humans since they had killed all the large meat-eating predators.

The people were a remarkable people. Although similar to the people who had inhabited the rest of the planet, their height was about four feet to four feet six inches. They had the modern-looking skull, without the low brow of the ape descendants, yet their skulls were larger almost rounded, unlike the people on the mainland whose hair was dark colors, blacks and browns, even reddish brown or black.

Unlike anywhere else, this group also had blond hair, and several had light skin tones closer to Jescan's people with whiter complexions than any we had seen. The lightness of hair gave the people of this area a different look than anywhere else on the planet, although several still had dark hair and skin. The crossing of the aliens did, on first impressions produce lighter-colored hair than the humanoid apes, but we had never seen blonds among a group before. The alien leader obviously carried a blond gene that through crossbreeding as well as interbreeding, blond hair had developed in this isolated group out in the middle of the ocean. Their chin and mouth were smaller, not protruding like the people of the other areas. I could tell that they were communicating with both verbal as well as telepathy, verbal being used the most as telepathic methods were not completely understood as it had always been a source of wonderment as it could not be explained yet on the other hand verbal conversation could be explained completely. Their bodies also had lost the bowlegged appearance giving them a taller stature.

Though their physical strength was not nearly as strong as their thicker-boned cousins on the main continents, one important factor was that they although not as strong, did not have to work as hard as life was a lot easy.

There was so much leisure time. There were no self-induced rulers gained by brute strength, as the people on the continents did but from the designation of land from their founding father, designated by him as pharaohs that ruled by lineage of birth not by overthrowing the present pharaohs. The people never challenged any of the kingdoms, as the rightful birth child was automatically placed into a leader's role, and everyone was a part of the growth of the future leader. The largest part of their duties was they decided upon the disputes of the individuals.

If the decision was really a difficult or complicated decision, the presence of all the ten kings was requested once every month according to their calendar.

Turning to Jescan, I said, "Let's observe the city from a ring-side seat." I turned and headed back to the *Genesis*.

We both decided that the entrance to the northern pyramid was the best location and locating the *Genesis* in the thick walls of the pyramid, allowing us to observe both inside as well as the outside.

The building was remarkable. It was made out of marble, red and green with blue flecks throughout the marble. It was four stories high, and each story had four balconies, each open to the inside, allowing indirect lighting to penetrate the inside. Outside, there were solid gold statues trimming the corners and pictures sculpted in the walls.

Looking at the pictures made of solid gold was the recorded history of the remarkable achievements and the culture of these people. It showed the first people learning the art of the spear and the art of hunting the different animals and techniques developed to hunt. The beginning was in a crude art form as the picture was copied from one of the caves that had been part of the original cave. Then a remarkable change in the art was the invention of a written alphabetical language, as the entire section was the formulation of the picture illustrations of the phonetic sounds that they had selected, straight and wiggling lines as well as the use of circles, triangles, and squares each with an explanation explaining the different words sort of like a dictionary, the first on Earth.

Further along was the remarkable leap with the smelting of metals, the charting of the stars with the star charts as well as the symbols depicting the layout of the stars, and the use of standardized measurements, showing the standard measurements like the cube, the area of a square, and a triangle, leading to the studies in mathematics.

The water buffalo and plants for the first time had been domesticated, boasting large fields of different crops, the advent of irrigation, and the final picture depicted the young child discovering that the light from the crystal could be used to start a fire.

The art was remarkable, and the skill of a rock hammer and stone chisels with the use of a copper type of chisel or punch to form the delicate shapes of the people and the animals struck a remarkably similar look to the later Egyptian works. Most of the statues were amazingly life like, most were without clothing but some showed amazingly intricate articles of clothing and decorative pieces adorning the statues. The artist even captured the expressions on the faces, which historically did not arrive till several thousands of years later.

The soft plentiful gold was easily manipulated into the forms that was both informative as much as it was beautiful.

Looking around, the island must have produced a lot of gold, as the precious metal adorned several plaques and trimming on the tables that had been hand carved with copper and flint tools with carvings inlaid in the massive tables whittled out of solid logs of a hardwood similar to ebony, giving it a black-and-gold contrast. Several tables in contrast were made of a solid block of marble.

The chairs surprised me as they being remarkably well constructed, were woven with bamboo and gold giving an illusion of a solid piece of work with amazingly intricate artwork, worked into every part from the top to the bottom.

This was obviously a palace of one of the pharaohs with the sentries posted at all the doors, mostly for looks. This must be the public court of the pharaoh, as the ten thrones made out of gold were set against the wall, each one adorned differently with jewels. Each of the pharaohs must of had special colors, as each throne was distinct each with varieties of rubies, diamonds, turquoise, and crystals of all sizes and shapes, placed so that the dais would be remarkably comfortable.

The cushions on the seats as well as the back upright were made of the finest soft saber-toothed fur, a fur that was preserved from what was the last of the tigers on the island which because of the deep golden look, enhancing the gold from the chairs, giving them a soft glowing look on top of the fact that they had been strategically placed in the indirect light, making them almost glow translucency.

The people in the building talked low as not to disturb the pharaoh and his family as they were inspecting the room, obviously the ones designated to take care of the pyramid, as they were cleaning and polishing the seats and benches, getting ready for the pharaoh's entrance.

On the floor, there was white marble checkered with the darker red-flecked colored marble. Also, the colors lightened the very otherwise dark room. The walls inside had been carved into large murals, and round pillars supporting the balconies, which ran from the floor up to the balconies, had figures carved into the marble on the base as well as on the top with the center of the columns smooth, perfectly circular, spanning exactly two cubits wide.

In the center of the checkered floor was inlaid with different colored stones, making a mosaic design of a large sun. Different designs similar to zodiac signs were in each of the four corners of the sun. Along the walls, there were also globes. At first, I thought they were globes of the earth, but with a closer look, I could see that they were navigational symbols for travel on the open sea with all the astrological symbols of the stars, placed exactly as the stars were in the sky, placed on marble stands. The red marble with the contrasting white made for a cheery pleasant atmosphere.

The water surrounding the building was not only used as a community bath but also for sections that had fish swimming in the fresh water moat. The fish was prevented from leaving by grids set over the overflow canals. Some of the fish were very large and would make a delicious meal. Since the looks of the fish added to the overall beauty, the fish were rarely eaten, as fish abounded in all the other natural ponds, lakes, and rivers. A short walk from the city, this island offered so much potential. I could easily understand why the alien had found it impossible to not use the natural raw materials to enhance his as well as his children's life. I unknowingly though could sense that the large bulk of the design was the work of the sons of the alien with no indications of influence from him.

The people went about their business till late afternoon when everyone started to come in from the fields. The people gathered at the base of the pyramid, and everyone took their baths in the refreshing water, parents and children laughing and playing in the water or sitting on the side of the pools, rubbing oil into their skin, or just splashing one another in fun and laughter.

The society was remarkable and very affluent with lots of leisure time something that was casually taken for granted, giving the people time to invent and time to sculpt. Truly, a paradise in such a virgin world.

As soon as they had finished bathing, the men started to dress in a formal cloth made of loosely woven animal hair. It was very similar to the later developed toga. After which, they filtered into the pyramid.

This was the time for the pharaoh to arrive, and the men gathered in a half circle quietly waited for the entrance of the pharaoh.

The pharaoh made a grand entrance with his personal guards entering first displaying their wooden shields and spears with pounded silver and gold metal tips, one of the guards announcing the pharaoh's arrival.

The people all bowed as the pharaoh entered. The people stayed bowed till the pharaoh sat in the throne, raising their heads only when he was seated.

Some of the individuals knelt before approaching the throne and we watched as the pharaoh, in all his glory, listened to the complaints made by one of the men, and then he listened to the other man. After a long pause, he gave his decision. The man making the complaint was definitely disappointed. Bowing, he accepted the decision and pulled several stones out of a pouch he carried around his neck.

This went on for quite some time, as the people approached the pharaoh, accepting the verdicts sometimes angrily but always controlled in the presence of the pharaoh.

This society had developed a calendar that was similar to the later Jewish calendar, and there were people designated to keep track of the position of the sun, the moon, and the stars. Occasionally, the pharaoh would confer with the people who studied astrology and then would make a decision based on their information.

One thing that the alien had done on first impressions was explained the basics of government, or did he as I could sense no influence from the alien. Although they had the basics, and overall the court was simple, the people took and elaborated on all the knowledge known to them, things like the remarkable architecture and the concept of standard measurements. Seeing the society and realizing that the people had catapulted themselves into a modern-day society, that would be envied by almost every future society on earth that knew of the rumors of this remarkable island. The island with all the riches and the climatic conditions would contribute to the most idyllic society, not to be rivaled for several thousands of years even then never as utopian, as was this setting.

"Before we carry on to the next period, let's go back and see this man and watch what he does as he has caught my attention," I said as I looked out at the amazing society.

Jescan looked interested, as he could finally find out what really happened with the man who had gone against everything that his people stood for as well as what he personally was taught. Touching the controls, the buzzing noise sounded our arrival.

Looking out, I laughed as I realized that we had landed in the middle of the mountain. Resetting the controls, we relocated the ship on the top of the mountain.

Looking out, we could see the man's camp. He had collected several females from the mainland and had moved them to the land, isolated only by a narrow strip of land slowly sinking, as the island was still in its infancy, as it still had a small fraction of the land that was still connected.

The land though was through several massive earthquakes shortly after their arrival and was completely separated within a period of a hundred years after their arrival had moved out to sea a good fifty miles already isolating the island. I could sense that later, it would settle just on the other side of the horizon, as it could not be seen from the mainland, although if the people had been aware of it from the tops of the highest mountains, it was still within visual sight from the island although restricted by the weather usually allowing a mirage image to give the sometimes usually clear image of the land to the east of them.

The small band of settlers had set up a camp in the crevices and caves of the same mountain we were sitting upon, giving us a perfect observation point.

The females ten in total, set about their various tasks from collecting firewood to collecting eatable vegetation and herbs to improve the flavors of the meals that they cooked. The lush jungle of the island assured them of a continuous and bountiful harvests.

Several of the females were already carrying siblings, and observing one of the females, she had the coloring of a light washed-out brown with a dominant large white birthmark covering most of the upper front of her body, part of her face, and part of her back. She was unusually marked, but it was her sibling that caught my eye as the child was I suspected, the oldest of the children on the island. The child she was carrying was a definite albino with the characteristic red eyes, because the child could not stand the sunlight to any great extent, she spent most of the time in the shaded areas of the island.

The child was almost four years old and was starting to discover the wonders of the island. He was well formed straight legged not as bowlegged as his mother. His face took on the characteristics of the alien father more than the others, as his cheekbones were set higher and his mouth smaller and not protruding as much as his mothers.

The people changed their attitude when he was around. They believed that animals of any kind that were white-skinned white haired, although extremely rare, were a good sign from the gods. They looked upon this boy child as a good luck sign from the gods, as he was the first born on the island, and the rest of the clan revered his presence and beckoned to his every wish. This could be the occurrence of the blond people, not from the alien as I first thought.

The man spent his days hunting and fishing, generally alone, because his oldest children were not yet old enough to leave the side of their mothers. We could see him, looking at the land, observing the landscape, and then sitting down, he would use the dirt as a means to transcribe the ideas so he could look at his idea. Shaking his head, he would erase what he had sketched in the ground and then would carry on hunting.

There was little that this group needed, as the island supplied for their every wish with the variety of fruits and vegetables as well as the bountiful fish in the seas and lakes as well as the animals on the land they had little trouble feeding themselves, and the people were strong and healthy. Their routines were easily accomplished in a very short time, leaving them with most of the day to laze around, playing most of the day away.

Some of the women had collected seeds that they liked to eat and had stashed them in the ground and was amazed when they started to grow. Fascination prompted them to allow the plants to grow and to their amazement, turned into the same plants that produced the same seeds. With this discovery, several of the women started their own gardens, and most spent the leisure time of the afternoons tending to the plants that they had started.

Each time they planted their seeds they, with sticks would work a larger area of ground. The weather allowed for them to grow year round, so they continually were planting and harvesting the small crops.

Looking at Jescan, I said, "We should see what they have done in ten years, as they have only been here about five years, and they have already started to grow crops. None of which had been influenced by the alien father." Touching the controls, we moved ahead another ten years.

The people had not changed much, although the children were now adults and were starting to take mates for themselves. They in turn, were starting their own families.

The group was now over thirty strong and, although very attached to the rest of the group found that the cave was starting to become very cramped, and they started to make extra room by smashing rocks against the cave wall and found that they could increase the size of the cave without finding a different location. The little rooms continued to grow as they found that the stone although very hard would crumble under the constant striking of another rock. They also discovered that within the stone was hard shiny stones that would not break as easily as the red marble and was excellent rocks to chip away at the walls.

Also, they discovered if the shiny clear stones were struck in a certain manner, they would expose brilliant stones that shone in the light and looked impressive.

They had also discovered a very heavy shiny material that was easily pounded into different shapes as gold and silver were abundant in large veins buried in the mountain walls. This was the discovery that started them into using the soft pliable metals at first practical purposes like a bowls to hold water or food and some then carried it even further as they could make rings to wear around their arms which the sounds of them clinking together delighted them, and several then started working the metal, making all sorts of interesting things.

The father was teaching the young men the basics on how to hunt and to fish, and the boys learned very fast, and there was always fresh meat and fish served at every meal. The hunts usually never lasted longer than a half a day as the island was abundant with game.

The albino boy had grown to the stage of taking a mate and he had carved out a little cave for him and his new mate which had pure light reddish brown hair with light red skin mostly she had a very large birthmark that was completely white covering several parts of her body still very apelike in coloring, although she had a slender, more upright build. She was carrying their first born which was born a whitish blond colored hair with eyes that were predominantly blue with slight streaks of light almost hazel brown, around the pupil in the unusually wide eyed baby boy, the first true blond to be born on the planet as far as the *Genesis* records indicated.

She soon was pregnant again, when the child was almost a year and a half old. She was preparing for the arrival of the second that from the looks of her would be in about a month's time.

"This was not directly from your people at all. It was from an albino who started the first blond children," I said, looking at Jescan.

"Our people do not have hair, although originally we must have had similar hair follicles. Although, through evolution it has completely disappeared from our species. We have developed a skin that will withstand the hot rays from our sun. Our makeup is that we do not need to have hair follicles that allow perspiration to escape.

We have oil follicles that produce an oil that protects our skin as well as cools us down." Jescan understood the implication of the hair, realizing that I had thought that it was because of his people's genes that the color of the hair was inherently decided. "We as a people, do not transfer color, as we have a lack of pigment which gives us a whiter look. Although the white birthmark of the mother may have some of the characteristics of our people's lack of pigment, genetically, we do not transfer color."

"Amazing. I thought that it was because of your people that the hair was lighter . . . Interesting." I moved to the console. "Let's see what happens in the next ten years," I said, touching the controls.

Looking out the window, the group had now grown to over one hundred. Most of the original females were still alive, although they were very old for the life expectancy of the time. Life was very good in this place and because of the unhurried lifestyle, the people were living longer. The major predators like the saber-toothed tigers were almost wiped out from being hunted as the dens were raided and the young usually being killed. The crops had been organized in neat rows and covered now several acres of land with the women taking great pride in the very productive gardens.

The women had the men carved out special rooms that they stored the crops in so that the seeds would not germinate and could be planted as they wished, whenever they wanted.

The women had also discovered the rising power of soda collected all over the island and when they cooked, they threw some in to the finely ground flower that they had recently ground and found it was making it rise and was very light and became a favorite bread.

The women had also discovered that the water buffalo could be milked and given to mothers whose milk had dried up too fast or could not nurse for as long as was common among the childbearing females, even the females that did not have children and even the men found it to be a refreshing drink when the milk was cooled in the streams. The women also found that added to flour, it made a tastier, fine, light bread.

The females had several children each and there was no slowing down as the young were now starting to take mates that had been approved by the leader and were having their own young.

The population would continue to grow unlimited because of the overabundance of food the island offered.

The men had started to plan a way of diverting the water so that the women didn't have to walk so far. The alien had taught them the differences between one item and several items using their fingers to indicate how many they wanted, in a very rudimentary way how to add and subtract. Basic though it was, it was the start of an educational program that would continue to be elaborated on for thousands of years.

The people, with a lot of thought had decided to start to divert the water with groups of men and young boys pounding the hard rock of the island to develop the start of what would become a remarkable undertaking. Their father sat back although watching intently, was only advisor and used to settle the disputes as to whom should do what or deal with which of the many suggestions on how to make the water run with the least amount of resistance and would be used.

Watching the man with the people, I realized that within this setting and situation the men would have made the canal anyway. His were suggestions that they had already decided upon and would have eventually found out for themselves. Watching Jescan, I realized he was re-evaluating his perception of the means by which the people had acquired so much knowledge.

Looking at me, he smiled then looked back at the men working on the canal. "He never suggested that they do it. They had decided to do it with or without his help. This is a different picture of what I had been told. The literature that I will someday write suggested that he was not all to blame, but I was so positive in my beliefs that no matter what I read, I had a hard time accepting his innocence. I realize that I must get the message across much better than I did," he said, contemplating how he would reword the literature.

Smiling, I turned and walked to the controls. "Let's check out the next hundred years instead of ten years," I said as I touched the controls.

Looking out, we could see that the people had developed the canal, and the mountain had been gouged out into several apartments.

The group had decided to start work on making the mountain into a grand meeting tower, starting with a square base a start towards a pyramid shape, that it somewhat resembled as the people had carved out individual homes now on all four sides of the mountain with water running to each of the four sides. Surprisingly, the decision was to start at the bottom and to build up.

The water had already been diverted and was running through the small apartments of the people which now have exceeded a thousand people. It was the consensus of the people that the individual apartments must match the design set out by a master plan that they came up with as a group, and with the construction of the canal, the people built close to the canal and started building freestanding buildings, as the rock was easily stacked to form walls instead of carving out of the mountain.

The dream that was drawn on the thin sheet of bark was what the city would finally look like as we saw it, although there were some changes, as the eventual tower was not a tower as much as a pyramid-shaped tower. The tower was eventually incorporated into the later developed pyramid.

The plan worked well, and the city developed over the next three hundred years. Everything that the people developed, their father, only made suggestions limiting his input to possible options, never did he suggest things, although he spent more and more time with the animals of the sea and his love for the animals, like the whales and especially the dolphins, and a branch from the humans that had started to live back in the ocean and had adapted unique qualities, allowing them to dive deep and to stay underwater for longer periods similar to the dolphins, which were increasing as did his experiments, artificially inseminating them to also increase their intelligence.

He seemed so very old, yet he was so very healthy. He had outlived generation after generation and was considered, rightfully so the ancient one. He now devoted his time to simply observing. The people came when they were stuck or had a problem to overcome. Not once did he break the laws of the Edan people. As the centuries passed, the people came to him purely out of respect, most often to help solve their problems similar to a child asking a parent for help.

The people had developed boats that they fished out at sea with. They never ventured further than the ability of seeing the land, and for all intent and purpose, there was no need to go any further as the sea was so bountiful that they only had to drop a basket into the sea and pull it out, they would have a loaded ship within hours.

When they had come to the stage that the population had grown so much, it was no longer practical for the population to live in one city. It was at this time that one of the blond descendants directly traced from the albino child came to the now ancient one and showed him something that both surprised and impressed him.

The boy of sixteen set a piece of wood down on the ground, and he reached into his pouch and pulled out a crystal. He caught the sun's reflection and, holding it for several minutes, started the wood burning. The boy was so excited he wanted to have one in each of the homes so that when the people get up, the fire would already be started and ready to cook on.

At this stage the ancient one looked at each of his most astute descendants of the ten founding females. His selection was relatively fast as he knew each one individually, and had made his selection from the different lines as each generation came. He knew that each one was capable of the task at hand, and he expected no objection from the people as he knew each one. As they turned of age, around thirteen, each was told that they would carry on the legacy of their ancestor.

A lot of time was spent explaining how each one descended and their history. Each one was given a document of bamboo paper with their lineage set out. Only the first son of each family was given the paper, which was handed to his first son. He called upon the ten. The decision would be made as time would be the judge not letting them know that this was as much a test as much a method of finding out how compatible the groups could get along together to solve mutual problems. The ancient one decided that there would be a five-year limit.

The group set about figuring how to use the crystals that were extremely abundant on the island. The ten made remarkable advancements and even discovered a method of using the light to open small hiding places within buildings as well as in large storage rooms filled with jewels as well as gold and silver.

They never did develop a perfect heating system, as the clouds would hinder the crystal effectiveness but on the whole they did remarkably well. Over the course of the five years, the two oldest passed away, one from a heart condition and one from appendicitis which burst causing him great pain, before dying. Each was succeeded by their firstborn son.

The ancient one decided that each should set up a city within the ten boundaries that he described in great detail. All the people would, within reason follow the king whose ancestors they descended. If one of the families from one ancestry decided to live under another king, for personal reasons, marriage or preference it would be allowed, but the kingdoms were set aside for each of the ten families. The first born of the entire ten families would take over the existing city, but it was the responsibility of each king to help the other king even after the cities were built and if disputes arose, all ten must be involved to solve the problem without fighting as each family started out with the same father. Each was a brother to the other and each shall abide by the decision of the court of pharaohs. "This, as you are all my children, is the fairest for all and mates should only be taken from one of the other groups, not from your own group."

Watching the ceremony and the exactness of equality was impressive, and the skill of the ancient one was now approaching his one thousand thirteen hundredth year. He still solved most of the problems and helped with the construction and design of the cities, as they all wanted to make a city that was better than the original city, although none ever met the same quality and beauty of the original city with all its history. Each in their own right had uniquely different characteristics, which made them extraordinarily individual.

The father of this small group of humans passed away before the cities had been completed and long before it was discovered by the Edan people.

This island disappeared as the earth's crust was constantly moving, and the island would simply be covered by water possibly just sinking. The legends and rumors would strike the spark of excitement and romance of discovering the ruins of the lost city of Atlantis. The rumors gave rise to a myth, giving rise to a legend, did it really exist.

"I think that it is time to check out when the island actually sank.

The original history will fascinate several cultures." With this, I knew I was reflecting on the literature that I had read when I was in school, but now there was a certainty about the facts. As in any legend, within the legend, there was always some truth, no matter how remote. This made me glow with a good feeling that impressed me as to the legend that I had the actual documented knowledge about.

Contemplating the possibilities, would I be able to find out the secrets that have fascinated me as a child, for that matter, even up to the present age? Before I happened to connect with the sixth plane, this would have been a dream, a dream that most people at one time or another wished for.

Within myself, I realized that I would see all that I wanted to see.

This really surprised me, as I had always believed that I would have the ability of seeing it for myself. Possibly, I somehow knew my destiny before it became a reality. I remember as a child I did not really disbelieving what

I was told but just that I always wanted to actually see it for myself and be able to draw my own conclusions of the situation.

This remarkable gift, or was it a gift? I now can see and do everything that I could ever desire with so much still to learn about. I can actually see, although it still seemed so outrageous. Why me? What is my purpose?

Do I think that I could be so privileged as to be the only one out of this entire plane to be chosen as the one to witness and record the history of our existence? Does this mean that there is a purpose for me other than to live as I am or was? I asked myself, touching the controls to take us to the collapse of this beautiful paradise-like island.

Jescan turned to me and looked deep into my eyes. "I fortunately have the privilege of being a witness to the unique things that have been a history of both your people and my people, although the story has just started in the interrelationship of our people and your people. As the world would look upon the incidents that happen and will someday be such an eye-opener for everyone, the reality of our connection is quite significant," he said, looking away as he spoke.

"Okay. Fill me in on what you mean. Is there more interference, or should I say how much more interference did your people do?"

"The history is the history, although it is surprising that your people were not more aware of us as we tried to let your people know of our existence."

"You mean that your people have tried to explain that their presence was, and still is here?"

"Yes, we have tried. I regret with dismal failure," he said, looking back at me, almost like an apology, although it was more like a matter of fact kind of a statement.

Looking out the window, the island was just as beautiful as it was the last time that we had seen it.

"Warning, this location is not stable enough to exit. Land is melting two feet every hour," the computer cautioned as it reported that the danger was eminent.

Touching the controls we moved up sitting just about cloud level.

We could see the entire island dissolving like an ice cube on a hot day.

The island was dissolving in front of our eyes. People were scrambling to reach the boats, although there was not enough room to hold all the people, and as soon as a ship carrying the kings were full, they headed out to sea. People were scrambling to find anything that floated small boats and large logs. The people were panicking like nothing I had ever witnessed.

The island seemed to have certain areas that were disintegrating as we watched. Looking closer, the reality of what was happening was quite surprising.

The people in the quest to discover the unique effects of light from the crystals, were causing the island to simply melt. Even though the island would have been covered with water eventually, it was not the melting of the ice caps that was causing this disaster. It was the laser beams generated by the crystals.

The streams of light were reflecting into all areas of the island.

The people had set up a relay of light so that if the island was partially covered with clouds, they were attempting to transfer the light to furnish all the homes with heat. The relays ran from one end of the island to the other. The intense amplification of the beams was passing through the rock, and the earth below was heated up, as the molten lava was exposed to the intense heat. Watching the direction of the beams, the people had placed seventy-five of the largest crystals in different areas of the island. As the light was intensified from crystal to crystal, it was literally melting the very ground that they stood on. The realization of what was happening only came to them on the second day as the testing had run across clouds, covering most of the island the previous day, except that there was one crystal that was relaying to most of the island. The people were rejoicing, as they had thought that the problem with the clouds had been solved. They unfortunately never calculated on the next day. Being sunny all over the island, the beams of light were generating enough energy that it dissolved everything around them, as they had been placed to accept light from all different directions.

No one even thought that they could have stopped the melting and, in some cases, stopping the light from traveling through the crystals.

No one had thought of covering the crystals. They panicked and ran to the water, as they knew that the trembling island was starting to melt under them.

The ten kings and their staff and all their families boarded their private ships. The fishermen loaded their ships with as many of the panic-ridden people. People left with rafts and logs, basically anything that could or would float.

The ships returning from trading on the main continent of Egypt and Italy, were near enough to see that there were problems on the island as the shock waves were already making travel on the sea difficult.

The island suddenly heaved and like sand dropping to the bottom of the sea with large tidal waves crashing in from all sides. Some of the fishing boats loaded with people sank as the tidal waves struck the small boats. The majority of people did make it though, and the new quest for a new home would now start.

Most of the ships had basically lost sight of the other ships. A few found one another, struggling to stay within sight of one another as the waves crashed and heaved all around them.

As the day wore on more and more of the ships came into contact with others slowly regrouping as the waves crashing all around them.

Each small frail group finding companionship with the other ships' presence set off, each group traveling in a different direction as most were completely disorientated. Three ships laden with people headed off to the west as in all the catastrophe they were pushed west, floating out to the sea that had never been traveled before. Their trip would be the longest, yet with relatively little loss of life, they would land on the South American soil.

One group from the northern end of the island traveled northeast, ending up north of Spain, not even aware that land was just over the horizon, headed farther north than they expected, ending up in a mountainous land that would later be known as Denmark.

One group landed on what would become Spain, traveling south around a jetty of land and ended up in a country that would become Greece, another in what would become England, two groups landed on mainland of Europe, and the majority of ships went east to the continent of Africa, traveling around the northern tip and ended up along the opening of the Nile River. One group tied logs and rafts together and made it to what would be called Sweden. Another made it to what would be called Finland.

Although the groups most would, in their lifetime never see one another again, the one group that had the most significant influence on the world as a whole was in the area along the river Nile, where the largest group consisting of several of the soldiers had traded in many of these areas. Some of which were still in that area, not knowing of the disaster, and were informed that the island had sunk to the bottom of the sea. These people set up residence near the mouth of the Nile River the start of a seven thousand year dynasty.

The stories from the people of Atlantis kept alive the memory of the marvelous city of Atlantis and of the rich land that was lost to the sea.

CHAPTER ELEVEN

The areas that these people landed had small clans scattered throughout and as of yet was still not very populated. With their ability to control their surroundings the children of Atlantis quickly controlled the areas that were to become their new homes.

The people on the continent were primitive and easily manipulated, allowing the Atlantis people to introduce their pharaohs or kings and have them accept them as their own new leaders.

With the use of their telepathy, it was easy for them to understand their perceptions and the use of their language almost instantly.

Although the locals could sense a difference when these new strange people were around for the most part, they did not even realize that they were having their thoughts scanned when they were in their presence. They simply knew that they were in the presence of a different type of person than they had ever experienced. They not only understood that something was different but they also mistook it for a true deity to be revered and listened to as these people held so many powers that they could use as they wanted. To them, it was like being in the presence of a god.

The areas that they did land almost immediately started to prosper and within the first year, started to dominate and influence the culture and lifestyle in many areas.

The kings started to gather large tracks of land, enslaving several people in their quest, as the people were already in the mode of warfare. As well, the people from Atlantis had learned extremely fast the advantage of war with the spoils going to the winners.

The new transplanted people soon trained several fine soldiers and started to overtake several new lands as there were no defined countries as of yet. The areas where the leader was able to maintain their borders were referred to as the land of whichever leader was in power.

The main continent really had not changed much, as the people of the continent were still a barbaric group of people that was quick to go to war. If some area looked like an easy take or they desired something that they had they would raid the area, taking whatever they wanted.

The majority of people worshipped all sorts of gods, and with the introduction of the people from Atlantis the pagan worship was quickly absorbed as the main religion, which would remain so for several thousands of years.

Watching the way that these people controlled their new homeland was an amazing feat. With their air of superiority, it was easy to influence the local people who showed their new guests their most polite manners and unknowingly, were manipulated to follow these newcomers blindly surprisingly never questioning. This also was the first time on Earth that there was a class distinction. As the king and queen were at the top, the others who had arrived with them were the second class, and the local people became the lower class referred to as the workers or commoners later to be called peasants, which were the working class. As well, there were the slaves, sometimes treated worse than animals, or to put it in proper perspective animals were treated with more respect and dignity.

One of the ships from Atlantis had continued on to an island which would be called Crete, and from there proceeded to a land that they had traded with, later to be known as Greece, within a very short time was controlling the territory and surrounding areas.

Taking a walk in a territory later to be known as Greece, which was an isolated territory with little invasions, as the land was a place where everyone voted or made all the decisions as a group and worked well because the majority ruled, this was the area where democracy had its beginning. Life was basically very simple with very little disruption from the outside influences.

Wandering up and down the small narrow streets among the citizens was a unique experience, as we had not been among people for quite some time it seemed. As we had stayed secluded on the island, we would have been noticed immediately as outsiders, and although we were noticed as outsiders here, it was accepted, as wanderers were quite common. Although watched and observed cautiously, we were allowed the freedom to travel the small town at our leisure.

Something surprised me as we overheard a small gathering of people talking about the different gods. One man was making a remark which all the others listened to so intently, as they had never thought or heard such a statement before. The discussion was that instead of all the different gods there was one the divine ruler, and was all the gods showing himself as many different gods but really was one in the same.

I immediately could sense that this man had been in contact with Jescan's people, and even though he could not remember the entire encounter, he had obviously pondered for some time on his loss of time.

As he was trying desperately to explain to himself what had happened, he was exercising his mind as he pondered over his lost time. I could tell that this had happened several months ago, and although he never divulged his secret, he was now trying to explain the weird occurrence by suggesting to himself that he was somehow changed.

Through this discussion, he was venting a possible concept from the overstimulation of the brain, as he tried desperately to answer questions that he had on his mind, and although completely not associated he had deduced that everything that he thought about must be of a relevant nature. So many thoughts had traveled all the used pathways of his mind. Obviously, this idea had kept coming up over and over and still, he did not have an explanation as to what had happened to him during his lost time . . . what was he secretly introduced to.

He was still searching for the answers, answers that he would, in his lifetime never answer, although he was to become a thinker and a philosopher.

The basis of the story as I was filtering through his mind, was formed through the legends passed down from generation to generation, the first man called Adam. It was a logical conscious conclusion that if one man started all mankind, then one God started everything.

Even though he had it in his mind that he had been made to think this way, there was definitely no influence by Jescan's people in his idea. It was strictly his own thought.

One thought that was subconsciously planted was that they were not the only creature that were intelligent in this universe. The concept of universe from his perspective meant heaven or in heaven where the stars were, and he could not imagine that it was not solid, as it looked solid from his perspective.

I could understand what the aliens were trying to do to prepare the people of Earth to meet part of their history. Although the thought was planted there, it was not easily solved as first they had to understand that the planet was floating in a vast empty space a concept that would not be realized till the invention of the telescope or for that matter, to realize that the Earth was round and not flat.

One of the characteristics of the aliens' ways, was for the truth to be discovered, not taught or explained.

"Jescan does this movement toward one god have anything to do with your people, or is it a natural occurrence?" I asked, knowing that most of what I had witnessed made me extremely leery as to the concepts that I had just witnessed and relaying to myself what I had been taught from a very young age being totally changed, never to be as innocent as I was before.

"The concept of a oneness is part of our philosophy as we believe that the universe is the creator of all. Our people have been trying to directly handover the facts for centuries. The people have in most cases misinterpreted the things including the objects that we left for them.

The people of this planet, as the size of their brains are getting larger, they are trying desperately to figure out why and how they got here.

As the original manipulators are no longer here to explain, and no one asked as they did on the island of Atlantis, he was there to answer the questions nothing more, nothing less." Jescan relaxed a little bit and continued, "We as a people do not intend to hide anything from any of the planets that we visit. The answers must be asked though, in order for them to be answered. There comes a time when the answers will be asked and the answers will come. The people of this planet did ask, and the answers were coming. Interpreting them was taken in several ways, as several things did happen. The time in history is very close."

"You're saying that when your people are asked questions, like Atlantis when the people asked him questions they got their answers?"

I paused for a moment. "The ancient one only answered questions when he was directly asked. You thought he had told them, without them being asked."

"From the evidence, we could only speculate that he had told them. We had no idea that he was following what was set out in the rules. He was falsely accused and this will be straightened out.

He also never gave them more information than they asked for which is how we have believed it should be. Because of the abundance of everything the extra time that was available, allowed the people the luxury of thinking. The questions were not direct questions as much as they were problem solving." Jescan paused, thinking of what he knew in regard to the history he had read. "Our people used the naïveté of the people to continue to study them physically as they matured. Your people have started to advance in some areas at this period. Our experience is that the more a group of people are occupied, the slower the questions. If it is harder for the people to survive the fewer questions are asked."

"You mentioned that the people did ask. What happened and why did the answer not come?"

"I believe that we should see it as it unfolds rather than me repeating something that could be different than reported. Your people all of a sudden have been overtaken with the people of Atlantis, which were not used to hard labor. They were thinkers and philosophers, and artists.

Although they were and are capable of heavy labor they spend more of their time finding out how things can be done easier, or faster as the case may be, due to the fact that they were technologically ahead of all the other populated areas throughout the planet. This is a new concept for most of the people of the large continents as they existed from meal to meal, season to season, most of them not thinking of a way to make it easier as much as that is how it is done, as they were taught.

"The people from Atlantis bring a lot in the way of questioning how things are done. These people are now spread all over the world.

It is like the arrival of the first occupant of my people. He had no concept of what he did. Although being isolated, and very self preserving, he, in a small sense, was the reason our people actually proposed starting to develop life on other planets. He lived his life not knowing that he would affect his people in this manner or as much as with your people."

Sifting through the information that Jescan had brought up, I knew many other questions would still have to be asked and answered, one included someday if a man from Earth landed on another young planet, marooned and alone, would the same situation arise?

"The largest group of Atlantis people landed in the Nile river area. Let's visit these locations and find out what happens," I said, touching the controls to land on the northeastern area of Africa. "Let's take a walk," I suggested.

Opening the door, the heat of the day was stifling, as the sun was reaching the high point of the day, and the heat rising from the land made the land move as the heat waves rose to a clear cloudless day.

The local people were very much wanderers following the herds of animals across the land setting up camps in convenient areas, most often used in the past year as they had for generations past which was close to the herds as well as near the watering holes, an essential necessity for all animals, man, or beast.

This nomadic lifestyle made the people take great pride in the herds that they followed as though they owned the herd and, in a way they did.

The small bands traveled light. The camps consisted of tents made up of usually soft light furs formed in a circle with fires started outside the ring to fend off any animals, although usually, there was a main fire in the center for cooking even then, the outside fires would take priority, if wood was limited, especially at night.

These camps were able to be moved within minutes because of the scarcity of caves in this region, especially near the watering holes. The makeshift tents could be folded up and packed onto their backs, as the people had not yet tamed any animals.

They did, to a certain extent follow the wild dogs as they could scavenge their kills and the dogs hung around the camps as they tried to reclaim their kills. The scrapes of food that was left was quite often thrown out for them as their way of thanking them. Even though they did not realize it, there was a bond that was slowly evolving between the dog and humans.

One particular clan was along the coast of the ocean and had seen the floating logs, as in their perception was all that they could comprehend, with people standing on top of the logs on the water or, at least in their minds, could be the only explanation of what they were seeing. The men started to follow the floating strange-shaped logs to find out as much as they could about this strange vessel, possibly help them if they could possibly come close enough to reach shore.

The small band of people could be seen close to the horizon, and they were heading toward the mouth of the river, about forty miles away, where the sea and the river formed a large delta. They had seen that it was stopping along the mouth of the river and was running so as not to lose sight of it.

The people from Atlantis landed near the mouth of the delta and quickly sent out a scouting party to make sure that the land was not inhabited with people that were not friendly as well as to discover the best location to set up a new city, as the location was primarily a good location with plenty of good soil, water with lots of vegetation, as well as the wildlife seemed, on first glance, to be abundant. The ideal spot it would seem. They cautiously observed the small group of people coming over the horizon still very far away to present any immediate problem. The wanderers were still a long way off. They were proceeding to the site that they had last seen the floating log.

The new group set up a camp with all the abilities to defend themselves near the mouth of the river, of course, leaving the river as their means if necessary to retreat into, if these people proved to be to strong or too many to overtake.

The scouting party reported that there were only fifteen people in the group coming toward them with limited arms or none at all. It was a group that they would not likely have to worry about. Although they proceeded to unpack, they did ready for a battle.

The people had already surveyed the area and were ready to move to the location that they had agreed would be a good location on first impressions for a city. When they had made their escape from the island, they also brought some of their animals as well as some of their seeds that they had stored. Some had brought some chickens and some geese, but the ones that would change how people looked at them, of all the animals, were the three giraffe camels and the water buffalos that had survived the swim and had landed safely, as the people coaxed the animals to follow them. Several were packing their things in the hull of the ships and on the rafts and were preparing to load them onto the camels, after they had rested from their long swim, when they spotted the wandering nomads coming ever closer, running in a slow easy gait that allowed them to cover several miles in a very short time.

Being prepared for the strangers, they gathered their spears and held them visible but not aggressively. They just wanted them to know that they were armed and ready for them.

When the small nomadic group of about fifteen people arrived, they stayed well back from this strange group that to their great surprise and wonderment, had the power to control animals. This was the most unusual thing that they had ever witnessed, as never before had anyone ever been able to control a wild animal. The expressions on their face were totally mystified by what they saw. *Were they gods?* they thought, as coming from the sea was like coming from the sky.

"Who are you? Do you need help?" the leader yelled from about two hundred feet away as the leader stepped forward with his hand outstretched in a friendly gesture, not approaching too close.

The king motioned one of his staff to approach the man offering his hand in friendship. The introductions stumbled along, as they had trouble understanding each other's language. I could tell that the man from Atlantis was starting to use telepathic means to communicate, and the Bedouin, although not realizing that his mind was being read, was amazed, as the man started to communicate verbally as he started to understand portions of the unfamiliar language.

Curiosity had brought the group, as they had seen them traveling along the sea and saw them landing on the beach. They, in very simple terms, were wondering where they had come from, as ships had been sighted in the distant horizon, because the people from Atlantis had been in this territory before but never been seen up close as this ship was.

They studied every part of the circular-shaped ship that had a pole in the middle supporting a tent like covering. The ship had been built large enough to carry heavy loads and had enough room to carry grain as well as livestock, such as the water buffalo, which ordinarily not be on the ship except that it had already been loaded with the other gifts, that were to be given to the pharaoh of the fifth group. Luckily, it could still hold several people, as they had filled the hull from wall to wall with about thirty people, and several had held onto the sides of the ship as these were one of the few floating objects that was at the time was also the closest.

Their curiosity started out on how they were in possession of such a fine means of transport. They dubbed it a floating abode, or house, that made them seem to have come from the horizon of the sea, which to them was like coming from the sky. Standing looking at the ship was secondary to the animals that they had tied up to some bushes along the bank beside the river with their attendants standing beside them in case they had to be moved quickly, something they had never imagined possible. This encounter would change forever how they would look at animals.

The soldier turned and approached the pharaoh, explaining the curiosity of these people. Understanding the message, the pharaoh welcomed them to have a drink of a strong cup of tea with them. He never got up, as one of the staff relayed the message to the visitors.

Accepting the invitation, the small group huddled together, cautiously moved closer to the larger group, avoiding the animals, as they had never been so close to an animal that they had not killed or another animal had killed, and they had chased away the predator stealing their kill. Slowly, they finally came to a stop in front of the pharaoh.

The small group had never seen anything as grand as the king dressed in these remarkably beautiful furs and jewels around his neck, arms, and legs with a large tube like white hat that was flat on the top trimmed with gold and gems and diamonds covering most of the crown with a fur lining that allowed the fur to form its own ring at the base of the crown. Never had they seen such things. In their minds, they thought that they must be gods. What had they been sent here for? Were they good gods or bad gods?

The staff explained to them that he, the pharaoh from a distant land of Atlantis, had decided to settle on this land to make his kingdom on these banks of this river.

The people were impressed by the pageantry and the unique skill at which they could talk to them, and they immediately, without even a second thought, asked if they could join the king and his clan.

The pharaoh pondered for a moment, as he thought of how he was going to accomplish all that he would like to see happen. The more people that he had willing to serve, the better it would be.

This was a good start in the process of building the city he could already envision. He studied the group as he poured the tea, making a unique ritual that would be watched and copied from that time forward. These men were mostly naked. Some had furs arranged across their shoulders and wrapped around their heads to protect them from the unbelievably hot sun, a few in ragged loincloths. Looking in the direction of their weapons, mostly sticks that had been hardened in the fire, some large rocks used to beat a beast to death. In all respects to the life that he had just come from, these people were so primitive it would be very easy to control them, especially with their ability to read their minds, an ability that was rarely used, an ability mostly forgotten by them.

"I will give you my decision as soon as I have a conference with my council. We shall reconvene in one-half hour. You shall have your answer at that time." They took their leave, leaving the guards to explain what was going on as they entered the ship, the king, his wife and his sons, as well as the head of the military and two cousins.

As the group of nomads had no concept of time, they stayed close by just in case they missed something.

Using my telepathic powers, without alerting them of my presence, I focused on the inside of the ship where the king was talking.

"We need to increase our population, and these people could be a good start. As well, they will supply a start to the workforce that we will need. If necessary, we must allow the people of this area to join with us. These people must have contacts within this area. We could set it as an invitation to any and all that would like to join with us. In return, we shall offer them our protection."

The queen spoke next. "We with extra help, can start planting our seeds even before we have built our homes. We have more than enough to feed us, and after the first crop is harvested, we can increase our fields to handle many people. This valley looks like it offers an adequate food supply."

"I agree. Let's offer sanction and protection to anyone who joins us in our rule of this rich valley" came the voice of the eldest son of about fifteen.

Leaving the tent, the head of the military announced that the king would now meet with those requesting to join the clan.

The small group moved closer to hear the decision of this strange new person calling himself pharaoh.

With the majesty of a great leader, with great pomp and deliberation, he decreed, "My decision is based upon my deepest extension of our friendship . . ." He took a long pause as though contemplating something. "My decision is . . . yes," he said, pausing to study the reactions on the faces of the new proposed members to his clan.

"First, you will prove yourselves worthy of serving me. I shall request that each of you shall be welcomed, as I shall extend my hand in welcome to any man, woman, or child who would like to join our group, as from this day, whoever joins shall have our protection. You must swear to uphold our laws that we decree for the good of all. If you swear to uphold these laws, you can report to the chief of the military and document your name as well as any skills that you can offer."

A bewildered look swept over their faces, as for the most part, they understood, but what was this about skills and documents? These were somewhat beyond their comprehension, and they were directed to a table that had been brought out of the ship and set up. Then to their amazement, a thin sheet of bark was laid out on the table, and a feather was laid out as well with a small strange shiny container with a liquid inside from the sound of the sloshing, as it was shaken before it was placed beside the sheet of bark.

The leader of the group started to explain that they could track animals, and they were excellent hunters. They knew where the fresh water was inland from the large river, as their families had wandered the lands for as long as anyone could remember. They knew almost every person or clan that wandered the territory around this area of the river.

The pharaoh again offered a ceremonial tea that would become a tradition that would survive to modern day. He waited till the tea had been drank and the exchange of agreement that they would come and join their group had been completed. The newest members of the land that would become known as Egypt.

The next week, they would move to the location that they had surveyed and would decide if this would be the site in which to build their city.

The nomads had no idea what a city was but agreed to go with the group, setting out that it was understood that they would retrieve their mates and families as soon as they arrived and helped set up the camp, as this was all they knew of a thing called city, thinking it was their name for a camp, and in a real sense, they were right, just that this camp did not move like they were used to.

The pharaoh instructed his people to finish unloading the boats. The supplies that had been loaded on to the boats, which were supposed to have been delivered to one of the other kingdoms, now became the start of a new life. The grains and the rocks of gold, the crystals of all sizes, which were to have been used in the heating of the homes, and the animals that the people had been quick enough to grab before they boarded. The king's wife had brought her favorite pet, a large feline similar to a small panther, which she had raised from birth. She had used the milk of the water buffalo to raise her, as the mother was killed, and she had taken pity on the young animal.

The pharaoh had also brought two buffalo. Fortunately, they were two prized pregnant females, which were to be a wedding gift to the one of the other kings. The three giraffe camels had been forced to swim, as the keeper stayed with them, herding them into the ocean. The large beasts were loosely tethered to and followed the ship and were almost lost because of sheer exhaustion. The exhausted people and three heavy-laden ships, ten makeshift rafts strung together that later were tethered to the main ships, and now this unique group of people had landed in the lush riverbanks of the Nile.

Several weeks later, the site was finally decided upon. The location that they had selected was several hundred miles south of their original landing site, and it was finally decided that a site twenty miles farther down the river would become the first spot to camp, as they proceeded to the chosen location.

The animals were herded down the banks of the river. The animals as well as the ships made for a spectacular sight. Never had these things been seen before, as live animals had never been seen in the company of humans.

The people the local inhabitants who had started filtering from all the different territories including the original wanderers and their mates and families, as the information traveled fast, though out the land, they traveled down the river as they had heard of these strange new people who had arrived on the shores, where the large river meets the sea.

The people who had been traveling along the banks of the river were met by this strange entourage. As they came closer, they started to follow them down the river, totally amazed at the sight, as the string of rafts was being pulled by the lead ship as the rowers worked against the current, allowing the people on the shore to make better headway than on the water.

By the time the boats had reached their destination, several days later, there was probably a hundred or better following this strange group of people.

The people started to set their things down as the ships came to a stop and was turning toward the shore. The people who were herding the animals started to make ready for the arrival of the ships and rafts, which waited patiently for the preparations to be made.

The people were lined up in two rows along the shore by the ones who had walked with the animals in preparation of the pharaoh's grand exit from the ship. The people who had been caught up with the unique assemblage were awe-inspired as the ceremony proceeded, something that had never been seen before.

As the pharaoh and queen exited the ship, the pharaoh placed his family colors on his cestrum in preparation for the land to be claimed in his name with such a calculated timing and showmanship, as the entire crowd was watching every movement of the pharaoh and his family.

With all the color and showmanship that were possible with such few props, the procession started as the guards walked in front of the pharaoh and the last guard announcing the arrival of the pharaoh.

The pharaoh, followed by his wife and family of three sons and two daughters, paused before stepping onto the ground and, with loud cheers, stepped onto the land of his new kingdom. The first task was to claim the new land, and with the colors flying from his cestrum, he held it high as he walked to a high point on the bank just above the flood line and raised it high, plunging it into the ground. As the king's cestrum or staff was strategically placed on the bank of the Nile River, the pharaoh claimed this land to be his and for all generations that follow bequeathed to his heirs from this day forward.

The local people had no idea what was going on but were not long in joining in all the pageantry, as they cheered and danced and clapped at almost everything that was said, even though several of them did not even know what was said, as the language was very mixed with the purity of the Atlantis language and the mix of the local dialect, so as the new members could understand parts of what was said.

Within a short time, they were also starting to take articles that were handed to them as they started to unload their heavily laden ships and set up a temporary camp for the pharaoh and his followers. The makeshift tents were set up by late afternoon. The pharaoh ordered the work to commence on the construction of the new city.

The pharaoh walked to a grove of a larger stand of trees and ordered it to be cut down. Several of the guards ran forward with a copper-edged sword, cut and hacked at the smaller tree of about five inches wide. After a short time, the tree had been made into a very large cestrum with one branch that was chopped off to a sharp point, projecting about six inches from the base of the staff, and the rest of the staff was stripped clean of branches as well as bark, almost resembling a small stick plow.

A couple of water buffalo were brought to stand beside the makeshift plow and were securely attached to the stick. Walking behind the buffalo, he carved a trench in a very large circle that would become the new capital city, his first city in his new kingdom.

As the late afternoon drew near, the men had set up small rock boxes consisting of a flat large rock with four cut rocks placed in a rectangular shape on top of the flat rock. These rocks were bound together with the strong cords from hemp to be the cast for his bricks, each being measured to the same width and depth as the first one.

The collection of dry grass was started, and large haystacks were quickly formed, ready to start the blocks used in the construction of the buildings.

The pharaoh was quite involved with the architectural design, knowing exactly what he wanted, and everyone was falling into some aspect of making the brick casts, or gathering grass, or collecting clay from holes that were dug along the shore of the Nile River.

A large pit was dug that would be used in the mixing of the clay and the grass, which would allow enough water to seep in to make a nice moist clay brick.

The pharaoh spent the next week with his group of stoneworkers, starting to lay out the plans. The local people watching this strange group had never seen plans or people drawing pictures on the bark of bamboo before and were quite often shooed away, as some got so close that the people who were writing and drawing were unable to see what they were doing, as usually a head would appear in front of them as the totally fascinated onlookers would be bent over, studying the markings that had been made. It was a very comical thing to watch till the pharaoh ordered the guards to keep the people back so as they could complete the plans.

The pharaoh and the men walked the area back and forth. The water was a main concern that the pharaoh had, and was dutifully agreed with by all the workers. The area that they had surveyed was higher and safer than most of the flood-prone areas of the river, and they squatted and squinted and walked and discussed.

All the other people gathered large amounts of grass and clay or stomped on the gumbo-like mixture of grass and clay every so often, stopping as another group would carry handfuls over to the casts and fill the casts, leveling them off as they had been directed to do. The clay would stay in the cast till it had started to dry enough to be able to hold its own shape then was carefully sliced with a hemp cord, forming perfectly shaped bricks, then along the base of the flat rock, carefully lifted, was gently carried then set the clay bricks placing them carefully on a flat surface where they dried in the sun.

After the bricks had dried for about two days, they were gathered and stacked carefully in an ever-growing pile, preparing for the day when they would start building the start of the city, which would first be the palace for the pharaoh and his family.

As the sun was setting on the sixth day of their arrival, the pharaoh had finally agreed on the location of his palace. The spot was on the highest part of the hill and was overlooking the desert as well as the river. The area was staked out, and although massively different from the pyramids that they had come from, they had their start in the land of Egypt.

The pharaoh declared a day of rest, and the building would commence the following day.

I turned to Jescan. "Let's see how they do in five years," I said as I headed to the *Genesis*. "But let's get some sleep first," as we had been awake for nearly twenty hours, as the workers had risen before the sun came up, and they had not slept too much, as the excitement was mounting, as the material for the construction was reaching a point that the bricks that were made would carry the builders for a good two weeks, giving them a good head start and plenty of time to keep well ahead of the construction.

Looking out the window, the city was coming along very nicely, as the palace was functional now, and the people were building their homes around the palace, completing the look of the city.

The local clans, mostly wanderers, must have attempted to attack and capture the new city, as it was becoming a remarkable-looking city. There were guards to patrol the area around the city and were stationed every two hundred feet or so.

There must have been several attacks on the city, as the homes under construction in several areas of the city were pushed over and looked as though they had been rammed by logs. Some of the areas also showed signs of recent fighting as bloodstains still were on the sides of the buildings and on the ground.

Several groups of people had been shackled together with ropes and were being guarded around the clock.

During the day, they were used as slave labor, usually stomping in the mud and grass, making the bricks for the palace as well as the houses, which they had probably damaged, and now were the main workforce.

There were four classes within the clan—the pharaoh, of course at the top his nobles, which were his relatives from the island of Atlantis, the overseers, the people who had joined the group after they had arrived, and then the slaves.

This morning was cooler yet the heat waves over the desert could be seen starting to distort the land, and the promise of a hot sweltering day was eminent.

Jescan and I noticed a small band of people crawling along the banks of the river and another group sneaking from the other side and one group coming from the desert side. The group had armed themselves with spears and shields. One of the groups started the attack, and the guards all started to defend the side facing the desert.

The opening left by the guards running to help fend off the attackers was quickly taken advantage of, as the other two groups rushed the palace. Killing the guards at the entrance, they quickly gained access to the inside, and they swarmed the palace.

The queen was sitting with her maidens and was taken totally by surprise, as the men approached the maids all gathered around the queen.

Just as they were about to grab the maids and the queen, several of the feline panthers crossed with the wildcats of the desert started attacking the men. With the fear of these medium-sized cats coming out of no were, it was as though the gods had possessed these animals as two of the men with their eyes scratched out crumbled to the ground. The wild instinct took over the cats as they went for the throat, suffocating the attackers. Nothing like this had ever happened before. The rest of the men, seeing what these cats were doing and had done, scattered, fleeing for their lives, as the cats seemed to come from everywhere.

The attackers, scrambling through the streets of the new city, most were caught, as the guards stopped them before they could leave the city, running right into the guards as they were looking behind them, looking for the possessed cats.

It was as if they knew that these men were going to harm the queen, and after the attackers left the cats settled down almost as though nothing had happened. They pranced around the palace as their adrenaline was still running through their veins.

The pharaoh and his guards ran from the fields as he had seen the commotion and was surprised to find everything under control.

People rushed toward him telling him of the remarkable cats.

Looking a little bewildered, as the queen came forward and told him what had happened, he could hardly believe what he was hearing, although the attackers' bodies were still in the palace room and visible claw marks, as the cats had scratched their eyes out as they hung on their victims' throats till they had finally suffocated the attackers as well as the captives that were rambling on about the possessed cats.

The pharaoh was so taken aback. He sat on the bench in front of the queen's room. The cats had saved his queen whom he really loved.

With a long pause, he finally stood, and he proclaimed to the crowd of people that every patrol guard surrounding the palace will be escorted by a cat, as the cats shall help scare any potential attackers. As a matter of fact, he continued that because of the surprising acts and the completely remarkable story that had unfolded. The cats would now be honored with the dignity deserving of a protective god, for obviously, the sun god was speaking through the cats to protect all the city dwellers from attacks. All the guards at the doors of the palace shall also be escorted by a cat, as from this day forward, it is law to protect the people of the palace and the city.

I turned to Jescan. "The cats saved the day, and it's still only the early morning," I said, smiling, as I found the pun funny.

Jescan smiled and said, "This is a very special day, as scientists have been trying to figure out what role the cat played in the Egyptian history."

"You mean that cats were an integral part of the history of the Egyptians? I had no idea. I must have missed that in school," I said, pausing as I remembered statues of a cat, the mummified cats, and drawings on the walls of the pyramids. "That's right. I do remember now. The Egyptians domesticated the cat, which was the foundation of the modern cat. Interesting, but . . . raised to the status of a god?"

"Let's see how they are doing in the next five years," I said, touching the controls.

The city had risen to a magnificent city. The followers had increased in vast numbers, as the king now had absorbed several tribes in the surrounding area. The city was bursting with these new arrivals, and new houses were increasing at a surprising rate.

In the distance we could see the base of a pyramid was in the beginning stages being built in the desert to the south and west of the city.

"The pharaoh must be starting the pyramids. This interests me, as the scientists could never figure out how they built them."

Jescan showed mild interest. "The people of Atlantis had already built pyramids. Why would it be hard to figure out how they were built?"

"Before I left my time there was never any information, only speculation that the city of Atlantis ever existed. Now to find out that they were the reason Egypt flourished like it did, is a remarkable feat."

"That is why you were so interested in the island of Atlantis. I'm sorry I never understood why," he said, looking at me, apologizing. "In our literature the island was well documented as there was such an uproar over the person believed to have told the society the things that were not allowed by our people. We have volumes of text of the surprising accomplishments of these people. I thought it was common knowledge."

"Looking back, I realize that we knew very little about our history. There were new discoveries every so often, but the real truth was not their only speculation. When I left, people were still not sure that you existed. Although in the trance that your people use, it gives them very little opportunity to ask questions."

Thinking of the life I left behind, I realized that I would never be able to return to the simple uncomplicated life. "We will return someday to my period, although I will look at things from a different perspective. We'll see if the planet is ready for this information. My intuition says that they are not quite ready, but we'll see."

Jescan looked out again to observe the city. "Should we take a walk?"

"Yes, let's walk but first let's change our clothes so that we can blend in to the people."

The heat was bearing down, and the dryness of the air made sure that there was no question in our minds that we were in a desert. The heat radiated from the ground as much as from the stifling sun. The garments that we wore felt like they were going to be too hot, for a day like today, although as we walked, we found them to be quiet comfortable and protected us from the heat of the sun. The sandals, although protecting our feet from the hot sand, were a little thinner than I thought they were. Next time, I'll make them a little thicker, as the heat from the sand penetrated the soles.

Walking toward the construction area of the pyramids, we could see a large raft of logs with the circular ships at each of the four corners, carrying the large blocks of granite carried from a quarry up the river a ways, arriving at the shore where they were about to unload.

The workers had already set out a road from the previous block made of timber coated with animal fat strung out across the desert.

There was a large number of men as well as buffalo all lined up with long hemp rope tied to a block of granite. There was also a long line of men mostly young boys along each side of the timbers, each holding a clay pot. As the men pulled the block across the land, the boys poured lard on the timbers to reduce the friction. I was impressed as I watched the men. I noticed that an unusually tall man placed a box on the large block before they proceeded, and the animals then started to pull the huge block across the desert.

"What is going on here?" I commented as I watched the man as he walked beside the block.

"I am going to say that looks like an anti-gravitational machine."

The man was also very tall, "I think that he is a Blue Avian as they promised to help the pharaoh build the pyramids.

Again, I was caught off guard.

The block, once started, slowly slid along as the men and animals labored with almost all their strength. The process was slow and very exhausting, and the men and animals were changed every four hours, allowing the one team to rest before their shift started again, as they traveled the long trip to the pyramid, which had a ramp already raised to the second layer.

Standing on a sand dune, we watched the men laboring as the block slowly moved toward its destination. We could see the lard buckets being passed back, as they were emptied, and new ones being passed up the lines, as the need for lard was extremely important.

We could see the masons working on the block that had just arrived the day before and was meticulously chiseled with copper tools.

The process was almost slower than the block being moved over the desert, although they skillfully handled the tools although not unheard of, rarely made a mistake.

The women were also present rendering the fat for the timbers and cooking the vast amount of food that was necessary to feed the large number of men. They had set up a small city of tents, as the men never left the base of the camp, except to bring a block from the ships. The smoke rising from the ovens and the cooking areas were impressive, as the cooking area was almost half the size of the city of tents.

The smell of cooking barley and the smell of bread and meat cooking were even reaching us, all of about a mile away. In the fields by the river were the water buffalo herds, not only for the labor but also for the meat that all the men received each day. The one thing that was the most powerful smell was the garlic as it was used in almost everything. We could also smell the odor of the men, as the sweat was reeking of garlic, which also reached us through the slight breeze blowing our direction.

The pharaoh was watching the proceedings from a tall hill just outside of the city and was sitting in a gold chair with a man slave cooling him with a large ostrich fan. The pharaoh sat under the shade of a covered gazebo drinking a red wine, the sweat dripping off his brow, as the alcohol was showing in his actions.

The pharaoh was sitting with his priest, the overseer, and his eldest son.

Taking a closer look I could sense that the priest was not who I thought. This was a taller person, and his head was that of a bird. He also had what looked like feathers. Looking at Jescan, I could see he already knew what I wanted to know.

"This is the Blue Avian people. They play an important role in the history of the Egyptians and Aztecs as the pictographs on the walls portray. They actually traveled to many locations throughout the world. They are the ones who teaches them calculus, trigonometry, and mathematics and basic scales, levels, and they also taught them the rudimentary electrical battery for lighting, which they forget, or lose after the Blue Avian people left," commented Jescan, looking at the group.

The pharaoh was now an old man in his late forties and knew that the pyramid would never be completed before he died, and his young sons of twenty and eighteen and ten years were watching at his side, as their task would be to complete the pyramid, hopefully before he died, as this was to be his burial tomb. Listening to their thoughts without them being aware, the Blue Avian called himself Ra, the sun god.

The pharaoh and his eldest son watched with great interest as one of, the blocks had finally been finished, and was being moved into place as the one that would succeed his father. The one side of the second level was almost complete, as the base had just about been completed.

The base was almost complete. The last two stones would complete the base, allowing for the second level to be completed, and the work seemed unbelievably slow as the work had been started about six years earlier.

We decided to go back to the ship and follow the progress as it will be in the next five years.

"This is a remarkable era for your people during this time. The island of Atlantis advances the different societies in countless ways," commented Jescan as we entered the ship.

"This is the time when great areas were being built up," I said, thinking about the remarkable accomplishments that the world was going through. "Have you noticed that the young children are looking more like the modern man even more with the amazingly promiscuous lifestyle of the people, as orgies was a very big part of their life? The children produced were definitely offspring from the Atlantis people, as the brain was larger as well as the lower jaw was slowly giving way to a higher cheekbones, characteristic of the Atlantis people, although natural development was also occurring, as the brain size was growing due to the increase of calories obtained from the meat that was becoming a normal part of their diet now and, although several remarkable physical changes overall, was at a stage that man was now protected from the animals with the power of the larger clans, which stayed together building in numbers as the population grew, the refining of weapons for defense against almost any animal or human. .

Overall, the influx of the lighter-boned Atlantis people was becoming the norm, as the males chose lighter-boned women, as it was not necessary for them to be as powerful as was required in the past.

As well, the promiscuity of the women's preference was given to the men who had a larger skull, as well as higher cheek bones. In a way, it was becoming a norm to select a mate that was in fact a form of selective breeding. The large-boned people with apelike appearances were slowly being breed out of the society."

"Come to think of it, the Atlantis people also landed on the shores of South America. Let's take a trip to South America where, if I recall, they too are building pyramids," I said as I touched the control.

CHAPTER TWELVE

Looking out the window, I could tell that there was a large population of people in this area, and the influence of the Atlantis people could be seen in the overall look of the place. We landed on the west coast of the continent where the people had started to build their start of the pyramids. This fixation with the pyramid was as it was in the African continent to build a city as beautiful as the first city of Atlantis, although it was somewhat different here in this southern continent, the circumstances were quite different, I turned to review the information gathered by the computer.

According to the computer, the bulk of the southern and western parts of Atlantis had grouped together, consisting of two pharaohs, their immediate families, and their followers. There were 260 from the one kingdom and 272 from the other kingdom. Regrouping several miles out to sea, as the waves had pushed them far out into the open sea, there were 5 ships with 10 makeshift rafts as well as the 30 loose logs that people had grabbed onto. Floating in close proximity to the other ships, they managed to tether the rafts and the loose logs together, allowing some movement among the people, as it was very crowded.

The ships did contain the normal compliment of supplies that were standard on each ship—two bags of grain, two bags of onions, a jug of water, and some tools—but most of the cargo were fishing supplies, as they had been fishing along the island's coast. The livestock consisted of a few chickens and geese, which some of the people had grabbed.

Everything was limited, as these ships had not been loaded down as the ships were that had carried on to the Nile River. The few chickens and geese that the families had snatched up would be the first to be eaten. On the whole, the people had gathered their precious stones and jewelry. As well, some had grabbed some supplies, such as a sack of grain or bread that had been made, although most of the articles brought were of no use to eat, as most were prized possessions, such as gold plates and utensils. Some brought articles that were aesthetically of value yet were of no use to them on this floating ship.

The people were thrown out to sea with very little in regard to supplies, and water became the main priority, as there was little on board, and dehydration quickly became a factor. It was discovered after the first night as the sun rose that the dew had developed on the canopies over the ships, and catching containers were used to gathered as much as it would give, using any container that was available; and although water was available, it was less than adequate to sustain the large group of people. It, though, meant that there was fresh water, which was the difference between life and death for this stranded group.

Within a few weeks, signs of scurvy started to set in and was to become the major concern of the people, especially the young and the old.

Fish was plentiful, as they could almost reach overboard and grab them, they used the nets and baskets to net the fish, and although there was no way of cooking them, the moisture contained in the fish was enough to help curb the ever-present problem of dehydration, as the sun was relentless, as a high-pressure system covered most of the ocean area and was dominating the skies. The ships had been carried by the currents, and during the third week out to sea, scurvy started to dominate the main ailments of the people. The ability to even eat the meager rations that they allowed them, most were too sick to eat. People started to expire.

A young girl was the first. The people suddenly realized that their lives too were very close to this little girl, as they too did not know how long they would be stuck out in the open sea. Each person gave their sad and sincere regrets, as there was a real possibility that they too would be next. Accentuated by their own sicknesses and the heat that had become unbearable, adding to the cramped conditions, the stench of sickness was ever-present with an occasional breeze to carry it away, only to return, as the wind would die down again.

The fourth week had arrived, and most of the people were very sick and could barely raise their heads when one of the people on the raft spotted birds flying over the ships, causing a minor stirring of the group around him as they watched the birds, and within a half hour, land was spotted, causing even the sickest to take notice. As many as possible started to row to the land and soon was grinding to a stop, as the boats ran aground on the rocky beach. The people had landed in an area that would be called Venezuela.

The people helped those who had trouble standing or walking to a nearby river that was running into the sea, from somewhere in the interior, and drank and drank most of them, making themselves very sick, as too much water too soon was not good for them. Afterward, they started washing themselves of the saltwater that they had used to bath with, getting the smell of vomit, sweat, and strong body odor off their skin.

The people then turned ravenously to the plants and started to even eat the leaves off the bushes and trees. The need to fill their stomachs as well as the need to have vitamin C was so great that they craved green plants. Any plants would do at that moment. Although they needed fruit to give them the larger amount of the vitamins, at this point, they were ravenous for any plants.

Within a very short time, coconuts and bananas had been spotted and were shaken off the trees as well as some that were able to climb for the bananas. There were also berries that had started to ripen and were devoured as quickly as they were picked.

The people were so caught up with the excess food that their painfully bleeding gums and lips did not stop them. Slowly, as they had their fill, many still would eat only to have it come right back up, as most were still suffering from scurvy and dehydration, as the water that they had drank was still not in their systems yet. Things did start to settle down as the wild feeding frenzy was over.

The men started to survey the land, looking for any inhabitants, possible smoke rising in the sky, or any signs of activity; yet all that could be seen was lush trees, undergrowth that blocked out most of the jungle behind it. There seemed to be no signs of humans anywhere and, although on a continual watch, would not find any in this area.

After several weeks of simply recovering, the hunting was good as their first kill was a slow-moving sloth that started to rebuild the proteins lost from their time at sea, and fruits were collected, as there were many different varieties present in the lush jungle.

Surprisingly, they only lost twenty-one in total, and the remaining group was gaining in strength as well as their health was improving on a daily basis. The women were the ones who suggested that they move to a better location, somewhere that they would be able to plant the few remaining seeds as well as an area that was more open, possibly a location that they could build a city. The discussion was started and was soon agreed to move to a better location.

The group had devised some spears as well and had made some machetes to be used against the jungle undergrowth.

They started to use the ships to move farther west and even attempted to travel up several of the rivers that seemed large enough to allow the ships to travel up the rivers, although most of the rivers had several waterfalls that would stop the ships. It was decided to abandon the ship and as many belongings that could be salvaged was.

They traveled west along the coast for as long as they could, but because of the terrain, they started to travel across the land, going through unbelievably scenic land but none that they were satisfied with to stay. They traveled for nearly two years. As the terrain was so unbelievably rugged, some areas took two days just to cross a raven, let alone the thick jungle undergrowth, until they reached the west coast, where they started heading south, where the land started to give way to more open areas of grassy land. This was an area that was more to their liking.

The human habitation of the southern continent was still very limited, as the migration from the North American continent, which was limited, was just starting to trickle down along the west coast.

The people from an island heavily influenced by the aliens known as the Annunaki, on the west side of South America, calling it self, Mu also knew their island was slowly sinking and they had started transporting all they possessions to the larger continent

All in all, there may have been a total population of twelve thousand humans, and these were spread out over the middle northern areas, several inhabiting the areas along the Amazon River. Some had moved south and were as far as what would become Argentina. Several lived in the mountainous areas of the Andes usually in isolated small pockets. The people from Atlantis never came across any of these pockets of people till they had traveled along the western coast, where the land gave way to the plains, just to the south of the thick jungle lowland terrain.

The Atlantis people had decided to build their city on the southern part of the plains in a beautiful valley later to be known as Lima, then they traveled inland to an area which they called the Cusco Valley, and the two kings decidedly would work together to build two cities as soon as the first city was completed.

They would split and form two kingdoms always being connected but similar to the island they had come from, would control their own areas as the survivors were almost equal in their numbers, each from the different kingdoms. The first city was built in the middle southern area at the base of the mountains to the west, and the river being their chosen location, accessible to most of the northern regions in the land that would become Peru.

As well, there was a little known landmass very similar to Atlantis, which also was situated over the titanic plates, but on the west side of South America. This island they called Mu', was also sinking but the people were aware of the slow disappearing of the land. These people were exiting the island with ships that they had built and used to in the past to travel to the larger continent for gathering some of the plants that the shamans used for medication and health concerns, as several of the plants did not grow on the island that they lived on, but the people were now in the process of moving to the larger continent.

The first encounter with local inhabitants came just after the construction had started on the first city and was a small tribe of about two thousand people, as they were following and moving with a herd of wild llamas. The people could not believe that these strange people would like to be stuck in one location. After they figured out what they were doing, the logic was incomprehensible to them. Although, some decided to stay and help, unbeknownst to them that they would quickly be absorbed into the new society, as life was well structured, and was surprised at how these people could feed themselves without following a herd although to start with it was their curiosity that kept them interested enough to stay.

The remaining about three quarters of them carried on to the north, where they spread all over the northern continent as well, as the southern continent.

We had arrived about fifteen years after they had landed on the west coast in the northernmost part of the continent. The population, now with the additional people from the island that they called Mu', was breaking the three thousand mark and growing, as the remaining people from the island continued to arrive, and the second city was under construction, inland and farther south in the area that would become the Cusco Valley.

The kings had decided to have and keep some communication between the two kingdoms, and they had set up paths that would be able to be run as well as with the capture of some of the local llamas, which they domesticated as work animal similar to what they did with the camels of the island, giving them a means to transport goods from one area to the other. The llamas though were restricted and reserved for the exclusive use of the royal families in the beginning.

Eventually, the local people would continue to domesticate them, but as it was now, the royal families had control of the animals as well, most of the inhabitants of the west part of the continent came under their control.

The unique setup was remarkable, as the communication and trade networks became an integral part of this new life on this new continent, and would stay that way for thousands of years. These links would eventually spread all down the interior, the west coast and the east coast linked. The northern area was not infiltrated as much because of the dense jungles, and the terrain was very treacherous.

Although the west coast was accessible, it was not used that much. As well the connection of the north and south continent was still very recent as the two land masses finally came together. The unique lifestyle was almost, in a way, paralleled that of Atlantis in that they built their large cities, and they had a remarkable trading arrangement soon in time with all the cities that would eventually span the west coast. Although, nowhere close to the size they would become with cities reaching a population ranging from 50 to 150,000 people, these cities were still relatively small with populations, averaging maybe 10,000, at most, although grew to remarkable sizes in the future reaching several hundred thousand people.

They also discovered a plant that produced a sweet cob and would be called corn, that they saved the seeds and started to grow them, which would become a mainstay of their diet. They also discovered a plant that produced a large red fruit that was added to their diet, later to be the known as a tomatoes. They also discovered the coffee bean, which became a drink that they called Jaffa. All in all they added several plants that they started to grow, which is still grown to modern times. The undertakings of these people, although was as remarkable as that of the eastern continents. Though the leaders used their managerial skills in remarkable ways, the cultures of the local people also influenced their way of life, and the sacrificing of live animals was a practice that was adopted, as the people were very sure that the sacrifices were what gave them such a bountiful harvest and good fortune.

The local people believed that blood was the life's energy flow, especially from the royal family, and over time became part of the Inca's beliefs, as they called themselves Incas.

This belief I realized was because the different aliens always wanted a blood sample as the people believed that they were gods, this became a very strong belief. In order to please the gods, it became a means to show the gods that they need their good favor for the crops, or for rain, or a number of different things, each having a meaningful importance to the individual making the request or the offering.

Even though it was never a part of the life on the island of Atlantis, the local people did have a strong religious background that was pagan in that they had many gods. Although they were very proficient in the transcendental healing, they worked a lot with the centering of the body and was remarkably adept with the laying on of their hands similar to what I did when curing certain ailments.

This fascinated me as this gift as I looked at it, was as far as I had assumed me being the only one who had the control that was necessary to work the tremendous amount of energy that was released.

How unbelievably arrogant of me, as I suddenly realized that the energy that I was using, was something that was within every human. The knowledge and the practice was all that was needed, I commented to myself.

Watching the priest, or shaman as they called themselves, use the healing energy was a unique experience for me, as I could tell that he knew and understood what he was doing. Sensing the chemicals surrounding his hands, and although invisible to the naked eye, I could visually see the energy flowing from his hands.

It was, at this point, that I had recalled meeting a man, in my time who had done a lot of work with the government as well as with the police, who had said that the energy generated was a physical energy that could be recorded and measured and he physically could bend a fork from about four feet away. At the time I had pasted it off as a line that he was feeding me. I was surprised that I had not connected the encounter with this man, with the power that I had used several times. This was no gift. It was the natural part of the brain that could generate and focus vast amounts of energy. Most people though would live their entire life and not realize that this ability was something that everyone had within them. All that was necessary was to access the part of the brain that could control the energy.

I watched this man perform a minor operation, breaking up a bad case of gallstones. Through the use of the energy, he pulled the stones out of the patient's body without any physical cutting of the skin. The priest soon held three large stones in the palm of his hand the patient got up looked at the stones and thanked the priest, accepting this as a natural common practice not even realizing that this was unique as it was, as I discovered only used in three other continents.

Although versions of this practice were common throughout the world, none was as competent as the shamans of South America, although North America was the origin of such talents, as they had studied the inner body. India and Tibet would later be able to claim a similar mastery of the ancient practice of shamanism.

The next operation was one that repulsed me, as it was a young boy who looked normal, but by the slowness of his mind, I could tell that he was a product of severe interbreeding and was not able to perform the way that the other children did. The shaman had decided to pound three holes in the top of his head toward the back of the skull. The idea was to let the evil spirits out and to relieve his mind of the evil slow spirit.

Taking a pointed stone, he pounded three holes in a triangle shape, and as the boy lay there with the blood flowing from his head, the shaman started to chant, and slowly the bleeding stopped and so did the chanting of the shaman as it was believed that the flow of blood, was cleansing his body of the demon. I could tell that the boy would be all right, but the holes would stay, and only a layer of scar tissue would cover the holes. This I knew would not other than cause a very large headache, help the boy as he was limited by genetics not by a physical problem. One thing that I did notice was that the boy would be expected to only do simple things as a result of the operation, allowing him to live the rest of his life with little responsibility.

The population was continually growing as the people prospered, and although it was a hard life compared to other areas it was a very aggressive lifestyle with lots of variations compared to the other continents.

We decided to see the progress in the next hundred years. Touching the control, the buzzer sounded our arrival.

We decided to take a survey of the area. As several cities had popped up fractions of people had separated or isolated themselves from the rule of the Inca kings, and although they dominated the entire continent it was possible to avoid the routes and the traveling caravans of llamas.

Some of these isolated groups had decided that they would build a better society and although far less educated as they lost interest in use of writing which slowly deteriorated, as life was very wrapped up in controlling the people, and the royal family and their people were the only ones, who were educated in the written language and as each generation passed, in the isolated groups, it became evident that written text was used less and less, as life was becoming more of a complicated manipulation of the people, more than learning new things. The text that had been written was mostly lost by these people and was only used by the descendants of the kings, and as there were now ten kingdoms, the verbal messages served their needs without the

need of written documentation although not totally as they used a rope
with knots, which was the most used communication over the long
trails that they traveled.

The Atlantis people not only printed many books on different areas
like astrology, mathematics, even school books for their children to
read which they lost when the Spanish came and burned and destroyed
everything they had, leaving almost nothing except areas that they did
not know about. They even had cups with funny things marked on
them. But that is what happens in real time, and I cannot change it.

As we traveled over the land, we came across one of these isolated
groups that had broken away from the kingdoms and had started their
own society.

The new society was the start of what would later be referred
to as the mound builders, which were people that would fill their
containers with dirt, and they built large dirt pyramids, as the local
people imitated these new inhabitants, although the kings built them
with blocks of stone that their masons or rock carvers meticulously
crafted, and built beautiful but smaller pyramids as compared to the
undertakings of the African continent.

In this area, at least in the beginning was very little need for
conquest, as there was so much land and so few people many ready
to follow these new and enterprising people. These people had been
influenced enough to still want to build pyramids. These people would
spend several hundreds of years building these pyramids, and they
would be their ritual sites as well as their center of worship, where the
gods could properly be honored, and astrological studies were the main
focus, as the alignments of the solstices was very important.

One thing that was consistent among all the differences was the
study of the astrological maps and how they were observed over the
year with the four solstices, and this contributed to the architecture of
almost all their temples and their layouts of their amazing cities.

They also devised a calendar that even in modern times was
accurate too seconds within several hundreds of years, although
was almost lost when the Spanish people came, destroying almost
everything that these people had developed.

Covering the landscape, the *Genesis* came across another small
isolated village near the mountains that were used by the aliens as the

runways for their airplanes as they had used air travel to cover the wide expanses with a very affordable method of travel used by the Edan people as well several other aliens.

These people were clearing a great path through the dense bush, totally catching my interest, as it was not like anything that I had seen before.

"Let's take a walk," I suggested, as I could sense something was not right, as the people were not doing normal things.

Walking along the ridge, we had a full view of the village. The village was a common village with small leaf-covered huts in the shape of a circle with all the activity taking place in the center.

Approaching the village, I once again had a feeling that something was not right. The women were preparing food and washing some of the utensils for eating and overall there was nothing out of place.

Then as I looked closer at the children I could see that the small babies from infant size to about three years of age, all had a bounding around their head.

Looking closer I noticed that the majority of women and the older children had very deformed heads. Very few men were present as they were out clearing the large path in the bush, but even the older men had very deformed heads.

"This is very unique," I said as we came to the entrance of the village. "Look at their heads."

"This is a culture that we knew much about," Jescan calmly stated.

"Our observers stopped and conversed with this group several times.

They have a longing to be part of our culture. That is why they bound the heads of the children so as they would look more like their gods that resembled the ant people, which mined for minerals making amazing tunnels underground, and were the first aliens to meet them, and spent a lot of time with them, or the Annunaki, but could be the Blue Avian people with the longer skulls, but they resembled birds more, our people was not the influence, this time.

The airport was used by several aliens over the years, but most importantly, the people here spent their lives, generations actually, building the runways."

Stopping, I looked hard at Jescan. "Your people and the other aliens have influenced another society. This is not like your people to affect a society, especially in causing them to change their physical looks."

"These people were aware of us as well as the other aliens when we, and the other aliens used and had the airstrips and they visited with our people often. They were curious, as they observe us as we them, and they would strike up conversations at every opportunity.

I will be very welcomed here, as the people have not seen my kind for several earth years, although after they finish the large raven, we did stop by and acknowledge the impressive undertaking, we left so suddenly, as lasers were used to give the lines needed for them to clear the land as the introduction of the hover ships was used more, as well as the decision to not observe from the ground we and the other aliens did not use the air strips leaving them without any explanation.

It was a surprise to them as one day we and the other aliens were no longer around. That is why they are now in the process of sending out a message to be seen from the sky from which we had arrived and they knew we traveled. They are imitators like the mound builders imitating the Atlantis people. These people wish to look like us to keep our interest and not to leave. They think, we are workers of the sun and moon god and have great powers as we are able to travel in the sky."

Being spotted, we were soon surrounded by everyone in the village, everyone more interested in Jescan, than my presence. The older men and women started to communicate with telepathic language. The young looked on with wide eyes focused on Jescan.

Jescan was bombarded with questions as to where we had gone, and why we had all left, including the other aliens. Raising his hand, the questions stopped, taking his time deliberately. "I am a visitor traveling with the caretaker of the land. We have come to meet you for a short visit, and to answer some of your questions. I reassure you that in time, we shall visit with your people one more time. I am a guest of this man. He is the keeper of your planet." Jescan turned in my direction, and all the eyes turned to look at me.

"Come join us as we shall offer something to drink and eat at our fire," announced the oldest man present. "We welcome you to our hearth."

Following the elder, we arrived at the fireplace where he motioned for us to sit. As well, he gave instructions to an older plump women, to get something to drink as well as to start preparing something to eat.

The reception was very formal, yet it was more like a welcoming of an old friend, than new strangers. The man joined with the others of the tribe, and sat down waiting for the wine to be brought as messengers had been sent to the men working on the massive clearing of bush.

The older woman brought out a large leather bag and was holding some cups made out of wood in her other hand. Passing out the cups, she proceeded to pour us a fermented berry wine, starting with Jescan and me, then to the men and, finally, the women.

"It has been such a long time," started the older gentleman whose face showed the nearly forty some years, as the hard life was showing heavily on his body. He was one of the few who had not had his head bound as a child, as the practice had been incorporated after the aliens had left. "Your people left suddenly with no farewells, and many questions are left unanswered." Taking a sip of the under aged dry wine he proceeded, "Our people have been watching every night and day waiting for your return as you did for so long. Have we done something wrong to offend your people?"

"I assure you our people have in no way been offended. They had out of necessity had to return to their home. Someday they will return, but for now we have come to visit for a short time. We will only stay for a drink and something to eat," Jescan said as he took on an air of authority. "We will be traveling to a newly built city in the direction that the sun sets."

"You are referring to the newly arrived people. They have strong powers. They have control of many, many animals," remarked a boy of about twelve, his eyes as wide as they could be, talking from thought, rather than consciously thinking of what he was saying.

As the women started to bring out the meal, the men from the field arrived, and were so jubilant at the fact that Jescan was there, that the questions started to come so fast that Jescan could not answer them all.

Raising his hand, he said, "I can only answer a few of your questions, as our time is limited."

The first of several questions started. "Where have your people gone? Are they going to return and when?"

Jescan took his time as he proceeded making certain that he was not going against what his people had laid out in their laws, and I could see him almost squirmed as he was very uncomfortable being placed in the center of attention.

The meal was served with great care as we, being the guests, were treated with the same respect given to a chief or a high shaman of high status. There were wild fruits, nuts, and berries that had been picked within the last day and an assortment of meat in a stew-like mixture, a very common practice, to preserve the meat, although the unique flavor was one that was pleasantly unexpected, as most often food was very tedious, almost to the extent of boring. I was treated to a taste similar to a sweet and sour sauce with the sweetness from sugarcane and the sour from a wine that had turned sour, turning to a vinegar, which gave it a thick syrupy texture. They also served us a coffee made from the dried beans of the coco bean mixed with a coffee lacquer made from the coffee bean.

"My friend and I are only passing through, as we are traveling to a city far from here, and we do not have much time to spend with you, as we will be leaving shortly. My people had to leave, although they will return as soon as they see your work that you have been doing. My people have had to travel far away, as they had to return home. Someday they will be back, for a short time."

"That is why we are doing what we are doing, so they can someday find their way back. When will they return? When will they come to have the long talks that we once had?" piped up one of the older men that had formed a circle around Jescan.

Knowing that he could not reveal the knowledge that he knew, he looked at me for reassurance then turned back and proceeded. "It will be some time before my people can return, as they have to travel a very long time before they can return too, and once again spend some time with you and your people."

"Where have they gone that it will take them so long to return?" a younger man asked, as he could not conceive of anyone traveling for so long a time.

"They had to travel to their home, which take several years to reach."

With a puzzled look on his face, he asked, "What is this year that you are talking about? How long is that?"

"It is equal to two rainy seasons, and it will take them several of those to reach their home, and in time, they will return and from what I have seen, they will be impressed with what you are doing.

When the time is right, they will return."

This last statement seemed to please most of the men gathered in a tight group around Jescan, and the questions were quickly changed to immediate questions like one young boy who had been watching and studying Jescan intently.

"How is it that you are not with them? What brings you here?"

"I am privileged to be traveling with the caretaker of the land. We are traveling to a large city that is to the west of here, and we are going to leave very soon, as we have some business to attend to."

One of the older men turned, and was rather put off, at the fact that we would associate with the people who they avoided, and had separated from several decades ago. "How come you are associating with them, as they have taken over most of the land and are very cruel to the people who serve under them? I do not like the way that they do not care about the people who have built their cities, and still cannot have the luxury of a comfortable life, that was promised to them, as was promised to us, and as we never saw anything to indicate that we would live like they had told us, we after several rains, we finally left."

These people had taken on such a lot of the rituals, and lifestyles of the local people that several generations later, it was a rule of complete dictatorship, a cruel and arrogant group of kings.

Several of the original Atlantis kings had, through battles been slain to the hands of the local people. It was nothing like they could have imagined when they landed on this continent. Although the kings ruled the people, the priests were the direct rulers even though they took the subservient role.

Gesturing to Jescan, I indicated that we should be going and that we should say our farewells, as I wanted to see how the other continents were doing one that was not influenced by the Atlantis people, and would not be influenced for many thousands of years. This was of course the North American continent.

Taking our leave, we bid them well and happy life.

Walking back to the *Genesis* it occurred to me that each of the main groups from the island was initiating a philosophy that would fascinate societies in the future, and each group played an interracial part in what society would become.

"We should check out what is happening on the other continents as well. What do you say?" I commented.

Jescan nodded his agreement as he was preoccupied and fascinated by the people who we had just left. The alien influence had affected them in such a different way than anywhere else, since they had come from the island of Mu, and had separated from the kingdom started by the Atlantis people, the encounter with his people and other aliens they had accomplished so much in fifty years, they were so stifled, by their obsession to communicate with a group that originally had no intention of showing themselves until the people knew of them, and was ready to accept them. "Yes," he said as he thought again about what a tangled web his people had woven, some intentionally, some unintentionally. "If they are anything like these people, it could be very interesting."

I calmly looked at Jescan. "The influences that your people have had is tremendous, yet they are the bases that our modern societies are based upon especially the Egyptian and Inca societies which ruled these southern continents with a control that would not be rivaled as they ruled for thousands of uninterrupted years ingraining their principles and laws. One area that was not influenced by the people of Atlantis was the North American continent, as these people lived a calm uninterrupted life, surpassing even the great rain of the Egyptian or the Inca and as these people lived a harmonious lifestyle that would last until the fifteenth century.

Touching the control, we arrived in the northern continent.

CHAPTER THIRTEEN

"The people should not resemble this last group of people if you are looking for similarities as these people have not been influenced by the people of Atlantis. Although were influenced more from the people of the island of Mu, with a large influence from the Annunaki, who had migrated and settled in the northern continent, they had a great respect for the land and nature, trying to maintain what the Mother Earth had given them, as well, mingled with the groups that had crossed over the ice bridge between the European continent and the North American continent as the ice caps melted."

Looking out the window the breeze was moving the grass almost like looking at a green sea swaying back and forth. "Let's take a walk and see what these people are doing. This is a part of history that we had little information on as everything was destroyed over time, leaving only fragmented information on such an amazingly long culture."

The fresh dry air was refreshing as the breeze carrying the smell of wild grass, flowers, and sage brush hit our nostrils with a pleasant tingling. The land was rough, untouched and unchanged by man.

It was as though there was not a human around. Herds of buffalo could be seen grazing in the lush prairies. They made the hills look like they were dark brown almost black, instead of green. There was deer browsing and playing in the meadow by the lake, and then we saw the smoke from a clan, or tribe of Indians as they referred to their groups as a tribe.

Dotting the landscape along the riverbank were thousands of teepees as the large tribe was almost as large as any city in any part of the world, reaching over a hundred thousand, some reaching two hundred thousand. The only difference was that these people left the land exactly as they had found it except for the fire pits that would be used the next time they stayed in this spot.

This lifestyle was so radically different from any other continent as well as the serenely peaceful atmosphere, the animals wandered leisurely across the land disturbed only by the carnivores. The descendants of the saber-toothed tiger such as the wildcats similar to the lynx, bobcat and the cougars, as well as the wolves and the bears which had descended from a small bearlike animal, and there was still saber-toothed tigers still around but where declining or changing more than declining, these were among the limited predators. On the whole, there were so many herbivores that the predators kept the herds in check as well as culling out the injured, sick, and old animals.

Most of the animals could feed comfortably within feet of one another for protection in numbers as well as there was nothing for them to compete with as there were vast areas of grassland that were lush with grass, and after a herd had cropped the grass within a few weeks sometimes days depending on the rain, it was usually as high as it was before the herd had past.

The people too were in harmony with the land. Their philosophy of life was so different, as there was no land to fight over since they had the belief that they were there to tend and care for the land. I reflected on what I had first told the first people that we had encountered.

The people were a mild, caring people who had the belief that everything had a spirit, and that the spirit came back to take on another life, each new baby that was born had a spirit from an animal revealed usually at puberty. This was what determined how the person lived their life.

"These people are so different from the others I have seen. There is no fear in their body language. They are confident and very amiable," observed Jescan.

"Yes, they live in total harmony with the land. There is no land grabbing here although there are territories, that they have sometimes heatedly disagreed upon the territory with the other tribes as to who would look after, as well as protect certain areas.

These people have the philosophy which would or should be the template for any society. Although they do not attain the knowledge of the other societies they are quite content to live within the limits of the land and have no desire to change what is already good and their concept is, if it is good accept it, if it is bad leave it alone."

"These people, they seem to move from place to place. They are like the nomads on the desert of Egypt."

"In a way that is true although some tribes did set up permanent homes, mostly along the coasts, although the majority did travel with the herds or you could say they set up where the animals would be.

These people changed little till the men from the European continent arrive."

"Our people talked of these people too and they were a group that was content with the way things were and did not try to change anything. It was observed that they were very in touch with themselves extremely disciplined within their mind and body as well as with their surroundings. Their society was not very progressive as little was changed from year to year decade after decade. They did, though, have a very busy and fulfilling life noticeably not really advancing as other societies did."

"These people consider themselves to be the caretakers of the earth. It was simply unheard of to take more than you needed, and to their way of thinking it was of no value to have more than you could use, although if you could give it to someone else it was considered the highest reward. They have no enemies although the tribes did have disagreements they tended to avoid the other tribe, except at special potlatches where all the tribes traveled to one spot to celebrate. The biggest was in the summer, although there was one in the winter as well.

Usually they were completely isolated from outside influences, as they had no desire to change the world as there is plenty for everyone with no desire to move mountains as the statement from the modern world would be completely laughed at here."

"You seem to hold a lot of admiration for these people, yet they are not as interesting as other areas of the world. They, all in all are rather mundane."

"Yes, I guess I do. They have a good life that would appeal to any person if they could live as peaceful a life as these people do." I paused as I reflected on a dream I had as a child living off the land, being able to wander throughout the land with no one to bother me.

These people though were a very industrious group of people as they wasted nothing. They had a very simple life with the chief deciding all that they did, like when to move and what camp they would move to next as they had favorite spots for each of the four seasons which on this continent was very prevalent.

During the fall, the women would gather large quantities of roots, legumes, berries, and herbs that would sustain them over the winter months where they would usually travel to the southern areas, where the winter was not as harsh as it was in the north, and the hunting was good. They through thousands of years knew where the animals wintered, as well as where they migrated, as each season descended on the land. This group did have a good life filling their days with daily, monthly and yearly tasks all extremely important to them.

One of the unique attitudes of these people, was that if you wanted something you simply had to ask for it, or if the person was not around you took it and in turn, would leave a supply of wood or some other kind gesture, to pay in a way for what you took. If the people were there it was as simple as asking for what you needed and usually without question was given freely."

I noticed a young boy of about twelve years of age saying good-bye to his family and friends as this was his time to enter into manhood.

This was something that every boy would do at the time when puberty was at its peak, and the desire to become a man was allowed as the chief would be notified, and a council would be convened whereby the request was discussed and the smoking of the pipe as well as the ritual of the sweat lodge to cleanse the body, and to purify the sole for the new phase that the boy was to enter. The following day the boy without any food, carrying only a small pouch of water would start his quest to find out what animal spirit would help him in, and through his life.

The boy started to wander off into the west and he walked for almost two days as he never stopped to eat and only drank when necessary, filling his pouch at a stream if necessary.

It was as though the boy could sense the spot that he was looking for, and soon he grabbed a stone and scraped a circle into the soil.

Within the circle, he would strip down, setting his clothes to the side as well as the pouch of water.

Sitting in a cross-legged manner, he would start chanting and was soon in a deep meditated state of consciousness.

I listened to his mind, which was almost to the point of unbelievable hunger. The control the boy contained both mentally as well as physically was surprising.

My mind suddenly linked with his, and he saw the images of me as well as I could see his images. He calmly asked me which animal spirit was to be his. I said that I would help him to find his contra as he called it. I could see the unique shape of the eagle soaring overhead. Pointing up to the image, I quickly separated from his mind, as I felt I should not have been in his mind.

This surprised me, as this link with his mind was not intentional, completely by surprise. Although I knew the concept, including the mechanics of what had happened, it caught me off guard when he could actually see and talk to me.

Because of his meditative state of mind with total tranquility descending on his body and mind, the vast space that he surrounded in his mind was analyzing all the chemicals that existed around him.

Because I was listening to his mind, he absorbed my energy, in turn, becoming part of his mind.

This posed an interesting problem. Should I have even been listening to his mind? Would this in time, change his people? I decided I will wait to see.

Jescan studied my face as he had heard me talking to myself.

"That is a technique that our people have used many times. Although we use the technique when we are visiting with them, studying them it works very well as you have just witnessed.

"Our society uses it to visit among ourselves, as your people shall someday use this part of the brain to do the same as you have done.

It can be transferred to most anywhere in the universe, allowing for study over very long distances, although at a closer range it is not as physically exhausting."

I turned to watch the boy and was amazed as the eagle too had connected with the boy's energy and was summoned by the boy. Even though he was not aware of it, he was controlling the bird's mind. As the bird came closer he stretched out his arm, and the eagle landed on his arm. Reaching underneath, he plucked a feather from his tail feathers.

The eagle was almost hypnotized and did not even blink an eye.

Then the spell was broken, and the bird took flight once more leaving claw marks on his arm. It started slowly circling rising higher and higher.

The boy slowly stood, dressed himself and drank the water that he had saved. It was time to return, and now he was so lightheaded that he walked with a lightness, as though he was floating. He stopped at a berry bush, eating leisurely contemplating the events that took place. Taking his time walking home he spotted a large young lone bull buffalo.

Remembering a cliff that was on the way back to the camp, he started to herd the buffalo straight toward the cliff. He ran as lightly as he had walked, most of his body cleansed of most impurities that build up within the cells of the body. The large amount of water, which with the start of the sweat lodge, and allowing only water to enter the body was thoroughly purified. His energy level heightened to an all-time high.

He ran behind the buffalo till it ran over the top of the cliff. The cliff was within eyesight of the camp, and the people had heard the running of an animal and was surprised to see the boy appearing at the top of the cliff stopping to check his kill. The animal was killed almost instantly as it had broken his neck. The boy grabbed a round stone and striking it with another stone, a sharp edge appeared and the boy set off down to the animal to drain the blood and to gut it.

As the people from the tribe arrived he held up the stone now covered with blood holding the feather in his other hand, beaming with pride at his first kill.

Within a short time the females had carved up the buffalo, and the men picked him up and carried him back to the camp as he had proved that he was now a man, and would as of this day showed would be a great hunter.

The celebration was started. The boy, now a man as the darkness of night settled in and the fresh buffalo kill had been eaten, would tell of the spirit of his contra explaining the eagle feather and of the vision that had come to him.

The story he would tell would be the envy of everyone present, as his was the highest totem or contra that you could have.

It fascinated me as I watched how, in his mind he transferred his thoughts to several of the elders, that in turn, started to interpret the vision, as they I could tell, could envision the complete vision, me included.

Surprise was the expression of the elders, as my image was one that had never had been seen before. They decided that I must be a guide a very special guide, one completely unknown to them, a mystery to all that was allowed to witness the vision.

I turned to Jescan smiling, as it was doubtful that I would have caused a radical change to this peaceful society. "I suppose that it is time for us to travel to the European countries. They on the other hand have been influenced by the people of Atlantis."

Returning to the ship I set the controls, and the buzzer sounded our arrival.

Looking out the window, we could see that it was lightly raining and the clouds were starting to break up. This was a good time to grab a light lunch.

The sweet smell after a rain hung in the air. Everything felt fresh and clean. The smell of wet soil was strong as the rain still dripped from the trees and the plants. The grass made a distinct wet sound as we walked to the top of the hill where we could observe the land. The plants had the look of modern plants, and the animals were changing closer to the modern animals that I knew, I could recognize a lot of the modern animals. Although they still had a lot of changes to go through, they did look more like the animals I knew.

The people from Atlantis had arrived setting up a small clan although they had wanted to set up a city, it was a very harsh and cruel area to live in, as most of the clans were very aggressive very warlike in everything that they lived for. As long as they had everything to sustain their life like food, water, and shelter they would go out of their way to disrupt any clan that was nearby, especially if they had infringed on their territory. The new inhabitants found that it was of utmost importance to have a protective barricade around their homes and although crude, was in a historical sense was one of the first castles to appear on the continent. It unlike the modern castles had been made of logs, as it was the easiest and most accessible material available.

The influence of these people soon gained a lot of respect, as the new structure was something that could not easily be penetrated at least not by anything they knew of.

As time would allow, rocks would become the material of choice, as it would be found out that fire could penetrate the structure. For now though, it was a very safe haven for the new residents.

The large cities that they had thought they would build would be waylaid, although would someday be viable it was a constant battle just to protect themselves from the local clans. Without the raw materials to manufacture metal tools after several generations, it would be lost in time and forgotten for several centuries.

All through the rough times, though the royal families did survive and was the start of the royal legacies that would continue throughout history. Even though there were several throughout history that would self-proclaim themselves as royalty some building remarkable societies, the Atlantis people even though spread out were the seed that started the dynasties that countries would develop.

This area as it was now was full of several segmented clans as they called themselves, they were always leery and very aggressive toward strangers. So we decided to again just observe from a distance.

The first group that we came across, was that of cave dwellers that was heading back to their camp, as they had just had a very successful hunt, five of the ten men were dragging a carcass of a deer.

The men were chanting and kidding with one another as they were approaching their camp. A young boy was the first to spot the hunters and started to run to the men. As he was running the earth started to shake as an earthquake started to open up the land. Seeing what was going to happen as the boy, felt the land started to open and he was starting to fall into the open crevice in the earth that would, I could sense close very soon, holding my hand out I levitated the boy and moved him as he was grabbing for the edge of the ground. As the ground started to close he was out of danger, and the earthquake was over as quickly as it had started.

The men collecting themselves, ran as fast as they could to the boy and realized that he was safe and nothing had happened to him. They had all seen the boy falling into the hole and miraculously floated to the other side landing safely. The men started thanking the gods that the boy had been saved. "The Mother Earth gave back this boy," they kept saying over and over to one another.

One man held the boy of maybe six and rocked him till the others from the clan arrived. The boy eyes wide with fear of what could have happened looked down at his hand, which held a rock that he had been chipping away at as he was waiting for the hunters to come back, and even well he was grabbing for the ground had held onto the rock.

In a crude way it resembled a small female with large breasts and a large tummy. He held up the statue and showed the people around him the object.

Such an object had never been seen before in this region and they all took a very close look at the object not only studying it, but they also looked at it with reverence and awe. They all decided that the

Mother Earth had given them a sign and that this stone resembling a woman was the captured form of the Mother Earth the giver of all life, the Mother Earth, that had returned this child back to them.

He would be, from now on, revered as the boy that was saved by this donii as they called it.

As the people looked at the rock, the earth again trembled as an aftershock came. The people all shuttered as this boy was truly connected with the Mother Earth, she was letting them know that this was a chosen child, they looked at him with a different look one of reverence and instant respect.

Jescan looked at me and said, "Did you give him the stone shaped like a pregnant lady?"

"No, the shape of the rock is completely a product of the child's work. It was just a fluke that it had been carved in the shape of the female, I had nothing to do with the stone I did help him to stay on top of the ground." I paused as I looked at Jescan. "This, I can assure you was as much a surprise to me as it is to you, for that matter as surprised as the boy holding the stone was. This was the start or birth of the donii. in this region"

"This statue would be prevalent all over this continent in the future. Could you have been the start of it?"

"Since this is the first time I have been here, the statue, although a coincidence, may have solidified what their symbol would look like," I said, realizing that this may have been the person who started the look or design of the statue. I had simply saved the individual. The statue would become the savior.

"As it is now the boy lives, and the statue is now a part of the culture. Although I can see now that I have changed this boy's life." Maybe I was destined to be here. I could now understand how the smallest of things could change and affect the future. I, though, had no regret in saving the boy's life.

"This boy's life has been elevated to a very high status, which may or may not have an effect on the future. The computer will be able to help us on this matter."

"Look," Jescan said as pointed to the north. "There is part of the group from Atlantis." A small band of blond hair, blue-eyed people were busy surveying the land.

"I think you are right. Let's see what they are up to," I said as we headed to a higher point to get a better view.

We could see that they were obviously looking to set up a new sight. As I read their minds, I could see that it was a site, not for building, but a site for mining. This would have been in the area of Sweden in modern times although they also would later inhabit areas of Norway. These people of the northern region of Atlantis, also the strongest, most dominant blond people, had traveled up the European coastline and landed on what would become Sweden and Norway.

They had thought that this land was an island, although later they found that it joined the mainland to their disappointment.

The people were semi-isolated as the area had been inhabited by a few isolated clans. Most of their structures would be built out of wood which they also discovered had an insulating effect compared to the cold drafty conditions that the caves and rock buildings had. The wooden homes were very appreciated as the winter brought storms, snow and cold weather. The likes of which they had never experienced before.

The land was harsh but the small colony flourished and grew. In fifteen years of occupancy they would increase their population to four times its original size, as the long cold winters had a part to play in the small population explosion. The people had adapted to the climatic changes very well. The food supply was adequate and could even be added to in the dead of winter as the wildlife was plentiful, and the ocean stayed unfrozen for most of the year, allowing some fishing. These people were doing very well, and the change in climate temperatures also added to their body size, which was a natural adaptation needed to winter the colder winters of this area.

Jescan commented, "These people too do not fear anything even though there are clans that attempt to lout their homes on a regular basis. They unlike the other groups which incorporated the local people into their society, have stayed relatively to themselves."

"They did not have to conquer and protect the land like the others, as this land had few humans living on it, and definitely land that was not in demand although very spectacular, scenery-wise." Looking at the massive mountainous landscape I turned back to Jescan. "We should see what is happening in the south, as I am interested in the progress of the pyramids," I said as I turned toward the *Genesis*.

CHAPTER FOURTEEN

Looking out the window, a sandstorm was in full force, and the intermittent view of the landscape appeared every once in a while as the small low-pressure system picked up and then eased off, only to pick up again repeating itself again and again. "I think we should maybe try after the storm has subsided and moved out of the immediate area, maybe later on in the day."

Sensing that it would not last that long I touched the control, arriving later that day to a completely different view, a peaceful calm day with a cloudless sky, as the storm had dispersed. The low-pressure area had been pushed out of the area disappearing with the approach of a high-pressure area that was presently over the northern area of the continent.

Opening the door the dryness of the air was a reminder that we were close to the equator and on the edge of a dessert. I had exchanged the sandals for a pair with a thicker sole, and we were all set for the walk.

The people had accomplished a lot as the construction of the pyramids had almost completed, the base of the third step pyramid, which was the last step pyramid before they would undertake the large pyramids with several buildings all around at present resembled a large square building, called a mastaba, and the city surrounding the pyramids was enclosed with a wall that was built to a massive thirty-five feet in height. The city was remarkable with open courts everywhere, and the priest which was not a Blue Avian but a hybrid human named Imhotep, was the main designer and had started the second level, which was placed upon the square building, forming the second level of the pyramid.

The people were still in large, well-organized groups. As the storm had delayed the work for most of the day, it was approaching late afternoon they were shutting things down for the night, as they were leaving for the great walls surrounding the city.

The anticipation of the evening meal was on the minds of most of them, heading toward the camp between the river and the city.

They used the river to clean themselves, and their attention was to the fermented barley drink of beer, which was being passed around as the beer was part of their daily rations, an appreciated ritual after a hard day working in the heat of the day, the beer was a pleasure that most of them looked forward to.

The plateau where the pharaoh sat was now replaced by his youngest son, Sekhemkhet, who was sitting now in his place looking out at a legacy of the pyramid, that was his responsibility to complete, as the pharaoh and his first two male heirs had passed away, to which he was to complete the three-step pyramids. I could sense that he would rather be with his royal dog, running through the palace courtyards and gardens, or bathing and playing in one of the many pools or baths that surrounded the palace. Yet the strong desire and belief that he would also need a tomb to prepare him for his reincarnation, coupled with the deep sense of responsibility to his father, as well as to his inherited country, it would become his legacy as much as his father's.

Touching his mind I could see that behind the lavishly designed toga and large crown upon his head, his mind was anywhere but on the pyramid, as the priest was the one who was making most of the decisions, which at this moment, although very dedicated he was simply a boy, but a boy with absolute rule. He was extremely self indulgent and very rude with no respect for the people around him, with one exception.

It was his mother who was his mentor, and it was she that subtlety could manipulate him, without the advisers becoming upset at her intervention.

The pharaoh King Zoser was buried in his chamber about ninety feet below the surface in a tunnel that had been dug deep into the earth, made out of granite with several corridors leading to other burial chambers, which were members of his family. A total of eleven would eventually be buried with him, as each tomb would be sealed. Eventually only one man would be left to seal the entrances.

He would slide several large thin rectangular slabs down in strategic locations, all the way to the surface. The open courts and the buildings surrounding, the rectangular shape in the center of the base, were now starting to be filled over by his son, although the passage way would be left for him as part of his place of burial.

The young pharaoh, nearing his fourteenth birthday, was very restless as the short day was coming to an end, and his mind was thinking of the meal that would be waiting for him when he returned.

He strutted and paced back and forth. Losing interest, he climbed down to play with his cat. Tiring of that, he then picked a stone and threw it trying to hit a tree that was growing near the base of the summit. Then as the work was ending, he his guards and the priest headed to the city entering within the protective walls for the night.

"He looks quite busy, wouldn't you say?" I commented.

"Really . . . I would say that he looks very bored and would like to run or play anything else but be here," he said seriously as he took the statement at face value not realizing that I was being sarcastic.

Smiling as I turned to him he realized that I was not serious, he shook his now lowered head, returning the smile.

Looking down at the slave camp, the men were getting drunk, and their women were preparing their meals. The sun was setting, and the hot winds from the desert started to blow in gusts, moving the hot still air, slowly cooling off the land as any breeze was a relief.

The smell of garlic as well as the fermenting barley used for the malt drink similar to modern beer started to disappear as the breeze carried the strong pungent odor away.

Some who had completed their meal had started to wander down to the river and were soaking in the river or relaxing along the banks of the river all under surveillance by the night guards.

The slave's life was hard with few liberties, yet under such adverse conditions, they did live an almost secretive life, as their mates also lived in the camp and several were raising families. It had been decided by the pharaoh, that the more children that they had the more people to do the work, since they had so many slaves, every resident could afford to have a slave. Slaves were abundant, although animals were not.

It had been a long day and I realized that it was time for us to get some food and some sleep too.

The buzzer announced our arrival some ten years hence.

We started our walk, as the *Genesis* made its surveillance of the planet.

The morning, still held the chill from the night, as the sun was just above the horizon. The camp was stirring and the women were setting the dried camel dung with dried grasses into the smoldering remains of the previous fire from the day before. The women and children were the first up the men followed. As they rose, each used a path that was set aside for relieving themselves.

Several of the men, and even some of the women, were trying to clear their heads from the beer of the night before, as they tried drowning their extremely repressed life. The camp was slow getting started yet this was the only time that was allowed for them to be in control of one aspect of their life, which they looked forward to and appreciated as they cooked, and ate their morning meal, virtually uninterrupted, which usually was the only time they had till they shut down late in the afternoon.

The guards as well as a large majority of people from the town had started a routine which after they had been drinking vast amounts of wine, would come down to check out the slaves, crudely grabbing and groping whoever took their fancy especially the young females and males equally, as they were the most desirable as every late evening was a free for all, for the normal routine of the bored orgy going crowd, the citizens of the city. It was their form of entertainment, thinking nothing of entering the slave's sleeping quarters, dragging out their choice for the night, or sending the rest of the family out of their bed, to stand outside till they had completed raping the victim. If the parents objected or gave the drunken person any hassles, the ritual was that a guard would be called, the family would be chained and made to watch, or was chained to a post just outside of the sleeping quarters to be released after they had finished raping the innocent victim that they had chosen. It was such a relief for the slaves after a night of perversion to see the sun come up and they could let their children out of hiding spots, that they had devised to protect the very young.

The taskmasters and or the overseers now patiently waited till the meal was completed then arranged the men, giving them their duties to be carried out in today's schedule. The sick were not allowed the luxuries of sleeping, although the sick usually was assigned to lighter duties upon request, as they were lined up. to walk to the base of the pyramid where they each went to their designated spots. The people had a long and backbreaking day with little or no breaks.

The last few years of the former king's life, was lived in the opulent luxurious enclosure within the base of the pyramid, where all his prized possessions were placed everywhere it would fit to be observed by him, as he was progressively failing in health. This place would become his tomb.

Their beliefs were similar in some ways to the North American Indians, believing that a person's life would again be reborn although unlike the Indians they wanted to believe, they would again become a real breathable person, as reincarnation was part of their adopted adaptations from the local people, which had deep-rooted beliefs concerning these matters.

The people believed that the objects that they were buried with would allow the new life spirit to see clearly the position and status of the past life, as well as explain to the new life that the slaves that were killed and laid to rest beside the coffin, would be there to serve his every wish in his new life. It was also believed that the objects that were buried with him would be reclaimed by the new life and once again be for his use. This shrine that he had spent most of his life working on would become his property once he arose, but for the time being until it was time for him to rise, this would now become the first pyramids made of stone to be built in the world, although it would take several years that would run into decades to complete.

The priest with the help of his overseer as well as the architect designers or masons, was held and admired by the wealthy citizens of the Nile, including other countries such as Greece and Ethiopia.

The priest selected the finest artists which scribed all the pharaoh's remarkable achievements in his life on the walls of the tomb.

He would never complete the pyramid in his lifetime. It was the duty of the first born to complete the remarkable undertaking of the pharaoh, his father. I noted that there was no reference to the island of Atlantis. Then I realized that the original king had passed away shortly after his arrival. His son Zoser had become pharaoh which his son was the main builder and it was the third-generation son who was now the pharaoh in charge of completing the pyramid. The island of Atlantis was simply ignored as the achievements of the new pharaoh never started till his father had passed away. The young boy when he arrived with his family was considered a man as he was eighteen years of age when he became pharaoh. Now his son of thirteen was born in Egypt, was to complete the pyramid.

The Egyptians as well as the neighboring cultures were very impressed with the priest's accomplishments, so much that later on the Egyptians even deified him to the status of their god of medicine as did the Greeks which associated him with their god of medicine named Asclepius. As he had been the first son of the shaman of the original group from Atlantis, he was noted for the healing medicine that he used with knowledge from the Island which his father had taught and passed on to him as well as the remarkable buildings that were designed and built by him. The remarkable achievements of the descendants from Atlantis had started the foundation of a dynasty that would last for several thousands of years.

The citizens of the Egyptian country lived a life that was full of art, picture writings and hieroglyphics that adorned the walls and the temples. One of the amazing things was that the majority of the lay people, could not even understand the writings, but they did take and use the innovations that the people from Atlantis had brought with them. Their calendar was also a little off, as they were short a quarter of a day each year, as the calendar was three four-month seasons, each month had 30 days, and they had 5 days added to make 365 days, which meant that they lost 25 days every hundred years.

Although they never corrected the calendar the New Year was over the years, celebrated earlier than the actual New Year causing several problems with the astrologers and some of the priests as religious ceremonies were not exact. This would not be corrected till the Greeks solved the problem several centuries later.

Looking out the window, I pondered the evolution of life, now mostly the humans including the aliens. The complication of the human race arriving with the interjection of the aliens, I found myself concentrating on the humans more than I did all the other animals and plants. I did keep track of the new species as the computer updated each time we landed, but the reality was that the humans were becoming the main focus of our attention, as in every part of the world, humans were finding their way there. The island of Atlantis was a major factor which advanced most of the societies that they came in contact with.

It was the aliens that lived with the humans before the aliens decided that that is not what they should have done and banned it.

The people of earth started to kill their newborn children if they looked like their distant relations of apes, as the norm looked closer to the gods, as they considered them to be gods, that came out from the sky, possessing so many powers that legends and myths had developed because of them. What the aliens did was taken by the naive people, as only a god had the power to control the things as they did thus becoming a god in their eyes.

The aliens wanted to tell them everything, especially the reasons for them being there. The people though had to ask, in order to be answered. This was because of the ignorance of the people not that they were not intelligent, but that they had never explored their minds enough to question the implanted thoughts and ask why. The people did explore the country, or were more concerned with organizing a hunt, or in just keeping alive. It was that "keeping alive" that most of the people spent their time at.

They lived in a real world with real consequences, and the idea that there was life on other planets, was beyond their comprehension, as well as an easier way to do the task that they were doing was simple and uncomplicated. It just didn't occur to them to change what the aliens had shown them. These two concepts were the same, as the people only knew what they knew and not knowing any better, simply lived for the day hoping to survive till the next day. Age was a large factor since the average life expectancy was under thirty and also contributed to the slow progress of the intellect, as the older and wiser usually had the time to ponder life, yet due to several circumstances usually died before they could really accomplish any significant discovery.

Take for instance the medicine men or the shamans. Their knowledge was taught and handed down from generation to generation. In most cases the transfer was done telepathically in order to transfer the most amount of knowledge, but rarely did the teacher have time to teach everything that was handed down relying on the mind's ability to absorb more than thought possible, although they did rely on mystical experiences a common practice of the people of Edan, and although introduced to the children that were born to their selected mates, and to be able to communicate with them as their ancestors. From these experiences, they were able to access and remember the teaching of the one who passed the information on to them in the first place, in time the actual dawning of mankind's knowledge.

The people in the last two thousand years were in total amazement of the newborn child which all of a sudden from a female who suddenly started to become fat, did not bleed monthly, and from inside her gave birth to a new being. This was a mystery and was looked at like magic, a gift from the gods, as they really didn't understand exactly how the life was capable of being created.

They had a vision of the spirit being released by the Mother Earth. The spirit would wander the earth till it found the right female. If the spirit looked kindly on the female then the spirit would start growing within the chosen female, which was the start of the new life as they saw and believed it to be. In the last four thousand years it became more of a norm, that if a bad spirit entered the body and a throwback to the apes came from within the female it was simply killed and was completely forgotten about as the bad spirit was now dead. The gift from the Mother Earth started as in their mind a small miniature human, complete with arms, fingers, legs, and toes. The act of sex was not considered in the conception of a baby. Although this was expressed differently in different societies, all the societies believed the same concept that the child was complete when it entered the chosen female's body, though the people in different societies took and elaborated on the events that were happening at the time when the female realized she was pregnant were the deciding factor.

The volcanoes erupting and earthquakes shaking the earth each had a significant meaning especially to the innocence of the people.

Less dramatic situations such as the movement of the animals and the location that they ended up at were significant. These the people could comprehend as well. They were something that they could touch and feel as well as see. This concept even when a female had a miscarriage it was usually after the child had developed the arms and legs, and if it was before the fetus was fully developed it was considered that the female's body had rejected a demon or an evil animal's spirit as it did not resemble a human.

Women did not change their everyday routine in many cases especially nomadic tribes, having their children as they were on the move or well tending the crops, leaving the group and having their baby, in most cases on their own, sometimes with the assistance of another female to accompany the expectant mother.

After the child was born there was usually a ceremony on the birth of the baby. The male whose mate had had the baby, and who was responsible for the female would organize a celebration with the help of all the other females and would gather together offering gifts to welcome this new person to the living world and to their clan. If a female gave birth to twins the whole tribe or clan celebrated with large long-lasting feasts and the gifts were showered upon the female. The children were usually revered and most often attained a high position of responsibility when they reach maturity.

Each child was assigned a totem at the ceremony. If the child, through the experiences of life found that the totem was wrong, the totem given to the child was able to take on another totem.

This in a way changed when the people from Atlantis arrived into the mainstream of civilization. Although they understood the basic concepts of conception, and that the male and the female both had a part in the conception, they were reluctant to share the information with anyone other than from their own kind. As generations went by, the general public overhearing small pieces here and there came away with remarkable stories, rarely based on all the facts, but nonetheless were absorbed into their beliefs, and the male was accepted in incorporating the transferring of the spirit that would enter the female's body as the males were the dominant factor, meaning that the females were only the means by which the male whose body had allowed the spirit to enter the female was now the link with the spirits, that allowed the female to become pregnant.

This too was the start of the worship of the male body which was revered in most societies. In several cases it was normal practice. In the last thousand years if the first child was not born male, the child was usually killed without a second thought. After the firstborn male the woman was in most cases allowed to have a female child.

This practice would take thousands of years to change or disprove, still practiced in many cultures of modern times repressing the truth to be known. The average person took these beliefs very seriously as the way it was. Man was advancing to a remarkable stage and yet in the same breath was set back at the same time.

The influences of the aliens were such an integral part of the way the people of Earth lived not really understanding the true meanings behind the planted ideas, that they were misconstrued so often they were in most cases, slowing down the progress of the people. Mankind was starting to control the outcome of future societies and starting to mold their future of course with man in charge.

It was the dawning of the modern man and each society held the beliefs of the stories and legends that were from a time so long ago, no one could answer when they started. It was a time long since forgotten when life was very simple and uncomplicated.

The pyramids of Egypt were a remarkable undertaking, not to be rivaled for thousands of years. People though followed anyone who seemed to know what was right or fact, and people could change their minds from one minute to the next depending on who was talking.

The *Genesis* had landed on the same high ground as we had landed before. Although the pyramid was almost complete, the last of the stones where being readied to complete the five steps above the ground floor, and although other step pyramids would be made, the pharaohs would not have any major influence on the Egyptian society.

The Ethiopians would conquer and rule with minor changes, although the original Atlantis people would indirectly reclaim the throne again as direct descendants of the original kings would marry into the dynasty once more, coming into power. The most spectacular pyramids were yet to come, as the modern pyramids were built within the next thousand years.

The *Genesis* had indicated an important date that was to be our next stop. The buzzer sounded our arrival.

Looking out the window, a different scene was unfolding. The slaves were not laboring on any pyramids or laying a new trail from the river to the newer pyramids. The large group of slaves that would be laboring on the stones hulled in on large barges were, instead gathered on the far banks of the river.

Hundreds of thousands of them were moving east, almost 70 percent of the population of the country, as the slaves outnumbered the general population.

Adjusting the controls we moved up and observed from the high hills along the journey pathway. They traveled for several days and were just approaching the shore to the sea. We could see the large armada of Egyptians that was moving much faster than the slaves.

It was just about noon when the Egyptians were spotted by the freed slaves. Hurrying, they came to the banks of the sea trapped between the sea and the Egyptian troops and bent on reclaiming their slaves. There was complete bedlam as the slaves feared the reproductions of the exodus from Egypt. There was nowhere to go with the sea blocking them from going forward and the advancing rush of mounted troops.

Standing by the river fear present in everyone's thoughts including the man who was leading the throng of frightened fearful people who was standing on the large rock on the bank of the sea, they had been trapped into a corner with nowhere to run and hide.

Touching the controls we absorbed the rock as we landed. I could sense the presence of aliens and although hidden in the sky above the hordes of people were ships hovering in the clouds. Looking at Jescan, I asked, "What are your people doing here?"

"This is the start or the beginning when our people tried to arrange a setting that would allow our people to introduce themselves to your people. It was a time when my people thought that we could let ourselves be known showing our technology, as well as letting them know that we mean no harm to anyone. As soon as we arrive we will start the questions that need to be asked in turn to be answered.

Time is not a factor and this our first stage of our plan our appearance without placing the people into a trance. It had been planned to set the stage for our introduction. The people, though are stuck on the banks of the Nile, and our people are going to land shortly and to allow these chosen people across the sea to safety."

The familiar music came from the sixth plane, flooding my mind with images. *Your presence here is already written. You cannot allow history to be changed. It must progress as it happened. you are a part of this.*

"It is not the right time. I cannot let them show themselves at this time." The people were starting to get excited as the soldiers were advancing from the south west and could be seen emerging from the crest of the hills and entering the valley.

The leader of the group started to climb higher on the *Genesis* so that he had a better view of the soldiers. I started to read his mind although he was nervous he had complete confidence in the belief that he had seen and talked with god.

Using a technique of suggestive controlling his mind was very susceptible. As I started controlling the body movements he turned to the river raising his hands as though to give a final try.

This was when I raised my hand and opened a passageway across the sea. Even though the ships hiding in the clouds pulled closer to the people, and was in full view not one person looked up as all eyes were glued to the river and the opening large enough for them to walk across.

The people with all their worldly possessions, from cattle to jewelry ran across the seafloor. As the final people were setting foot on the far side the soldiers had made it just about a quarter of the way into the opening and were moving fast as the horses could move.

Lowering my arm the water flowed normal once again washing the men down the river as it resumed its normal flow.

Jescan looked so surprised. "You have just changed history. You must change it back!" he said, looking at me as though I had gone crazy.

The ships were communicating among themselves, as they were not sure whether there really was a god as they did not have the technology to open the sea and allow the people to walk across. The aliens were prepared to show themselves but had intended to transport the group across the sea. Not surprisingly this event caught them completely off guard.

Jescan smiled as he was reading my mind and I explained to him it was not time to expose themselves right now. He watched his people's ships retreating back into the clouds staying well hidden in the clouds as they talked back and forth not sure what had happened.

"This was the first time that you have interjected in any of our people's activities on this planet. This will be documented although the men are not sure what exactly happened. It will cause a great respect for your abilities."

"These people needed to be freed. Even the Egyptians were uneasy almost terrified of the large number of slaves, as their numbers exceeded the population of citizens many fold over. The arrangement of the different illusions by the aliens would cause significant changes in the beliefs as the general public goes. This one act that I did would start a whole new way of thinking.

From the aliens' thoughts, I could tell they were speculating that I had been involved with this occurrence. I realized that I had only one actual meeting with them which was when they had removed a female from Earth to be studied on their planet.

The musical sounds started in my brain, images of a young baby boy. *This is your son. He was born nine months after you made contact with us. His DNA was confirmed with the same genes that allows him to connect with the different planes the same as you did. He was ten years old when he was tested. This would not ordinarily cause a problem except that he even at his young age is communicating with two of the planes. He does not realize that he is or whom he is communicating with yet.*

There is more to see before you return to Edan, though as it has a bearing on your meeting with the Edan people. The music subsided.

Looking at Jescan, I said, "It might be time to go back. There is other things that they want me see, before I go there though."

CHAPTER FIFTEEN

The unification of one God who rules over the earth came hard to most people as they had always had a statue or something physical to look at and observe. To observe an entity that was not symbolized by something physical was within the grasp of the human mind, and once the idea was presented it was understood even by the very young.

The older people still wanted something physical to relate this entity with. As well being very superstitious basically was covering all the aspects just in case the other gods were strong as or even stronger than this one God, and mostly in secret the statue of a male deity with the statue of a female deity at his side was a very common collection near the altars. Even though the concept of one God was developing, it started to grow in leaps and bounds. Several people still had a statue of Ashara the female goddess, which stood beside God in the statues still made to deified the images of God, which started to spread discretely under a cloak of secrecy so that the fallen dynasty could somehow justify the release of all its slaves from the land of Egypt.

The loudest proclamation of the deity was mostly from the land of Jordan, where the slaves had traveled to presently squatting on the land now fighting for space to call their own in this new land.

The aliens had arranged for rules to be written out for them, which were meant to guide them in their daily lives, giving the people something meaningful and constructive to follow laying out the rules on a tablet that would become a major part of history.

The Egyptians losing their huge workforce slowly digressed, and the undertakings of the remaining cities and future pyramids would take them decades to complete as it was unusual for the king to be buried in a building that he started. The kings would be secretly hidden in surrounding valleys, away from all the attention, grave robbers, and thieves. Usually, it was his descendants that completed the undertaking with a cloak of secrecy as well as a charade of guards being posted as well as visits from the royal family.

"Let's keep a closer eye on the activities of your people," I said, looking at Jescan, knowing that this was just the start of things to come.

Touching the controls we landed where there were a lot of alien activities recorded in the sensors of the *Genesis*, some that I wanted to watch very closely and I knew that they were especially occupying this general area.

"Let's take a walk," I said as I turned to open the door.

We walked out to an unbelievably hot day. Although this was the start of the colder rainy season, the temperature was over a hundred degrees in the shade, and the hottest part of the day was yet to come.

The stifling heat almost knocked us over as it was so unexpected. Stepping outside the sunlight was so strong that we pulled the hoods of our clothing over our heads for protection from the sizzling heat, sneezing as our eyes adjusted to the bright sunlight.

The people were carrying on their regular routine lives doing normal everyday things, and the life on the whole was relatively quiet, completely oblivious to the observers watching from high up in the sky. Although their life was a hard life the people were prospering.

Life was relatively simple, as the areas of power were several hundred miles to the west in the land that would be called Italy, where the Romans had dominated most of the continent in the last few centuries ruling with a control that was not rivaled before on Earth.

The Egyptian reign had ended several thousand years ago although maintained their country and with that most of the knowledge of the ancient building techniques had also been buried with the pharohs.

The Romans had almost emulated the great Egyptian culture. They had developed the basis of modern-day civilizations even though it would be the Greeks that most of the political concepts would be based upon. Although they too were to have their pitfalls that would crumble their empire at this time, the empire was well into its prime. The people under Roman rule were attaining great strides economically as well as technical accomplishments.

"Let's walk through the town, starting down the hill to the mud brick houses gleaming white from the white wash, making the city stand quite noticeably out from the reddish background of hills surrounding the town.

"My people have been interested in this area for some time, as the people are basically good people being that they had before being freed, been dominated by the Egyptian rule, now Roman rule. My people decided that these people are the meekest of all cultures which would be introduced to our people, so they might introduce us to the world," Jescan commented as we started to enter the city.

The people had mostly an agricultural society with the majority of the people farming and tending their crops. The town was built around a large town well, which was not only a place to get water but was a favorite gathering and meeting place. In their regular routine the people usually made at least one trip there during the day to draw their daily drinking water if for nothing else, to hear the local gossip.

There was a marketplace set out all around the well offering produce as well as trinkets, pots, pans, wool, salt and materials imported throughout the Roman territories. Exporting goods from one market to other markets was commonplace items such as rugs, wooden carvings, art from Persia and especially Rome, and even a few articles from European countries as far north as France and Germany although they were not called that at that time.

Looking up at the clear blue sky a shiny reflection caught my eye. "We have visitors observing us," I commented, and I could see Jescan suddenly looking up into the clear blue sky.

"Where?" He focused, adjusting his large eyes to the bright sunlight.

"It almost looks invisible. I just saw a glint of it as I walked from back here," I said, retracing my steps. "Here, stand here."

Jescan stood on the spot that I had pointed out to him. "Yes . . . I now see it. They are waiting for the right time. This is a very important undertaking for my people. This is at first something that had never been done on any other planet. Mind you, this was the first of any planet. You later on this afternoon will be a witness to the start of the most remarkable history-making event of your planet's history."

"You mentioned later on in the evening. You already know the time?"

"Yes, this had to be documented, as we had never introduced ourselves to any species on any other planet, as this would sort of become our benchmark of how to proceed. Your planet influenced by the basic knowledge of Atlantis have matured to the stage that our presence could be known and not change the direction that your planet is taking. This was a very significant decision as our people now prefer to be strictly observers, documenting events and not willing to influence any planets' direction socially."

Walking toward the marketplace the people dressed in a variety of different apparel some in long tunics, some similar to a toga some simple with only an opening for the head as well as the arms held at the waist by a cloth rope. Most had sandals, but many had nothing on their feet.

There were two tax collectors dressed in a white toga with the Roman insignia incorporated on the ends of the toga. They were surrounded by six Roman soldiers who had been designated to help them on their collections. They were standing in the middle of the marketplace beside the well watering their camels and horses that were laden with goods they had collected. The locals trying to avoid contact walked around the edge of the market stopping at different booths, not wanting to run into these two men.

We walked along the main line of merchants casually inspecting their wares. As we wandered through the market an older couple well into their mid—to late forties, were checking out a clay pot for water and were bartering on the price. The man had on priest's clothing and was obviously of high status and listening to the minds of the merchants was held in high esteem, as with the status of his position.

The jewelry was draped around her, as well as his neck. Their hands were covered in large rings. The two made their way over to another merchant and the price of the pot was negotiated, a deal was almost sealed when the first merchant yelled out a price and then the second lowered his price. The priest and his wife finally decided on the first one that they had first picked.

Watching the people was an interesting study of history as some of the clothing was interestingly decorative denoting their position of wealth or lack of wealth, as most people wore a simple pullover blanket type of tunic with a slit for the head and arms. There were also many males as well as females who wore a simple towel-like wrap worn from the waist to just above the knees. The heat was unbelievable and the signs of sun-burned skin were starting to show on the mostly nude people. Several had a cloth thrown over their head to protect them from sun stroke.

The large baskets that the women placed on top of their head held the bread, fruit, some of the meat or fish that was to become their evening meal.

The merchants dealt in pieces of silver which the Romans had developed and adopted from observing the practice in Egypt where they used gold as well as silver, although there were still beakers of salt that several of the people used to trade with as salt almost carried as much buying power as silver or gold.

Nothing struck me as unusual but I was surprised to see some of the people removing their clothing to use as a trading item and it was not uncommon to see a naked person wandering around with a basket or a bag as a means to carry the goods home. To my surprise no one even seemed to take notice as nudity was an accepted normal part of life, as several areas were available for public bathing, was not a surprise that they were walking around with nothing on except, some maintained their shoes or sandals. It did seem out of place as I was not used to such openness something that in my time was not an acceptable practice in public. Getting over the initial surprise of such an open society the currency that was most often used was gold or silver pieces, that was the main trading commodity.

I had no idea whether this was a normal day in the market, although I could sense that nothing out of the ordinary was going on. It was a very busy place as there seemed to be a steady stream of people moving in and out of the square. At any given time I figured about five hundred or so were in the small square at any given time.

We had wandered through the largest portion of the market, and it was approaching the middle of the afternoon when it was like everything suddenly was rolled up. The tents were closed, and the goods were put away. It was as though the people were getting ready to leave. Catching me completely off guard the marketplace simply dissolved as the people disappeared into their homes, and it was kind of like they rolled up the streets. Within minutes the streets were empty the tables all shut down and the people just vanished.

Looking at Jescan, I asked, "What did we miss? Where did everyone go?"

"I believe this is their afternoon break. This is when everything shuts down for about two hours as the heat of the day is at its peak."

"Speaking of heat let's find a place where we can get shelter from this heat, maybe some shaded area," I said as I noticed people starting to look at us from the tents and the windows watching us as we looked for a comfortable place to rest.

Finding a tree near one of the community baths we sat leaning against the trunk and watching the silent streets hearing the odd muffled sound of someone talking in the buildings. A cat could be heard growling as another cat was crossing into its territory. It almost felt like the town was an instant ghost town as not a person was in sight and just as we started to appreciate the quiet, I could sense the presence of aliens in the sky coming closer, as they approached with a high-speed quiet hum as a ship hovered over the town.

The aliens flooded the area with a pulsing energy wave that stimulated the urge to sleep. Knowing what to expect, I protected both Jescan and myself with a protective shield. The aliens were only about an hour as the ship continued hovering. Listening to the conversation telepathically, the aliens were artificially inseminating a woman. As soon as they had completed they communicated to her as well as to the husband that she was to have a baby. I could tell that it was from the priest's house as the ship was sending a beam directly to that area.

Levitating I pulled up high enough to see the beam hitting the priest's window from the top floor. The ship stopped the light beam stopping the sound waves as it shot straight up into the clouds.

Looking down I realized that I had not left the protective shield around Jescan and he was just waking up as though from a deep sleep.

Landing beside him, I helped him up. "Why have they fertilized this older woman?"

Moving his shoulders and head as he woke up he said, "This was originally going to be the chosen one although this lady had lost her virginity many years ago. The council decided after the insemination that it must be a virgin that must carry the chosen one. This as was decided by the council would be a possible backup plan. He was conceived with the intention of a protector to the chosen one."

"Why did they pick such an older woman?" I queried.

"At first, it was believed that people would not believe that a women who was past having any children would be able to have a child. Although it was almost immediately accepted, and the council realized that it would not work in the way that they wanted it to, there had to be some other way to introduce themselves, and seeing that mankind with all it had attained, had become very complex. They had to have some way of assuring that the chosen man, could emulate knowledge. This man had to make them understand themselves, before they were able to accept our people. This child is a selected child but was not the one to be the spokesperson or the deliverer.

"Man had achieved remarkable things, although it was nothing to what they would attain because of the chosen one which at this time they had no idea, what was in store in the future.

Your people had evolved into developing the remarkable ability to control their destiny which gave them the ability to manipulate their surroundings attaining what our people had taken several years to reach. It was attained through the teachings of our people.

Although the basics had been given, your people have improved several aspects which my people in the beginning had struggled with as well as almost any civilized society, no matter which planet they are on.

Your people did achieve what takes most planets thousands of millions of years. Your planet had achieved that state in less than one million years. The achievements are in this period remarkable as we have the advantage of knowing the outcome. We have learned a lot from your people more than any other planet and the other planets did not have the close connection that your people have except that we now realize that people or living humans have a destiny that cannot be changed but must evolve. The child, the chosen child, is a protégé of millions of years, evolved in all the things that mankind will attain.

Our people were treading in a territory that had never been crossed before. The attempt was to calumniate all the most unique qualities enhancing each one to the ultimate qualities of all the humans that now dominate the planet Earth a direct link to our people."

"Your people, including the other aliens, thought that this was the time to teach my people about their roots so to speak so why would they not land with the spaceships and introduce themselves?" I asked, realizing that I already had the answer to my question knowing that it would have giving them a look at the technology that they must achieve on their own and not be introduced, prematurely as was nearly the case on the Nile River.

"This chosen one . . . is the man they called Jesus?" I commented, knowing the answer before I said it.

"Your people needed guidance. This man was everything that man would be and able to attain. This child will be his cousin. The women were genetically altered and transplanted into the wombs of their mothers. They are of our kind although the mother of the chosen one was recently introduced. These women had been selected to carry a child who carried all the abilities that mankind will someday achieve.

This man child," he said, turning to look at the older lady, "will set the path for his cousin. The women were preselected, although this was on a subconscious level, and although in the deepest part of their mind that was buffered, from the conscious, they really did not know which one would be the mother of the chosen one. They did know that they were different and it was part of their conscious beliefs that there was going to be as they put it, 'The coming of the Lord savior of the people.' Even they had no idea that they had been selected to become the possible mother of the chosen child. The age of this lady was not really a factor. The significance of the birth to an older lady who was well past the age of having a baby should have been enough to convince the majority of people that there was an outside influence working. There was great skepticism especially in the people of higher rank or in control. This was a large factor in the decision to have one prepare the way for the chosen one."

"Your people are not very direct are they?" I commented. "It is like you must have everyone observe the uniqueness of the situation and read into and question every incident. This is all well-orchestrated, yet there are no signs other than insignificant signs that really do not have anything significant, nothing like being completely subtle."

"Our people will not interfere with the development of a planet's social life. Although it was a calculated plan it was plagued with problems as the people became more leery even questioning the validity of the virgin birth."

"Your people should have anticipated the outcome as well as the natural reaction of the people to a secretive outside influence showing nothing except intangible things that can neither be touch nor studied only discovered."

"Yes we were aware of the independent thoughts of the people. Our problem was how the masses of people reacted which, caught us as you often comment, off guard."

"Let's see what happened when Jesus was born," I said, turning toward the *Genesis*.

The *Genesis* landed just outside of a small town along a limestone overhang. The houses, a short distance away, were made out of mud bricks neatly made and placed into position with a clay mortar. This was then whitewashed with a compound of white dye. The buildings seemed to be all well organized and some had large open courtyards.

Most used a sloped roof with open spaces on the second level, although several had flat useable spaces for a roof. The areas in the courtyards were where they grew fig trees and shrubs, flowers and some vegetables. These were mostly a shaded retreat from the unbelievably hot days especially in the summer months. The width of the streets was interestingly narrow especially to me being used to streets much wider. Although it was more than adequate to walk down it was also large enough to include a donkey or a camel. Some of the streets were wide enough for a pair of animals to walk beside each other.

Traveling down the narrow intermittently cobbled streets, we could see that several of the streets were under construction.

The people had gathered desirable rocks to be chiseled and laid, one at a time beside each other to cover the narrow laneway. It looked like each house was responsible for the area in front of their own building, as stones were piled in front of each resident with visible signs that people were forming each stone, as beside the pile of stones, there was a pile of broken stones and small fragments strewn about.

Presently there was no one working on the streets as they were all having their afternoon nap a tradition common to the areas close to the equator as well as in other continents such as the South American as well as the southern part of North American continent.

There were hemp ropes strung across the street, allowing them to hang their clothing that were just washed, although most of the clothing were washed sparingly as water was a valuable commodity, as the well was the only means of fresh water, as fifteen miles down a steady decline they would come to the Dead Sea which contained a lot of salt and with little rain, was a very harsh area to live. The area to the north and east was a desert.

The unique homes looked remarkably well built and resembled the homes of the modern-day homes in this region. The countryside had many caves that had formed in the limestone. Most of these were used now to shelter the farm animals as most of the people had built homes and at this time no longer lived in the caves. It was very convenient for the animals as the largest mainstay of the economy was of the herds of sheep and goats. Most of the people were either shepherds or something involved with the herds like yarn makers, or weavers and status was attained by the number of sheep or goats a person owned.

There was a main gathering place and market in the center of the town and like Rome, had all the roads leading to the center where the well, was located.

The smell of curry and garlic as well the aroma of baking bread waffled though the city giving a comfortable homey smell as people suddenly crowded along the streets. As the nap time was over the town came alive once again. The main conversation that everyone was talking about was about the taxes and the continual movement of people heading to the plaza.

The Caesar had declared a census to be taken as the taxes were in the process of being calculated. The people some very unwillingly had to travel to the place that they had been born.

People were coming from all over the country. The travelers found lodgings with relatives and friends, several setting up their nomadic tents, extending the town limits with little camps dotting the landscape.

The late October afternoon was starting to cool as the night approached and the cool unique wind, as I could sense the threat of snow although only a skiff could be detected in the low-pressure area, that was moving in, causing stronger gusts of winds than was normal for this area coming off the desert, making the afternoon cool down at a rapid rate as the people held their robes closer to themselves.

The trails from the other towns had a steady stream of travelers, as the people traveled to their hometown of birth. The majority of people had traveled many days and most were tired, and the talk among themselves was somewhat disgruntled that they had to travel at this time of year, but the anticipation and deep down gratefulness to be able to re-associate with old friends and relatives was one of the bright sides to the journey, yet the trip was a long and arduous one, as the terrain was very hilly and was a constant climbing or descending.

The countryside was filled with people both leaving as well as coming. A unique sight caught me by surprise, as up in the sky off in the distance was a glowing radiant light reflecting from a ship that slowly moved across the sky. "What . . . is that?" I questioned as I turned to Jescan.

"That is the ship that was designated to watch over the virgin carrying the chosen child. This was a way of recording the very movement of the hours before the birth of the child, as it will be written. Although your people will write it in several different ways it was also a way that we could introduce ourselves without becoming a threat."

"You're telling me that the people are not aware of the ship even if it is almost within visible range?" It was so bright that it even showed quite visibly during the daytime. Looking at it I remembered the stories of the trip that Joseph and Mary made, then I realized that it was the ship disguised to look like a star that followed the unborn baby to his birthplace, as well as the people who were attracted to the star as was planted in the subconscious minds of several of the initial players in the stories that would be recorded in history.

"Your people had no idea of what it is, as in a way it does resemble a star. This was the explanation that your people could understand.

Most of the speculation was contributed to the fact that there would be the coming of the king of kings the savior.

Subconsciously we had planted seeds of the concept that the savior would arrive soon. Very few people actually could understand the truth in the words, as each person had a different perception or vision of what they expected. They had no idea that it was a carefully selected genetically superior human."

"Why are your people not showing themselves if that is their goal?"

"Our people could not show themselves till the right time. Although we are showing ourselves it is not received like we had anticipated, and the anticipated excitement of introducing ourselves to the descendants of our people our relatives, it is an emotion that our people wrote in great length of the anticipation of finally completing the secret link." The true feelings were very dominant in Jescan's voice as he thoughtfully interpreted the readings of his youth recalling from the considerable capacity of his photogenic mind.

We looked out from the bustling city as the late afternoon sun was sending shadows across the streets. The ship disguised as a star, I could tell was not going to make it before dark. The large number of travelers congested the markets as well as all the rooms available, completely oblivious to the star shining in the western sky.

Walking to the street heading out of town we walked a short distance from the city. The night had started to arrive with a quickness common to the desert terrain as well as the lateness of the year. The light was now starting to stop and start as they rested at regular intervals and although very visible few people paid much attention to the light, or even thought, much of the light in the sky as they were consumed in the arrangements for the night accommodations that they were making as well as how they could bed and board the large amount of people in the small rooms available. The crowds diverging on the city, was what occupied most of their thoughts. The statement of "could not see the forest for the trees" struck me, and I shook my head at the total lack of observation present in these people.

I noticed one of the children watching the light totally fascinated, but no one noticed him as he was one small child in a large throng of people, and children's whimsical infatuations were dismissed by most parents who thought that children were to be seen and not heard.

The light was just about at the edge of the city, lighting their way as they were approaching a house that was renting out rooms along the side of the road. Curiosity came over me as we walked closer and could see that the mother-to-be was in heavy labor. The man was in a rush to find a covered shelter, as the expectant mothers water had broken nearly an hour and a half ago. The child would be born this day late in October, later this night.

The man had sympathy for the mother-to-be and offered the man a space in one of the caves converted into a barn at the back of the inn. They were almost ready to go on to another inn, when the mother sank in pain with a very strong contraction. The decision was made quickly as the man carried her to the stable where he quickly spread out the straw, laying a large blanket over top for the comfortable straw bed then helped her lay down. Turning he closed the slab door to give them privacy. The screaming of last stages of the trimester labor, which was muffled by the limestone walls, echoes produced within the cave was even heard above the sounds of the people in the inn. The animals all seemed to sense the infant's arrival as they quietly watched the proceedings in the barn. Even the people in the inn seemed to be quiet, as most were settling in for the night. It was like the calm before the storm although no storm was coming. The animals and the surrounding land were uncommonly quiet with no spectators to witness the proceedings within the cave. In a way I thought it was very fitting that the chosen child should be born within a cave, as most of the ancestors lived, and was raised in caves. Possibly although not planned it was destiny, for the savior to be born in a cave similar to that of the very first child who was born to an apelike mother and an alien father.

A very loud scream waffled through the still night air, and moments later the cry of the baby's first breath could be heard, filtering through the wooden slabs for a door. As the crying started, the light from the ship increased and lit up most of the area around the cave including the city, and some of the late-night people gathered to marvel at the light, watching with the same response that would be given to someone watching the aurora borealis, or a comet shining in the night sky, observed yet totally accepted without any major emotions or even the slightest questioning of what it was doing there.

The animals again carried on as though nothing was out of the ordinary, accepting the light as part of the daytime and the sounds of the animals returned to a normal foraging through the hay like nothing out of the ordinary had happened.

The inn was still uncommonly quiet as the light was shining into every opening of the inn. The occasional muffled sound of someone talking in their sleep would come from one of the rooms. It would seem as though most of the people had all gone to sleep, as it was late in the evening not noticing the light from the shuttered and curtained windows.

As the virgin mother cleaned herself and the infant, shepherds from the surrounding area were starting to arrive attracted by the light in the sky. As they were starting to arrive, Joseph opened the door wanting to tell someone that it was a boy, the son from God himself.

He proudly announced the arrival of the boy child. The shepherds drew closer, leery of the statement of the man standing inside the cave, questioning his sanity as they huddled around the door way, not really sure what to think with the bright light surrounding the barn. We too also mingled in the small crowd for several hours. As the shepherds got to look at the new baby, we observed mostly from the back of the crowd. All the time the little cave or barn was illuminated from the bright light similar to a spotlight, close to the intensity of the sun itself emanating from the ship, as everything was lit up like it was daytime.

Suddenly, I could sense that something was not right and that something needed to be looked after as soon as possible. As I communicated to Jescan telepathically, two other people turned and looked at us. I knew they were from the Edan council and they were as surprised as we were, that we were there, as we were, that they were there. Reading their minds I knew that they were simple observers with nothing else on their agenda. We politely acknowledged one another, not wanting to draw any attention to ourselves.

Backing off we were heading back to the *Genesis* when off in the distance we noticed three travelers on camels traveling in the direction of the inn. We both turned and watched the three majestically dignified kings approach as we stood, watching in front of the camouflaged *Genesis*. The approach was one of such dignity as they majestically trekked across the hill, heading up to the small lighted inn. The sight was unbelievably impressive. They were definitely a fitting trio for the remarkable historic evening. Although the stories portrayed them as magnificent, the truth was more than could be verbally described, as the stories of this momentous occasion were to be written down. There was no way they could justly write of all the unique atmosphere present, as the kings arrived to give their homage to the king of kings and only the facts could be transcribed, not the feeling and emotion of the moment. Like a picture can take the physical images, yet the emotions can only be imagined.

Turning we entered the *Genesis*. I once again could sense that something was not right, heading to the monitor, as I was eager to find out what this strange feeling I had. It was like something was about to happen. The energy flowing through my body increased, as I knew I was tensing up with anticipation.

Checking out the results of what we had witnessed as well as any other changes, it was obviously not to do with the happenings that were presently unfolding outside of the *Genesis*.

One of the lights was flashing a warning signal, which meant that history was not progressing as it should. It was flashing continually as the computer noticed something that was not a natural occurrence, which required my immediate attention.

Jescan was surprised at the beeping. "This has never happened before. What does it mean?" He was slightly excited, as he could not figure out what it meant.

Musical sounds started bouncing in my head as the sixth plane, in solo, made an appearance as the other planes only listened. *Calmly, he started to communicate the task at hand. "You have learned, experienced, and utilized such a large amount of knowledge, and overall, it is still a small amount. Your mind has agreed with everything that is as it is. You must now allow yourself the luxury of acceptance. With acceptance, there are also limits. Unless you intervene, your planet will be railroaded into a life that is not of their making, as the situation about to present itself is not necessary for the good of your people. You must work with these people, convincing them that there is another alternative to the handling of the situation. There is a way that both planets shall prosper, grow as well as interact.*

The beeping from the computer became the beat, which was consistent with the images that were bouncing off every neuron in my mind. The images flashed, showing the life that would be if nothing was done.

Then images of the way in which, it was to unfold started to show itself. A formal treaty or contract bounced back and forth as each event happened. The outcome was very straightforward, although implications were presenting themselves, and a decision needed to be decided on each issue as it presented itself, as the images of no agreement showed itself, then if the agreements were in force, the outcomes were very definite and very clear leaving no question of what had to happen. There was a need for a direction not only for the people of Edan but also for the protection of the people of Earth. A tentative contract of scattered pieces started to formulate, starting by saying that there was another way to address the importance of the situation on Earth.

Introduction of the Edan people at this time was not to happen, in time it would come to be, but the timing was not to happen at this time. The contract was going to be a very big surprise, as your intrusion will be of great importance to the way that the universe evolves. The music slowly subsided.

Looking at Jescan, my surprised look made him uneasy. I sat back and allowed a small amount of the images to transfer to Jescan, including some of what I had heard and seen, allowing some of the images of what the sixth plane was interpreting the situation, and my mind started racing again, as I knew what had to be accomplished.

"What is wrong? What is it all about?"

"You knew that your people have set up a base on the opposite side of the moon in order to control the direction that the people are going to be forced to take," I said, observing the monitor as it still flashed, and the screen revealed what showed the increasing number of ships landing on the moon. A reasonably large complex of buildings were being constructed with remarkable technology incorporated in the rapidly constructed buildings. This was to be the start of a difference of opinion, something that the people of Earth was not yet capable of conveying yet. This, I knew was going to change my concept of all my experiences traveling in time, which had enriched my understanding so much. Now I must act on these experiences to better help and protect the people of Earth. On the other hand it would also help advance the people of Edan, as beliefs would start to change some of the tactics that they are starting to incorporate as a justification for exploiting an unsuspecting society." I paused as I contemplated the implications of what the sixth plane had conveyed. Unknowingly, the people of Edan were heading in a direction that even they did not know the consequences, nor the final outcome of the actions that they were contemplating. They needed direction as much as the people of Earth. The council in control, would have to be led in a different direction, as I fully knew that they did have the good of all, at heart, but what was happening was wrong, with complications that they could not comprehend or anticipate at this time.

"Your people are fortunately not going to place our people under their complete rule." Leaning forward, I touched the controls on the control panel, and the *Genesis* announced our arrival.

Landing in the hallway at the headquarters of the high council, of the Edan people. Looking at Jescan, I began placing my thoughts as well as total conviction to my proposal very carefully, so he understood how serious I was.

"You are about to change the council's rulings in a way that is undeniably for the better, I must say." Jescan was smiling, as he knew what was about to transpire.

"You knew what is about to take place?" I asked, realizing that I should have read the logs of the future, yet was content in the fact that this was something that I needed to do to change the future. "You know about the changes that will occur, and you do not object?"

"As you learn the ways of our people you in turn gain such support that it is something that will enhance your status and respect among our people. Your people as you have already written with this document, the destiny of your people is secure as well as our people.

You are going to embark on a very enjoyable journey, so you will tell me in the future, as I now know how some of the things turned out, at least a small part of the history."

Looking out the window of the *Genesis*, the hallway to the council was directly ahead. Relaying the remainder of the proposal to the computer and several copies of the document started to materialize, the time had arrived to visit the council. My understanding of what must be was crystal clear more than ever before.

"This is the end of our trip together, although it is known that we will meet many times before I die and several years later when

I am born once again. This is a very difficult time, as I have grown to admire you and what you do. Our friendship will always be in my heart, as I have been privy to your first experiences as you have learned your capabilities. It will be written."

Looking into the face of a friend, who was truly a friend and shall endure all the changes that must occur I said, "This is the start of the awakening of my people, and it is a time when they must accomplish on their own, not with the influences that are proposed by your people."

"Your people have come so far as the result of our interference. It is time to protect the future of your people. It is time to let the young learn for themselves, on their own, sort of like a child growing and in time leaving home to make a life of their own to decide their own future."

Understanding more than he was saying, I knew that this is when Jescan would write his book, which for generations would influence what happens in the future encounters with other life forms. I knew as well as he, that he will stay and shall raise children who shall produce an endless cycle of his life, as his ancestor will again enter the *Genesis* some two thousand years in the future, forever and eternally caught within a circle of living and dying, although there will be other trips, that we will take in time.

All the thoughts and situations that we have encountered, he will be able to relive over and over his time with me. His life will be a complete and full life with many rewards. I removed and rolled up the copies of the proposal I had the computer prepare, knowing it was time to meet the new council.

"Come, we must meet the council, and fulfill the destiny that will influence all intelligent life forms for the rest of eternity."

"My pleasure," he said, as he knew the importance of his return to his people.

Walking down to the council room, Jescan turned to me and thanked me for an unbelievably enjoyable trip that was such an important time, or period as he put it. Opening the council's door, we caught the council off guard one more time, as I could sense a surprised look on everyone's face.

The council was completely different, as the years had made way for new faces, as the average life expectancy changed every thousand years or so. The council was new, but we were well known and invited to come in.

"This council welcomes you, as we have been aware of your presence but we as a council, have never had the opportunity to meet you."

"The honor is all mine," I said as I greeted the council, turning to introduce Jescan.

"I am Jescan. Pleased to meet you," interjected Jescan as he politely and formally bowed.

"We have some important documents that need to become legislation, passed by your council. This will help both my people as well as your people. I need to set up an ongoing constitution, proposing the guidelines of an agreement between your people and my people."

"What are you proposing?" questioned the head of the council with the full attention of everyone on the council.

"This is a list that I have compiled and approved. It will help both our people as well as other societies throughout the universe."

The head of the council reached out, taking the documents, that I was handing to him. Reading the document, he passed the other copies to the next person beside him. The copies were passed around the table, each letting the whole room read the information before talking, each sitting patiently as the paper was read by each individual.

The leader of the council calmly said, "We have all read the documents you presented. Our people are one of discovery because of you, as well as the man who crashed on your planet. Our lives have been closely linked to your planet, and you were the first planet that had significant intelligent wildlife, and plant life to sustain entire continents of life, all sizes and shapes. The discovery of your planet is one of such remarkable importance that your presence is always appreciated, although usually only briefly with several years in between."

Nodding my acknowledgment of the invitation, I carried on with the purpose of my visit. "This document is important in that it sets out a clear direction and responsibility of both societies on the path to beginning to understand each other without confrontation or disagreement, as most solutions are present within the document, limiting the involvement between the two cultures, till such a time as the two of them are in a position that each side can add to this legislation with an awareness of each other's intentions."

I looked around at the council members. "Is it possible for us to be able to study the proposal in depth, as we too need to protect our interests?" the leader of the council asked.

"I have no problem with that. How long would you like to have?"

"Would two weeks be enough?" he asked as he looked around to the other council members. Everyone nodded on the time frame allowed to study the proposal.

"That will be satisfactory,. I do want you to transmit to all that are on earth, and the moon base now, that they will stop all the activity that had been planned and new instructions will be forthcoming. I shall return in two weeks' time."

Looking at Jescan, I noticed him watching a female council member as well as I noticed her looking back, not being offended at all. In both cases, each was flirting with each other.

The statement of falling in love at first sight was definitely the situation as I watched the chemistry of their bodies meet and mingle with such emotion, completely captivated with each other.

This was not what Jescan had expected, although he knew that he was to stay behind and write his book. He had not written about the reason for him staying behind, as it was this beautiful council member, which was the main reason for him staying, something that he must have wanted to leave out, so he would not have any idea of why he made the decision.

At this time, he was not thinking about anything else but this woman who took his complete attention and was intoxicating him in a way that he never knew could happen. The old statement of love at first sight was most accurate in this particular case.

The council members had agreed with the approval of the document to be studied thoroughly all the conditions I was proposing, and the head of the council turned to me and said, "Your conditions have all been agreed upon, although we must study it. I am certain that we will have questions on some of the topics covered. Is it possible for you to stay and fill us in on some of the contents of the contract?"

"Which is not possible due to the fact that I need to be somewhere important at this time? Though, I am certain Jescan would be able to stay here to answer any and all questions. I will return shortly to check in on the progress. If any question arises that Jescan cannot answer, I will answer them at that time," I suggested. "I will give you the time you request."

Moving towards the Genesis, *the music started in my head, all of the planes were communicating, at the time that we were transformed,*

Evelyn had an amazing infatuation over us that she impregnated her egg with your sperm, as in each of the other planes the same occurred as well.

Not really the issue, but when the child reaches ten years of age, he has our same genes that allowed you and us to communicate with other planes, unheard of as he is unknowingly communicating with two planes. Rarely even with the genes would it be able to communicate with more than one plane. We will incorporate him into our lives, and teach him all that we know as he will be separate, but a part of us, and will be part of our lives.

The music notes subsided, as I approached the Genesis.

The Genesis was announcing my arrival, as I had landed on the large planet known as Edan, I knew the location of Evelyn and my offspring, which in each plane was a part of history now and could not be changed.

THE GENESIS (THE BEGINNING)

Adam is abducted and finds out that he has special abilities that are unique to him. He discovers that he has counterparts in other planes and finds out that he is connected to six others. With these connections with the other planes, he gains the ability to travel anywhere in the helix of time. He will set out to discover his new abilities, discovering how life started on Earth and events that changed the evolution of man. He has many things that he wants to do, so he and an alien travel in the *Genesis* to different times, discovering several things that, through observation, change how things unravel throughout the beginning of life.

The influences of the situations also change the destiny of mankind through the people of Atlantis and Egypt and the Mayans.

There are so many things that have changed the history of mankind. Adam and Jescan, the alien, experience many things, and Adam's abilities increase as they proceed through these changes. As he discovers his abilities, he, in turn, evolves with the help of the other planes.

ABOUT THE AUTHOR

Cameron Munroe loves animals and the outdoors, is a novice artist, and is a big Star Wars, Star Trek and Dr Who fan. He was born in Oyen, a farming community in the Southeastern area of Alberta, then moved to Calgary where he spent most of his younger life and some of his adult life, going to school and university there. He is presently living south of High River, Alberta, Canada.

Printed in the United States
By Bookmasters